SWEET ENCHANTMENT

Swaying, chanting softly, Riana moved closer to Wolf, planting her leg between his thighs. Like a snake, she writhed up against him, rubbing her body against his, driving the blood through his veins like a raging torrent. He kept his arms at his sides by sheer force of will, letting her slide around him, chafing hip against hip, back against back in wildly erotic fashion. As she moved, he could feel her heat radiate into him, melting them both, fusing them together. Soon, the dance would be over, he thought with a leap of excitement. Then it would be his turn to weave an enchantment.

She wheeled to face him again, her eyes wide and open as she pressed against him, her lips parting invitingly as she uttered the last, hurried chants. Feeling her building urgency as she rubbed against him, Wolf's brain reeled.

Riana cried out suddenly, thrusting back her head and leaving her throat exposed to him. Clutching her by the arms, he rained kisses on the soft, white skin she offered. He could feel her trembling, could feel his own, and he reveled in the moment of shared triumph.

Their souls had joined.

It was time now to link their bodies . . .

Books by Barbara Benedict

A TASTE OF HEAVEN

DESTINY

ALWAYS

ENCHANTRESS

Published by Zebra Books

ENCHANTRESS

Barbara Benedict

Zebra Books
Kensington Publishing Corp.
http://www.zebrabooks.com

ZEBRA BOOKS are published by

Kensington Publishing Corp.
850 Third Avenue
New York, NY 10022

First Printing: December, 1996
10 9 8 7 6 5 4 3 2 1

Printed in the United States of America

To Gram Riley,
May the warmth of Spring always find you
And to my hero, Scott
Just because.

One

Lightning flared across the western sky, piercing the darkness for an interminable instant. Riana tensed, waiting for the accompanying roar of thunder, but the eerie silence remained undisturbed.

An omen, she thought uneasily.

She hesitated, unnerved by the isolation of the hill she was about to climb. At her back stretched the fertile farmland and endless forests of the river valley, but up ahead, only the most hardy and daring of shrubs clung to the barren slopes. The hill was known as Dragon Crest, for it was as if some huge scaly monster had breathed upon it and scorched all in its path.

The valley inhabitants all avoided this place. The summit was said to be haunted by the Old Ones, mystical spirits who once practiced the magical arts here. Only her guardian, Sela, wandered among the abandoned ruins, searching out the plants and herbs of the ancient priestesses for her healings, convinced that she'd grown too old and near her own final rest for any lost spirit to covet her meager life force.

If Sela could survive her visits here, Riana thought defiantly, then so would she. Nothing would stop her from scaling this hill tonight.

She knew the old woman would chide her for it, accusing Riana of being too impetuous, too inclined to the rash impulses of heedless youth. "Only a fool dabbles in magic without proper training, Moriana," Sela would say, using her full name to express her displeasure. "You'll come to no good, toying with forces you can neither understand nor control."

In her mind, Riana understood the logic behind the warning, but in her heart, where urgency dwelt, she knew only that she had secret, hidden powers that must be tapped and trained, so one day, she could answer the call to save a kingdom.

With a determined sigh, she gathered her cloak tighter about her and secured her grasp on the sack of stones she carried. It grew heavier with each step upward, and she longed to relinquish her burden, but she could not spin a proper enchantment without the sacred stones. And a proper enchantment was all that would get her back to Camelot.

The urgency built as she climbed. More and more of late, she'd had the sense that King Arthur needed her, as did his queen, and she had to find some way to reach them. Riana had never known her parents, having been abandoned as a babe at the castle kitchen doorstep, but she'd often hoped them to be Arthur and Guinivere. Hers was not an ambitious craving for royal standing, but rather a wish to be a part of the two she loved most.

As a child, she'd never stopped to wonder why she, the court foundling, should be brought up from the kitchens to be raised with the other noble children, but now, grown into a woman, she pondered on it incessantly. Was it the loneliness of having no children of their own that prompted Arthur and Guinivere to single her out to entertain them, singing songs and spinning stories? Or had such special treatment more to do with the king's sisters, Queen Morgan or Queen Morgause, who listened to her occasional predictions of future events with more than a casual ear? Or, as was sometimes rumored, could she be connected to Arthur's stern, ever-frowning magician, Merlin?

Too well, she could remember her last interview with the Great Enchanter. She'd gone to Merlin on some errand for Arthur and the magician had gazed at her with a somber expression. "Study life and hone your craft," he'd said in a voice that seemed to float around her, "for one day, Arthur shall call upon your help."

How thrilled she'd been at those words, how determined to

become an enchantress. Yet before Morgan and Morgause could offer much in the way of training, the guards had come to the nursery in the wee hours of the night and whisked her off, with neither warning nor explanation, to this frontier settlement. A remote outpost where she could be raped—if not murdered—by the dreaded Saxon hordes.

Though at first she'd felt abandoned, like at her birth, she came to believe that this was a test from which she must emerge strong and victorious. Merlin must have sent her here to learn her craft, she'd decided, since Sela had some skill in the art of healing.

Though it did give her pause, how the old woman had yet to begin her formal training.

Riana halted midway up the hill, turning to view the village below her, anxiety churning in her gut. Sela had frustrated her often in these many years of their exile, but today she'd outdone herself with the announcement that she'd arranged Riana's marriage to the dull and oafish Gaston, an aging farmer with barely a hide of land to his name.

And before Riana could protest, or even digest that dire news, a horse and rider had come charging through the village, pausing only long enough to send rumor racing like some loathsome plague. The Saxons had begun their raids again, he told his horrified audience. His own Lord Eckwid was cut down by them yesterday. No doubt the barbarians were marching here now—the wise would flee while they could, or be swallowed by the murderous Saxon swarm.

At his words, the weight of cold fear had brought Riana's future into focus. She couldn't die and neither could she marry Gaston. She had to reach Camelot, so she could be there when Arthur came to need her.

But how? A female alone would never make it past the Saxon raiders, nor did she know the way to the far distant castle. Before she could take a step, she must find a male escort.

Staring up at this very hill she now climbed, it had struck her that she was an enchantress—or at least, the beginnings of one. If Arthur would not send a knight for her, why not summon one herself?

And so here she was, climbing this fearsome hill in the dark. Smiling as she continued upward, she imagined her rescuing knight. Tall, golden-haired, a gentleman of the highest order, he would not see a peasant, despite the coarse homespun wool of her tunic, but rather the lady underneath. Dipping over her fingertips, brushing them with his lips, he'd swear to offer his life to protect her own. He'd be kind and considerate and all she had ever dreamed of, and he'd never once hesitate to take her back where she belonged.

Of course she must summon him tonight. He was the one man who could make all the difference in her life.

Reaching the summit, she crossed to the area where the priestesses once gathered. The night seemed darker here, and a great deal cooler, but she could feel the ancient energies pulsing in the soil beneath her feet. Unlacing and kicking free of her leather sandals, she held out her bag, offering up the stones for the Earth Mother's blessing.

As she did, lightning again streaked across the heavens with no accompanying thunder.

It must be a sign, she thought. If only she had the skill to interpret it.

The Goddess did not normally favor heavenly omens, she knew, so it might be the brutal sky gods who thus expressed their desires. With an involuntary shudder, she thought of the recent Saxon raid, that proof of their savage cruelty. If their sky gods felt Riana meddled in matters that didn't concern her, they'd show no more mercy than the barbarians who worshipped them.

"No matter," she said defiantly as she set the sack of stones on the ground. As Sela accused, she was a creature of impulse, of action. Better to seize the moment, take control of it, than to wait to be overrun. Come what may, she would go to Camelot.

She looked around, finding the area adequate for her needs. Scattered about, small scraggly juniper bushes clung to the soil with stubborn determination. Another might yank them from the

ground to get them out of the way, but Riana admired their te-
nacity. She decided she could just dance around them.

Removing the first stone from the sack, she ran her hands over
its polished surface. Sela would be furious with her for taking
her "spell-makers." Having searched far and wide for the perfect
shapes and textures, the old woman was fanatical about her
stones and guarded them zealously, convinced that the loss of
even one would destroy the power of the rest.

To take them, Riana had slipped a sleeping draught into the
woman's ale earlier. Sela should stay abed long enough for her
to complete her enchantment and have the spell-makers back in
place undetected before the sun rose in the hills.

One by one, Riana set the stones in a circle on the ground
around her, counting out three steps between each. She needed
an area large enough to dance—the Goddess must hear the message of her footsteps—but not so extensive it would create gaps,
through which an earthbound demon might enter. One ran great
risks by creating an opening into the dark world, Sela often
warned. A proper magician took the necessary precautions.

When the last stone had been set and the circle could hold five
of her lying head to toe, she raised her arms to the sky and began
to chant. If she'd learned nothing else from reading Sela's leath-
erbound collection of runes and spells, she knew these particular
incantations summoned the energies of each stone and joined
them to form a secure border.

At the end of her chanting, a bolt of lightning split the sky to
her right, so close she could almost taste its acrid scent. Daunted,
she thought again about the Saxon gods, and prayed their pagan
force could not penetrate her enchantment.

A chill breeze began to stir, tugging at the ends of her cloak.
Looking about, seeing naught but the black and threatening sky,
she knew a sudden strong need to be home in their hut, huddled
on her straw mattress with the covers up to her chin. The air grew
cooler by the moment; the breeze swirled about her, gathering
force, coming alive.

Urgency overcame her. She could scarce think in her haste to perform her spell and be away from this place. Her hands trembled, her mind went blank. Try as she might, though she'd pored over the runes in Sela's book, she could not remember how the spell began.

Inhaling deeply, trying to gather her thoughts, she recalled that some conjurations required certain herbs, either crushed, left to scatter, or brewed in a tincture the magician must swallow. She had no herbs, nor even knowledge of the ones she should use. Sela was right; Riana always *did* rush into things unprepared. By the Goddess, this could be the single most important act of her life—what if she did it wrong?

"Sweet Mother Earth," she found herself praying, "Please protect me and help me achieve what I need."

All at once, she could feel the ground beneath her feet vibrate. Tingling from head to toe, she reached up, forming a link between earth and sky.

The scene before her blurred, became a mass of sensation. Colors swirled through her brain, rich, earthy hues interwoven with a deep, ardent red. The breeze tugged at her cloak, lifting it, coaxing her to untie the strings. No sooner did she pull at them than the cloak billowed out, dancing free off on the breeze. She felt light and airy, as if an enormous weight had been lifted from her shoulders. Indeed, she felt she too could be swept up and blown away by a current of air.

Magical air. She knew it, reveled in it. The breeze wove around her, not frightening now but instead softly whispering. It prodded her feet in a circular pattern about the confines of the stones until she found herself swaying, a willow in the breeze, the air soughing through her outstretched arms.

Intoxicated by the bittersweet scent of the juniper berries she inadvertently crushed beneath her feet, she danced to the drumbeat of her heart. Every part of her felt that mystical cadence, every part responded until ancient incantations came brimming to her lips.

Bring him here, she ended in a voice so deep and commanding, it could well belong to a stranger. *Bring forth the man who will make a difference in my life.*

At the words, power surged within her, vibrating up from her toes and out into her fingertips until earth and wind merged into a palpable force. Caught up in the sensation, becoming part of it, her feet danced faster and faster, her movements grew more driven. She jerked at the rope at her waist, unable to bear the restraint. Even her tunic seemed to weight her down, so she yanked it off, tossing it into the breeze. Tearing the woolen strip from her head, she let her long, golden hair whip wild and free about her shoulders. She was as the Earth Mother had created her, as primitive as any of Nature's creatures, at one with the gathering storm.

Somewhere deep inside, Riana was aware that she had never danced like this—been like this. Some unknown force pulled at her, probed into her, delved into her secret needs and desires. She ached with the hurt of her parents' desertion, the utter loneliness of having no family to call her own.

Make him want me, she heard herself whisper. *Never, ever let him leave me.*

As if in answer, the earth shook with the sudden roar of thunder.

Jolted as if struck by lightning, Riana stopped dancing, frozen to the spot. The world and all its painful realities came crashing back; she could now feel the rain, one chilly drop after another, striking her vulnerable skin. She shivered, the tremor snaking through her body. Suddenly, she felt a presence, a heat—as if a dragon lurked in the shadows, waiting to eat her alive.

Striving for calm, she told herself it was more likely Sela, come to chastise her for taking the spellmakers. Yet even as she braced herself for the old woman's admonitions, she realized that it could be her spell, already bearing fruition. He was here, the answer to her prayers!

With a rush of hope, she turned, the words of gratitude forming on her lips.

They froze there. Before her loomed a giant of a man, dark

and fierce and intensely real. Radiating with strength, with brute force, he stared at her hungrily, as if he were the dragon that meant to devour her.

With growing horror, she grew conscious of her naked state. Her cloak and tunic, she now remembered, had been offered up to the wind.

He reached forward with a powerful arm but as his fingers touched the stones' protective barrier, lightning erupted around them. He jumped back, roaring his own thunder, raising his sword in the air.

Blood running cold, she recognized that weapon. One tribe carried the fearsome seaxe, wore the leather cuirasses adorned with feral animals. With a gulp, she relinquished all hope. There would be no messenger from Camelot, nor any other savior.

Only this savage standing before her, this ruthless Saxon warrior.

Two

Penawulf, warrior chief of the great King Cerdric, stared at the wraithlike vision. Logic insisted that he return to the bottom of the hill, to the comfort of the night's fire and flagon of wine he shared with his men, yet the same inexplicable urge that had drawn him here kept him in place. One moment he'd been relishing today's raid with his warriors; in the next, he stood on this hill with a storm raging around him, unable to move.

It had come as a shock, the sight of smooth, pale flesh, her hair trailing like a golden cloud behind her, but his surprise swiftly turned urgent with lust. Filled with a need so fierce and sudden, his first impulse had been to take this female as an animal would claim its new-chosen mate.

Yet he remained immobile, the rain dampening his tunic and wind whipping his cloak, as he battled conflicting emotions. It was madness, surely. Watching her dance, he'd sensed she was a fey creature who would bring him nothing but trouble, but he could no more banish her from his mind than he could turn now and walk away. He knew only that he craved this female and had to have her.

On that thought, the hammer of Thunor crashed down from the heavens, the earth reverberating with its force. Convinced it must be a message from the great god himself, Penawulf thumped a hand against his chest, the gesture of obedience. His duty was plain. He must claim this girl, as Thunor expected.

Eyes round and wide like a startled deer, the girl eyed the area as if searching for where and how to bolt. Determined to prevent her flight, he reached out, but as they touched, a bolt of sky-fire shot between them.

Leaping back, arm raised and ready to use his seaxe, he roared his surprise as fire sped through his veins. The girl shrank back, her eyes like twin pools of reflected flame, glittering with her fright. Concerned that she would flee, he reached again for her, only to be burned by a second bolt of sky-fire. Its source, he realized with no little confusion, emanated from the ring of stones surrounding her.

Frowning, he studied the invisible wall, wondering why Thunor would lead him here to claim the female, and then keep her encased in trickery. Could it be some trial of wits? In King Cerdric's feast hall, the bards sang of the immortal blood that ran through his veins. Wodin's seed, they called Penawulf, and who else did the gods love to test more than their own?

They sang also of the many times Penawulf had met divine demands, both in the hunt and in war. Surely his patience and cunning, honed by the demands of forest and battlefield, would prove ample match for a collection of enchanted stones.

Circling the barrier, he poked with his seaxe, only to be met by the inevitable spark. The girl followed his every movement, clutching herself to shield her charms from him. Had he mastery of her tongue, he'd have told her she had no need to so bestir herself. She could be covered in a wealth of furs and still his mind's eye would see each inch of her graceful body. Her image had been branded on his brain and there it would stay forever.

Still, she must be cold. Though the storm showed signs of abating, the chill would merely deepen the nearer the night grew to dawn. Surely she must have brought clothing; this early in Spring, she would hardly climb the hill unclad. He glanced about and a splotch of brown caught his gaze. Striding over, he found a cloak, snagged by a juniper bush. The girl's alarmed expression proved it belonged to her.

A subtle whiff teased his nostrils as he lifted it, a mixture of field herbs and roses—her scent. Resisting the urge to bury his face in the soft folds of wool, he turned back to the circle. She glared at him, her wide eyes now accusing. She seemed to blame him for her captivity.

He held out the cloak to her, but of course, he had no way to give over her clothing. He had yet to find a way through the barrier.

Refusing to look at him, her gaze darted from the cloak to the stones, as if trying to reach a decision. Could it be that she held the power to do away with the walls of her cage?

Witchery, he thought with distaste.

His hands tightened on the cloak. To face the magic of the gods was one thing, but this . . . this reeked of mortal mischief, the pernicious influence of the ancient Druids that had caused such trouble for his tribe.

Yet as much as he despised and distrusted such sorcery, the fact that it was earthbound and not divine, made him smile. If this girl had designed the ring, if she could come and go on a whim, he need merely show that it was more desirable to be *outside* the circle.

Was he not the king's finest hunter? Hadn't he made his name and fortune in baiting the lure and setting the trap?

He set her cloak on the ground, just beyond arm's reach of the stones. She might not enjoy being snared like some prey, but this went beyond petty womanly pride. This female had been granted to him by the god Thunor, and by fair means or foul, Penawulf was destined to claim her.

Backing away from the circle, he dropped in a crouch, the stance he adopted when stalking wild beasts in the forest. He liked to be near the earth, to hear and feel its rhythms. Much could be gleaned when a man cleared his mind and left his instincts open to the secrets of nature.

Bring the girl into my keeping, he chanted silently, planting the fingers of his right hand deep in the earth.

And having made his prayer, he remained where he was, motionless and silent, waiting and watching.

* * *

Shivering with both fear and cold, Riana watched the Saxon go into his trance. Her panic eased—his failed attempts proved she was safe enough within the circle—yet he seemed such an intensely determined brute. She could not like that he had yet to give up and go away.

What could he want that he must crouch there, sizing her up like the hawk would a dove? She'd have voiced the question, but his mutterings had been in the harsh, unfamiliar Saxon. Besides, what wish had she to communicate? Better the untamed beast just go and leave her alone.

Unnerving how quietly, how intently he watched her.

She shivered again, blaming it on the chill air. Damn him for taking her cloak and leaving it there, too far for her to reach, but near enough to tempt her. He had to know she was freezing. Cruel and cunning, he was teasing her, trying to lure her out of the safety of her circle.

Never, she thought, hugging herself tighter. He'd pounce the instant she moved, and with his long, powerful legs, he'd overtake her in a heartbeat. She knew what befell maidens caught by Saxons in the dark of night—and those unlucky others at least had the veneer of clothing.

No, she'd be safest where she stood. He could not penetrate the circle, so she'd just wait him out. These barbarians were infamous for their lack of patience and restraint; surely she could outlast a witless savage.

Unfortunately, this brute seemed not the least impatient. The way he crouched there, watching her every blink and breath, she began to fear that she could freeze beneath the winter snows before he ever tired of his game.

Desperately, she tried to picture Sela's book of spells, struggling to remember the incantation to lull an enemy to sleep. She could wait for the Saxon to drift off, remove a stone from the circle—the farthest one from his reach—and venture out with the stealth of a snake.

Of course, Sela would rail at her for leaving the stones behind—not to mention wandering about the night without a thread to her name—but those worries held little precedence over the need to escape.

Biting her lip, she forced her mind to function, but the incantations came haltingly. Each word had to be dredged from the mire of memory, and by the moment, she grew more exhausted until she could barely keep her eyes open. Fear of her captor was all that kept her from falling asleep.

After some time, she looked up groggily to see the Saxon stiffen. Her heart leapt at the prospect that he'd at last given up and now meant to leave. A good thing, too, for he seemed not nearly as drowsy as he should.

As she herself felt.

". . . haven't the brains the Goddess gave you," Sela ranted suddenly behind her. "By all that is sacred, what am I to do with you? Stealing my spellmakers, disturbing my runes, and now I find you lying on the ancient summit. It's a miracle you weren't struck by lightning while you slept."

"I wasn't asleep." To her dismay, Riana's protest came out thick and clotted. Belatedly realizing that she was indeed lying down, she popped up to a sitting position, struggling to regain her wits. She noticed the first rays of dawn in the distance, streaking red across the sky. Just how long had she been lying there?

"Look at you." Sela tossed a bundle at her, which Riana recognized as her tunic. Fighting lethargy, she slipped it over her head.

"I warned you not to meddle in what you don't understand," Sela continued. "Who knows what other mischief you conjured in your sleep."

Riana wanted to deny again that she'd been sleeping, but it was difficult to argue when every muscle and bone ached from her time on the cold, hard ground. She wasn't the one who should have been lulled to sleep; she'd meant the spell for . . .

The Saxon!

Horrified at having forgotten him, she looked back to where

he'd been crouching, but of course he was no longer there. Hair rising on her neck, she turned to find him *inside* the stone barrier, looming right behind her.

She scrambled to her feet, meaning to flee, but he snared her wrist and clasped her close to him, making her feel his strength, his heat. Helpless in his grasp, she could only listen as Sela spoke to him sternly in what she assumed was his native tongue.

Odd, that her guardian should know Saxon. Odder, the way he smiled down at the old woman, as if her words amused him. From her tone, it would not seem Sela meant them to be a joke.

Riana watched them exchange words, the Saxon seeming a giant next to Sela's stooped and aging form. She could be a crone, her gray hair poked out at wild angles, her gnarled fingers wagging in accusation. Most of her displeasure seemed directed at the cloak he now held in his hand.

Still grinning, he draped the cloak on Riana's shoulders, then tied the strings like a parent would tend their child. A gesture amazingly gentle, but perhaps in her grogginess, she'd imagined it. She found no such tender concern in the large, powerful hand that clamped down on her wrist.

Nor did he bother to look at her as he spoke to Sela. His tone remained quiet, but she could not mistake his message for anything less than a command. His strong grasp made it clear Riana was his prisoner.

Still, escape might have been possible—it was one mere man against two clever magicians—had not a troop of Saxon warriors come charging up the hill. Impressive, the way they raced forward, gathering round him in marked concern for his well-being. Their instant obedience, the way they stepped back from her when he barked, proved he must be their leader.

Holding her cloak snugly about her, she prayed he had complete command of these warriors, for she could not like the way they ogled her. Relieved when Wolf moved his men away to confer with them, she turned instantly to her guardian. "What is happening, Sela?" she whispered. "You must know what is it he means to do with us."

Looking decidedly uncomfortable, Sela refused to meet her gaze. "As far as I can tell," she said, her words and shrug meant to be offhand, "he considers you his property and means to take you with him."

"But why?" Riana asked in bewilderment. "I have no fortune, no name to earn a ransom."

"Perhaps he sees you as his slave. In view of his blatant virility, and the fact that you were dancing naked, I can well imagine what your duties will be."

Blushing fiercely, Riana shook her head. She'd kill herself before submitting to the Saxon savage. "Surely you won't let it come to that."

The woman continued to look at the trees, rather than Riana. "How am I to stop him when I shall be here, all alone?"

"You won't be coming with me?" It betrayed her, that squeak. "But Sela, you've always been with me. And how can I protect myself when I don't know his language, or what to expect?"

Sighing, Sela gestured down at her stones. "These are things you should have considered before stealing my spellmakers. How many times have I warned that when one toys with the forces of Nature, one must be ready to pay the price? Ah child, just what did you hope to accomplish?"

"I wanted . . ." No, Riana thought angrily; she had no need to offer excuses. "It wasn't a silly whim, Sela. You know I am desperate to reach Camelot. I was setting a spell to summon a knight."

Sela's gaze was now trained on Riana's face. "You called for a royal escort, but summoned this Saxon instead?"

"I didn't summon him. He happened by while I was dancing." Even as she made the protest, Riana suffered qualms. In truth, she'd never been certain about her spell. Clasping her cloak tighter, she let the words trail off. No sense saying more. The old woman saw far too much as it was.

Sela grunted, but her eyes reflected fear and worry and perhaps resignation. "Very well, I suppose I must go with you. Someone must protect the poor Saxons. I hate to think what will become of the innocent women and children if you insist upon trying your magic on them."

Riana wanted to bristle but all she felt was relief. "You'll stay near?" she heard herself ask. "You won't let him hurt me?"

She was beginning to dislike the woman's shrugs. Anyone could see she meant to come with Riana—that in truth, the Saxon had probably given her no choice—but how like Sela to pretend she did them all a great favor.

Riana decided not to tell her about the sense of power she'd felt as she swayed and swirled with the storm. If Sela refused to take her talents seriously, then she'd keep their manifestations to herself.

Besides, she fully intended to outwit her captor. When she managed to get them to safety, she wanted the old woman surprised and properly grateful. Then, perhaps, she'd hear Sela's long overdue praise.

As if reading her thoughts, the Saxon left his men to come grasp her arm, providing no opportunity for escape. Saying nothing, he pulled her behind him down the hill, assuming the others would follow.

His confidence proved justified, as each man fell into line without a word, their silence infecting even Sela. Marching to their camp with barely the snap of a twig, they paused only to roll up their sleeping furs and gather their cooking implements. At his nod, they again formed behind their chieftain, and making little sound, leaving no sign that anyone had been in the area, they hurried down to the river.

It unnerved Riana to think these raiders might have come and gone in the past, with no one from the village guessing they'd been here. Indeed, with so hushed and hurried a departure, who would know she and Sela were gone? There would be no alarm raised, no hope for a rescue.

Three longboats sat on the bank, oars set and ready, the vessels waiting only to be boarded to be set into action. With the same silent efficiency, the Saxon raiders were soon seated and pushing off, the boats gliding away with barely a splash. Separated from

Sela, Riana sat in the lead boat facing her captor. His intent gaze made her look away, for she found it hard to marshal up plans for escape with the brute watching her every breath.

Time passed with each dip of the oar. As the morning mists lifted, and the sun rose high in the sky, her captor removed first his fur cape, then his cuirass and upper tunic, until he sat before her in only a thigh-length kilt. A thin sheen of sweat covered his bare torso.

Watching him ply oar to water in a slow, efficient stroke, Riana became distracted by the sight of all that gleaming muscle. She'd helped Sela with her healings, so was not a stranger to a man's anatomy, but no farmer in their village had shoulders that wide, or a chest so firmly planed. This Saxon would be a bear in combat, whether the battle be fought in the field, or, she thought with a shudder, at home in his bed.

Horrified by the thought, she forced herself to again look away.

But as the day wore on and the uninhabited shoreline provided little to hold her attention, she found her gaze drifting back to his features. Hard not to wonder about him. Odd, that his black shoulder-length hair would be shot with gray when his face held too few lines to wear the badge of age. And why was he alone clean-shaven? Surely it was a Roman trait, not often practiced by these barbarian louts.

Too, his features were sharper and more defined than the others. Where their eyes were blue and green, his gray glittered with silver glints. His angular bone structure hinted again at a Roman influence, creating features so hard and controlled, they could have been cut from stone—chiselled, like the carvings on the huge ancient monoliths on the plains.

When he smiled, his was a handsome face, yet woe to the fool who forgot his penetrating scowl. Life would not go well for one who defied him, she sensed. In vengeance, this man would be harsh and unforgiving.

At his shout, she jumped, jolted out of her thoughts. To her relief, it was not at herself that he pointed, but rather to the shoreline ahead.

A tiny village sat nestled on the bank and as the Saxons rowed their longboats up to it, the villagers—mostly female—ran from all directions to greet them. Amid shouts and laughter, the longboats were beached and several buxom young maids crowded around Riana's captor. He shrugged them off, reaching down to lift her from the craft. Tugging her behind him, he led the way into the hamlet.

He brought her to a rickety bench, then gestured for Sela to join her. Clapping his hands, he summoned a pair of giggling females, whose faces fell as he barked orders. When they stomped off, he pointed to the bench, looking from her to Sela.

"He wants us to sit," Sela explained. "I suggest we obey, for he appears to be in no mood to be crossed."

Openly displaying reluctance, Riana took a seat. The two females returned with a weak rabbit stew and vinegary wine she could not gulp down. It was not that she was nervous, she insisted to herself, just merely too intent on their escape.

His men claimed his attention and with great relief, she watched him sit with them on the far end of the village. She could see they were deep in argument, but the source of the conflict didn't interest her. With their captor so occupied, she and Sela could not find a better time to take flight.

Yet when she suggested fleeing, Sela laughed. "We'd not last one hour in these woods," she snorted with her finest scorn. "Unless you wish to be dragged about trussed up like a bird, I'd eat their food and give Penawulf no excuse to bind you."

"Pena *Wolf?* That is his name?" Irked that the woman had scoffed at her plan—and annoyed that Sela might have good reason—Riana gave vent to her anger. "It suits him. I saw how he waited with sneaky cunning to pounce and strike. And I bet he growls when things don't go his way."

"He's not the only one."

"I never growl." Affronted, Riana drew in a calming breath. "Take care in how you bait me," she snapped. "When I get back to Camelot and earn my true place in the court, I shall have tallied up each insult."

"Camelot's a long way away, girl, and your Saxon has no intention of letting you go there."

"He cannot stop me. I mean to escape, Sela, whether or not you choose to come with me."

Penawulf listened absentmindedly while the others argued over whether to bed down in the hamlet tonight, or push on to Cerdric's fortress. He was anxious to face his king, but many of his men had girls waiting in the village who had been warming their beds for them too long already.

Though he wished to be done with his royal duty so he could deal with the girl he'd captured, Penawulf knew also that the raid's success owed much to each man's contribution and his warriors deserved the reward Cerdric promised them. Too, it was long-standing custom to let the group make the decision.

If one could be reached. From the vehemence of each argument, the debate seemed likely to continue throughout the night.

His thoughts strayed, even as his gaze did, finding the girl at once. Hands on hips, she spoke sharply to the old woman, as if they, too, were in conflict. Trouble brewing, he thought, rising to his feet. He could see how the girl eyed the trees. The old woman might have sworn not to escape, but he'd wrangled no such concession from her charge.

Concerned, he strode to the females. Two men rose to follow at his heels—Tadrick, the eager youth who dogged his every move, and Ranulf, his lifelong friend and loyal companion, who must be confused by his interest in the hostage. The girl held little value, save for the brief pleasure she'd provide, and his ambitious chieftain rarely put pleasure before profit.

Understanding his own motives no better, Penawulf came up behind the women in time to hear the younger one speak angrily. A small grin played at old Sela's lips as she nodded in his direction. The girl spun to face him, her skin paled but her mouth unaffected. Rattling off a string of invectives, she spat her derision into the leaf-covered ground.

Scowling, Penawulf asked the old woman for a translation.

"Hearing your name, she's decided to call you Wolf."

Beside him, his companions chuckled. He silenced young Tadrick with a frown, but Ranulf had been a friend too long, and his humor was harder to stifle. "It suits you," the man said, "though I daresay she hadn't meant to compliment you on your skill as a hunter."

"That is enough—"

"I like it so much," his friend went on, not the least daunted, "I think I myself shall call you Wolf from now on. What is her name, I wonder?"

A good question, and one he had not yet thought to ask. He turned to Sela. "Tell me, what is it you call her?"

"She is known as Moriana."

He said the name slowly, the syllables sensuously rolling off his tongue. Plainly puzzled, Ranulf stopped laughing, but it was the girl's face Penawulf studied. He could see it unnerved her, him knowing her name.

Eyeing her, she reminded him of a cornered cat, wary and unpredictable, ready to strike rather than ever surrender. It would take time and patience to tame her, neither of which he had in large supply.

"Enough of your foolery," he barked at Ranulf, gesturing to the trees. "Gather the treasure bags. We must be on our way."

"But the men—nothing has yet been decided."

"I have decided. We march at once for Cerdric's fortress."

Though clearly bewildered, Ranulf and Tadrick went to pass on the news. It would cause strife, his going against custom, but Penawulf was in a fever to settle things with his king. To get home to his village.

"Wait," the old woman called when he, too, would turn away. "The girl would know what you mean to do with her."

"That will be for the king to decide," he told her curtly. "And we shall know his decision soon enough."

* * *

Hours later, stumbling behind him and ready to collapse, Riana decided her captor was worse than a wolf. He was a cur, a vile, foul mongrel she would destroy once she got the chance. He was also strong and capable and she'd neither opportunity nor courage to openly defy him.

Hurrying through the forest, he set the pace, his warriors following with a low, unhappy grumbling. Riana could scarce breathe trying to keep up with his long, sure strides, but she had no trouble seeing his scowl. Like his companions, she saw no wisdom in complaining to his face.

He did it on purpose, she grew convinced, forcing her hither and yon over such unforgiving terrain so when they finally stopped, she'd be too bruised and weary to flee. That he was determined to keep her prisoner she could no longer doubt. What she didn't know was why he would want her.

And why such hurry? she wondered as she again tripped and he dragged her to her feet. The man seemed driven, as if some demon rode his back with a penetrating lash. Did he chase the sun, striving to reach his home before it soon dropped behind the distant hills? No, she found it unlikely that nightfall would bother one of his ilk. Like the wolf she'd named him, this Saxon creature would be equally at home in the dark.

Just when she thought she could bear the suspense no longer, they came upon a wood-framed settlement of huge dimensions. A tall buttressed wall with towers in all four corners protected the collection of mismatched structures inside its mammoth oak gate.

Along the perimeter, in haphazard fashion, sat odd little timber-framed huts. Short and squat, with their sloped thatched roofs touching the ground, they looked as if they'd been sunk half below the ground. Roughly dressed churls stood outside these meager dwellings. Weary and mud-stained from their days in the fields, both men and women waved eagerly to the returning raiders—though the females, Riana noted, seemed particularly anxious to welcome her captor home.

He pressed on, driving them past the byres and working sheds, to the huge, wood structure in the center. Three stories tall, it towered over the settlement with an air of importance. Riana assumed it must be their meeting place, a grand hall for meetings and celebration, since behind the huge oak door, she could hear muffled music and laughter.

At a question from one of his warriors, Wolf nodded, gesturing back to the others. Simultaneously, they lifted the sacks to their shoulders and filed past into the building. Holding Riana back, Wolf looked at her long and hard, his expression grim, killing any hope that she could stop whatever he intended. With a clenched jaw, he clasped her arm and tugged her behind him. A cacophony of shouts erupted around them as they entered the hall.

She found herself on a wide, raised step, looking down on the feasting hall below. Thirty or more men sat at the benches lining the side walls. Before them, long trestle tables groaned under the weight of food and drink, while on the walls at their back, shields and swords hung from hooks. The king's warriors, Riana thought, noticing their scarred faces and powerful forms. Tonight, they had laid down their arms for a communal feast, with their ladies sitting beside them.

A fire had been set at the central hearth, and at a shout from the raised dais at the far end of the room, servants scurried to light it. Riana's gaze was drawn to the large bearded gentleman seated at the dais table. The sudden hush as everyone in the room turned in the same direction indicated that he must be their king.

The fire sprang to life, giving light and life to the room, but the king's broad smile offered the warmest welcome. Standing, raising his goblet, he shouted to Wolf. Everyone rose, echoing the greeting in a rousing cheer.

Wolf stood quietly beside her, giving no sign of his emotions as he waited for the noise to subside. He must be accustomed to homage, Riana decided resentfully. From his aloof manner, one would think he considered himself the king instead.

As the room quieted, Wolf gestured to the man who had teased him earlier. His friend stepped forward, holding out a sack. Taking the opportunity to slip free of her captor's grasp, Riana went to Sela, apart from the warriors.

"That is Cerdric, their high king," the old woman explained in a whisper. "A boy from the hamlet raced ahead with word of our arrival and the king has gathered his men to celebrate. Wolf was sent out to avenge the death of Cerdric's nephew, murdered by a roving Briton tribe. A great reward was promised on his successful return."

"Was he? Successful, I mean?"

"See for yourself."

Her gaze followed to where Wolf reached in the sack. Everyone leaned forward, the anticipation audible. Dramatically, Wolf yanked out his prize, holding it high for all to witness. Another round of cheers erupted.

It was a head . . . a severed human head.

Bile rose in Riana's throat and nausea threatened. All this time, he'd been carrying that gruesome trophy. No wonder Britons feared and hated Saxons. It took a monster to mutilate another human being, then display such work with so little remorse. Nay, with such pride.

She could not bear to look at Wolf, much less contemplate a future at his mercy. Each time she thought of his hands on her, hands that now held what was left of his victim, she grew more desperate to flee. Only the certainty that it could as easily be her head next kept her in place.

A servant appeared with a pole, to which Wolf relinquished what remained of his enemy. Riana had little time to see where it went, for with another clap, King Cerdric summoned Wolf forward.

He reached for Riana, dragging her behind him, separating her once more from Sela. She found it impossible to wriggle free, but not for a lack of trying. Hating him, resenting every new turn in her life, she wished now she'd married Gaston. Sela was right; she was a fool to meddle with magic.

They stopped before the dais. Above them, the king stood flanked on the right by two females, one draped in jewels and fur who must be his queen, and a younger plain-faced woman who eyed Riana with suspicion. The tall man to the left, clad in an immaculate white tunic, seemed polished and refined enough to pass as a knight of the Round Table, until he raised his goblet to toast with the king and his raucous shouts proved him as coarse and rough as any Saxon warrior.

Wolf bowed to the king and his ladies, ignoring the man entirely.

Though Riana could not understand the words, she sensed Cerdric must be offering a reward. Wolf's frown implied that it did not meet with his approval. The king's tone grew heated, his manner more insistent. The room hushed as he pounded a fist into the table.

Wolf stood silent throughout, merely shaking his head in refusal each time the king paused. It was not until the man on Cerdric's left leaned over to speak in the king's ear that Wolf showed emotion. Riana now sensed his rage, tightly checked and barely visible, but awesome nonetheless.

Wolf's words to the king were cool and clipped. Glancing from his stiff profile to the two men united against him, Riana could feel his resolve tighten with his grasp. From the glint in his gray eyes to the taut set of his jaw, it was clear her captor wanted something—something he'd do all in his power to achieve.

As if Wolf had found the right words, the king broke into a wide, approving grin. The man next to him narrowed his gaze, focusing on Wolf. He did not seem pleased when Cerdric shouted to the others and cheers again broke out around the hall.

Too suddenly, everyone's attention shifted to her, as if her fate had at last been decided. Riana felt her throat go painfully tight. It did not bode well that the king and his thanes now leered at her, that the queen gazed down with a pitying expression.

Riana would have cried out, demanding to know their plans, but four guards appeared at her side to whisk her from the room. Panicked, she reached for Wolf—now suddenly the lesser of two evils. He might still be a Saxon savage, but he was big and strong and earlier, his single glance had kept his men from touching her.

Now, however, he merely shrugged off her grasp, making no move to protect her, nor even so much as turn to look her way.

Desperate and afraid, she resorted to anger. How dare he ignore her. His possessive grasp, his intensity as he'd dragged her through the forest—where was it now? To learn he had stolen her from her home to use as a bargaining tool, some trinket he could barter, seemed an insult, a betrayal. And now that her usefulness was at an end, he acted as if she'd never existed.

Biting and kicking whoever was unfortunate enough to get within range, she fought as her newest captors tried to pull her away. "Don't make it worse," Sela hissed as Riana was jostled past her. "Don't give them the excuse to kill you."

"Wolf!" she was horrified to hear the scared little girl in her cry out. "Please, you must help me."

He had to have heard the fear in her voice, if not the full content of her words, but as if he'd gone suddenly deaf, he stood still as stone, never once turning to face her.

"You shall pay for this," she shouted, hating him with every ounce of her being as she was dragged from the room.

Three

Wolf steeled himself against the girl's cries as the guards carried her from the hall. Though unaware of her actual words, he could guess their content, but he dared not reassure her. Too many eyes watched him, assessed him—the queen and the princess most intently. One complaint from either and all could be ruined.

"This is madness," Princess Gerda protested, her thick hands tightening on her goblet. "Father, you can't mean to go through with this."

Gazing over the hall, Cerdric grinned ear to ear. "And why not? This is what my warriors need, not some bard spinning the same tired tales. These men are starved for real entertainment."

Gerda's broad cheeks flamed with resentment. Everyone in the hall knew the princess designed each night's activity. "Where is the thrill in watching two men battle over a mere slave?" she asked haughtily. "And a rather puny one at that."

Wolf stiffened, disliking that she should speak of Moriana with such derision. Envy must drive the princess. Where Moriana had the beauty and grace of a gazelle, Gerda reminded men more of the royal oxen. Solid and sturdy, plain of face and disposition, she rarely inspired her father's thanes to engage in competition.

Yet in all truth, it had once been Wolf's plan to ask for her hand in marriage. He had ambitions, lofty ones, and wedding the king's daughter seemed the simplest means of achieving them.

"It is unseemly," Gerda went on, casting a desperate look in his direction. "Mother, make them stop this."

Ignoring Gerda completely, Cerdric frowned at Queen Anya. "Tell your daughter not to presume on my affections for her. These are matters for me to decide. It is not for her to criticize a royal command."

Anya smiled sweetly. "Gerda did not mean to interfere, my king. We have all looked forward to Penawulf's homecoming, and here it must be spoiled by some petty argument over a slave. Why not give the girl to Vangarth and the land to Penawulf, as you first decreed?"

Wolf struggled against the protest rising to his lips. It would do little good, he knew, for he'd made that mistake earlier. He should have taken the land the king offered and thanked him, instead of demanding Moriana as well. In all likelihood, she'd have come to him anyway, since it was his right as warrior chief to have first pick of the loot. His insistence, on the other hand, merely raised the girl's value in his rival's eyes.

Vangarth had always sought what Wolf wanted. And from boyhood onward, the knave had taken great pleasure in flaunting each acquisition he wrangled away.

Not this time, Wolf thought determinedly. Not Moriana.

Yet Vangarth seemed equally set upon having her, though what he would do with her, Wolf did not enjoy considering. How could one read such a changeable toad—now the simpering diplomat to charm the queen when only moments before he'd been the proud, blustering warrior toasting his king?

"It is kind of you to take my part, my lady." Vangarth dipped a courtly bow, his words dripping like honey from his facile tongue. "But surely you must see how I cannot resist? Why refuse, when I can have both the girl and the land, merely by defeating Penawulf? Yet again, I might add."

The man had bested him a mere two times, both when they were youths and only because Vangarth had twice cheated, but Wolf saw the wisdom in holding his protest. After all these years of aching for the opportunity to prove his true strength, here was his chance at last to wipe the smirk off that strutting peacock's face.

Queen Anya made great work of pushing the food about her plate. "It seems a pity," she said airily, "when the competition could be made doubly interesting. If you men must fight, I would think you'd wish the prize to be something worth battling over."

Cedric eyed her with surprise. "Isn't a hundred hides of prime hunting and grazing land along the river worthy enough?"

"Perhaps." Sighing, the queen lifted her goblet to her lips. "But only think," she said, pausing to sip and swallow. "This competition could be twice as exciting, were the stakes raised. Why fight over a mere slave? Your warriors should vie for your daughter's hand in marriage."

A shocked silence blanketed the hall. Wolf could hear the logs behind him, sizzling and popping on the fire, keeping pace with the thoughts racing through his mind. How slyly the queen had maneuvered them. He should feel flattered that she'd be so certain of his victory, for Anya made no secret of the fact that she wanted him for her daughter, yet all he knew was an urge to run. Once, the prospect of marrying Gerda had seemed advantageous, so why did it now loom more as a trap?

Cedric turned from his wife, but the gleam in his eye betrayed his interest. Pacing behind the table, he seemed to give serious thought to the queen's proposition.

It was Vangarth who asked the question uppermost in Wolf's mind. "The girl—the slave—what is to become of her?"

"Give her over to your warriors. They deserve a reward." The queen shrugged, dismissing the thought as beneath her consideration. "When they are done with her, she can serve in the kitchens."

"If I might offer a suggestion?" Vangarth nodded in Wolf's direction. "In light of his recent raid, it would be unfair for Penawulf to walk from this night with naught but his humiliation. Let the slave be offered in consolation to the loser."

Wolf wanted to argue, to insist the winner take all, but the king instantly shouted his approval. Surrounded by the cheers of his fellow warriors, Wolf waited in angry silence. How like Vangarth to make certain that whatever the outcome, he would win and his opponent could only lose.

Wolf had to defeat his lifelong rival; pride demanded it. How could he face that constant smirk, or live in a kingdom where Vangarth might one day be king? More importantly, what would he tell his tribe when he returned empty-handed, with neither the wealth nor land they needed to prosper? It was not for his future alone that he must fight; many others depended upon his success. Win, and he could achieve all that his father's death had lost them. Lose, and he could forfeit what few hopes remained for his people.

Even knowing all this, he kept hearing Moriana's pleas as she was dragged from the hall. It caused him physical pain, imagining her locked within Vangarth's selfish embrace. Yet saving her, he knew, carried too high a cost.

At the king's shout, Wolf turned and strode down the hall to join his men. His fellow warriors continued to shout as he marched by, offering their cheers, as certain as the queen that he would win the competition. They, too, depended on his victory, he realized. The thanes lining those walls knew Vangarth's cruel streak and few wished to risk that he would one day lead them.

Surrounded by his men, receiving a bracing clap on the back from each, Wolf felt as if a trap had indeed been sprung about him. After long years of faithful service, they had their expectations, these men, and as their leader, Wolf must fulfill them. His father Exar, were he still alive, would demand that he purge his mind of such romantic nonsense, that he think not of the females involved but rather of the consequences should he be defeated. He was Penawulf, warrior chief of River Ford, and he must do what he'd been trained a lifetime to accomplish.

He must fight to victory, or fight to the death.

Riana could hear the cheers behind her and the din filled her with dread. The brutes in the feast hall sounded so like a pack of wild dogs, she half expected her guards to set her loose in the forest so their fellow savages could chase and track her down.

It was with great surprise, and no simple outrage, that she found herself dumped unceremoniously in one of those strange little huts instead.

Since the dirt floor was indeed below ground level, her entrance included a brief but unpleasant fall. Kneeling on all fours in the dark, she stifled a sob. They could do what they must, but she'd never let these Saxon brutes see her whimper. Rising to her feet, brushing herself off, she decided she might better occupy her mind trying to escape.

It was no easy thing, feeling her way through the dark. She reached out with her hands, seeking any opening that might lend itself to an exit, forcing herself to go slowly. Which was as well, else she'd have been knocked off her feet when the door was again thrust open.

Light from a lone candle filtered across the room. Poised in the door frame, Sela seemed like a gift from the Goddess. It had to be a sign, her fortuitous appearance. If magic could bring her guardian here to her, magic would help them get away.

As if to dash that hope completely, Sela shook her head. "We can go nowhere," she whispered, nodding back over her shoulder. "Two armed guards wait outside."

To emphasize this, the door slammed shut behind her. Although unnerved by the sound Riana refused to let her hopes be deflated. As long as they had the light of the candle—and Sela's magic—they could yet escape.

With far more grace than Riana had shown, the old woman stepped down into the hut and crossed over to the pile of straw mats in the corner. Ignoring her, Riana studied their surroundings. No windows, she noticed with disappointment. Just four wattle and daub walls, a damp earthen floor, and the mats. She supposed they were to sleep on them, since she saw no other furniture. Stark and barren, the room seemed more than ever a prison.

The word did not sit well with her peace of mind.

"What is happening out there?" she asked, preferring not to

dwell on the implications. "What are they saying? Why are they cheering?"

"Trust me, you don't wish to know."

Though Moriana winced, she would not be daunted. "Must you always be so provoking? I need to know what they discuss to better prepare myself."

Muttering softly, Sela stuck the candle in the dirt, then took a mat to set on the floor beside the candle. "It was hardly a discussion," she said as she sat, settling her voluminous skirts about her. "They were scrapping over you like dogs over a bone. As I told you, Penawulf considers you his."

"That savage?" Riana could not get enough contempt in her voice. She would never acknowledge his ownership of her, not when she knew he could discard her with the same disregard he'd shown for the severed head.

Nay, she'd far rather kill him first—and failing that, she'd as soon kill herself. "If so, he was foolish to argue with his king over me," she told Sela coldly. "Given the chance, I shall make his life a living misery."

"You may not get the chance. That other one, that Vangarth, he wants you, too, enough to challenge the returning hero to mock battle. Though his interest, I fear, is suspect. Vangarth cares for none but his own concerns."

It had ceased to surprise Riana how swiftly Sela could sum up a man's character; through the years, the old woman had remained so accurate, Riana would be foolish to doubt her now. Besides, she'd seen the same greed in the man's lascivious gaze. Vangarth's lust held all the generosity and comfort of a bitter North wind.

"Wolf will not let him win," she blustered, pacing from one side of the hut to the other. "You said yourself he considers me his own."

"Perhaps." Sela flashed her secret smile, as if knowing far more than she let on.

Riana halted, uneasiness gripping her. "We're both in danger here. Don't forget, you, too, are their prisoner. You too will suffer should the wrong man win."

"Perhaps," Sela said again, pinning her with her gaze. "But who do you consider the *wrong* man?"

A probing question, and one Riana would rather avoid. "I want neither, and you know it. Stop trying to irk me and help find a way out of this hut. We must be gone before their battle is over."

"And what do you suggest?" Waving a gnarled hand, Sela gestured about them. "Shall we dig a trench with our hands, butt our heads against the timber frame? Or perhaps you would like to engage in combat with the two burly warriors at the door?"

"Don't mock me. You know full well I want you to use magic. Can't you melt a hole in the wall, or perhaps lull the guards to sleep? You must have some enchantment that will get us safely away from this place."

Sela shook her head. "Do you truly think it that simple? That I need merely chant a word or two and all will be well? This is heathen land. Even were I so gifted, the powers of the Goddess hold little sway here. Besides, as you no doubt remember, thanks to you I have lost my sacred stones."

"So you will do nothing?" Riana pressed, refusing to be stopped by such a blatant attempt to make her feel guilt.

"Did you not hear me? There is nothing I *can* do."

"Very well, if you insist upon playing the coward, perhaps I should try. I'd likely do a better job of it anyway."

If she'd hoped to prod the old woman to action, her boast had the opposite effect. Sela shrugged off her words with a grin. "One would think you'd have learned your lesson. Or have you forgotten we would not be here now had you not proved your ineptitude by summoning that Saxon?"

"You can't know that. He could have been out for a stroll."

"In the rain?"

The fact that the old woman could be right made Riana determined to prove her wrong. "Who can know what these savages will do? Our people might shy from a rain-soaked amble, but then, no knight of the Round Table would engage in mock battle over a mere prisoner."

"You flatter yourself. Their battle is not to win you."

"But you said . . ." Riana faltered, thinking back to what the old woman had actually told her.

"The argument might have started with you, child, but it soon became a larger battle of wills. They fight now for the princess Gerda's hand in marriage. Both men entertain ambitions for Cerdric's throne. You are merely a consolation to the loser."

Consolation to the loser? Bristling, Riana could hear distant shouts as the warriors cheered the combatants to victory and she prayed the contest would continue indefinitely. In her mind, there was not much to choose between the two. Which could be worse, Vangarth's icy regard, or Wolf's passionate intensity? Neither would take well to losing, she feared, and being Saxon, both were liable to take out their defeat on an innocent victim.

With a grunt, Sela stated her intention of getting some much needed sleep. Her suggestion that others might benefit from rest was ignored as Riana continued to pace across the hut. She felt too nervous to close her eyes, too unsettled. Each shout had her jumping. Every cheer sent her thoughts racing, certain that this was it, the moment she dreaded, the time when the loser would come drag her away.

Yet the contest went on, wearing down her nerves until she knew she must do something. It should be easy enough to lull the guards outside to sleep; surely she could remember the proper spell this time.

And when she escaped, she thought spitefully as she eyed the dozing Sela, perhaps she would not wake the old woman.

Her spite lasted less than an instant, for in her mind, she could see Vangarth kicking and beating that tiny, frail frame, blaming Sela for letting his prize slip out of his grasp. No, she'd no choice but to take her guardian along, despite her complaints and taunting. In her own way, Riana supposed she had a certain fondness for the old woman.

Besides, how could she resist the chance to prove she was right, and Sela was wrong?

Determined to show that she could indeed weave an enchantment correctly, Riana lifted the candle as she stood in the center of the hut. Chanting softly, she stared at the door, willing the men outside to grow drowsy. As she listened for the thud as their bodies hit the ground, the door wavered before her vision. Vertigo threatened, so she sat, poking the candle in the dirt beside her. Her chanting faltered, dropped off altogether. She found it harder and harder to mouth the words. Her tongue felt so heavy, her thoughts seemed mired in quicksand.

So much so that she barely noticed that it was her own body that dropped to the ground with a thud.

Panting fiercely, Wolf stood at his end of the field, guarding the circle in which the wolf, his new marking, had been etched. After an hour of fighting, Vangarth lay prone, badly winded before him. All Wolf need do was plunge his spear into the ground on the opposite side of the field, in the circle bearing his opponent's poorly-drawn lion.

Yet he stood frozen, unable to make the move. He wanted to, knew he had to, but it was as if some force reached out to stay his hand. Where he should be seeing blood-lust and victory, he saw only the golden flecks of Moriana's eyes.

Gathered around them, the warriors leaned forward, sweating with worry and hope, sensing that the contest would soon be ended. Act now, and Wolf could be lifted up onto their shoulders to be toasted as champion and granted all that any king's thane could desire.

And what then would happen to Moriana? a voice whispered inside him, even as her image swam hazily before his eyes.

From far away, he could hear the shouted warnings, could feel the crowd's apprehension, but he was held captive by the vision. By the time his head cleared enough to realize Vangarth was charging toward his circle, it was too late. Wolf had more than lost his opportunity for victory; he stood poised on the brink of defeat.

Gathering his wits, he moved to block his opponent, but Vangarth had charged unimpeded from too great a distance. They collided with tremendous force, and both went crashing to the dirt.

Badly winded and seeing stars, Wolf shoved Vangarth aside and staggered to his feet, determined to defend his target. Groping for the spear he'd dropped when he fell, he turned to find Vangarth had gone for his own weapon. Yet as he came at Wolf, screaming as he charged, the man seemed to change before Wolf's eyes, transforming into Moriana's fragile, shimmering image.

Vague longing swamped and confused him, coming as they did with a sense of peril, as heavy as a cloak closing around them. Reaching for the hazy vision, he cried out her name, meaning to alert her to the danger.

At the sudden, bloodcurdling war whoop, the girl's image dissolved. Bemused, Wolf stared at the spear piercing the ground behind him, quivering there with the force of its delivery. He whirled to see Vangarth's upraised arms, his wide, gloating smile. Wolf's confusion swiftly became guilt, then shame, as Cerdric stepped forward to declare his hated opponent the victor.

Wolf flung his own spear away from him in self-loathing. From this day onward, he knew, he would be made to suffer the fool's tauntings.

And he'd no one but himself to blame. One moment he'd held the world in his hands and with an instant's inattention, he'd watched his future—and that of his people—slip out of his grasp.

And all because he could not stop thinking about his strangely beguiling prisoner. What had come over him to make him lose sight of the importance of this battle? And why did he now, despite his ignominious defeat and his warrior's obvious disappointment, feel a measure of relief that the girl would be free of Vangarth's sadistic urges?

Confused and unsettled, he watched the others file back to the feast hall, duty-bound to honor Vangarth's victory. Some looked back at Wolf with derision, some with pity, others with mere confusion. The king scowled, while his women ignored Wolf entirely, proving that whatever aspirations he might once have had about joining the royal family were now crushed forever.

It worried him, yet Wolf still found himself in a fever to get to Moriana. Considering his king's current displeasure with him, he could not trust that the girl would still be granted as his consolation. He might be wiser to take her and go, on the implied assumption that royal permission had been granted. Let Cerdric come to River Ford to retrieve Moriana, if he were that determined.

Barking orders at Ranulf, Wolf saw the bewilderment on his old friend's face. To command his men to leave in the midst of a feast, especially when they had yet to be rewarded for their raid, was ill-advised at best. The men were too spent to make the long trek home, and Vangarth—not to mention the king himself—could well take their departure as a slight.

Repeating his command, brooking no argument, Wolf turned on a heel and strode to the prison hut. He had no need for Ranulf to point out that his thinking was irrational and self-destructive, most of all to himself. No one could be wearier, since he'd had no rest the night before and his body had been battered by the fight with Vangarth. Too, as their leader, Wolf stood to lose the most should the king take offense.

Stay, act the diplomat, and he might mend the necessary fences, yet irrationally, he remained determined to take Moriana and go home.

Flinging open the door of the prison hut, he found her sleeping on the earthen floor, knees gathered into her chest like a child, looking small and defenseless and completely alone. It struck him forcefully that he had to be her champion. The girl had no one else.

Walking up to her, he resisted the urge to touch her face, to stroke her golden hair. She might seem soft and compliant in her sleep, but he knew better than to hope she would wake with a smile of welcome. Better to wake the old woman and let her rouse the girl instead.

His reasoning proved faulty. Though the woman spoke gently, she could not have chosen the words with care, for Moriana jerked up to a sitting position, first alarmed, then confused, then spoiling for a fight.

"What is it?" he asked Sela, deciding he must soon learn the Briton tongue. "What is she shouting about?"

The old woman shrugged. "She refuses to go anywhere with you."

Wolf gazed at them both in disbelief. "Have you explained? Does she understand what may happen if she stays?"

"Go. Stay. She can't see that it will make a difference."

Wolf did not bother to keep the irritation from his tone. "I will not hurt her, old woman. Tell her that."

Sela rattled off her explanation, to which the girl curled her lip and spat her words to the ground at his feet. Wolf had no need to ask for a translation. From the way she crossed her arms at her chest and planted her feet, it was clear what position she meant to take.

Thinking of what she had cost him, his own anger and resentment came to the fore. "Your young charge is too proud for her own good," he told Sela. "Perhaps I should leave her to her fate and be done with it."

He thought he saw a flicker of fear in the woman's gaze, but her eyes were deep, with many hidden fathoms, and it was hard to guess the contents of her mind.

"Be patient," she said soothingly. "She's young and can't see what's best for her."

But his patience was strained, and he was too weary and worn to argue further. Striding over, he reached down for her, intent upon escorting her from the hut. As his hands encircled her waist, a throbbing began in his groin. He knew he should take her and go, but all he could see was her soft, quivering mouth. It seemed suddenly vital that he taste her soft, moist lips, explore all of her delectable body, right here, right now, on the floor of this hut.

She spared him such insanity by kicking out and clawing at him like a treed feline.

With a hearty sigh, he hefted her onto his shoulder like a sack of grain. A twisting, biting, screeching sack of grain.

Carting her off, he could feel his anger feed on itself. After all he'd sacrificed for this girl, this was her gratitude? His tribe would suffer long for this night's work, and so, too, would his pride. Everywhere he went, people would look away, knowing he'd shamed himself by his defeat. Were his father still alive, he'd have ordered Wolf out of his house, for no true chieftain would consider the needs of one—a mere female, at that—over the needs of the tribe. Exar would have dumped the ungrateful shrew in the mud and left her to her well-deserved fate.

So why did Wolf clasp tight to her wriggling form, determined to drag her across England with him? How could one single female continue to distract him from the sane and sensible? Knowing he had no real answers, Wolf carried her to where his men waited.

Knowing her struggles and screeching could draw attention and prevent their departure, he gagged her mouth, then bound her wrists and secured a rope at her waist. He set off, dragging her through the forest.

This time they skirted the tiny hamlet, knowing how swiftly news carried from there to the king's fortress. Reaching the river-bank, Wolf relinquished the rope, ordering Moriana dumped in his longboat. Perhaps the trek had subdued her, for she made no attempt to resist.

As he took his seat before her, their gazes locked. Recognition that he was the hunter and she, the captured prey, glittered in the gold-strewn depths of her eyes. He could see her fear, her panicked desperation, and he knew a sudden wish to unleash her. She was like the wild, untamed creatures of the forest who would wither and die if not left to roam free.

Yet even as hope flickered in her gaze, he knew he could not let her go. Were she captured here, Cerdric would give her to Vangarth. Too, the gods had granted Moriana to him for a reason, and until he learned what it was, he must take her, and keep her.

However miserable it made them both.

* * *

In the longboat behind them, Sela smiled to herself. From the men's chattering, she knew where they were headed. There were places farther away from Camelot than River Ford, she supposed, but few so conveniently remote.

Her old bones might feel stiff and brittle from all their travels, but in the main, she was well pleased with how things had turned out. Trust the Goddess to send a capable champion like Penawulf.

Or had his summons, she thought uneasily, shifting her weight on the wooden plank seat of the longboat, been less than divine intervention?

Sela remembered finding Riana on that hill, lying amongst the juniper with the spellmakers circled around her, and Penawulf watching the girl like a man possessed. Was it possible, in her ignorance, that Riana could have inadvertently trapped the Saxon in an enchantment?

She told herself it did not matter. The end result was all that should concern her, and Riana must end up married.

Gazing at the Saxon's powerful frame, feeling as if the Goddess herself had whispered the order, Sela became convinced that the girl must wed this strong warrior. There were forces at play, darker forces than the girl could fathom, and the day might yet dawn when she'd have need of such a protector.

Though circumstances forced Sela to hide it, she loved the girl as fiercely as she would her own daughter. She might taunt and tease, but she'd fight to her grave to save Riana. Sela could find comfort, though, in knowing Cassandra's son would be there to help her.

If only the girl were more biddable. They might still be at Camelot had Riana stayed quietly in the shadows, minding her own affairs, but bright and lively and far too impetuous, she'd too soon drawn the wrong attention. They'd had to leave the court before it was known that Riana did indeed have magical talent, powers she had not yet begun to realize.

Sometimes Sela wondered if she'd been wrong to discourage her, to pretend Riana could never master the magical arts. Had she explained the lesser known forces of nature, or trained the girl how to use her talent for good, perhaps Riana would be better prepared to fight her own battles.

Moot point, for it had never been Sela's decision to make. The edicts were handed down to her by one who held a far greater right to decide. Besides, how could Sela ever explain anything, when it had long since been decreed that the girl must not know her true beginnings?

Yes, it was better if this bold, virile Saxon mastered her, kept her from ever returning to Camelot. Poor Riana had no idea of the peril that awaited her. Naively, she thought King Arthur's interest would protect her.

But in truth, it could well mean her undoing.

Four

Riana woke with a panicked sensation, not knowing where she was, hazily aware that the vessel had stopped. She looked up to survey her surroundings, only to meet gray, flinty eyes.

Wolf, she thought with a clutch of fear—the hunter who had snared her, and brought her here to . . .

With deepening dread, she remembered the man's rage as he'd dumped her in the boat, the same fierce, dark expression as when he'd presented the severed head to his king. By the Goddess, could he be planning the same fate for her?

Wolf yanked out a knife. She cringed, but she would not let herself whimper. A small point of pride, especially when he used the blade to slash through the ropes at her wrists and the gag at her mouth. He was none too gentle at the task, however, and she cursed him under her breath.

Little did he care, or even notice, for just then, a female shouted his name. A favored female, judging by the joy lighting his features as he leaped from the boat. Curious as to who could elicit such a smile, Riana scanned the shoreline. People rushed forward, laughing and shouting, as the warriors jumped from the vessels to greet them.

Against her will, her gaze drifted back to Wolf, now clasping his female. Small, dark-haired, and near Riana's own age, the girl laughed as he swung her high in the air and spoke with animated gestures when he set her back down on her feet. From her adoring gaze as she welcomed him, Riana supposed she must be his young wife. Unnerved by a vague sense of discomfort, Riana pointedly looked away and climbed out of the boat.

She counted a good hundred men, women and children rushing at them from a narrow path between the trees. Gathering on the shore, the Saxons embraced one another, all talking at once. Unable to decipher their foreign, guttural speech, Riana stood among them feeling awkward and unnecessary. How close-knit everyone seemed, how blatantly happy to greet each other after what must have been a long separation. In all her life, she could recall no one ever waiting to welcome her so warmly. Were she to die tomorrow, few would care, nor even know she was gone.

Glancing at her captor, she realized she *could* be dead by tomorrow.

How foolish of her to stand here feeling sorry for herself. She might better use this distraction to make her escape.

"I wouldn't consider it," Sela whispered at her side.

Riana jumped. "I hate how you creep up and startle me like that," she said with a frown. "Besides, I have to escape, Sela. You know that."

"Where? Through these trees?"

Dark and dense, the forest hemmed in the beach, stretching as far as the eye could see in either direction. The only break was the thin path behind Wolf, through which Saxons continued to straggle. Knowing it must lead to their village, Riana dismissed it as a possible route of escape. Nor could she like her chances of getting through the trees on either side of it. She might slip into the woods without notice, but once inside the cover of the forest, it would take no time to become hopelessly lost. "I will steal one of the boats," she thought aloud.

"It only took ten strong warriors to row and navigate the vessels, men with ample knowledge of the unpredictable currents and countless forks that plague these rivers. Think, girl. Even in your wildest optimism, can you truly believe a sole, ignorant female has a prayer of survival?"

"You could use magic to help us."

Sela threw up her hands, exasperated. "Once again, you overestimate my power. How many times must I tell you the magical arts cannot be tapped on a whim? Besides, have you never stopped to wonder if perhaps the Goddess brought you here for a reason? That your destiny might actually lie in this village?"

Riana felt a tug, thinking of how warmly the Saxons greeted each other. She shook it off, focusing on the more dire aspects of her possible fate. "Camelot is my destiny. He . . ." Riana nodded back at Wolf. "I think—no, I know—he means to kill me."

Part of her hoped the woman would deny this, but with a thoughtful gaze at Wolf, Sela merely nodded. "He's certainly capable enough, and you've done your best to rile him. If I were you, girl, I'd just smile sweetly, do as you are bid, and wait to see what happens."

"Like his woman?" Riana asked. "Look at her, so sweet and meek and docile. What happens when they're in bed? I can't imagine the savage rewarding her with a gentle touch. Want to wager he devours her whole?"

Sela's brows raised. "Odd, that his mating should so interest you."

"It does not!" Riana colored instantly, denying even to herself that she cared what Wolf did in his bed. "Even you must see it will do me no good to be amenable to that brute. Look at my wrists. They're rubbed raw from where he bound me. And see my feet, scraped and bruised from when he dragged me through the forest. I despise him, that . . . that . . . Wolf. It will make me ill, pretending to obey him."

"Your decision, of course. Still, I can't help but notice how gentle he is with his woman."

Hearing Wolf laugh, Riana's gaze returned to him. Sela was right, she noticed; he was amazingly tender with his female. Feeling suddenly more alone than ever, Riana found herself wondering what it would be like to watch his slate gray eyes melt, to go soft with concern, even longing.

Uncannily, his gaze met hers, as if something inside her had summoned it, and like it or not, she had her answer. It was not a wise thing, staring into his intensity. It sapped her will, made her feel weak and fluttery.

Still, she could not bring herself to turn away.

With a growl, Wolf called to his comrades. His gestures in her direction must have been orders to escort the prisoners, for the warriors began dragging her and Sela to the path through the trees. Wolf then ignored Riana with brutish insensitivity, leading the way with his arm about the dark-haired female's waist.

Hurried along the path, Riana found her appraisal of the forest dismayingly accurate. Other than the rough, narrow lane they trod upon, there was no clear way to cut through the dense foliage. It might be good defensive strategy for the village, she supposed, for it kept all unwanted intruders out, but she could not like how easily it kept unwilling guests in. Wolf need post but one guard at the path's opening and she wouldn't get far without detection.

Soon, she heard a change in the grunts these people used for language, then answering shouts from the other side of the rise. Seeing Wolf smile again as he crested the hill, so obviously happy to be home, she found herself curious about the village in which he lived.

Reaching the crest, she saw little cause for excitement. The wooden fence about the clearing seemed sturdy enough, as did the two guard towers at the gate, but the structures inside looked apt to blow down in any good wind. Most were mean little huts, held together with sticks and mud with a rough thatch roofing, though a sturdier, more sizable structure dominated the center. Still, if that were his grand hall, it was a crude collection of wood and stone, even by Saxon standards. It made Cerdric's rough meeting hall look like a palace.

Obviously, she had overestimated Wolf's power and position. His churls might think him godlike, but he ruled over a poor, mean little settlement, barely worth the effort of defending. Arthur and a few of his knights could trample it down in the blink of an eye.

Small consolation, considering how far she was from Camelot.

Swamped by a wave of longing, by the need to be with her own kind, she looked again for an escape route. Scanning the countryside, she became awed in spite of herself by the expanse of green pastures and furrowed fields beyond the enclosure. Even with the sun setting in the distant hills, she could see how dark the soil was, how rich. The village might be one gasp away from total poverty, but they could find wealth aplenty in such fertile land.

For her own interests, she found the vast area of those open fields a bit daunting. Until the crops grew tall, it would be impossible to cross them unnoticed. A curse on that cruel and heartless Saxon. Must he leave not even a slim avenue of escape?

Dragged down the hill into the village, she was surprised by how much larger the huts seemed now that she walked between them. Most were divided in half, with one side for living quarters, the other for housing the livestock. Steadily lowing, the cattle must be reminding these farmers that it was fast approaching twilight and time to be milked, for most of the group splintered off, going here and there to the various huts.

Wolf led on, stopping suddenly in the center of the clearing, before the grand hall. Built of pine logs and twice the height and length of the surrounding huts, it towered over the village, commanding attention, but to Riana, its windowless walls seemed merely dark and ominous, almost as threatening as the man waiting for her in the doorway.

Poised there like a king surveying his realm, Wolf trained his gaze upon her, his features narrowing into a scowl. She fought the urge to squirm, to flee like a frightened rabbit.

He clapped his hands once, and six of the women scurried past him into the building. Clapping again twice, he barked out orders. The other villagers dispersed, while the two warriors holding Riana herded her none too gently toward the door.

Battling fear, she called out to Sela, being led in the other direction. "Don't let him do this," she urged. "Tell him we must not be separated."

Hope flared as the old woman paused to face Riana, but Sela

once again disappointed her. "Penawulf has spoken," she said solemnly, acting as if she now owed her allegiance to that hateful barbarian. "I shall try to come to you, but until I can, you must stand tall. Remember who you are, my child, and greet your fate with the same proud dignity of your forbears."

"What forbears?" Riana spun, yanking her wrists free. "How can I emulate them when I don't know who they are? This is no time for your riddles, Sela. Can't you see I need your help? Use your magic to save my life."

"It is in the hands of the Goddess now," was the only comfort the woman would offer. "It is her magic in which you must trust."

At another clap from Wolf, Sela was hurried away, and rough hands once more ensnared Riana's wrists. She fought the urge to cry. All well and good for Sela to insist that she must be proud and dignified, trusting in the conspicuously absent Goddess, but she didn't have to stare into the grim-faced Saxon's eyes.

Approaching him, Riana gazed instead at his bare chest. Bad mistake, as it merely increased her awareness of his size and brute strength. One swat of the hand and he could crush her completely.

Loathing rose up in her throat. What injustice. She should be on her way to Camelot, not marching helplessly to what could well be her death.

And Wolf was to blame. This very moment, Arthur's emissary, conjured forth in her enchantment, could be on his way to their hut in Milford, but thanks to this meddling savage, Riana would not be there to greet him. She'd come within a breath of making her triumphant march home, until Wolf barged in and spirited her off.

Throwing back her shoulders, she eyed him defiantly. No easy feat, for his gaze was fixed on her, intense and steady, commanding a heated response from deep inside her body. A strange need pulsed out and upward, consuming her, until lurid images swirled through her mind. She pictured herself once again dancing for the Goddess, only this time, this overpowering male breached the circle to capture her in his unyielding grasp. And rather than fight, she melted against him, offering up her softness to his rock-hard strength.

So strong was the image of their bodies entwining in their own hot, writhing dance, she had to blink her eyes to be free of it. Had it involved anyone other than this hateful Saxon, Riana would have sworn she had just had a vision. She would never feel such things for this man—she could not. Her future, her duty, lay at Camelot. *That* was her destiny.

Before she could fully recover, the dark-haired female set a hand on Wolf's arm and spoke low and urgently. His expression tightened, as he gestured at his men to guard the entry, then took possession of Riana's arm and dragged her behind him through the door. With a brief, apologetic smile, the dark-haired girl followed them both inside.

The interior was one huge, long room, dimly lit, with an open pit in the center. Two of the women were scooping ashes out of it, while two others carried logs to pile at the edge. The last two females, she noticed, had busied themselves at a long stone table at the far end of the room.

The dirt floor, littered generously with stones, offered no rushes to cushion the foot. Rough partitions formed alcoves along each wall, save behind the stone table. Seeing mats in most of the cubicles, she reasoned they must be the sleeping quarters, though she could spy no rushes, rugs nor any other comforts in them. Such cramped quarters were fit for a peasant, she thought with derision, taking perverse pleasure in the thought that Wolf must bed his woman in such squalid surroundings.

Riana stole a glance at the girl beside him. She returned the gaze, her dark, pretty features breaking into a smile as she hurried over to take Riana's hand.

Concerned by such sudden eagerness, not knowing what they meant to do with her, Riana tried to pull away, but the female would not let go. Gesturing to the long stone table, she nodded encouragingly and tugged Riana with more insistence.

Wolf watched them intently, but showed no real expression on his strong-boned face. His bold, authoritative stance, arms folded across his chest, made it plain that all eight females—Riana included—were here merely to follow his orders.

Keeping in mind Sela's advice, Riana decided to pretend obedience so he might relax his guard. Although it went against her nature, she lowered her gaze meekly, and followed the girl to the far end of the room.

As they neared the table, Riana could see the grotesque pagan figures lining the shelf behind it, the ceremonial urns and braziers parked at its base. Noticing dark, reddish-brown stains in the dirt, she found it suddenly hard to swallow. It was no table at all, she realized, now queasy. This stone slab must be an altar. A savage, heathen altar. The Goddess alone knew how many sacrifices had been made here.

Acting as if she delivered her prisoner for just such a rite, the girl abruptly dropped her hand. Feeling abandoned, Riana reached for her, before regaining her dignity—and wits. The girl had merely gone behind the altar to retrieve a flowing white tunic, which she held out to Riana. She motioned Riana to remove her own tattered clothing and put this on her body.

Again, Riana's gaze went instantly to Wolf. Did the arrogant wretch expect her to disrobe in front of him?

Noticing her hesitation, the girl laughed softly and made a shooing motion at Wolf, gesturing at the door. He spoke sharply, but didn't move. With a cheerful shake of her head, the girl again motioned with her hands, until Wolf muttered darkly under his breath and strode out.

Watching him go, Riana felt a moment's exhilaration. This would be her best opportunity for escape, left alone with his simple, trusting female. Riana should be able to outwit—if not overpower—this mere girl, before Wolf even dreamed of returning.

"Permit me to make myself known to you," the girl said when he'd left the hall. "I am Greta. Our Penawulf, he is . . . I believe you would call it ox-headed."

"Mule-headed," Riana corrected, before realizing the girl had used her language. "You speak Briton?" she asked, stunned.

"I try. I have little chance to make use of my ability, since my mother alone spoke your language and she has since left this world. She spent many years among your people, though her own family hailed from Rome."

"Roman?" Riana blurted out, unable to contain her surprise. "Why would she marry into the barbaric Saxon horde?"

Greta frowned, looking suddenly like Wolf. "You speak as if we are useless clods with one small, collective mind. Saxon, Briton, or Roman, we are people, we all fall in love. My father was Saxon, yes, but he loved his Roman prisoner. He found her too beautiful to kill, with or without her ransom."

"You kill your prisoners?" Riana asked, her voice small.

"Not this one," the girl told her vehemently. "Exar would never execute the woman who carried his heir. Their marriage took place the day she delivered Penawulf into this world."

"Wolf is your brother?" So Greta was not his wife, Riana thought, instantly denying she felt any relief.

"Wolf?"

"It is what I call him. To me, he is like a predator, an animal. A wolf."

Greta giggled. "You are right. It is a good name for him." She sobered, looking Riana in the eye. "You should know also that the wolf is amazingly loyal to his pack. And when he chooses his mate, it is for life."

Riana stiffened, annoyed by the girl's fatuousness. Her brother could commit the foulest murder and still she would worship him. "Be that as it may, your brother took me from my home against my will. For this, I shall loathe him to my grave."

"Perhaps," Greta said softly. "But if you took time to know him—"

"I'd as soon make my escape."

The girl placed a gentle hand over hers. "My mother would say that it's a wise woman who knows when to give in, and when to fight. She'd tell you to accept your fate, and in so doing, learn all you can about your new surroundings. It is hard for a woman in this man's world. Knowledge is our only real power."

Taken aback by such wisdom, Riana saw she might have underestimated this girl.

"But where is my head?" Greta asked suddenly, removing her hand to tap her brow. "I waste time, babbling on about this, when we must prepare you. At this rate, you will never be ready for the ceremony."

Riana stiffened. She'd heard rumors of gruesome practices in these Saxon rituals, some of which even included human sacrifice. "These stains," she asked, pointing to the dark spots by the altar. "Are they from sacrifices?" At Greta's nod, Riana's voice became small. "And this ceremony? Will it include blood-letting, too?"

Concentrating on Greta's uneasy features, Riana nearly jumped as one of the other women called out behind her. Clearly relieved by the distraction, Greta rattled off words in that rough cadence, directing the women to place the large basin they carried by the hearth. Turning back to Riana, Greta explained that they'd brought water for her bath. "It would be best that we do not speak in your tongue just now," she added quietly. "My people distrust all things British. They feel your people have committed too many atrocities against us."

Riana too had noticed the glares the other females gave her. "But how unjust. You Saxons started the violence."

Greta shrugged. "The hostilities have gone on so long, does it matter who started them? Here in our remote outpost, we have only our own experiences to go by. Helga, the tall, hefty woman with the graying blond hair, lost two sons and a husband to a British raid. It will only hurt her to see me chatting to you like a sister."

Riana eyed Helga's girth and militant stance, and decided Greta had every good reason to fear this woman's displeasure. Things would not go well for the hapless soul who fell afoul of this Amazon.

Still, when Greta left her, smiling warmly as she joined the others, Riana again felt that sense of isolation. How swiftly they shut her out, these women. How acutely they reminded her of her lack of importance, that she was a prisoner here who could well soon be dead.

One of the guards poked his head in the doorway, calling to Greta. Shaking her head, the girl hurried back to Riana. "I must go now," she whispered. "My brother needs me." Nudging her unwilling guest toward the tub, Greta went on to suggest that Riana could bathe while she was gone. Leaving her no chance to argue, the girl hurried off, abandoning her to these blatantly-hostile women.

From their glares, they were no happier than she with the situation. Lighting the logs they'd set in the hearth, they gestured emphatically that Riana must submerge herself in the tub.

She found it no comfortable thing, undressing before one's sworn enemy, but it was merely the first of many unpleasant experiences. Impatient fingers grabbed her hair and scrubbed it—as well as her tender, travel-sore body—with gritty, unscented soap. Shivering as Helga dried her with abrasive towelling and harsh hands, Riana fought a building apprehension. They took such pleasure in being rough with her, as if they knew she was helpless and unable to seek retribution.

They shoved her into a chair to apply paint to her face. As Helga yanked a comb through her drying hair, Riana wondered afresh about the ritual they planned for her. Fighting dread, she glanced up to find Sela had entered the room.

No one glared at her guardian, she noticed, though perhaps this was due to the fact that Sela spoke their tongue. Gesturing at the huge open hearth, the old woman soon had the others feeding the fire, leaving her and Riana a few moments alone.

Smiling conspiratorially, Sela whipped a small flask from beneath her robes. "Here, I was able to brew this for you. It should help you get through the ceremony."

Riana clasped the woman's bony wrist. "Sela, you must tell me. What is this ceremony?"

"I am no member of this village," she said, looking away. "Why would they tell me of their plans?"

"I can't bear this. See how they bathe and dress me? This fine white wool, the elaborate paint—I feel as if I'm being trussed up for a holiday feast."

"Drink up, child. Trust me, it will make it easier for you if you do."

Realizing it must be a product of a magic, some talisman against harm, Riana tilted the flask and downed the liquid. It was all she could do not to shudder as a sharp, pungent aftertaste invaded her mouth.

"That was awful," she said, tasting it again on her lips. "Do you mean to poison me?"

Sela merely smiled enigmatically as she took the flask from her hand. "Remember your dignity," she said as she turned to leave. "Your mother would expect no less."

"Mother?" Riana asked, stopping Sela at the door. "Are you saying that all this time, you've known who my mother is and didn't tell me?"

Sela shook her head, refusing to face her. "As always, you let your thoughts run riot. I meant the Goddess, the Great Mother-of-Us-All. Put rein on your fertile imagination, Riana. It will do you more harm than good in the night ahead."

"Sela—"

Infuriatingly, the woman swept out the door, fleeing her questions.

It struck Riana that she might have been wrong to trust her. Sela seemed to have grown quite comfortable with her captor; perhaps she and Wolf concocted some plan to drug her into compliance. She'd make for an easier sacrifice, after all, if she didn't go kicking and biting her executioner.

Already, a certain haziness began to steal over her mind, calming her, making her wonder if it truly mattered if some drug now snaked its way through her body. The Goddess had laid out her path; all she could do now was to follow it.

And in truth, it seemed more pleasant to revel in the soft white wool being slipped over her head, fluttering down her skin to nestle against her legs. She wanted to twirl in the voluminous new tunic, for it was more luxurious than any she'd ever owned, but with the haziness came lethargy, and a strong need to lie down.

It was the oddest thing. Part of her knew she should try to escape, but an equal part could not find it worth the effort. A strange languor had stolen over her, making her limbs feel both heavy and weightless at the same time. She need only lift up her feet to fly off, far away, but it was warm and cozy here inside the hall and it seemed more pleasant to curl up by the fire. It felt as if she were already half-dreaming; why not stop fighting and give in to the comforting sleep?

Backing up to the table, she leaned against it, watching the women stack log after log on the fire. How like ants they seemed, a constant line of busy, eager workers, building a blaze that would soon reach the roof. Mesmerized by the flames, she happened to notice the one called Helga, her grim face darkening more so as she marched to the altar. With surprisingly-gentle hands, she lifted Riana up to the stone slab, forcing her to sit. *Stay there,* she seemed to be saying in that foreign tongue, her dark eyes snapping with anger. *Don't move if you value your life.*

Faint-headed and weak in the knees, Riana was happy to comply. Rather than watch the women bustle about the room, she preferred leaning back, then lying down and stretching out. She might better let her thoughts do the flying, she decided. Her weary body could rest where it was.

Though vaguely aware of voices in the room, of the blaze burning brighter, her mind had already drifted to where she most longed to be. She went back to Camelot, to those happier days when she was cosseted by Arthur and Guinivere, when his sisters, Morgan and Morgause, secretly revealed bits of their mysterious world of magic. Watching the women work, hearing their incantations, an awed Riana knew this was her calling. She must risk all she had—and would ever be—so that she too might become an enchantress.

Indeed, she was mouthing those chants when she realized the voices came not from within her mind, but rather the room around her. Turning her head, she discovered the hall was now filled to bursting with Saxons.

How primitive it seemed, all that pagan chanting, the steady distant drum setting cadence for the figures dancing about her. With the sole light in the room coming from the fire, she could scarce make out faces, but she could see that the dancers wore a great deal of feathers and fur. Their gyrations and the strange shadows cavorting upon the walls made for a lurid combination. The drum's beat, too, was darkly sexual in nature.

Heat filled her body, an oozing heat, pulsing deep within her.

Voices rose in pitch and fervor, working themselves into a frenzy. Spread out on the stone altar in lethargic abandon, she wished she could join the shadows on the wall in their dance.

Their dance of love.

Intrigued, fascinated, she longed to feel those gyrating limbs brushing against her prickling flesh. Her blood heated by the fire, by the music and chanting, she squirmed on the altar as she pictured herself being lowered to the ground, twisting and writhing beneath . . .

At that moment, the Amazon Helga hissed in her ear. Grabbing her arms, she yanked Riana up to a sitting position, then roughly to her feet. Swaying, still needing Helga's support, Riana slowly realized the room had now stilled to an electrifying silence. Following their gazes, she, too, looked to the doorway.

Framed in firelight, Wolf stood in the threshold, tall and commanding, every inch the proud warrior come to claim his prize. Clad in a leather loincloth, his hair unbound and his bronzed skin glistening, he looked wild and savage and completely untamed.

Deep within her, Riana felt an answering wildness. It urged her to go to him, to rub his hard, naked flesh thrust against her own.

Even as she struggled against the strange, overwhelming sensation, Wolf raised an arm and the room went wild with cheering. Her gaze following the long, lean line of his glorious torso, up the firm shoulder and muscled forearm, Riana froze at the sight of the wickedly gleaming knife in his hand.

All desire dissolved as she realized this man hadn't come to make love to her; he meant to take her life.

Rage welled up in her, and with it defiance. Refusing to die like some beaten dog, she gathered her thoughts for one final battle. With a bloodcurdling scream, she pushed free of Helga, intending to charge past her attacker and out the door, but Sela's drug, combined with a recent lack of food, caused the blood to flee from her head.

In the midst of her finest moment, she stumbled and fell to the ground unconscious.

Five

Stirring slowly, Riana grew hazily aware of the darkness around her. No, not quite dark, for she could hear the distant hiss and crackle of a fire behind her, could feel a comforting warmth on her back. Beneath her side, the surface was soft and yielding, urging her to reach out and caress it. Animal pelts, she thought with a languid smile—a wealth of luxurious fur. In a groggy corner of her mind, she recalled Sela's drug, and the reason for taking it, but if this were her death, she could not bring herself to mind it.

Floating in this dreamy state, she grew aware of things gradually, the pieces fitting together in a puzzle of building pleasure—a scent of musk, a soft, whispering breath at her ear, the warmth gaining focus until it became a long, firm body molded against her back.

A strong, masterful hand stroked her shoulder. It glided down the length of her, massaged the back of her knee, then brushed up her thigh, her hip, her navel, to graze the tips of her breasts. With a delicious shiver, she felt her nipples peak in the cool, evening air.

Her entire world seemed to concentrate on that hand and what it would do next. Each breath heavy with anticipation, Riana waited as featherlike fingers again traced the circuitous route, down her side, her legs, up to cup her buttocks, then caress the soft mound of her belly. Moaning softly as the hand worked its magic, she shut her eyes and leaned back into the solid warmth behind her, burrowing into a cocoon of sensual bliss.

What sweet torture, waiting as the hand inched upward. Tingling with awareness, she thrust out her breasts to meet it. She moaned with delight as the hand slid over one breast, gasped when a swollen nipple was caught between deft fingers. Arching into the touch, she pressed into the hard, throbbing insistence behind her.

She heard another moan—deeper than her own—and suddenly, two hands grabbed her arms to shift her weight so she lay back on the furs. Soft lips now traced a path to her breast, sucking her taut nipple into a moist, welcoming mouth, lapping and licking and teasing it to its ultimate erection. Lost to sensation, Riana arched ever upward, craving more of the clever tongue, that obliging mouth, the magical hands.

They led her actions, those hands, making her writhe on the furs as if dancing an enchantment, though she was the one bewitched. Roaming freely over her, they wove their uncanny spell, stirring her blood to pulse to an ancient rhythm, bringing lust, hot and urgent, blazing to life inside her.

Delving deep into her most private parts, the clever fingers fanned her need to a fevered pitch. Intoxicated by a deep, musky aroma, she reached for the head above her, digging her fingers into a thatch of thick hair, feeling the sleek, silky strands. Her mind awhirl, every sense filled to bursting, her hands read the clues. The hair, the firm torso, the enticing scent . . .

She tried to open her eyes, but her lids felt heavy and in truth, where was the need to see? The man haunted her every waking moment, why not her dreams as well? She knew his eyes burned with hot intensity, a deep, consuming desire she somehow shared. Pulling his head down to her own, she took his lips, matching his hunger, marvelling at how much she wanted more of this, more of him.

He spoke to her, his harsh, guttural Saxon softening, becoming love chants in her ear. It drove her to a frenzy, this spell he cast upon her, and she ran her hands over him, glorying in the taut skin and rippling muscle, avid to see and touch and taste all at once.

And with each new display of her boldness, he grew more insistent, more greedy. Kissing her mouth, her breasts, her thighs, he marked her for his possession. Wantonly, she offered herself up, gripping his back, eager to be locked forever in his grasp. She wanted this man more than life itself, needed him driving deep inside her.

As if she'd voiced the thought, he moaned low in his throat. Pulling away, he parted her legs to kneel between them. He paused to look down at her, his breathing swift and shallow. For a moment, she thought he might speak, but with another moan, he thrust inside her, the sheer, pulsing size of him forcing a cry of alarm.

But it was far too late to stop now—both of them knew it—and fear and pain swiftly subsided in the flood of warm, liquid desire. Throbbing with it, she responded to his hoarse whispers, meeting him thrust for thrust, exulting in the heat they bred together. An eager captive of his magic, she dug her fingers into his back, keeping him close, not wanting even a breath to come between them.

Wild with longing, she rose higher with each new thrust, growing closer to the heavens. She cried out *Wolf,* shouted it over and over, certain she could never get enough of what he offered. Clinging with all her might, she felt herself soar, flying far above the mortal world.

Then there it was, a precipice opening up before her. She felt herself falling, tumbling in glorious abandon, traveling through wave after wave of incredible pleasure, her body rocked by a thousand tingling spasms.

Laughing and crying at once, still clinging to Wolf, she sank with him to the furs, filled with a sense of satisfaction so complete, she drifted back into the deep, untroubled sleep of the drug.

* * *

Not so blessed, Wolf stood beside the bed watching Moriana sleep. In his mind, she was his now, this beauty. As the old woman had urged, Wolf had taken Moriana, loved her, branded her his own. And having done so, there was no turning back.

Yet too easily, he could foresee trouble brewing. Earlier, listening to his people speak of their woes, he'd seen their frowns and scowls as they gazed at Moriana, the sole prize brought home from Cerdric's council. The village needed the spoils from that last raid to help survive the winter, but instead of land and gold coins, their chief had returned with a mere female—a despised Briton, at that.

How could he ask them to wait and be patient, to share the conviction that Moriana was a gift from the gods who could one day prove their salvation? There were many who would ask if it were indeed Thunor who spoke to him the night he'd found her— or if it were Penawulf's lust that had done all the talking.

And their lovemaking tonight did little to allay such doubts.

There was the crux of his uneasiness. After such a tumultuous coming together, his hunger for her should be sated, yet disturbingly, he found it far from appeased. The need to feel her sweet body against him again was an ache, festering and building, taking over his thoughts and clouding his judgment.

Wolf needed all his wits about him, for he could ill afford to lose another challenge as he had with Vangarth, lest other tribes perceive him as weak and see profit in attacking his village. Nor dare he risk angering his king further. Cerdric might no longer deem him worthy of his daughter, but he'd expect a decent interval before Wolf chose a replacement for Gerda.

On one hand, Wolf had the god Thunor urging him toward the girl, on the other, he had the edicts of his king and the needs of his people. His instincts found value in the girl, but Moriana made it clear that she saw him only as a loathsome savage.

Then there was his father, always his father, haunting him from the grave with his warnings and accusations. Exar would insist that only a weakling would enslave himself to a female, for even a moment. A lesson he'd hammered home repeatedly, each time Wolf questioned the man's harsh treatment of his mother.

No, Wolf refused to fight that battle again. He was chieftain now and he would rule his village as he'd been trained to, unconcerned with the reactions of others to his decrees. Having made his decision, he must stand by it, strong, proud and unyielding.

Gazing down at Moriana's sleeping form, he hardened his resolve. He would demand that his people accept her.

And one way or another, this female would bend to his will.

"Rise, slug-a-bed! Wake to greet this glorious day."

Grimacing at Sela's cheery voice, Riana opened one eye and instantly regretted it. A blend of nausea and head pain left her wishing for death.

The sweet, throbbing death she'd experienced last night.

Before her smile could form, the sting of reality erased it. Whatever had happened the night before, she wasn't in the afterworld now—or even in a dream. She groped about her, recognizing the luxurious furs, the musky scent. The soreness between her thighs did little to calm her. Nor did the breeze blowing across her body—her naked body.

She forced her eyes open, wincing against the sunlight spilling into the room from the two windows before her. The whitewashed stone walls and huge hearth where Sela revived a fire, indicated this was not the squalid hall with its pagan altar. Indeed, the folded tapestries on the benches spoke of wealth and elegance, as did the ornate coverings at the windows and colorful woven mats warming the stone tiles of the floor. A matching red, blue, and gold coverlet had once graced the bed, she saw, though it now lay discarded in a rumpled heap on the tiles.

If she must die, she thought, better to spend eternity here in this pleasant room. No rough and tumble Saxon retreat this. Its bright, airy dimensions and tasteful furnishings were more the home of a wealthy Roman, or a Briton of Latin descent.

Greta's mother's family had hailed from Rome, Riana recalled—a mother she shared with Wolf.

Alarmed, she searched the bed for her clothing, but the white tunic lay on the floor beside her sandals and the fallen bedcoverings. Holding her head against the pain, she sat up, slowly relinquishing all hope of the afterworld. She was very much alive, and still very much a prisoner.

Wolf had taken her, used her, relying on that vile tasting potion to make her respond. This was worse than turning his back on her in Cerdric's stronghold, or dragging her bound and gagged through the forest. By lulling her with the drug, he'd robbed her of the ability to choose wisely.

Sela spoke suddenly in the hoarse, clipped Saxon tongue. Following the woman's gaze to the corner, Riana gasped aloud.

Wolf leaned against the wall, arms folded at his chest as he leveled his cool, gray scrutiny on her. She found not a trace of guilt anywhere in his expression.

Whereas she felt as if every drop of blood she owned had rushed to her face. By the Great Goddess, how could she let him . . . let herself . . .

Even now, her body tingled betrayingly.

With a wry grin, he unfolded his arms and neared the bed, reaching down to scoop up the tunic. He offered it with a courtly gesture worthy of any British knight, so out of character for the brute she knew him to be.

Be wary, she told herself, *he's trying to trick you.* Ignoring the tunic, she gathered the furs about her and edged to the other side of the bed.

His features abruptly hardened. Dropping her tunic, he turned to Sela and rattled off a string of Saxon. The woman scurried to obey him.

"Where is your loyalty that you must rush to obey his every bark?" Riana asked, stung by the woman's betrayal. "Are you blind to the fact that this monster attacked and raped me?"

"Odd, I found you purring in your sleep this morning. I was of the impression you'd enjoyed yourself immensely."

"Enjoyed myself?" Riana rose to stand on the bed, the furs clutched against her. "This man defiled me. Will you stand back and watch while he beats me senseless?"

"No one has abused you. Penawulf has done nothing more than what he has every right to do. He is your husband."

Riana could barely breathe. Married? By the Great Goddess, so that was what last night's ceremony had been, a marriage. She almost wished they had sacrificed her instead. Better to be dead than to be trapped with this Saxon savage for the rest of her miserable mortal life.

Sela must have known. The woman had come to her last night, not to offer comfort, but to trick her with that noxious brew. "You drugged me," Riana accused. "You wanted me meek and compliant. Nay, not just compliant. You had to make certain mine was complete capitulation."

Unruffled, Sela faced her squarely. "You know as well as I that a spell can do no more than enhance what is already there."

"No!" Riana refused to believe that. "He used the drug to take advantage of me, to force me against my will, and you helped him."

"He didn't know of the drug, Riana, any more than you. In his mind, I am sure he found you gratifyingly eager and willing."

This, too, Riana refused to accept. "I hate him, Sela. I always shall."

Straightening impatiently, as if he grew weary of female chatter, Wolf grated out another order. Sela's tight expression proved she was far from happy about relaying his message.

"What is it?" Riana asked. "What does he expect now?"

"He said it was time for you to bathe and dress. He will return upon the hour and take you to greet his people. They will want to hear from your own lips that your marriage has been consummated."

"He expects me to publicly admit what we did last night? I'd rather roast in the Christians' hell."

"Ri—"

"No, you tell him I'm appalled by what he has done to me. He tricked me into this marriage—with no little help from you—and I will never honor our union. And this time," she added, her voice quivering, "there's no drug on this earth that can make me comply."

By the tightness about Wolf's lips, Riana could see that Sela had made the translation accurately. His reply was brief, and clipped, his gaze directed at the fur Riana gripped in front of her.

"He wants you to know," Sela explained, "that while your appearance would be a courtesy to his people, it is not required to claim consummation. The blood on the furs will be more than proof enough."

Virgin's blood, Riana thought in dismay. Even in her own culture, it was sufficient proof of their union. Dropping the pelt and pulling the white tunic over her head, she realized that once again, this man had won out. "I detest you," she told him, putting that emotion into her glare.

Ignoring her, he muttered to Sela.

"What is it?" Riana demanded. "What now?" But Sela also ignored her, following Wolf across the room. Watching them exchange words at the door, Riana felt more than ever deserted. Just like that, they would march off, dismissing her feelings and fears as of no importance. She could never survive here, she thought desperately.

"My, my," Sela clucked when he was gone. "I can't say you handled that at all well."

"You tread upon unsteady ground, old woman." Riana climbed down from the bed. "Do you think I can so easily forget the part you played in this?"

"Admit it, the man intrigues you. I can't see what you can object to, in any case. A simple peasant could do worse than the wife of a chieftain."

"A *Saxon* chieftain!" Riana ground out the words. "Our sworn enemy. Our brutally cruel enemy."

Sela shrugged. "Cruelty, I've learned, is in the eyes of the beholder."

Riana leaned down to lace her sandals to her feet. "My eyes

beheld that severed head. I doubt the victim, or any of his family, is singing Wolf's praises tonight."

"You are young and sheltered, with no knowledge of what happens in the heat of battle between hardened warriors. But that is war. Here in this village, you'll find only simple people, much like ourselves, with dreams of living a good life and raising their families to be proud, strong and happy."

"I am nothing like these people," she protested. "But you, Sela, I can't believe how quickly you've changed loyalties."

Sela shrugged. "I am what I've always been, a chameleon. It's the way of survival, to adapt to your surroundings. A wise man studies his boundaries before trying to cross them. What is the hurry, child, that you cannot wait and watch? Do you fear you might enjoy your time here, that you might actually come to like these open, hardworking people?"

"I shall always hate it here." Into her mind came visions of a laughing Arthur and Guinivere, calling her their favorite bard. "Camelot is my home," she said, her voice breaking.

Sela shook her head in exasperation. "You live in this world now. Use your brains, not your pride, and take the future your husband offers. Never forget that he holds the power of life and death over you."

Riana held up her chin. "I won't be under that man's thumb, Sela. I must escape."

"Then I despair of you."

Sela quit the room, the sadness in the woman's tone and resignation in her slumped shoulders making Riana uneasy. She had to remind herself that she was the one wronged, the one cheated of her true fate. Why couldn't Sela see she felt more than a whim to go home? It was her duty.

And glancing at the bed, remembering last night's weaknesses, she knew she could never stay here now.

Determined to leave at once, she looked to the door. No, Sela would be waiting outside, along with half the village, all ready to snicker. Riana might better try the windows. As she crossed the room, she knew Wolf had likely stuck her in some isolated tower on a steep, dangerous cliff, but she'd rather plunge to her death than spend another moment at his mercy.

Reaching the window, she found her room to be on the second floor, the descent manageable. She grabbed the bedcoverings, as well as the linen toweling Sela had left for her bathing and fashioned a rope. Attaching it to the table, she flung the other end out the window.

Unfortunately, either she hadn't secured the knots, or the linen proved flimsy, for halfway through her descent, the makeshift rope split in two. She hit the ground with a painful wrench, sliding on a section of moss a less impulsive soul might have avoided.

White hot pain blazed up her leg. Lying there, clasping her ankle, she cursed the fates for conspiring against her. Wolf had so many advantages already, why must she be robbed of the ability to walk?

Fighting tears, she rose to a sitting position. She had to regain her wits for she'd never survive without them. Now that panic had left her, she could see how dire her situation could grow with no supplies to sustain her journey. Glancing behind her, seeing the smooth stone surface of the wall, she knew she could never scale her way back up to the window. She had to go forward; retreat was impossible.

Somehow, she had to circle back around the village, to the river where those longboats waited. With luck, they might not all be unloaded; there might be a bag or two of food or treasure left inside. And even if not, she could push off in one of those vessels, taking her chances that the river could bring her to a British village, from where she could arrange transport to Camelot.

But she must hurry, before her captor discovered her missing.

She tried to put weight on her ankle, finding that while she could walk, she could not depend on her speed. Limping slightly, she set off for the river. Despite it being the longer route, she kept close to the woods, knowing she'd be less likely to be spotted there than if she trudged across the open fields.

Glancing back, she found her prison had been built into the hill. With each step she took, the dwelling blended more with the terrain until she could no longer discern the line where stone left off and hill took over. Camouflaged thus, it seemed less a fortress and more a hideaway. No prison now, but rather a lover's haven.

She felt a sudden fierce longing for last night's magic.

Quelling it immediately, she thought instead about how Wolf used her, how he stood in the way of her destiny. She could not let herself be content to sit in some Saxon hole in the back of nowhere, as Sela would have her do. She had to return to Camelot, to make certain she was there when her king and queen needed her.

So she pushed on, despite her tender ankle, until a glance downward confirmed her suspicion that the bruised flesh had swollen over the strap of her sandal. She stopped to untie it before the leather bit into her skin.

Dismayed to find her ankle was now twice its original size, she removed the sandal. Carrying it in her hand, she hobbled on, driven by a need for haste. Sensing Wolf's rage as if the demon breathed down her neck, she knew she must lose no time putting vast distances between them.

Yet her ankle ached so, it grew harder to believe she could survive the trek to Camelot. With the hot sun pricking at her neck and hunger growling in her belly, the need for food and rest grew unbearable. *My king needs me,* she chanted over and over in her mind as her resolve weakened.

Her will had ebbed to its lowest when she saw the horse nibbling the meadow grasses before her. A magnificent animal, strong and well-muscled, it beckoned her closer. Had she not been so hot and weary, she might have wondered at its owner's whereabouts, but all she could think of was that with such a fine steed, she'd have no need to hobble. Certain this noble steed had been sent to bring her to Camelot, she went to it gladly. She was standing before the beast, daunted by its height and wondering how to mount it, when she heard the growl behind her.

She turned with a sense of foreboding, knowing in her heart who would be there.

Who else but Wolf?

* * *

Glancing at Riana, now sleeping fitfully, an exasperated Sela shook her head. This marriage could be the answer to everyone's prayers, but trust the girl to make a mess of it already. Grumbling, Sela prepared the poultice for Riana's ankle, that swollen symbol of the girl's rash behavior.

"Can I watch you?" The girl, Greta, stood at her side, smiling shyly. "My people have great need for someone skilled in the healing arts. If I observe you as you work, I might someday learn how to help them."

Sela couldn't help but wonder why Riana couldn't be more like this girl. Always a smile, her doe-brown eyes open and trusting, Greta did her best not to cause anyone trouble. No wild dreams of grandeur, no reaching into dark worlds of limitless power; hers was a simple desire to please.

Sela could feel safe teaching her humble magic to this one. Unlike the more volatile Moriana, there would be no danger here.

Showing Greta how to mix the ingredients, finding her youthful enthusiasm endearing, Sela nonetheless missed the banter in which she and Riana always engaged. Kept her sharp and bright, that imp did, challenging her set ways with constant questions. Sela only prayed Riana hadn't gone too far in testing her wings this time.

Wolf had certainly been furious when he brought her here to the hut he had granted Sela. Dumping the girl unceremoniously on the cot, he'd announced that he had matters to attend to in the fields, but he expected Sela to do what she could in mending his wife's foot. Be warned, he'd added darkly as he stomped off—it would not go well for Moriana or herself, if both were not here when he returned.

Sela thanked the Goddess for making Riana currently unable to walk. She would not put it past her young charge to try another foolhardy escape, and the look in Wolf's eyes as he departed was just this side of murder.

Gathering up her herbs and wrappings, she motioned for Greta to follow her to the cot where Riana now slept. As Sela began applying the poultice, Riana's eyes opened. "Why bother treating the ankle?" she said wearily. "Were I a horse, you would just put me out of my misery."

The note of resignation concerned Sela. It was one thing for Riana to accept her fate, but quite another for the girl to give up entirely. "Your foot's not at fault," Sela said, hoping to provoke a reaction. "Blame your brain. What were you thinking, heading to an area prowled by bears? Is that how you'd like to end your life, mauled by some great oaf of a beast?"

"Better than to be mauled by my beast of a husband."

Sheer bravado, but Sela left the girl her pride. Better this Riana than the pale imitation moments earlier. Besides, they both knew she'd go nowhere tonight. Her fate, like it or not, rested in her husband's hands.

"Why do you run from my brother?" Greta's soft question surprised them both. "Penawulf is a comely man and a just one, and chieftain of our tribe. Any girl I know would be eager to have him for a husband."

Sela thought Riana might snip at the girl, but she shook her head with a sad smile. "Those girls do not have my obligations. I am needed elsewhere and your brother stubbornly stands in my way."

"But perhaps he could help you."

Riana merely snorted.

"He always does his best to help me," Greta pressed. "Have you even asked him?"

"Shall I tell him I need to go to King Arthur's court at Camelot?" Her voice gaining strength, Riana sat up. "That I wish to one day become an enchantress, as powerful as the great Merlin himself? You tell me, Greta. Is your brother willing to help me do that?"

The girl shook her head. "Like most in our tribe, he distrusts all things magical. Too, it seems a strange ambition for a female."

Sela braced herself. She could have warned Greta how Riana would react to her statement, but this might better be worked out between the two girls. Riana needed to learn restraint, and Greta's hide could use toughening.

Riana leaned forward, her gold eyes spitting out more sparks than the fire. "Women are ideal candidates for summoning the force of the Goddess. Queen Morgause says that men merely usurp such power, exploiting it for the wrong ends, like conquest in battle. Women use the softer side, the gifts of creativity and love. In my mind, there is no finer ambition than learning and perfecting such magic."

"I see." Greta tilted her head, gazing at Riana thoughtfully. "But to create love, surely you must experience it. And for that, don't you need to surround yourself with a family, a husband and children?"

Good point, Sela thought, but before she could embellish on the thought, they were distracted by the sudden thunder of charging hoofbeats.

Riana looked to the door, her hand going to her throat. Knowing their visitor must be Wolf, and seeing Riana's high color, Sela wondered if it might have been wiser to keep her resigned, after all.

"Try not to provoke him," she said quietly when Greta ran outside to greet her brother. "You will serve no one, yourself least of all, by making him angrier."

Ignoring her, Riana sat stiffly, arms folded militantly at her chest.

Greta walked in before Wolf, smiling wanly to make up for his stern expression. "My brother wishes you to come with him," she said quietly.

"Is he so high and mighty, others must speak for him?" Riana asked bitterly. "Surely if you speak my language, he can as well."

Greta shook her head. "My father took great pains to separate Wolf from my mother. I learned from her, he did not."

Poor Cassandra, Sela thought. Proud, stubborn Exar would have been ruthless about making certain that none of her fey, foreign ways tainted his son and heir.

"In that case," Riana said proudly, "you can tell your brother that I am quite comfortable where I am."

"You don't understand." Uncomfortably, Greta looked from Riana to her brother. "This is not a request. Wolf has decided he must administer your punishment himself."

Riana rose to her feet, visibly pale, though it was hard to tell if her pallor stemmed from Wolf's visit or the pain in her foot. "It is not enough that he must kidnap and rape me. Now he seeks my complete humiliation?"

"But you must be punished," Greta tried to explain. "By running away, you defied him, the chieftain, in front of his people. He must prove he is master of his own household if he hopes to rule the tribe with honor."

Eyes blazing, Riana turned to Wolf, directing her rage at its source. "I cannot—will not—be your captive. I belong with my own people."

"It is too late for that now," Greta said flatly, not bothering to translate. "The ritual has made you and my brother one. You belong to Penawulf."

"Never!" Riana spit out. "Tell your brother he can keep me in chains, but I will never be his true wife. I will never come to him willingly. He can force me, but I shall merely run away, over and over, until I am free."

Sela braced herself, fearing where this would lead, but feeling powerless to stop it. Hot-blooded and impulsive, Riana would say and do what she felt was right, no matter how her guardian might warn her.

Wolf listened to Greta's translation, his hands tightening into fists. Striding closer, dark eyes glittering with a fury all his own, he stopped a mere breath from his wife's face. "Tell her she can try to escape, but warn that she can never run far or fast enough. If I must hunt her to the grave, I will track her down and drag her back."

He paused, breathing hard, as if fighting the urge to throttle her. "Tell her this also. If she owns any sense in that silly head, she will stop such foolishness and settle into her fate. If she cannot, I will have no choice but to mete out the proper punishment. Warn her that being my woman will not save her from suffering under tribal law."

Riana's chin merely thrust out further with every word Greta uttered. "Better to die," she hissed, "than submit to his will."

Sela fought the urge to grab the girl by the ear and pinch some sense into her. It was obvious that Riana desired the man—anyone standing too close to the pair could be burned by the heat generated between them—but her proud, willful charge had much to learn before she could work side by side with the equally stubborn Saxon.

"Wait," Sela called when Wolf reached out to drag his wife away. "Before you take her, let me brew her a potion."

When Sela repeated this to Riana, the gold eyes narrowed skeptically. "Another of your love drugs? Do you think me so foolish as to put myself in such a vulnerable state again?" Riana turned to Greta. "Tell your brother about Sela's potion. Make certain he knows I was under its influence last night. That it was the aphrodisiac in my veins that made me so eager."

Little fool, Sela thought. Couldn't she see how this small moment of pride could have untoward ramifications? That it would be herself most of all that she hurt with her declaration?

Apparently not, for she stared with utter defiance as Wolf listened as his sister related her words.

Dropping his grip on Riana's arm, Wolf stared long and hard into her eyes, as if seeking an answer he could not find. Riana faced him squarely, giving away nothing of the turmoil Sela knew must be plaguing her.

"Witchery," he spat, turning away to hide his own agitation.

"Moriana had nothing to do with it," Sela volunteered in Saxon before Greta could translate. "She has no real skill at magic, in any case."

"And why did you interfere, old woman?"

How could she explain to a man with such disdain for the magical arts that she'd had a premonition that their union was vital? She'd hoped the physical pleasure would bring Riana to sense this as well. "I feared she'd be unwilling," she said instead.

His features narrowed, went dark with disgust. Turning to his sister, he gestured at Riana. "Tell her I will not touch her, or come near her, until she issues the invitation herself. I have no need, and even less desire, to bed a cold, dead fish."

Riana stiffened as Greta translated, flinching at that last.

"But do not think this excuses her from her duties," Wolf went on, his deep voice booming across the tiny hut. "As part of our tribe, she must learn our ways. For her punishment, she shall be tied to her bed tonight, denied all food and drink. In the morning, she shall be summoned by the weavers to begin training at the looms. Warn her that should she cause further trouble, I will take a strap to her back."

He watched Riana's face as Greta spoke, nodding in satisfaction when she was done. "Ranulf shall escort her home within the hour."

"Ranulf?" Greta asked, clearly surprised. "Why send your thane to escort her? She is *your* wife."

"I want nothing more to do with her today." Scowling, he strode to the door. "But make no mistake. I can well become her shadow, her nightmare. Should she disobey my edicts, or try to escape again, I shall make certain she rues the day she was born."

Silence blanketed the hut as Wolf stomped out of it, the appalled silence of females when confronted with their lack of power. Even Riana seemed to sense she'd gone too far. That this time, there would be no magical spell to save her.

Wolf stood outside the hut, striving to cool his emotions. Foremost was rage, for he could not believe his wife would defy him by running off, but he knew also a good measure of frustration. Even now, lust quickened in his loins, despite knowing that her desire had been conjured by witchery, not by his careful, patient caresses. By the blood of Thunor, he should have raped her as she accused.

Yet even that thought caused his loins to throb.

It seemed unjust, a great joke of the gods, that he should hunger for a female so eager to be quit of him. How could she face him so coldly while he burned to lower her to the cot, taking every sweet inch of her, even there in front of his sister? She did things to his resolve, this Moriana, making him feel and act as if he no longer had a mind or will of his own.

Witchery, he thought with a scowl.

Forsooth, he would have no more of it. Like his father before him, he would control his house, his wife. Enchantress or not, he would tame her.

Six

"She burned the bread again this morning." Pacing before the council in the grand hall, the widow Helga worked herself into a tirade. "She does it to spite me, this Briton. She resents being forced to work in the bakery."

Wolf stifled a groan. This was not the first complaint—Helga alone had lodged a wealth of them—but he had no wish to be so continuously reminded of his wayward wife. Bad enough she must haunt his sleep, keeping him twisting and turning with unslaked lust, but must he hear her name tripping off every tongue in the village?

Suffering through Helga's diatribe, a frequent pastime in the weeks since he'd married, he wondered what he was to do with Moriana. He didn't doubt that she'd burned the bread deliberately; hadn't she tangled the threads in the looms, soured the butter in the barns and in general sabotaged every task that had been set before her?

And with each new report, his people would shake their heads and wonder anew why he'd brought this girl in their midst. All they saw was a shrew, a useless one at that, who tried their chieftain's patience. No one understood what had possessed him— still possessed him—to take such a she-witch to wife.

"I cannot have her in my bakery," Helga finished officiously, locking her hands at her thick waist. "Please, find some other use for her."

"Her bakery?" Ranulf asked under his breath, leaning close to Wolf. "I had thought the ovens belonged to the village."

Helga glared at Ranulf, exasperating Wolf further. This was not the first time the two had clashed over what to do with Riana. There was little love lost between them, of course, but still, many would consider it a bad omen that his new wife could cause such dissension.

Clearly, Riana's work must cease in the bakery, but what was he to do with her? The weavers would not have her, nor would the workers in the barns or coops. There was but one place left she could be sent. "Since her skills are not culinary ones," he announced, "my wife shall go to the fields to join in the planting."

"But Wolf," Ranulf hissed beside him. "For one raised in Camelot, it will seem like slave labor."

"You question my decision?" Wolf growled at him. Besides, old friend or no, it was not Ranulf's place to concern himself with his wife's feelings, nor should he be arguing with his chieftain before the village council. "Helga," Wolf said sharply, "go now and inform Yarrick that my wife will join the women in the fields this morning."

Helga objected, citing the importance of growing a good crop this season, but Wolf was in no mood to brook argument. "No one knows more than I how close this village is to starvation. Nonetheless, Riana shall join you this morning. You oversee the women in the fields, Helga, so if there is trouble, I shall know who to take into account. Now, since I must train the warriors before presenting my army at Cerdric's next council, I disband this council. I must be about my business, and you must be about yours."

Obviously surprised by his curtness, everyone shuffled out of the hall in subdued obedience. A puffed up Helga trounced off in their wake, making it plain that she found much to object to in his decision. Wolf feared it would not be the last he would hear from her.

Ranulf remained behind, shaking his head at the departing woman. "Helga worries me. She means to stir trouble."

It annoyed him that his friend had taken to calling him Wolf, as half the village had. Was there no end to the strife Riana caused him? "All I know for certain," he barked, putting his anger in his stride and speech, "is that my young wife is nothing *but* trouble."

Ranulf followed him out of the Grand Hall, his voice hesitant, as if knowing already his words would not be well received. "You are angry at her, and with good cause, but think, Wolf. Was it fair to send her to serve under Helga in the kitchens?"

Wolf stopped, facing his friend with surprise. "You speak of justice? The female refuses to obey her husband, choosing instead to devise more and more ways to thwart my wishes. If the woman will not act like a wife, she can have none of the privileges."

Ranulf raised a brow. Too late, Wolf saw how his rash speech betrayed him. No fool he, Ranulf could see the spite behind his decision. He knew that placing her under Helga's thumb had little to do with justice. Wolf wanted to punish her for not gracing his bed.

But this was something he chose not to discuss, even with his friend. Like most men, Ranulf would expect him to rule his household. He'd tell Wolf to take his wife and be done with it. How could he understand this reluctance to force Moriana when Wolf so little understood it himself?

But Ranulf surprised him by taking a different tack. "I see your point, but think of this. Greta tells me that Riana keeps failing because the other women taunt her. That they are not trying to teach her at all."

"Nonsense." Wolf resumed his pace, annoyed that Ranulf and Greta had obviously been discussing his marriage. "I know you dislike Helga, but this goes too far. Everyone in the village knows that Riana must be trained to act the part of a proper Saxon wife. If I cannot gain Cerdric's blessing for this marriage, River Ford can be expelled from the Saxon nation, a hardship we can ill afford to bear."

"Everyone in the village might know." Ranulf fell into step beside him. "But does Riana know what is expected of her?"

"I must pray not. Else, she'll try all the harder to thwart me."

Ranulf laughed, a contagious sound that had Wolf reluctantly grinning. "In truth, Ranulf, this is no laughing matter," he felt compelled to add. "My wife causes dissension at a time we must all band together."

"But Riana hails from a different world, and holds different values. Her willfulness could be less spite and more a lack of understanding."

"You, of all people, would have me show such compassion for a Briton?" Why was Ranulf so intent on defending his wife?

"I have no love for her race, it is true, but Greta says that Helga uses distrust and hatred to stir up the others. You know she leads the women, and you must guess how she must resent having a Briton in their midst. Can you doubt she'd do all in her power to make Riana's life miserable?"

Wolf frowned. "She would not dare. Riana is my wife."

"But that is the problem, Greta insists. You do not live as mates."

It struck Wolf that Ranulf derived a great many of his thoughts from his sister.

"Riana spends her nights at your mother's villa, while you sleep here in the village," Ranulf went on. "Seeing you shun your wife, the women feel justified in their scorn. Why display kindness to the enemy, after all, when her own husband ignores her existence?"

This gave Wolf pause. In this, perhaps Greta was right, yet how could he wipe out years of distrust, or even convince Riana not to provoke it further? His father would say to lock her away, to keep her isolated, but he found the prospect distasteful. As infuriating as his wife could be, Wolf could not bear to watch her zest for life fade, as he'd done with his mother.

Stopping before the barn where he stabled his horse, he shook his head. "Even were my wife this helpless victim, tell me, Ranulf, what would you have me do?"

"You could visit her, see how she's faring. Show the others you take an interest in her well-being."

Wolf cursed the leap his heart took at the thought of again

being near his wife, of gazing at her lovely face, touching her soft, warm skin. Was he a sadist, that he would seek such torment?

"Nor would it hurt Riana to know the man she has married," Ranulf pressed. "Greta believes that your wife knows too little about you."

"It would seem you spend a good deal of time with my sister, discussing my private affairs. Did Greta ask you to talk to me of this?"

A slight flush stole under Ranulf's blond beard, proving Wolf's suspicions. "We both feel that if you talked with your wife," Ranulf said firmly, ignoring the question, "if you showed her the man, not just the chieftain, Riana might grow more accepting in time."

"Have you forgotten we speak different tongues?"

"Greta tells me also that she's been teaching you Briton, that you've grown adept at it."

"I think you talk too much with my sister."

Ranulf again colored, but looked Wolf straight in the eye. "I think we can all benefit from speaking with Greta. The girl is wise beyond her age."

Wolf stared at the fields, remembering how his mother had said much the same the day he last saw her. Clasping his hand, she'd begged him not to dismiss the important role his sister, and all women, could play in his life.

Little Greta, his adoring sister. How uncannily she'd grown to resemble their mother. Greta, too, knew how to influence men with her subtle prodding, always appealing to their gentler side.

Their *softer* side, his father would say.

He remembered how Exar had put a stop to his visits to Cassandra's hillside sanctuary. Branding it a sign of weakness to seek female company, raging that it was past time his son cut all ties to the womb, Exar immersed Wolf in the harsh male world of hunting and battle, as befitted a future chieftain. Wolf embraced that world, knowing it his duty, but he remained haunted by the heartbreak he'd seen on Cassandra's face as he bid her farewell. And though he'd done all he could to please his father,

Wolf still craved the peace and serenity he'd known only with his mother and sister.

"Wise though she may be," he said gruffly, "Greta asks too much of me. I am chieftain, a Saxon warrior trained for battle. I cannot go begging like some hopeless swain for a woman's favor."

"Words can change worlds, Greta says, far more than swords. It's a wise chieftain who knows when to use each."

Greta might have said this to Ranulf, but Wolf had heard it before. From his mother.

"Your tongue is glib, my friend. Why not put it to use?" Ranulf grinned as broadly as if he'd delivered a joke, but Wolf heard the gentle admonition as if it came from Cassandra.

"Would you and Greta turn me into some greasy diplomat? Some snake, like Vangarth?"

"As if it is possible to turn you from any path once you've set your mind to it. Consider it merely a *suggestion* that you talk with your wife. Now that you speak her language, that you can hear her words and have your own heard directly, surely a clever lout like you can find a way to make Riana understand what you need from her."

"Understand, yes. But to accept it? To obey me? That, Ranulf, would take a miracle."

Ranulf laughed heartily. "She's a challenge, but isn't that how it is with anything worth conquering? In battle, when one strategy fails, we don't retreat and leave the field. We try again, hammering away at the enemy's defenses until we emerge victorious. If your current strategy does not work, why not try another? I'm told women respond better to words, to gentleness. They view the world differently than we men."

"Women!" Wolf repeated, exasperated anew.

"Just so," Ranulf clapped him on the back. "But can we dismiss their importance when they keep our households, bear our children, warm our beds? I, for one, do not care to imagine a life without women in it. Merely talk to Riana, Wolf. Where can be the harm in that?"

He could well see the harm—to his peace of mind.

"I will think on this," he said grudgingly. "But only if you cease badgering me about it."

Ranulf grinned. "I would not ponder long. Delay overmuch, and you could yet lose your lovely Briton."

Watching his friend stride off, Wolf denied the uneasiness Ranulf's words produced. He told himself he could not lose what he did not have. Yet he knew Greta would not have pressed Ranulf to speak to him had she not felt a need for the warning.

Riana, vanishing from his life? He would not allow it. As vexing as she sometimes might be, she had opened a door in his existence, a door he was not yet ready to close.

Nor would he. He would post a guard on her—young Tadrick, perhaps—who would watch her night and day. And Wolf would go to the fields to talk with Riana, to see for himself if she still entertained foolish notions of escape.

One thing was certain. She would not run off as his mother had done.

Sitting in a small oak grove, apart from the other field workers, Riana rubbed her aching limbs. Though they had stopped to eat their noonday meal, she could still feel the sweat of her morning labors glistening on her back and brow. Her brown tunic of coarse homespun wool could be a heavy brown sack, the way it looked and chafed against her skin. Cinched at her waist by a rope belt, it made certain to keep all the heat in her body.

I do not belong here, she railed silently against her fate. What sort of husband would exile his wife to slave in the fields like the lowest peasant? Wolf wanted to humiliate her, she knew, as if locking her away in that villa were not punishment enough. She might not know their language, but she could see in their smirks and sneers that these women knew the truth. Her husband had cast her off like unwanted clothing.

Then again, a tiny voice suggested, it was no new thing in her life to be abandoned. Her own parents had dumped her at the kitchen door to Camelot without a backward glance. Perhaps even the king himself had spurned her, banished her here.

No, she refused to allow that doubt to prosper. If she'd been sent from Camelot, it was for a reason. Merlin wished her to learn, to gather knowledge, so she'd one day be able to help the king.

Only what knowledge could be garnered working in dirt and manure?

"I must clear the scraps now, Riana." Greta stood above her, shaking her head. "Look, you've hardly touched your bread. Please eat something or you'll not last the day in the fields. You've grown thin enough as it is."

"And how am I to gain an appetite, facing such sour faces? I swear, Greta, each week, my situation goes from bad to worse. It's as if everyone pushes me from place to place so as not to be stuck with me."

"It's not as if you try to make friends with anyone," Greta snapped, surprising Riana with her impatience. "Maybe you do your best to make everyone dislike you."

Greta's quick glance at Helga explained her exasperation. She was still upset with Riana for calling the woman an overfed cow to her face, one of the few Saxon expressions she'd mastered. Greta was angry, for she'd cautioned her to exercise diplomacy when dealing with the hateful woman, but Riana could bear only so much. The burnt loaf hadn't been her fault, but who would take her word over Helga's? No one, it would seem, not even her new friend Greta.

Stung, she felt compelled to defend herself. "It's not fair to expect me to cook, or weave. I'm an enchantress. My skill lies in setting spells."

Behind them, one of the others muttered something to Greta. The girl called back an answer over her shoulder and the crowd of women giggled.

Certain they laughed at her, Riana demanded a translation.

"Ana asked what you were saying," Greta said distractedly as she packed the leftover scraps. "I merely repeated your claim to be a magician."

Riana rose to her feet, determined to be taken seriously. "You can tell them all I trained at Camelot. With the Great Merlin himself." It was far from true, but she saw no reason to tell these yokels so.

Yet instead of being impressed when Greta repeated her words, the women merely doubled their laughter.

Save Helga. Snarling, she challenged Riana to prove her boast.

In all the years Riana had bragged of her powers, she'd never before been asked to substantiate her claim. Taken aback, she tried to find a way to avoid answering the challenge, for thus far, her forays into the magical realm had not been all too positive. "I'd love to turn you all into toads," she said with false bravado, keeping her gaze trained on Helga. "But alas, I am not in my natural element. I'm not accustomed to this setting, your world is out of alignment. I find it quite likely my magic won't work here at all."

At Greta's translation, Helga set her hands on her beefy hips and spoke in her slow, lowing tones. With her graying hair tied tight at her nape and her pale skin mottled with righteous indignation, she seemed every bit the overfed cow Riana called her.

"She says you are using this as an excuse," Greta explained. "That you are nothing but a charlatan."

"I am genuine enough," Riana said with growing indignation. "If she wants a spell, then a spell is what she shall have."

Clearly uneasy, Greta translated. Helga smiled, gesturing broadly as if to say, *go right ahead.*

"You needn't do this," Greta said softly. "Don't let her goad you."

As this was so like what Sela would have told her, Riana felt instant rebellion. Nor did it help to watch Helga's gloating pose as she turned to speak to the others. Riana could have no idea what the woman muttered, but from their smirks, she doubted it was complimentary. "I have no need to hide from her challenge," she said defiantly. "Tell me, Greta, what is it your people need most?"

The girl bit her lip, glancing toward the sky beyond the grove.

"The ground grows hard and our new crops thirst for water. More than all else, we need it to rain."

A pox on them all, Riana thought angrily, she would make it pour buckets. And she'd keep it raining until they begged her to stop.

Rolling up her sleeves, she closed her eyes and inhaled deeply. Somewhere in her memory lay a spell for revising the weather, yet search though she might, she could remember only bits and pieces of Sela's sacred book. Desperately raising her arms to the sky, she decided to design her own enchantment. "Dear Mother Goddess," she chanted in a singsong whine. "Come bless this hostile land with thy bounty."

She opened one eye, guessing already that nothing had happened. The women watched with open skepticism. It would help if there could be even a trace of a cloud, but the sky remained as blue as a new robin's egg.

Squeezing her eyes with all her might, she concentrated harder. "Dear Mother, show these ignorant infidels your generosity. Reward their efforts with your bounty."

Her voice rose satisfyingly, ringing with solemnity and power. She felt no surprise when she heard the first plop on the ground, merely satisfaction. At long last, she had conjured the proper enchantment.

But the sound became thuds, growing more solid and frequent, and accompanied by shrieks from the women. Confused, Riana opened her eyes to see what caused them to scatter. It was then that the first wriggling creature fell from the branch overhead to land on her head.

She too shrieked as the creature slithered down her arm; she also fled with the others from the cover of the trees. Helga alone stood within the grove, laughing with undisguised glee. Bending down, she lifted up one of many harmless garter snakes writhing off to safety. She held it out, spitting out words in Riana's direction.

"So the great enchantress can rain down serpents," Greta

translated. "It would seem you are as good a witch as you are a cook."

Snakes? Riana thought, burning with humiliation at the renewed laughter. "What did I do wrong this time?" she said, voicing her doubts aloud. "Where did I make the mistake?"

"It was not your fault," Greta answered, no doubt hoping to make her feel better. "The snakes often gather in this grove. We should have thought about it before sitting here."

So she hadn't even summoned the snakes? Helga could be right, she feared; she wasn't much of a magician.

But if that were true, it made her dream, her whole life, a mockery.

All at once, she could not bear to be around these women. Indeed, she wondered how she would manage to face herself. Sick inside, she turned to flee, but as luck would have it, she ran straight into Wolf.

Steadying his wife against him, feeling her heart pulse against his chest, Wolf longed to lean down and banish the outside world in a sweet, drugging kiss. But conscious of curious eyes, and knowing Riana was capable of biting off his tongue instead, he set her away from him firmly.

He could see a glittering in her golden eyes, but her chin was up, her shoulders thrust back. It was as Ranulf said. His wife was a proud woman, too proud to suffer the taunting he'd witnessed.

Though in truth, he could not blame the women for laughing. He himself found it hard to stifle a chuckle as he recalled her expression as the snake fell on Riana's head.

As a result, he addressed the women sharply. "Your meal is over. Greta, take the scraps back to the kitchens while you others return to the fields. This village shall never reap Nature's bounty if our planters waste the day cavorting in the groves."

The women hung their heads as they walked off, outwardly chastened, though many shoulders shook betrayingly. Poor Riana, Wolf thought, knowing this was one stunt she might never live down. The village would swap this tale for years to come.

Seeing her move to join the others, he reached out to retain her. "Wait. I would talk with you."

Plainly surprised, she stared at his hand on her arm. "You spoke to me in Briton."

"I have some knowledge of your tongue," he said stiffly. "Enough, I hope, to make my needs known to you."

It was her turn to stiffen. "Indeed. And what of *my* needs? Will you listen to them?"

He dropped her arm in exasperation. He should have known better than to attempt this. Being female, there would be no end to her demands.

"You must have seen," she went on with a betraying tremble to her voice. "Those women have nothing but scorn for me." She sucked in a breath, as if hoping to draw strength from it. This time there was no tremor as she spoke. "I have said I will do my part, but I cannot work in your fields. You must find something else for me to do."

While impressed by her quiet dignity, as chieftain, he could not allow her to tell him what he must do. "We work where we're needed. There is much planting yet to be done if we hope to have stores enough to stave off winter's starvation."

"But I am not one of your villagers," she said stubbornly, crossing her arms in front of her. "My skills lie in other areas. As an artisan, I am not accustomed to dirtying my hands."

He crossed his own arms. "There is no honor in keeping your hands clean. The soil is our greatest wealth, a gift from the gods, and to work it is our blessing."

"You sound more like a common farmer than a chieftain."

He forced a smile. "For a Saxon, that is the ultimate praise."

"Saxon," she said with obvious scorn. "I don't know why you would claim kinship with these people. You don't act, you don't even look like them. You would be more at home in Rome, I would think."

She hit a nerve. All his youth, he'd strived to reconcile the two natures inherited from his parents. For Riana to suggest that he did not belong here, that he might have failed Exar's expectations, made him lash back at her. "I know who I am. I see no need to prove myself, to resort to tricks of witchery that fool no one."

She flinched, but her voice was hard with bitterness. "How smug you sound, when in truth, you are little better than a thief. Or do you deny you stole me from my home?"

"The god Thunor directed me to take you," he answered without thinking.

"Some heathen god has a whim and I must become your prisoner? You pride yourself in being a just man, but where is there justice in that?"

"You are no prisoner. You are my wife."

She made a dismissive gesture with her hands. "Is a wife sent out to perform all the tasks no one else wishes to do? Forced day after day to endure the taunts and jibes of your womenfolk?"

"My people see you as a stranger, the enemy. It will take time for them to know you, for us all to adjust."

He considered his words to be soothing, worthy of a diplomat like Vangarth, but Riana refused to be calmed.

"And how can you know me," she asked heatedly, "when I am shut away like some loathsome leper, kept out of sight on yon distant hill?"

"It was your choice," he said, giving vent to his exasperation. It had never occurred to him that she'd find his mother's quarters anything less than pleasurable.

But looking at her now, he saw that his sister could be right, that there might be too many misunderstandings between them. "You must not think I demean you by sending you to the fields," he added, gesturing to where the women now worked. "In truth, you should consider it an honor to be part of the planting."

She couldn't look more skeptical.

"Half of me might be Roman, but it is from my father's people that I receive my love for the land," he explained. "To every one of us here in River Ford, the soil is precious and coaxing crops from it is our greatest glory. Every Saxon, from the tiniest child to the oldest grandfather, knows the land is our true master and salvation. Revere it, bless it with hard work and dedication, and one day it shall offer us limitless bounty."

She tilted her head, studying him. "You speak of the soil as if it were a living, breathing being."

"Is it not?" He reached down to lift up a clod of dirt, holding it out to her. "Like a man, it has color and scent and is ever-changing."

"My people call the land The Womb of the Goddess. We see it more as a feminine entity."

She might mean to challenge him, but he could not dispute her claim, for there was much about the land to remind him of a woman's ability to give and sustain life. "Whatever its source, there is power in the soil, riches we dare not squander if our kingdom is to prosper again. It is my dream to watch my sons walk tall and proud through the waves of grain."

"And your daughters, who do all the work, will they be permitted to walk behind them?"

He almost told her that the men, when not called to battle, kept just as busy in the fields, but it was not for his wife to question and bait him. Her role was to listen to her husband and chieftain, to accept what she was told and act upon it. "Go join the others," he said stiffly, tossing the clod to the ground. "Your belly will thank you come the advent of the new year."

She looked at him with confusion. "You would send me back to their mocking laughter? You cannot find some other task I might do?"

"What is left for you to do?" he asked, annoyed that she would continue to badger him when he had explained his needs so patiently. "Have you not already failed at every task I've assigned? Go to the fields, Moriana. I will brook no more argument from you."

Her lower lip trembled, and he thought for a moment that she would defy him, but with a deep, inhaled breath, she turned for the fields.

Watching her go, Wolf felt a wave of satisfaction. Maybe Ranulf was right about altering his strategy. Riana had not been overly pleased, but for once, she had listened to him and acted upon his orders. They had communicated, he thought; he'd made a good start.

In all, he could be well pleased with this day's work.

"I tell you, Sela, that man is a pompous peacock."

Riana could not contain her indignation as she helped her guardian sort herbs. "If you had seen him, so arrogant and sure of himself as he spouted off his edicts, I swear to you, you'd have wished to scream also."

She did not add that she'd found the man endearing when revealing his hopes for the future, or that her hand had gone to her belly when he spoke of having children. For a brief moment, she'd imagined carrying his babe and the thought had filled her with a surprising sense of peace and contentment. Too bad he had so soon reverted to his usual arrogant form.

"He is chieftain, my girl," Sela said. "He could not rule this tribe were he *not* sure of himself."

"I should have known you would take his side."

Sela glanced up, as if surprised by Riana's bitter tone. "I take no sides, child. Indeed, could it be you look too hard for reasons to hate him? Can you not at least try to listen to what he says to you?"

"I listened. He expects me to produce sons for him, like some mindless brood mare. Yet when I spoke of daughters, he went cold and hard with disdain. I can't be wed to such a man, Sela. I beg you, can't you find some little enchantment that will set me free?"

The old woman shook her head. "It is in the hands of the Goddess. She has brought you here and here you must stay."

"You use the Goddess as your excuse for everything. Very well, if you won't help me, perhaps I shall just weave an enchantment myself."

Sela merely chuckled. "Yes, I have heard about your rainstorm. Do you hope to leave here riding a snake?"

Reddening, Riana refused to speak. Bad enough everyone else in the village must throw it in her face, but one could hope Sela would spare her the humiliation. That she did not made Riana feel more isolated than ever.

"Ah, child, your youth betrays you." Sela set down her herbs to smile gently at her. "In years to come, you will look back at these days and laugh at your angst, your impatience. Wolf is a good man. He will make a great chieftain and an even finer father and husband."

"I don't belong here," Riana repeated stubbornly.

"No?" Sela narrowed her gaze as if she could probe into her deepest thoughts. "Tell me you don't think of what it would be like to have him in your big, empty bed. Your body is young, and has known a man's touch. It must yearn to feel such magic again."

"No." The denial rang false, even to her own ears. In her mind, she could see his smile today, how even in its brevity it warmed her and left her aching for more. He was undeniably handsome, this man who called himself her husband, and had devastating charm when he cared to exert it. "You forget," she said in angry denial, "I'd have found no pleasure in his bed if you hadn't drugged me."

"Can you be so certain?"

Again Riana blushed, unable to protest with conviction. Anxious to change the subject, she gestured at the herbs spread before them. "Why all this juniper and monkshood? Are you preparing for the Beltane rituals?"

Sela glanced up, her gaze hooded. "How could I dare? You know your husband forbids such witchery."

"Use your protests on him. They are wasted on me. I've lived too long with you not to know the signs, Sela. You are planning something, and I think it is the ritual."

Infuriatingly, Sela merely shrugged and went back to her sorting.

"Far be it for *me* to object," Riana pressed, hoping to prod her into admission. "I think we need the ritual. These Saxons would yoke us to the same burdens their sky gods set upon them. We need the joys and freedom of our own religion. It's time to summon the Goddess to this heathen land."

"Indeed? Beltane, as you recall, is a rite of procreation. Summon the Goddess and she will merely tell you what I have been saying, that your place is with your husband, girl. The night of the ritual, you should lie with him, take his seed into your womb, and yield up the fruit of your union."

Riana fought the quick urgent warmth those words produced. "Never! I do not belong in this wilderness with that man who calls himself my husband. This is the message the Goddess will deliver at Beltane. Mark my words, there will be a sign that I am not meant to waste my days in this Saxon back of nowhere. My place—my future—remains at Camelot."

"You and your obsession."

"The Goddess knows, if you do not, that I shall be called there to serve the king. One day, Arthur will need me."

Sela's face clouded. "And what if I tell you there is danger in returning to Arthur's world?"

Riana stifled a shiver. "I would answer, what is my choice? Stay here, and I can hope for no more than what befell Greta's mother. I will not die as some glorified slave."

Her words rang across the room. Sela continued to frown at her, making Riana feel like a wayward child. Annoyed, she rose to her feet and prepared to leave. "I see there's no sense talking to you. I might as well summon the guard Wolf has dogging my heels and go back to the villa."

Deep down, she knew she punished herself more than Sela with her leaving, for it was too often lonely up there in her silent, empty villa. Still, she might have felt greater satisfaction in her proud departure, had Greta not walked through the door as she was preparing to storm out of it. It struck her that her guardian and friend oft kept each other company.

Looking from Greta to Sela, Riana was disturbed by the solemn glances they exchanged. "Go on," she said angrily, "hatch your plots without me. I won't be here long in any case."

"Don't be a fool, child. Did you not learn your lesson from your last attempt at escape?"

"What I learned, Sela, is that I'd rather die than live as a Saxon."

Sela stood, her face white and grim, her hand trembling as she pointed it at Riana. "Speak not so lightly of your death, child, for mark my words. Leave for Camelot, and it may yet come to that."

On the outskirts of Camelot, a cowled figure gathered the women about the flickering candle. Thirteen shadows danced on the walls of the drafty cave, cavorting like shades upon the grave.

Their leader spoke loud and clear, her voice echoing eerily against the stone. "Tomorrow, at the Beltane fires, we shall make a sacrifice. Be ready with your sacred knives for the signal to begin."

There was a low murmur among them, but none dared speak out. Smiling, the leader continued. "We need a tool, someone close to the king, young and unwitting, to serve as a pawn in our hands. It is hoped the Beltane sacrifice will summon this pawn. I have read the crystal and all signs point favorably in this direction."

"But Arthur has forbidden such sacrifice," one finally dared challenge. "Surely we risk much in disobeying his royal edict on so holy a day."

The leader extended a hand, pointing to each conspirator in turn. "I would have you consider instead what's at stake should we fail to act. Every day, the men of this realm grow more secure in their power. Thanks to Merlin and Arthur's priests, the old religion is all but banished from this kingdom. Heed me well, for I have seen also in the crystals that soon, all women will be persecuted for practicing the magical arts. Our daughters, and their daughters shall burn at the stake. I tell you, we must put an end to Camelot. The Great Goddess commands it."

"But this tool? How will we know we've found the unwitting pawn?"

Laying her hands on the crystal, feeling its icy power streak through her veins, the leader sought her own, secret answers.

And what she heard was the single word.

Moriana.

Seven

Riana walked through the dark fields behind Sela, the full moon lighting their way. She was glad that for once she need not have her guard, Tadrick, at her heels. Young Tad, as she'd taken to calling him, was an overeager pup when it came to obeying his chieftain's commands. Wolf had obviously given orders that his new wife was not to escape.

Sela had vouchsafed her good conduct tonight, but not even Riana was desperate enough to venture out alone on Beltane's eve. All over England, women would gather to summon the Goddess, and she'd no wish to encounter any dark forces the less-skilled might inadvertently conjure. She had woes enough without adding discontented demons to the list.

Besides, it made sense to stay with Sela. The woman had skills that she did not, among them the ability to summon the Goddess. Riana had good reason to hope for great things tonight, for the Goddess was her most generous during the Beltane ritual, favoring the act of creation above all other rites. In her ultimate wisdom and bounty, perhaps the Goddess would indeed see fit to present Riana with a sign—some visible proof that she was meant to go to Camelot.

Hurrying behind Sela, she followed the overgrown path up the hill behind the villa. Occasional branches snagged her cloak-like clasping fingers intent upon detaining her. Grabbed by one particularly persistent bush, she called out for Sela to wait, but the woman was caught up in her chanting and continued on without her. Riana yanked the cloak, tearing the wool as she rushed up the path, so anxious was she not to be left on her own in the dark.

With a sigh of relief, she reached the top of the hill. Sela stood on the rise, arms upraised as she chanted to the heavens. Hearing the sound of rushing water, Riana gazed over the lip of the crest, finding a waterfall cascading to the rocks below. From there, she realized, the stream must wind around the villa to form the tranquil pool she bathed in each day.

Water, Riana knew, was one of the four elements required for summoning the Goddess.

Air was another ingredient, she thought, feeling the healthy breeze stir her hair and play with her cloak. Blowing cool and damp, it made the night seem more like harvest end, than the heart of the planting. It swept across the land, whipping up scents of peat and fertile earth, causing the trees to bend and sway like handmaidens in an ancient dance. Clouds skittered across the sky, now and then obscuring the moon and leaving the landscape in eerie darkness. A perfect night for roaming spirits to prey upon the unwary, Riana thought with a shiver.

She gathered her cloak close and approached Sela, who chanted over a large pile of limbs and kindling set in a bowl-shaped indentation in the ground. Riana could not imagine this frail old woman digging the hole and toting wood, but who here in Wolf's village would help her? "Witchery," as they termed it, was deemed unnatural and unhealthy, and wisely avoided.

But Riana welcomed these comforting symbols of the old religion. Fire was the third required element, with earth being fourth and last. Glancing about, she found the soil had been upturned around the circle. Everything was in place, just waiting for them to begin.

The pace of the chanting altered, became deep and urgent. Taking the two sacred flasks, Sela poured the libation specially brewed for this ritual. Watching her, Riana held her breath. Drink the fiery liquid and they could then light the holy blaze. The dancing could begin.

Eagerly, she kicked off her shoes, letting her feet sense the rhythms of the recently tilled earth. Sela offered the flask and Riana drank it in one gulp, impatient to start. Dancing was what she enjoyed most in any ritual. It allowed her to step out of herself, to become wild and uninhibited, and to leave the cares of the world behind. Only in the dance did she feel free.

Handing the flask back to Sela, she licked her lips, surprised by a strange tang. Another time, she might have stopped to analyze it, as it seemed vaguely familiar, but her toes were already wriggling in the soil. She wanted to dance; she needed to summon the Goddess. "Light the blaze," she urged Sela hoarsely. "Fan the flames."

Awed and breathless, Riana watched the fire burst to life, drawing strength and energy from its heat, and from the earth, air and water surrounding it. For long moments, she stared at the blaze, transfixed. It seemed alive to her, its golden tongues licking the sky, its ruby heart pulsing deep in the earth. A languid warmth radiated up and out from her own heated core. It spread within her veins, fanned to life by Sela's slow, rhythmic chanting. More and more a hungry heat, the sensation spread through Riana like a forest blaze, leaping into her fevered brain, her tingling limbs, her burning breasts. Thrusting back the cloak, she arched her back, arms extended behind her, and offered herself to the moon.

The dance had begun.

No careful, practiced thing, her movements took on a life all their own, the steps pure impulse, coaxed by the elements surrounding her. Beneath her toes, she felt the ground tremble and hum, uncannily echoing Sela's chanting. Urgency built within Riana. Swaying like the trees, she welcomed the breeze. She knew a deep, hard longing to feel its cool breath along her limbs, at her breasts. Yanking off her tunic, she tossed it behind her. Bending and twirling, she extended her arms upward to the moon.

"On this night of Beltane," Sela chanted, her voice growing with power and volume, "your humble servants everywhere gather to do your bidding. It is time to plant the seed in the fertile furrow, to maintain the cycle of birth, death and procreation."

Procreation. As Riana's mind danced with visions of her marriage night, the heat in her body swelled.

"Man of Earth, Woman of Moon," Sela called out. "Join in holy union. Take pleasure in the sacred act."

Pleasure. It had been pleasurable, Riana now acknowledged. Indeed, so vivid was the lust she'd shared with Wolf, it throbbed now inside her with unfulfilled yearning. She wanted to taste his sweet, drugging kisses, longed to feel his practiced hands on her flesh.

"Come to her, Man of Earth." Sela no longer seemed herself, her voice stern and commanding, her face shadowed from the flames. "Come take this vessel of the Goddess here beneath the sacred moon."

Sela's voice tapered off. Looking up, Riana saw her vanish into the trees. The chants had been more than a prayer, Riana realized, they were a plea to an actual physical presence. Her whirling, dizzying dance came to an abrupt stop as she saw Wolf, a mere ten steps away.

Silent and still, he watched her with heated intensity, as if his gaze had the power to sear her body. Trembling with fear, and yet, anticipation, she hoped with her mind that he would stay where he was, while her heart and body prayed he would take a step closer.

But it was Beltane, a time not for intellect and logic, but rather for emotion and pleasure. Unconsciously, her hands went up and out to him.

At the invitation, a madness broke free in Wolf's brain. Done was the sheer torture of holding himself in check while she danced; in five long strides, he had her clasped in his arms, her sweet, yielding lips open to his own.

Like a man long starved, he touched and tasted her, his hands and lips roaming freely, demandingly. He'd waited far too long for this and he was in a fever to possess her.

Lowering them both to the ground beside the fire, he marvelled at her eagerness, thinking it well worth the long empty nights of waiting. That their lust could be a shared thing made him heady with power. The old woman was right; they were indeed Man of Earth and Woman of Moon. He felt he could go anywhere, accomplish anything, if blessed by the bright, shining light that was Riana.

Bucking and twisting beneath him, hungry for their joining, she fueled his madness. He lost all perception of time, of place; their mating seemed a recurring, perpetual thing. It was no longer a matter of wanting the sweet oblivion he found between her thighs, nor even of needing it—it had become his destiny, his purpose in life.

"You're mine," he ground out, parting her legs and driving inside her.

He gripped her eager thrusting hips, kissing her greedily, surging with the rising tide of their passion. He'd become part of her seductive dance; they were now one writhing, swirling entity. Stirred by the heat and scent of their joined bodies, he plunged deep inside her, sensation welling about him until he thought he might drown in a sea of pleasure.

His mind pounded with primitive rhythms, urging him ever deeper, ever faster. He heard her soft moans from afar, then her first startled gasp of release as she tightened around him. He burst forth, crying out her name in victory, thrusting and driving even after all his seed had been spilled.

Yet as powerful as his own release had been, he was not sated. On the contrary, he found he wanted her all over again, whatever limitations Nature might impose upon him. In a moment of total clarity, he saw he would want this female forever.

Gazing down at her, he took her face in his hands, tracing her features in a gesture of possession. "This is how it should be," he told her solemnly. "My woman, hot and eager beneath me."

But instead of meeting his gaze with an answering desire, she stared with fear and confusion. "Oh, no," she breathed. "What have I done?"

"We made love," he said, irritated. He saw no reason for her to turn missish now, not with her hot, moist flesh pressed against him.

"No." In a sudden panic, she pushed at his chest.

Surprised, and fast losing patience, he rolled aside to give her room to breathe. She took advantage by leaping instantly to her feet.

Rising more sedately, he watched her scramble about for her clothing, reminded of the first time she had danced before him. She'd hidden from him inside her magic circle then, even as she hid from the truth now.

"We are one," he said stubbornly. "You cannot deny that you came to me eagerly."

Eyes wide and round, she shook her head vigorously. "I got swept away by the dance, the sacred rite." Helplessly, she looked at the fire, at the tunic clutched in her hands. "By all that is holy, what have I done?"

"You have done as the Goddess commanded."

Wolf turned, even as Riana did, both of them startled to see Sela coming out of the woods. In the madness, he'd lost track of where the old woman had gone. "You wanted a sign from the Goddess," Sela went on. "And now here you have it."

"No," Riana cried, yanking the tunic over her head. "This is not the sign I sought."

"Don't deny the inevitable, child." Sela's smile held a note of age-old wisdom. "Accept what the deity wants from you."

Riana licked her lips as if tasting them, a look of hard suspicion coming into her eyes. "Juniper," she said icily. "You put it in the potion and drugged me again, didn't you? This was no sign from the Goddess. This was your trap."

Wolf went cold with disgust. "Interfering crone," he lashed out at Sela. "Bad enough you must pander my wife to me, but you must stand here and watch?"

Sela faced him squarely, showing no remorse. "In deference

to your ways, I retired to the trees and gave you your privacy. Though in our religion, it is our custom to share in the rite, all taking joy in the glorious joining."

"It is to me you should explain," Riana cried. "You had no right to use magic to bend me to your will. If this were indeed a sign from the Goddess, then you influenced her unduly with your dark arts."

"Enough of your witchery," Wolf growled, angered by the uneasiness her words produced in him. "You are on Saxon lands and will follow Saxon law. Let this fire die and retire to your chambers, both of you. I will have no more of your mischief."

Riana bent down for the cloak. It angered him further that she could gaze at him with such fear and loathing when they'd lain so perfectly together. "And you wife," he said cuttingly. "I forbid you to practice the dark arts. As the chieftain's wife, your sole duty is to bear me an heir. Tomorrow I will visit the villa and begin bedding you in earnest."

"I swear again to you," she hissed back, no frightened virgin now. "I shall never welcome you into my bed."

Smiling contemptuously, he glanced at the ground where they'd lain. "So you say. But welcome or not, I *shall* come to you, over and over, until my seed sprouts in your womb."

Eyes flashing, she started to speak, but the old woman pulled her away. He could hear Riana arguing as she stomped back to the villa.

Wolf watched the dying fire, wondering how the joy of their coupling could give way to such bitter disappointment.

He could tell himself that it mattered little what she wanted, that she was his wife, and must bear him children, but he would be lying to both her and himself. He craved more than mere obedience from his wife, and he feared he would never find it.

Leaving her young charge in the well-guarded villa, Sela smiled in contentment as she took the path to the village. The girl would have her feel abashed for the part she'd played in the night's proceedings, but in truth, Sela was well pleased with her work.

Trust Riana to confuse her herbs. No juniper had been in the potion. Any lust she'd felt had either been her own, or granted by the Goddess.

Either way, Riana's fate was sealed.

Sela actually envied her young charge, knowing the intense pleasure Riana was likely to experience in the nights ahead. Her virile husband, driven to prove his prowess, would do much to show her the magic that could exist between a man and a woman Like it or not, Riana was about to embark on a path of self-discovery, and hopefully, she'd come to realize how such knowledge served her in her quest to become an enchantress. A female must share in the act of giving and taking love before she could communicate with the Goddess. A woman at peace with her sexuality and its pertaining emotions, became a stronger, wiser mortal being, and a far more capable enchantress.

Approaching her cottage, Sela was not surprised to see the lamp still lit. She watched the door whip open.

"Did all go well?" Greta asked, reaching out to tug Sela inside. "Did the fire we laid spark anything between them?"

"Time will tell," Sela said softly, patting her coconspirator's hand, knowing they could plant the seeds and no more.

Riana stirred on her bed, slowly conscious of the ropes at her wrists and ankles. Naked and vulnerable, spread-eagled face-down in a sea of fur, she could see little of the room behind her, but she could hear someone stir there, could sense his large, dark presence nearing the bed. A quick beating pulse leapt to life inside her.

She felt his heat, then his breath on her ear, as he slipped into the bed beside her. Hot skin, as bare as her own, slid along her back, his coarse hair tickling, rasping, bringing her every inch to acute awareness.

Nuzzling at her neck, nibbling at her ear, his mouth whispered sweet chants against her tingling flesh, his tongue trailing along her side, up her arm. "Release me," she pleaded in a desperate whisper, shivering as his mouth reached the rope. "Please," she begged again as his tongue dipped back down her arm, but she could not tell if it were the ropes she wished loosened, or the aching tension within her.

He released neither, choosing instead to trace his tongue up her other arm. Moaning softly, struggling to resist, she cried out his name, the sound abnormally loud and foreign.

She woke instantly from the dream.

Sitting up, blinking her eyes, she rubbed her arms as if she could erase its images, still pulsing with lurid life inside her. How could she conjure up such a fantasy? Why would she want to? She hated that man, despised him. If she were his captive, the last thing she'd feel was such mind-numbing pleasure.

Uneasily, she remembered the night before at the Beltane fire.

She heard again the ungodly noise that had woken her, and as she made the identification, she stomped to the window with an oath on her lips. "May the Goddess strike you down," she shouted to the energetic cock crowing outside. Every morning, the foolish rooster felt compelled to strut about the countryside, calling his females to worship at his feet, forcing them to work, always work . . .

Much like the man who called himself her husband.

Before she could curse either Wolf or the rooster, she caught sight of a woman hurrying toward the village, a sack hoisted over her shoulder. Helga, Riana thought, bristling. What was the woman about, this early of a morning, so far from the village ovens? Ever industrious, had Helga gone out to grind the wheat herself, so she could brag about baking bread for the entire village and then spending a full day in the fields?

Frowning, Riana turned away from the window, wondering what new torture the woman would have devised for today. No matter what she did, Helga remained determined not to like her. Riana had come to recognize a few words of Saxon, enough to know the difference between a greeting and an insult, and most of what Helga said about her fell in the latter category.

How the woman delighted in taunting her in front of the others. Her favorite jibe was a writhing motion she made with her arms each time Riana strolled by. Her victim could hardly overlook this blatant reminder of the snake fiasco, not with the others hooting with laughter.

And from what Greta told her, Helga had spread it about the village that the only spell Riana had conjured was the one to enslave their chieftain's heart, for what sane man would want such a cold fish? Were he not spellbound, she claimed, Penawulf would have long since banished the useless Briton, casting her back to the nether world where she belonged.

No, she was not considered completely useless, Riana thought, recalling how Wolf meant to use her body to beget his heir. Over and over, like the village brood mare, spending night after night in her bed.

Against her will, her body began to throb, remembering the wanton creature she'd been last night.

Her gaze went to the bed. She had no juniper in her now, or any outside stimulus to titillate her thoughts, so why must she envision the two of them locked in passion, writhing amongst those furs? It was the dream, she insisted in sudden panic as she hastily dressed and quit the room.

Though why she should even have such a dream she stubbornly refused to guess.

She stormed outside, conscious of Tad trailing behind her. She felt a spurt of guilt for waking her ever-present guard so early, but decided the lad must blame his chieftain. If Wolf didn't invade her dreams, she too would still be asleep.

She went through the woods to the tranquil pool where she daily performed her morning ablutions. If she washed the scent of that pagan brute from her skin, perhaps she could stop her sex-driven thoughts and dreams. Else, she'd never get through the day's planting without Helga and the others laughing themselves silly.

Tad stayed on the path, giving her privacy at the pool, for which she was grateful. As she washed, she forced her mind to her most immediate concern—leaving this place. Now more than ever she must escape, but Wolf's appearance last night had prevented her sign from the Goddess. Hard to hear a sacred message, after all, lying flat on one's back, moaning with pleasure.

Unbidden, an image came to mind, her and Wolf in this glade, him laying her down on a soft bed of moss, stroking and caressing expertly . . .

Blushing, she reminded herself yet again that she mustn't be distracted by such base, physical yearnings. Her need for Wolf's touch could be like a drug in itself. Craving it more and more, she would soon lose sight of her goal, and then she'd never return to Camelot.

Yet as she stared into the pool, she found herself nonetheless wondering what would happen between them if he came, as threatened, to the villa tonight. Would he force her? Would he need to?

As if in answer, she saw his face in the pool's reflection, at first shimmering, then clear and exact as if she stood before him. It took some confused moments to realize that Wolf was not here at the pool, but in the grand hall, talking with his warriors. Wolf's friend Ranulf stood protectively at his side, while another man strode back and forth across before them. The second man was not of the village but she found him vaguely familiar.

With growing excitement, for surely this must be a vision, and therefore proof of her magical powers, she watched Wolf lean forward in his chair. "What brings you to River Ford, Vangarth?" he asked.

Vangarth, she thought with dread. The man from Cerdric's stronghold.

And all at once, she could hear Vangarth's thoughts, as if she walked within his brain. Aloud, he claimed to have come to offer Cerdric's blessing, but his inner speech revealed that the king was not aware of his visit. Vangarth had come to trap Wolf, to find some way to further blacken his rival's name.

And the tool he meant to use was Riana.

Poised amidst his thoughts, sensing his hatred for Wolf, she saw how this Vangarth could yet succeed, having the king's ear and knowing how to use it to best advantage. Cerdric might be angry at his warrior-in-chief for running off with a prisoner, but his fondness for Wolf had him seeking excuses. He could condone a love match, for it would produce many fine sons to one day serve him, but should he learn Wolf risked the fragile peace with Camelot by kidnapping a Briton who wanted no part of him, the king's disappointment—and punishment—would be severe.

Were Riana to tell this cool, calculating stranger that she'd been taken against her will, that she sought Cerdric's protection, she could leave this village at once and forever.

While Wolf would be stripped of his wealth, his position, and quite possibly his life.

"What are you doing here?"

She spun, heart going to her throat as she saw her husband standing before her. Suspiciously, he looked from her to the pool. Disoriented, she glanced back at its glassy surface. Nothing shimmered there now.

"I was washing," she began hesitantly, no longer certain what she'd seen. "I do so every day at this time." Recovering slowly, she stared up at him with her own suspicion. "What brings *you* here at this early hour?"

"You are clean enough," he said abruptly, ignoring her question. "Return to the villa and prepare for your day in the fields."

"The fields?" Exasperated, she stood, wanting to lash out at him. "First, a long hard day of work, and then a longer, harder ordeal tonight on my back?"

His cold gaze raked over her. "Would you prefer we begin your ordeal here and now?"

Going hot all over, remembering how she'd so recently imagined that very thing, Riana scrambled up and backed away from him.

"Go now," he said implacably, pointing at the villa. "Or pay the consequences of disobeying me."

Embarrassed by her reaction to him, blaming Wolf for it, she hoped she *had* seen a vision. When Vangarth came to call, she would indeed hold the power of life and death over this unreasonable brute.

Then they would see who would be suffering the consequences.

Wolf watched her go, feeling frustration. It was no oversight that he hadn't answered her question. He couldn't explain to her what he'd been doing here any more than he could explain it to himself.

Nor did he wish to admit that he'd slept at the villa last night, not trusting Tadrick to prevent her from bolting. Eyes narrowing, he glanced at the stream. What had she been doing, staring so intently into the pool?

More witchery, he wondered uneasily? The Druids were said to read the future from smooth reflections. Had Riana learned from them and could now summon magic from the glassy surface, enough to aid in her escape? And did she dare practice such an art when he'd expressly forbidden it?

He would not have her following in his mother's footsteps. His young wife would bear further watching.

Riana reached the end of her row, throwing all her remaining seeds in the furrow. She grew weary of this planting, of the dirt caked beneath her nails, the ever-present sweat trickling down her back. It annoyed her that Greta could remain so ceaselessly cheerful.

But then, a great many things annoyed her this morning.

Damn Wolf for interrupting her vision. If she could have seen her actions played out to the end, perhaps she'd be less irritable now.

"Why the glum face?" Greta asked as she too reached the end of her row. "Only five more rows and we can stop for the noonday meal."

Trust Greta to smile; she could find something worthwhile in a conflagration. Riana showed her empty hands. "I'm done now. Look, I'm out of seeds."

Greta frowned, more in confusion than displeasure, but she brightened at once. "Here, take some of mine. We can work on this row together and then get more from Yarrick when we reach the end."

Resourceful, ever practical Greta.

Seeing no help for it, Riana took the seeds and knelt on the other side of the row from her friend. They made great ceremony of this planting, she thought irritably, dropping each seed in its hole, saying a prayer as they mounded the earth over it as if they were tucking a child into his cradle.

Not sharing their reverence, Riana preferred to talk as she worked. She found herself curious about the players in her vision, and she realized this girl could likely enlighten her. "Greta, who is Vangarth and what does he mean to your brother?"

The girl looked up, clearly startled. "Why do you ask?"

Riana forced a shrug, hoping to sound offhand. "I saw him there at King Cerdric's camp. I had the impression Wolf didn't much like him."

"Like him?" Greta spat on the ground—not, one would think, a good start for a seedling. "He despises Vangarth. We all do."

"They fought a mock battle that night," Riana prompted.

"It was a trap. Vangarth gave Wolf the choice. My brother could either win, and take the glory, or he could lose, and take you." Greta frowned again. "I cannot claim to know my brother's mind, but I've watched their rivalry, and I know it must have pained Wolf greatly to lose to that slithering snake."

Surprised by what the girl implied, Riana stared at Greta. "Are you saying he lost to Vangarth deliberately?"

Greta eyed her as if she were the dimmest simpleton. "It requires but one look at both of them to know who *should* have won. Of course Wolf lost deliberately. It was the only way he could save you."

Stunned, Riana sat back on her heels.

"It was no easy thing for him to do, either." Oblivious to the fact that Riana had stopped, Greta continued on down the row. "The two have been vying against each other since childhood. My father oft used Vangarth as a measuring stick, casting his achievements in Wolf's face to make my brother try harder. Exar could not see how often Vangarth cheated, how he let others take the blame for his misdeeds. Proud to a fault, my father heard only Vangarth's smooth flatteries, not the lies underneath." She sighed, then looked up. "Look at me, getting so worked up I left you behind." She waited for Riana to join her. "Forgive me for running on, but I wished you to understand how Vangarth is a master of making promises he rarely makes good on. Wolf is a man of honor, Vangarth is not."

Man of honor? Riana wanted to shout. Did an honorable man threaten his wife? Or follow and hound her, take her without her consent?

He did not know about the drug, an inner voice reminded. He had every reason to think her willing and eager.

And every cause to feel his own rage at learning the truth.

"What is this sudden interest in Vangarth?" Greta probed gently. "Did my brother mention him to you?"

Riana answered without thinking. "No. Actually, I had a vision."

"You saw my brother's rival in a vision," Greta asked, her eyes going wide and round.

"In it, Vangarth was toying with Wolf. He meant to use me to destroy your brother."

"And you let him?"

She eyed Greta with surprise. "You talk as though you believe in my vision. I thought you Saxons didn't trust witchery."

The girl shrugged. "My mother taught me never to close my mind to any possibility. If there is threat to Wolf, I would know of it."

This, Riana could accept, knowing how deeply the girl adored her older brother. "I don't know what happened. Wolf interrupted the vision. I never saw it through to the end."

Greta stared at her, long and hard. "But surely, you must know in your heart if you could betray him."

Riana bristled with resentment. "Must everything revolve around your brother? How can I betray him when I am the one wronged?"

But Greta had ceased listening, her head jerking around as if someone had shouted her name. "Look, there is Sela," she said, rising abruptly to her feet. "She wants us to join her."

Riana looked to where she pointed to find Sela was indeed approaching. The old woman stopped at the edge of the field to wave her arms and gesture them closer. Rising, Riana hurried in Greta's wake. She hoped Sela had come with news that they could quit for the day.

As Greta greeted her, Sela reached for her arm and patted it soothingly. In all the years she'd been with the old woman, Riana had never seen this soft side to Sela—she hadn't even known she had one.

"I fear it is not you I have come for," she heard Sela tell the girl, her voice ringing with regret. "Go back to your planting, Greta. I must speak with Riana."

She made it sound a thankless task, a chore to be executed swiftly, then forgotten. Greta seemed to sense this. Touching Riana's sleeve, she smiled encouragingly. "Perhaps we can talk later. I shall come visit you."

"Come early, then, for Wolf comes to the villa tonight." Riana's voice went tight as she remembered the purpose of his visit.

At her tone, Greta betrayed a flicker of surprise, before turning to Sela. With a brief smile, she darted off back to her planting.

"Penawulf summons you," Sela said when the girl was out of earshot. "I must pray you've done nothing to aggravate Helga. By the Goddess, why can't you be a sweet, biddable girl like Greta?"

Riana felt her hurt and resentment erupting. "Must you talk of her as the Christians do their saints?"

Sela eyed her curiously. "It wouldn't hurt you to be more like her. It might stand you in good stead for your upcoming interview. I must say, it does not bode well that your husband asks to see you in the grand hall."

The scene in her vision. Could it mean Vangarth had already made his appearance?

But she wasn't prepared. She'd had no time to consider what she should do, to delve into her ever-shifting emotions. While part of her yearned to escape, an equal part kept seeing Wolf's face, proud and strong, yet so infinitely vulnerable as his world crashed down around him.

It was a clear cut case of her or Wolf, she told herself as she marched to the village. No question of betrayal here; if anything, it was a case of well-deserved vengeance. Perhaps even the Goddess herself had placed the power in Riana's hands. For once, the female held the power of life or death over her husband.

A heady feeling. Only, what did Riana mean to do with it?

even to rescue Riana, but once they're to have the girl and once
Cerdric became impatient, Wolf's punishment would be swift and
sure and terrible at best.

He was not immune, Cedric Vangarth thought as he stared at the
girl, picking her up. Once he was sure Riana had run the table
in front of king and court, his eyes, his cold blue eyes, gleaming
in the firelight. Perhaps, killed in private before them. This will
keep his wife happy, said a small, distant, diplomatic voice in the
king's ear, urging war, thinking mocking, your offering, imagine
the consequence.

Vangarth considered his alternatives, and all of his future
options turning...

Eight

Watching Vangarth pace across the Grand Hall, Wolf wondered what the man was plotting. He'd seen the shift in his gaze
when Vangarth claimed he had come to offer the king's blessing.
"The king wishes me to see this new wife myself," he'd added
ominously, "and hear from her own lips that she's happy."

Finding it odd that Cerdric would concern himself with a prisoner's happiness, Wolf wondered if the king even knew of his
marriage. It would not be the first time Vangarth had taken it
upon himself to pry into Wolf's affairs. The urgent haste with
which he'd charged into River Ford might indicate he'd only recently heard the news and rushed to take advantage.

Wolf glanced at the door again, wondering what kept Riana.
He hadn't wanted to summon her but his rival had been adamant
and Wolf could not safely deny him. Vangarth, soon to wed the
king's daughter, carried the power—whether assumed, or otherwise—of royal edict.

Sitting in the huge oak chair he used for council meetings,
Wolf gave nothing away of his inner emotions, knowing Vangarth would pounce on any perceived weakness.

"Where is the lovely Moriana?" Vangarth spun to face Wolf
with a smirk. "Such spirit, such fire, it must be difficult to tame
her. This delay worries me. I hope she does not mean to defy her
chieftain. Her husband."

In truth, Vangarth hoped just the opposite. He knew Cerdric
might condone Wolf's taking Riana if they'd formed some deep

bond between them, but were the king to learn the girl had been abducted against her will, Wolf's punishment would be swift and sure, and possibly deadly.

"We beg your patience, Lord Vangarth," Ranulf answered for him, "but keep in mind, we are some distance from the fields."

"Fields?" Vangarth widened his eyes, taking obvious pleasure in the revelation. "Is your kingdom grown so poor, Penawulf, that the wife of its great chieftain must dirty her hands in the soil? Or is forcing the Briton to help with your planting meant as a punishment?"

Wolf tensed, for this was Riana's own opinion of her duties. Had his wife been speaking to Vangarth?

No, it was impossible. They could hardly talk when she did not know Saxon, nor he Briton. Assured by this, Wolf eased his grip on the chair.

An ease that did not last long. Looking up, he found Riana had entered the room with Sela at her heels, both women pausing to eye the newcomer. Looking from Vangarth to Wolf, Riana seemed to weigh in her mind which was the better alternative.

"You remember my wife, Moriana," he said to his guest after Sela translated Vangarth's last speech to her charge.

Eyes narrowing, as if she recognized her opening, Riana marched up to Vangarth, beaming up at the man as she spoke in her own tongue.

"Welcome to our humble home, my lord Vangarth," the old woman translated. "I'm told you've been asking about my work in the fields. I am curious. What has my lord and master been telling you?"

Vangarth became all concern. "Precious little, my lady. Word has reached our ears that you have lived a time in Arthur's court. King Cerdric feels there is enough unrest in this land between Saxon and Briton without adding to it. He would know if you are here against your will."

Smiling like a cat with a mouse, Riana listened as Sela related that pretty speech. She turned to Wolf, her smile broadening as she neared him. He braced himself, waiting for her to spring the trap.

"Against my will?" she said in mock amazement. "My lord Vangarth, I am wife to the strong and noble Penawulf. Here, I am as like to a queen."

Wolf worked to contain his surprise. Perhaps Vangarth saw this, for he pounced the instant Sela stopped talking. "Indeed? It is not every ruler who sends his queen to work in the fields."

Listening to Sela, Riana stood at Wolf's side as if she'd always belonged there, straightening her shoulders when the old woman finished. "No, but then my lord Penawulf is no ordinary man," she said vehemently. "I *chose* to go to the fields. I find it a rare honor to work beside the women of our village. Indeed, I've spent many an hour with them at the looms learning to be a good Saxon wife. Have you told him, husband," she asked sweetly, gazing down at Wolf, "of the fine bread I bake?"

Why, she's enjoying herself, he thought, no little bemused.

Vangarth smiled, though the humor did not reach his eyes. "Clearly, Penawulf has every reason to be pleased with you. Tell me, does he teach his lovely young bride to use the bow, to ride a horse?"

Meeting Ranulf's worried gaze, Wolf realized his friend saw the trap. Until Cerdric gave his blessing, Riana was considered a prisoner and by law, it was forbidden to give a captive a weapon, or teach her any military art.

"Not as yet, my lord," Riana said sweetly, leaning down to snuggle her cheek against Wolf's own. "In truth, we are newly wed. I would hope he has other, more important things to teach me."

While everyone else laughed, Wolf grabbed for her arm, pulling her down to face him. "What game do you play now?" he whispered in Briton.

"Vangarth lies. He does not come at your king's bidding."

He gazed at her face, so close to his own. As he searched her eyes, he wondered how she could know these things—why knowing them would make a difference. Yesterday, she'd have fed him to the lions, yet here she was, standing fierce and proud at his side against the one man he hated.

Her gaze slid away, avoiding his scrutiny, and Wolf felt renewed frustration. There was no genuine feeling behind her speech to Vangarth. His wife played a game, using him as her pawn, and he must not allow it.

"Now that you've greeted our guest," he said gruffly, conscious of curious eyes upon them, "you may leave us."

"I'm dismissed, my lord and master?" she asked in Briton, straightening as he released her. "Am I free to go to my villa?"

"Minx," the old woman hissed, hurrying up to tug her arm. "Come along now. You and I must return to the fields."

Wolf raised a hand. "The hour grows late," he announced, feeling suddenly weary. "The lady Riana can go rest in her villa."

She looked at him then, as if trying to divine his motives. Either she found nothing, or was afraid he might yet change his mind, for abruptly, she grabbed Sela and marched from the room.

Vangarth eyed him with bewilderment. "What was all that?"

Wolf stood, not liking how the man watched his wife's every step. "Moriana asks that I join her in her chambers," he lied. "Ranulf, see that our guest receives food and drink, and oats for his mount."

"No." Vangarth waved a hand, preoccupied, his gaze still following Riana. "I do not stay. I must return to Cedric's camp by day's end."

"Then I shall not tarry long," Wolf tossed out, deciding to go after his wife. "Stay, share some ale with Ranulf, until I return to bid you farewell."

He left the grand hall, paying little heed to his guest's protests. Vangarth would be there when he got back, or he would not. Wolf's main concern was in catching up with his wife.

She seemed surprised to see him, and not at all pleased. "Am I not to have my reprieve? Am I to be sent to the fields after all?"

He stopped before her. "I would know. Why is Vangarth a liar?"

"He comes not on Cedric's orders, but rather to drive a wedge between you and your king," she answered bluntly. "He hoped to find me eager to support his accusation that you abducted me, making you guilty of treason. He's now angry, I think. He didn't expect to find a loving wife."

"He is not alone," he said, stunned by her grasp of the situation. "Why did you play the part?"

She shrugged, once more refusing to meet his gaze. "You once saved me from the man, a debt I felt compelled to repay. Whatever else may be said about me, I, too, am a person of honor."

"And now that the debt is repaid?"

Implicit in her smile was the warning that should the occasion warrant, next time, she'd take full advantage of the opportunity to escape. It irked him no end, yet he could not deny a grudging respect.

Typically, she did not let the emotion live long. "Do not let me keep you," she said coldly. "You must be anxious to return to your guest."

"How considerate you are today."

"Make no mistake. My sole consideration is a need to rest. I shall need all my strength to survive my ordeal this evening. Or can I hope you've forgotten your threat of last night?"

Threat? Was that how she viewed his lovemaking. He had the urge to throw her to the ground and ravish her now. Though he knew she meant to bait him, he found himself biting nonetheless. "Ordeal? Most females would consider my coming to their bed an honor."

"Then by all means, go to them. I am sure you'll receive a far warmer welcome."

Her words hung between them, cold and hard and calculated to hurt. It angered him how much they did so.

He would not have her holding such power over him. "You are right. I shall find some eager, willing maiden upon which to slake my lust. Even a tired, well-used courtesan can offer more warmth than the cold fish I wed. Go to your villa, woman."

She flounced off, but once she was out of sight, his anger abandoned him, leaving him aching with unfulfilled need.

* * *

That night, Riana sat on her bed, absentmindedly stroking the furs as she listened for Wolf's arrival. Darkness had fallen long since and the hours seemed to while away interminably. She wanted him to come and get it over with, she told herself repeatedly, yet it did not explain the leaping sensation in her chest each time she thought she heard a horse's approach.

Five times now she'd crept down the stairs to Tad. Communicating with the boy was no easy thing since they knew only bits of each other's languages, but she'd thrice said the name Wolf as a question. Red hair flopping in his eyes, her young guard had tilted his head in confusion, leaving Riana to trudge back up the stairs in frustration.

There was a time when she'd thought Tad's eagerness to serve her could work to her advantage, but unfortunately, the boy idolized his chieftain and would leap from the nearest cliff just to win Wolf's approval.

Everyone in this village adored her husband and took great pains to please him. This very moment, some eager maiden was likely lifting her skirts to ease his lust. Riana wished the girl good fortune then, for she knew from experience there was no end to her husband's passion. The man could service a kingdom of maidens and still go rampaging for more. The later the hour, the more she became convinced he must have sought another woman. Not that the prospect upset her, she insisted to herself. She didn't want Wolf panting down her neck at every odd hour; she was glad of the respite and hoped it would continue.

Hearing a noise, she jumped up and went to the window. Nothing stirred in the dark, still landscape. Strain though she might, she could hear no distant hoofbeats to indicate her husband might yet be on his way.

Gripping the sill, she told herself she would wait and watch no more.

* * *

Wolf did indeed seek out another female, but not for the reasons with which he'd threatened Riana. He was troubled, and when in such a mood, he often went to his sister.

Though Greta could find more ease and comfort in their mother's villa, she'd chosen to live here in the midst of the village, saying the villa held too many memories. This, Wolf readily understood, for he too had no need to be reminded of Cassandra's tragic end.

Greta was busy with her distaff, twirling the thick wool with deft fingers into a slim, wispy thread. Looking up in surprise as he entered her chambers, she graced him with a smile. "This is an honor, indeed, my brother. I was of a mind that tonight, you'd be visiting Riana."

"It is about my wife that I wish to talk."

She gestured to the chair beside her. "Come, sit. Do not stand there hulking in the doorway."

He realized he must indeed seem to "hulk" here in this dainty room. Though its proportions were small and the furnishings simple, his sister's renowned skill with dyes, not to mention her mastery of the loom and the needle, had created an oasis out of virtually nothing. More and more of late, Greta reminded him of their mother.

Wolf entered the room, but he could not sit. Most nights, he found the soft colors soothing, but a strange restlessness gnawed at him, had him pacing across the floor. Despite his best efforts, he kept imagining Riana on the yellow coverlet, Riana stretched out on the green rug before the fire. Even here in this room that bore the sure stamp of his sister's gentle nature, he continued to be haunted by his cravings for his wayward wife.

Greta paused her spinning to study him. "You love her, don't you?"

It was a statement, not a question, as if Greta were privy to some information that he was not. "Love?" he asked, annoyed. "What would I know of that soft emotion? I am a warrior, a hunter. I live by my wits, my senses, not my heart."

"Love is not something you *know*, my brother. You feel it inside you." Smiling, Greta put a hand on her chest. "Trust your senses, your instincts, and do not struggle so hard against the emotion."

Wolf stopped pacing, coming to the point of his visit. "Tell me, Greta. You know her better than anyone in the village. Is she a witch? Has she indeed set a spell upon me?"

At her laughter, a slow hot flush burned his neck.

"Stop making excuses, my brother." She gestured again that he should sit. "You love the girl. It's as simple as that."

Turning the chair to straddle it, Wolf sat, determined to prove his sister wrong. Love or no, he found nothing simple about his feelings for Riana.

"Whether or not she's a witch," Greta went on, spinning her wool as she spoke, "she would never use magic to trap you."

"Of course she would. She's a woman."

Greta eyed him with disappointment, like a mentor would a pupil who had failed at his lesson. "Did she tell you about her vision?"

Straightening, he remembered watching his wife as she stared into the pool this morning. "Did she tell you of this vision?" he prompted.

"She saw what Vangarth planned. Think, Wolf. If she truly wished to harm you, she had ample time to plan her vengeance. But she rushed to your side, choosing to support her husband instead."

"And made it clear afterward that she would not do so again. It was distrust of Vangarth dictating her action, Greta, not any concern for me."

His sister smiled knowingly. "Poor Wolf, our father made certain you would remain as ignorant as he about women."

He stood, pushing roughly back from the chair, which fell to the floor unheeded. "You go too far, Greta. As chieftain and Exar's son, I will not let you speak ill of him."

She dropped her distaff in her lap to look up at him. "He was not some god, Wolf. He was a great warrior and chieftain, but as a husband and father, he was a blind, narrow-minded tyrant."

Wolf generally avoided taking sides when it came to their parents, but he could not stand by and let his sister tarnish their father's memory. "Now that you are grown, you should have a mind of your own, with no need to parrot our mother's words. I loved her, too, but do not seek to place the blame for her weakness on Exar."

"Weakness?" Eyes flashing, his sister seemed suddenly a stranger. "Can you truly believe he was the stronger of the two? It was Cassandra who left Exar, never forget. She took that final, fated step."

"And in so doing, robbed us all of a kingdom."

"He drove her to it!" Her voice became hard, urgent. "Just as he drove you to put aside her influence. Even from the grave, he reaches out to rob you of the happiness he was too stubborn to grasp for himself."

Her words battered against him, ringing with the truth. How much of his father's harsh teachings, he wondered, had been prompted by hurt and stung pride instead of wisdom?

"He would have you be his puppet," Greta pressed, her tone softer now, "but you are not like him. I know you, Wolf. Your instincts must have conflicted often with what our father would have you do."

"Enough," he snapped, feeling as if she probed inside his wound. "You women would poke and pry and drag out our emotions for the world to see. Do you hope to thus control the men who rule you?"

Greta shook her head sadly. "Why must one sex control the other? It is by their union, by male and female coming together, working together, that our world finds its balance. The feminine assets, when joined with a man's own, can make for a formidable force."

He stared at her, long and hard, struggling with the concept she'd presented. In truth, he'd never been easy with his father's assessment of a female's lack of worth, but to raise her status to helpmate, to equal?

"It seems a useless effort, trying to master Riana," Greta went on, "when more can be gained from learning her ways, by teaching her ours, finding power in shared knowledge." She lifted up her distaff to resume spinning. "That's why you are drawn to her, you know," she added. "Riana is your other half."

"What nonsense is this?"

"Your life has become grim with duty and conquest, and you've forgotten the need for laughter and joy. Can't you see how Riana's spirit, her zest and imagination, can put magic back into your pragmatic world?"

It was true. Of late, he'd found little to smile about in his life. But to suppose that Thunor had led him to that hill for the sole purpose of finding the part of him that had always gone lacking was absurd. He had no use, nor even patience, for magic.

"My brother, open your eyes and you will see what the rest of us know already. You are meant to love Riana."

No, this he could not grant her. Love made a man weak, diluted his power of logical thought.

But then, in truth, did the source of this madness matter? Love or lust, he was obsessed with Riana and he would have little peace until he found a way to appease his craving. Bending down, he reached for the chair and righted it, slowly forming the words in his mind. "I doubt Riana considers herself my other half. She makes it plain that she'd rather bed down with a viper."

"Like you, she's too preoccupied with what she must accomplish in this life to take time to consider her true feelings. Then too, having had so little love in her life, she must be especially blind to the emotion."

The words gave him pause. Resting his hands on the back of the chair, he leaned forward. "How can you know of her past?"

"I listen."

It was true that he'd wasted little time hearing what his wife had to say. "And what did she tell you about her childhood?"

"She volunteers little," Greta went on, "but Sela tells me your wife was abandoned at birth. Unlike you and me, Riana has known neither parent. All her life, she has made her way alone."

Wolf frowned as he thought of the child Riana must have been.

To have no one to emulate, to identify with—it seemed an overwhelmingly lonely existence.

And it explained much about her prickly manner.

He spun the chair behind him, sitting slowly. "She speaks often of her mission in life. Is she so preoccupied with finding her parents?"

Greta merely shrugged, "That is a question you should ask her."

"She will not talk to me." Hard to keep the frustration from his tone.

"You have much to learn about women," Greta said with a grin. "Give us a reason and we all talk eventually."

That much he knew to be true, "I have no time for female prattle," he said impatiently. "Nor much skill in paying court, either."

"Conversation, like seduction, is an art you men ignore, more's the pity." Sighing, Greta held up her distaff, twirling the wool before his eyes. "The pursuit of a woman should be like spinning. See, you take coarse fiber and refine it into a long, delicate thread. It's the combination of the threads, woven with others, that makes for the snug, warm cloak you wrap around you."

"You try my patience. What would I know of spinning and weaving?"

"Very well, when you hunt, do you rush in, demanding that the forest accept your ways or your conflicting existence? You take time to understand your surroundings, to learn the needs and habits of your prey, their very essence and scent. You offer patience and respect, and when the quarry is lured into your trap, you find acceptance. Not of victor over vanquished, but of one offering his life so another might prosper."

Intrigued, he considered this. It was true that any good hunt must combine both male and female traits. In the forest, Wolf always took his time, deferring often to the ways of Nature. Stalking one's prey required exceptional patience, as well as understanding and respect.

He could see how he might find pleasure in this hunt called seduction.

"Take care to listen to her," Greta added quietly. "With your mind *and* with your heart."

Wolf stared at his sister. "Ranulf was right," he told her. "You hold a great deal of wisdom for one so young."

She lowered her gaze but not before he saw scarlet stain her cheeks. "Indeed, and how is it you and Ranulf were discussing me?"

"He tried to offer the same advice, though not near as eloquently."

She grinned again. "Did he tell you also that your wife likes jewelry made from shells, and mead sweetened with honey? Oh, and Sela tells me Riana's greatest weakness is walnuts. She craves their meat and can never get enough of it."

"Indeed," he chuckled, rising from the chair. "I think I shall retire to my quarters and think on this. Dream well, little sister."

"She's worth the effort," Greta called after him as he marched from the room. "In the end, Riana can bring more joy than you can dream of."

"Provided we both survive the battle," he bantered back, but while the words were sardonic, his heart was not. Feeling more hope than he had in a long while, he left Greta's chambers with a spring to his step.

Sela looked up, surprised to find Greta entering her hut when they'd made no plans to meet this evening. From the shawl shrouding her head to the furtive glances over her shoulder, the girl clearly wanted her visit kept secret. Sensing trouble brewing, Sela silently said the age-old chant to ward off the ill spirits of the night.

"I am glad you are here, Sela," the girl said, glancing again over her shoulder. "Quick, you must brew your potion for Riana. I think my brother will visit her villa tonight."

Sela fought disappointment. "Why is it you girls think all

problems can be remedied with a potion? Is it your youth that leads you to assume that with a few quick chants, you can abandon hard work and dedication?"

Greta blinked, clearly stunned. "But I have talked with Wolf and he is now willing to consider her needs. Will it not help matters along if Riana is as eager to please him?"

Sela sighed, feeling as if she had taught this lesson too many times. "I will say this but once, so heed me well. In magic, there is always a difference between timely intervention and useless meddling. We who would conjure must take care to use our skills sparingly for the greatest good, never for selfish gain."

Greta tilted her head. "But this *is* to everyone's good. You said yourself the two belong together."

"Perhaps, but their path is their own, and they must make their way accordingly. Would you cheat them by taking away the necessary steps?"

Greta glanced back toward the villa. "But Wolf is liable to lose patience. What if he says or does wrong and alienates her all the more so?"

"Then so be it. Your brother must find his own way or he will learn nothing. Succeed or fail, he will be stronger and wiser for it."

It was Greta's turn to sigh. "Oh Sela, you're right, as always. It's just that I feel so helpless, watching those two. I wish I could gaze into the crystal, as you can, and see that everything will turn out all right."

Sela smiled, for she understood impatience and frustration— what mortal did not? "It would do you no good," she said soothingly. "Their path is a long and murky one, as if they travel through some mist-covered bog. I fear there are more forces at work here than this poor magician can divine. Even with the best intentions, all we can hope is that we can be there when they need us."

Ever alert, the girl pounced at once. "You've seen something. Someone else using magic?"

Sela looked away, not anxious to reveal her fears. "The world is littered with would-be sorcerers, my girl. Anyone can alter the perception of reality. In truth, that is all that magic truly is."

"If you won't tell me anything," Greta said, visibly upset, "I might as well leave."

Though incredibly weary, Sela knew she could not let the girl go without understanding this most important concept. "It is an awesome responsibility to summon the magical forces," she told Greta, her voice shaking with strain. "We conjurers cast our spells like stones in a pond, never knowing where the ripples will end. More often than not, the disturbance you cause comes back in wave after wave of repercussion. In the future, my girl, I'd advise you to think long and hard before you act."

Greta nodded, her face thoughtful. Frowning, she turned back out into the night. Left alone in her quiet hut, Sela unhappily shook her head.

Oh yes, she had seen into the future and it troubled her dearly. This was a calm before the storm. One day soon, the ripple she'd unwittingly created was liable to return and strike them all with terrible force.

Wolf stepped inside his mother's villa, sensing the difference at once. In Cassandra's time, the place had held a restful air. Entering it, he had immediately relaxed.

But Riana now walked these halls, filling them with her vitality, her impatience. No one would ever call Riana a restful woman. If Wolf sought serenity, he would no longer find it in this house.

He thought of how Greta said that something drove his wife, which was what kept them at odds. It was why he'd come to the villa, wanting to take the first step toward learning about her. Walking here from the village, wrestling with his thoughts, he'd seen how his sister could be right. To break through Riana's resistance, he must soothe her, gentle her, and listen with all his senses. He would be the hunter who tamed her to his ways.

Young Tadrick jumped from his seat at his approach, all gangly arms and spindly legs. "My lady has already retired," he whispered, glancing up the steps to the door at the top. "But if you desire it, I shall go waken her."

Wolf shook his head. "I'll go. I've found my lady is not at her kindest when woken prematurely."

A quick grin told him the lad had suffered his own experiences, but swiftly remembering his position, Tadrick wiped his expression blank.

Nodding solemnly, Wolf turned to mount the steps. In all the hours he'd been pacing in the night air, he had known he would come here. He had to see Riana, be with her, even if only to watch her sleep.

Easing open the door, expecting to see her sprawled across the furs, he was startled to find her staring out the window. She spun when she heard him, blinking rapidly, as if she had tears to hide.

Irritated, he crossed the room. His father maintained that a woman used tears to manipulate a man. "Have you been weeping?" he asked bluntly as he stopped before her. "I would know why."

"I never cry!" she said proudly.

He reached out to turn her toward him. No tears on her cheeks, he noticed, though he found a telltale glittering in her gold-flecked eyes.

She flinched back, slipping away to stand defensively before the bed. "I am merely weary of all this strain. It has been no easy evening, waiting and worrying in anticipation of this visit."

Annoyed afresh, Wolf refused to follow her. In her nightshirt of soft, white cotton, she stood like a siren tempting him onto the rocks. His every swallow might ache with longing, but his pride would have no part of a woman who spurned him. "I have not come to claim my husbandly rights," he said, "so you've no need to assume your sacrificial air."

"I see," she said, unable to hide her surprise. "If you are not here to bed me, then pray tell, why have you come?"

Why indeed? "We have issues we must discuss," he said truthfully enough. "I have decided that Vangarth was right."

"You will send me away? Back to Cerdric's village?"

He heard the catch in her voice. Eyeing her, he looked to see if it were surprise, dread, or hopeful eagerness that caused it. She looked out the window, giving away nothing.

"No. Now that you're no longer considered a prisoner, it is time you learn to defend yourself. You will begin with instructions in shooting the arrow."

He could see he'd again surprised her, though she did her best to hide it. "Indeed. Is this before or after I finish the planting?"

"You can spare a few hours in the afternoon."

"Can I?" she said, staring up at him angrily. "It matters little if I have other plans. Our lord and master speaks and I must leap to comply."

"These other plans—what are they?" He could see the candle flame's reflection dancing in the golden depths of her eyes.

"You think me so worthless, so witless, I would have no life of my own?" she asked indignantly.

Earlier, he might have met her anger with his own, but her tight tone reminded him of his sister's admonition. By listening with his senses, by hearing with his heart as well as his ears, he realized his wife's defiance was less a desire to thwart him, and more an act of self-defense. When Riana felt threatened, he'd begun to discover, she lashed out indiscriminately, even if it meant hurting herself in the process.

"I have no wish to fight with you on this," he said quietly. "Indeed, you and I have been too long at cross-purposes, and it is time for it to stop. From this moment on, what concerns you shall concern me as well. If you have a problem, I expect to hear of it. While I cannot promise to agree, or always act on your complaints, I will do my best to listen."

She eyed him with suspicion.

"Today, with Vangarth . . ." He trailed off, searching for the right words. "Never think I was ungrateful, or even ignorant of what you did."

She watched him as he took a step closer, then another, her eyes as wide and wary as a doe's. "I told you. I merely—"

"Don't." Reaching her side, he risked a grin. "I find I like having you fight beside me."

Her eyes widened. "You don't seem the sort to indulge in fantasy."

"Ah, but I often dream of a time when we do not fight, when we stop crossing swords to no real purpose. We talk together. Work together." He moved closer, his body touching hers, both throbbing from the heat they generated between them. He knew he towered over her, that his sheer size must fluster her, but surely she was not unaffected by the memories of how their bodies had spoken to each other.

He took her hand in his, clasping it to his chest between them. "Tell me, why am I drawn to you? Why must I constantly fight the urge to throw you down on the bed, to know you as thoroughly as I did last night?"

"Why fight the urge?" she breathed, her voice tight with strain. "As lord and master, you can do what you want."

"Why do *you* fight it?"

"I feel no such urge!"

Her heightened color and breathing belied her denial. She could no more look away than he could. Indeed, if she'd bewitched him, then she'd been caught in her own spell, for she now seemed as trapped as he by the lure between them.

Lifting her hand to his lips, he kissed the softness of her palm. "I will not force you," he said softly, "but I shall live in your dreams, steady and true, until the fight has gone out of you."

"Never!"

Ignoring her protest, he released her hand and left her. He now knew that one day, she must inevitably come to him. And for now, that was enough.

The hunt was on.

Nine

Riana sat alone at the edge of the field, eating the tart Greta had brought for their noonday meal, surveying the rows she'd planted. She could not deny her sense of pleasure—nay, almost pride—at watching the tiny green seedlings sprout from the ground.

She held out her hands, inspecting them, no longer seeing the caked dirt and cracked fingernails but rather the power she held in them. With the help of the elements, she had coaxed life from the winter-freed earth.

Not that all the elements cooperated. Glancing upward, she knew the continued absence of clouds meant carrying buckets of water from the stream each night to irrigate her seedlings. She'd suggested to Yarrick that they should all work together, watering the entire crop by forming a line and passing bucket after bucket up from the river, but thus far, the overseer had chosen to ignore her suggestion—coming as it did from a female, and a Briton, at that. To Riana, it seemed useless spite. Couldn't Yarrick see the other seedlings withering while those in her patch prospered?

"My lady?"

Startled, she looked up to find Tad fidgeting above her, embarrassed at having to interrupt her thoughts. She toyed with the idea of not answering him, for she still hadn't forgiven him for not warning her of Wolf's arrival last night—a visit from which she had yet to recover.

Against her will, she gazed at the palm Wolf had kissed so gently. For an instant, for that brief, glorious fraction of time, she had looked in his eyes and seen how it could feel to be cherished by such a man.

But after offering such a lure, he had turned and left her aching with loneliness and yearning.

"Why are you here?" she snapped at Tad as she rose to her feet. "Has my lord and master decreed I must be watched at the fields now as well? Doesn't he realize that no warrior would guard me more zealously than Helga?"

The poor boy stared with helpless confusion, sensing her irritation but unable to decipher her words. Taking pity on him, Riana called Greta over to translate.

"He expects you to go with him," Greta said when Tad finished speaking.

"Does he now?"

"Rage not at Tadrick," Greta cautioned. "He comes at Wolf's command."

Command? Riana thought angrily. So much for talking about her problems, working together—it was back to master and slave.

She would not feel disappointment. "Am I some toy, to be bandied about on a whim?" she demanded of poor Tad. "First, I must go to the fields, then he needs me to gloat over his rival. Then it's back to the fields so he might drag me away to . . . to . . ."

She trailed off, losing steam, as she remembered why Tad had come for her. Today was to be her first lesson in self-defense.

Following Tad to the training field at the far end of the village, she marvelled at the strength of her anger. She told herself she resented being summoned at all hours at some hateful brute's whim, but deep down, she feared it had more to do with the fact that Wolf himself had not come for her.

Nor was her mood one whit improved upon reaching the training grounds and learning that Wolf would not be here either, that his friend, Ranulf, would be teaching her instead.

Like Tad, Ranulf had only a smattering of Briton, and was

often unable to communicate what he wished her to do. Though he tried to compensate with gestures, Riana grew more confused and frustrated as the lesson wore on. It did not help that the sun beat down on her brown wool tunic, or that the warriors training nearby had stripped down to short leather kilts. Riana tried not to be distracted, denying that all that unclad flesh reminded her of a particular warrior—until she glanced up to meet Wolf's intent silver gaze.

He stood on the ridge, clad in the same meager cloth as the warriors gathered around him. He made an impressive picture, bare chest glistening with sweat in the afternoon sun, silver-shot hair rippling in the soft breeze.

Try as she might, she could not still the quickening in her blood.

She turned, refusing to let his presence unnerve her. Yet the more she tried to concentrate on what Ranulf showed her, the less she could grasp his instructions. From his gestures, she assumed he expected her to pull back the string and let loose the arrow in a long, glorious arc, but his words and movements became garbled up in thoughts of Wolf dropping a gentle kiss in her palm.

I despise that man, her mind argued, but it was a poor protest, as feeble as the shot she fired. Hitting her forearm the instant she released it, the string sent the arrow straight into the ground not five paces before her.

She heard a round of raucous laughter at her back.

Crimson-faced, she trained her attention on the arrow, lying limp and useless, far short of the hay bale set up for a target. Listening to the braying mules on the ridge behind her, she knew it was like the incident with the snakes, all over again. What sadists these Saxons were to derive so much pleasure from watching her failures.

From now on, she vowed, they could find their pleasures elsewhere.

Barking at his men, Wolf strode down the hill to join them. He exchanged words with Ranulf, until with a frown, his friend went off with the other warriors. Taking his time, Wolf strolled over to the fallen arrow. "It will do you no good to quit," he said, plucking it from the dirt.

"How can you know that was my intent?" She tensed as he approached her, not at all pleased that he could so easily read her thoughts.

"It's what I'd be tempted to do." Handing her the arrow, he nodded at the bow clutched in her hand. "Most learning occurs through trial and error, however. If you wish those jackals to stop laughing," he said, nodding toward the retreating warriors, "then you must prove there is nothing to laugh about."

He moved behind her, taking her hands in his warm, sure grasp and moving them on the bow. Conscious of his half-naked body pressed tight against her back, she could feel the heat as if they again lay on the furs. Swamped by images of their coupling, Riana could scarce focus on what Wolf was saying. Knowing he could as well have been speaking in Saxon, she shook her head to regain her wits.

"Keep still," he coached. "Focus, and take care to keep your wrist firm where you clasp the bow. That, I'd have thought, would be the first lesson Ranulf taught you."

"And well he might have, but I cannot understand a word he says."

"I'd forgotten you speak different tongues." Wolf looked back to the hill, but Ranulf was already gone. "It seems I owe my friend an apology."

"You, the great chieftain, admit a mistake? I thought every word you uttered came down from your great gods themselves."

His grasp tightened, then relaxed, as if he willfully restrained his response. At least she could still rile him. A small thing, but it was the only power she had left.

"Pull the string with this hand," he went on, breathing the words in her ear as he guided her arm, easing it backward. "Keep the elbow up and maintain your sights on the target. Feel that?"

She could feel a good deal more, but she saw no reason to tell him so. How he would strut and crow, if he guessed how she longed to melt against him. It was all she could do to keep her arms from trembling.

"Hold firm," he coached, oblivious. "Good, now release."

This time, the arrow went zinging through the air. It fell to the right of the hay bale, but she could not deny the thrill of watching it fly toward the target. Pleased with herself, she spun to face Wolf, eager for praise. Instead, he offered another arrow.

"Try it yourself this time," he suggested.

Gritting her teeth, she took the shaft, taking care not to touch his hand. Wishing she could be back in the fields planting, or anywhere she need not be pinned by her husband's ever-watchful gaze, she readied the blasted bow. *Please let me remember all he told me,* she thought as she took aim. But of course, she hadn't been listening; she'd been preoccupied by thoughts of their joining.

She groaned as the string slapped her arm and the arrow again fell short. It was not the sting, or even her failure that made her uneasy. It was the knowledge that Wolf would once more be standing behind her. "What is the sense in such training?" she protested, tossing the bow to the ground before he could again grasp her arms. "You have a wealth of warriors at your command. Why must I act like one too?"

He frowned at the bow, then at her. "We live in a remote outpost," he explained tersely. "While it affords us the finest land, it leaves us too often prone to attack. Every man, woman and child must be able to defend the village."

"But I am not Saxon. I would be safe in a Briton raid."

"If they stopped to ask you. And keep in mind that we are threatened also by Jutes and Angles and Danes. Should our warriors be summoned to defend the king's stronghold, the women will be left alone to defend this village. You must be able to fight, and fight well, or our huts will be burned, our food storage looted. You could well find yourself raped, if not murdered."

He must have seen her shudder, for he gentled his tone. "At such a time, the women seek a leader. They will look to their chieftain's wife."

Riana shook her head. "To lead, you need others willing to follow. In case it's escaped your notice, your women won't ever follow me. Not when Helga still has them still laughing about those snakes. They think me a raving lunatic."

She thought she saw a grin as he bent down to retrieve the bow. "They will follow, once you've earned their respect."

She grew frustrated with his willful blindness. "They distrust everyone not of this village. Look at your own mother. From what Greta tells me, she lived among your people for many years and they never accepted her as their leader."

"Our mother was too gently reared to know how to lead others, and my father perhaps showed poor judgment in not training her in the art," he said in a quiet, though no less firm tone. "But never think Cassandra was not accepted by River Ford. Far from it, in fact. It was to my mother's villa that this tribe went for their remedies, her advice that they sought when they were troubled or heartsore."

"Your father allowed her to act as a healer?" she asked in surprise.

His smile went grim. "She spent part of her youth among the Druids and learned their art of secrecy. By the time my father learned what she was doing, it was too late."

"Too late?"

He looked away, grimacing as if he'd regretted saying what he had. "Suffice it to say that my mother was well enough loved in this tribe that she left a great gap, an emptiness we are still trying to fill."

She heard the pain in his voice. Whatever had happened with his mother had left more than a gap, she sensed; it had come close to breaking his heart.

He shook his shoulders as if to throw off the scars of the past. "Come, we dally," he said, handing her the bow. "We must continue until you master the lesson. Lift and straighten your arm. No, careful, watch that your wrist doesn't bend."

"But I've been at this for hours and the bow now feels like an iron weight. My arms can no longer hold it up."

"Then I shall help you." He stepped up behind her to guide her arm. Fearing how her body would respond to his nearness, Riana tried to twist away.

He grabbed her at the waist, spinning her around to face him. Whatever protest she might have offered was lost the instant their gazes met. There, in the smoldering gray, she could see their joining clearly, the two of them locked forever beside the Beltane fire.

He pulled her against his chest in a long, drugging assault on her mouth. Resistance melting in the heat of his grasp, she lost all thought of where and who she was. She could hear her heart pound, her blood sing with need, as she dug her fingers into his hair and pulled him closer yet. She wanted him to hold her, stroke her, take her—here and now, lowering her down to the soft, green grass at their feet.

As well he might have, if not for the forced cough behind them.

They broke apart like children caught at a prank, ready to deny their guilt before any accusation could be made. Breathing fast and hard, Riana stared at Wolf in disbelief, appalled that such hot, intense passion could flare up so swiftly. She tasted her lips, seeking the taste of juniper. Or could the effects of Sela's drug linger on, even days later?

Wolf turned, and belatedly, Riana noticed the old woman stood before them, grinning.

"What brings you here?" Wolf asked Sela, his tone as emotional as if he'd been asking about the weather.

"I have come to bring Riana back to the fields," the old woman stated simply, but her gaze travelled up one side of Riana and down the other.

"She is here at my request," Wolf said with that same lack of feeling. "I am teaching her to defend herself."

"So I see."

Wolf would have put anyone else instantly in their place, Riana knew, yet he allowed Sela to tease him, as if she'd known him a long, long time.

"Whatever you've seen," he said, his fleeting grin causing Riana to redden more, "it is time you took your gaze elsewhere. My wife must resume her lesson."

"Why have you come, Sela?" Riana asked, ready to seize any excuse to get far away from this unsettling man.

"Yarrick has decided to adopt your idea for irrigating the fields. This very moment, he has the women gathering every available bucket in the village. Though I'm not at all certain the dolt truly understands the line's function." She turned to frown at Wolf. "Your overseer, my lord, is a far from imaginative man."

"What is this about a line?"

"Ask Riana. It is her idea."

He turned expectantly to Riana.

"It's for irrigation," she explained. "I've been carrying pails of water from the stream to the seedlings, but I can wet only a small area each night. I thought if everyone worked together, forming a line from the stream to the planting, we could ensure the survival of a far greater crop."

He watched her as she spoke, his expression thoughtful. "A logical plan. Why has Yarrick not implemented it already?"

Riana shrugged. "Perhaps he hesitates in hopes that it will rain."

His brow raised, implying that he guessed the true reason his overseer hadn't listened to her suggestion. Wolf must know that like everyone in the village, Yarrick considered her an outsider, the enemy. A distrust that was mutual, Riana insisted to herself.

"Sela is right," Wolf said, dropping the bow and arrow. "We must go to the fields and make certain Yarrick executes your plan properly."

"We?"

He seemed more than ever the marauding wolf, smiling at her with a wide row of even white teeth. "We'll work together, shoulder to shoulder."

She took a step back, putting extra distance between them.

"Rest easy," he said, chuckling as he turned in the direction of the fields. "I will be there merely to work, the same as you.

Though I do find I am curious about how my village will respond to this idea of yours."

A curiosity too quickly satisfied, for with one glance, Wolf could see the hostility the women directed at Riana. With their chieftain at her side, they could not ignore her as they so blatantly wished to do, but it did not stop them from glaring at her behind his back.

And yet, she had come up with this plan for saving the village's crop.

When he asked her why, she shrugged, her manner deliberately offhand. "Having been forced to slave day after sun-scorching day planting that crop, I will not watch my hard work go for naught due to an unnecessary lack of water."

Her prickliness was an act, he decided, an attempt to disguise that she truly cared about those seedlings, perhaps even some of the people who had helped plant them. Whether Riana cared to admit it or not, her attitude was softening. It gave him a sense of triumph, nay joy, to think of how completely she'd surrendered in his arms earlier.

Standing to her right on the line, he pressed his advantage, making certain their bodies came in contact at every opportunity, pretending not to notice her discomfort if his touch lingered over-long. He meant to make her aware of him, to grow accustomed to the fact that he would not give up and go away.

As they worked, she grew more relaxed and less wary. She even managed to giggle with Greta, each time Tadrick ran back from the fields. Long arms holding the empty pails out before him, gangly legs bending as he scooped up water from the stream, the poor lad did indeed resemble the busy stork they called him.

It struck Wolf that he rarely saw Riana grin, much less chuckle. To see and hear her laugh so with his sister brought Greta's point home, that he was missing such joy in his life. He found he wanted to share in her laughter, to be the one to bring a smile to her sweet, sensuous lips.

Watching her mouth, caught up in thoughts of what he'd most like to do with it, he was caught off guard when Riana suddenly gasped. Sending her pail flying, she ran past Greta to jump in the stream.

It took the startled Wolf several moments to recover. Running to the bank, he watched his wife kick out to the deeper channel. The currents were deceptive there, he knew. A girl her size could be pulled helplessly along to the waterfall, and sent cascading down to the rocks below.

He shouted a warning, but she did not heed him. Cursing, he plunged into the cold stream after her.

Riana could hear only the sound of her own pounding heart as she swam with the current, searching for a sign of Tad. She had seen him hit the slick mud of the hill, and fearing that he'd be unable to stop his skid, she'd been braced for action before he'd gone plunging into the stream. From his flailing arms, his blatant panic, she'd guessed that he didn't know how to swim.

But in her haste to jump in and save the boy, she'd forgotten the water would be so cold, the current this strong. By the Goddess, why couldn't she find Tad's orange, bobbing head? She prayed silently. Had he gone under, she might never find him, much less drag him safely out of the stream.

With relief, she spied him breaking the surface ahead, but waving his arms in helpless abandon, he soon sank again. Swimming harder, she struck out for where she hoped he'd emerge next.

He popped up a few strokes ahead, but when she tried to shout out for him to hold on, her voice was lost in the roar of water. Swimming to him, she noticed the current was moving faster. The thunderous sound, the deeper water—too late, she remembered the waterfall she'd seen the night of the Beltane fire.

Even as she reached for Tad's flailing arm, she realized what little hope she had of getting them both to safety in time.

The panicked Tad grabbed at her, pulling at her hair, his weight dragging them both down beneath the surface. Taking in unexpected water, her first instinct was to kick free of the boy, but she clung to his arm fiercely. Though her senses were muted underwater, she could still feel and hear the current's power and could not bear to think of Tad's body crashing to the rocks below the falls. Somehow, she must drag them both to shore.

She kicked to the surface, dismayed by Tad's weight and lack of cooperation. In her mind, it seemed that they'd been struggling in the water too long already, that at any moment, the falls would loom, waiting to claim them, if the river didn't drown them both first.

Before she could lose heart completely, two strong arms encircled her waist to propel her upward. Coughing, gasping, she broke the surface, face to face with her rescuer. "Wolf," she rasped, wanting nothing more than to cling to him and never let go, "Tad—"

"I've got Tadrick," he shouted over the roar of the water. "You swim to shore."

She needed no further coaching. Though not a great distance, fighting the current took considerable effort, and she reached the shallows only a short distance from the falls.

Refusing to dwell on her mortality, she pulled herself from the stream to sit on the waist-high embankment, feeling like a snagged fish flopped to the shore. Shivering from the cold and wet, she wrapped her arms around herself as she watched Wolf drag the lad to safety. She realized she must look more like the victim of near drowning than the embarrassed but otherwise unaffected Tad.

Wolf, however, had never appeared more strong and capable. Emerging from the water like a god rising from the sea, with his hair slicked back and his bronzed skin glistening with moisture, he seemed suddenly the most beautiful creature she'd ever seen.

She found she could not take her eyes off him.

All this time, she'd resented his strength, knowing it enabled him to hold her captive, but all at once, she could now see how Wolf put his considerable might to good use. Nothing forced him to jump in after them, saving both Tad and herself from eventual drowning, but Wolf had done so quickly and efficiently and with a minimum of fuss. This was her husband, she realized with awe. A man of quiet courage.

She watched him survey their surroundings. Curious as to what made him suddenly smile, she followed his gaze to the right, instantly recognizing the cliff ahead. The hill, the scent of stale smoke lingering in the air—it was the site of the Beltane fire. It was where she and Wolf had made furious, glorious love.

As if the thought passed through his mind as well, he turned to look directly at her. She had the instant desire to run her hands along his taut flesh and straining muscle, to let her fingers trace the upward curve of his lips. She found all she could want in the gray depths of his eyes—the longing, the hunger, the inevitable fulfillment. It seemed she need only reach out a hand and this beautiful man would come lay all her demons to rest.

Distracted by shouts behind them, Wolf pulled his gaze away, leaving Riana to feel as if she were again being pulled by the river. Wading through a sea of confusion, she tried to regain her footing. She didn't want any part of this man, or the life he offered. He was her abductor, an unwanted husband; what madness had her lusting so badly, she'd surrender her will, her entire future to him?

He saved you again, the tiny voice inside her reminded. *Once more, you are in his debt.*

Shaken by the thought, she focused on the villagers, now running along the bank toward them. She saw Yarrick and Helga and Greta at the fore, all demanding to know if she and Tad were all right. No one asked after Wolf, though, as if they simply assumed he'd escape unscathed.

Wolf stepped closer to Tad, speaking to the boy in Saxon. The way Tad hung his head, looking guilty, Riana feared Wolf might be giving him a tongue lashing. "What is it?" she asked Greta, moving closer to her friend. "What is Wolf saying to Tad?"

"He's chastising him for endangering your life."

Poor Tad visibly squirmed, as if wondering if it were worth escaping death if it earned him his hero's disapproval. The poor boy looked so miserable, Riana spoke up without thinking. "It's not Tad's fault. I, er, fell in. I've always been too clumsy for my own good."

Tad smiled in gratitude. Wolf eyed her skeptically.

Helga stepped forward, her round face dark with sudden outrage. Rattling off a spate of Saxon too fast for Riana's limited grasp, the woman wagged an accusing finger in her direction. Wolf spoke out, but Helga would not be stopped. Giving vent to her tirade, she was soon appealing to every Saxon gathered around them.

"She's demanding you be charged with desertion," Greta translated for Riana. "Helga insists you were trying to escape, that you endangered Tad's life and our work in the fields by this selfish and foolish attempt."

"I can't believe that female. Does she stay awake all night, dreaming up ways to make my life miserable?"

"Worry not. I doubt Wolf will let such nonsense continue. It's an insult to his house to accuse his woman of treason."

"Treason?"

"You must understand," Greta explained, even while watching the proceedings. "Our tribe survives by banding together. To run away is to show no regard for the safety and welfare of others. Such selfish behavior is a danger and cannot be tolerated."

"But I didn't run away. Why would I, with everyone there to watch me? Wolf must have seen. Surely he will speak up."

Gazing at her brother, Greta looked suddenly uneasy. "We must hope so. Else, it will not go well for you."

Watching Helga rant, Wolf wondered if Ranulf were right. Did this woman feed on her bitterness, deriving joy in stirring up trouble for Riana?

His gaze went to his wife, needing to reassure himself yet again that she was unharmed. It had been a hideous few moments, moments he had no wish to ever relive.

He wanted to gather her close, to hold her tightly against his chest, but as chieftain, he could not dismiss Helga's accusations as absurd merely because he didn't want to believe his wife guilty. He'd seen Riana striking out in Tadrick's direction, not the other way around, but he owed it to his village to hear and weigh all the facts.

Holding up a hand to stop Helga's tirade, Wolf turned to Tadrick. "Is it true?" he asked sternly. "Must I punish your mistress for running away?"

Tadrick winced as he gazed at Riana.

"We argued," she said hastily. "Over . . . over who would take the bucket. I pulled too hard and we both fell in the stream."

A blatant lie. Wolf turned to Tadrick, seeing the boy was torn. He waited, hoping the boy would do the right thing.

"I was the one who fell," he said in a small voice, his body stiffening as if to brace himself against the others' scorn. "The Lady Riana jumped in to save me."

There was a gasp from the group and even Helga dropped her accusing finger. The woman did not seem one bit happy, though, to learn her would-be victim was somehow a hero.

Relieved that Tad had not let him down, and happy to have the matter settled, Wolf suggested they all return to work at once. With the excitement now over, the villagers complied readily enough, everyone falling into step behind Yarrick as he led the way back to the fields. Even the wet and drenched Riana.

"Wait," Wolf called to his sister. "Take Riana to her villa to find her dry clothing and something warm to drink to stop her shivering."

Watching his wife's face when Greta related his request to her, he saw her surprise blend with gratitude. For an instant, he thought she might even have smiled.

He longed to follow after them, to warm Riana himself, but he had work to do. First of which was talking to Tadrick.

As he called out for the boy to wait, Tadrick stopped where he stood, head lowered as if he expected—and deserved—to be hung by his toes.

"Are you aware of the trouble you could have caused for Lady Riana by not speaking the truth?"

"I would never let it come to that. Indeed, I'd lay down my life for her," he swore with endearing enthusiasm. "It was my lady herself who told the story. I think she saw . . . she must have known . . . I'm sorry, sir, but I just couldn't bear to have the others laugh at me."

Wolf nodded. Too well, he remembered that awkward age, the certainty that public ridicule was worse than death itself. Still, this lad was on the verge of manhood and a man did not hide behind a woman's skirts. "I am glad that you came to your senses at last," he told Tadrick sternly, "but it troubles me to think a warrior of mine would consider shirking the consequences of his actions. Is this the example we would set for the rest of the tribe?"

"No, sir." Poor Tadrick could not have hung his head any lower. "I will gladly serve whatever sentence you deem fit."

"Well, now, the Lady Riana tried not only to save your life, but your dignity as well. Perhaps you should return the favor."

"I shall do whatever you command. Sleep at her feet, carry hot coals to her grate with my hands, ride to the moon and back—"

Holding up a hand to stem his exuberance, Wolf stifled a smile. "I think you might first find yourself something less damp to wear, and then make your apology. Accompany this with a gift, something with special meaning. Jewelry fashioned from shells, perhaps. I am told Britons are partial to such adornment."

"Yes, sir," Tad agreed, brightening. "A brooch for her cloak, perhaps," he muttered to himself as he walked off. "Or a necklace."

Watching him go, Wolf wished he had a gift of his own to offer his wife. It struck him again that he would very much enjoy making Riana smile.

Something had happened between them today. Having seen that softening in her eyes as she'd gazed at him, he now wanted a permanent end to her resistance, to all the nonsense between them. Wolf ached to claim Riana, to own her, to live forever like man and wife.

Yet as eager as he was for these things, he could not force her against her will. Like the truly experienced hunter, he must wait for the optimal conditions, to when his quarry was warm, dry, and completely relaxed.

He might better wait until tonight to visit the villa.

Thinking of that soft bed of furs, he grinned. What an interesting pursuit, this game of seduction.

Ten

Riana stood by the window, fingering the necklace of luminous shells that a contrite Tad had presented this evening. Muttering in his incomprehensible Saxon, he'd thrust it in her hands before running off.

In the hours since, she'd gazed at it often, wondering how the boy came to be in possession of such a fine piece. A simple farmer's son, Tad could not own much of value; where would he find such jewelry? The thought flitted through her mind that he might be acting as another's agent, that someone else meant her to have this beautiful gift instead.

Someone like her husband, perhaps.

Abruptly, she chided herself for being foolish. Wolf was too proud and sensible to lavish gifts upon his wayward wife.

Yet she could not let the thought go. Ever since the incident with Vangarth, Wolf seemed gentler, more apt to treat her nicely. But offering gifts? And why send the boy, when he could as easily present it himself?

She gazed at the door, unnerved by how much she wished her husband would walk through it.

Pacing across the room, she insisted such longings meant nothing, that she was merely lonely here in this big empty villa, with only Tad for company. A boy who could not even speak her tongue did little to assuage her restlessness, her need for a friendly face.

Is it conversation you seek? logic asked as her gaze came to rest on the bed. *Or something altogether else?*

As if to test her, the door burst open behind her and Wolf stood in the frame. Fresh from his bath, hair slicked back, he looked much as he had when emerging from the river. Tall, powerful, godlike, he could well pass for a Roman deity in his crisp white tunic.

He wore little adornment, save a gold medallion hung from a thin leather strap, and a braided belt at his hips. From it hung a small leather sack, and the scabbard holding his sword. As he shut the door and strode toward her, the scabbard swung against his thigh, reminding her forcefully that this man was a Saxon warrior. He did not simply walk into a room, she decided; he stormed in and took it by force.

And woe to the unwary who stood in his path.

Hastily, she stepped backward, realizing her mistake as she felt the bed loom up behind her. She fled to the window, wondering how a room could seem vast and empty one moment and now feel so tiny and cramped. Amazing, how one man could fill it up with the sheer strength of his will.

"I spoke with Tadrick just now," Wolf said quietly as he stood beside her. "He claims to have recovered from his ordeal. Have you?"

She could not look at him. He seemed suddenly too tall, too powerful—too close. "I am warm and dry enough, if that is what you ask."

An awkward silence sprung up between them. Riana searched through her mind for a way to fill it, but could find no word or phrase that did not seem inadequate or inane. Where had it gone, the need to yell and fight? How could she still hold her own without her anger to sustain her?

"This afternoon, with Helga . . ." he began, seeming to have his own difficulty in choosing his words.

"I did not run away," she said softly, though no less adamantly. "I can't claim I won't try to escape in the future, but I did not do so today."

"I know."

She risked a glance at his profile. "You would laugh at me?"

He shook his head. "In truth, it's the thought of Tadrick tumbling down the hill and into the water that I find amusing."

She smiled faintly. "The poor boy doesn't enjoy being the object of humor."

"Few of us do. But if he hopes to serve as my warrior, he must learn to take responsibility for his actions. I cannot allow him to hide behind your kindness."

She met his gaze, saw the softening there, and let herself believe she'd seen his admiration. Odd, how the thought warmed her.

"I see he has given you a token of his gratitude," Wolf added, reaching toward the necklace in her hands. "May I see?"

Handing it over, she tried not to feel disappointment. She'd known it wasn't from Wolf. Indeed, from his puzzled expression as he inspected it, he must find it hard to believe anyone would think her worthy of such a gift.

"This is quite valuable," he muttered, turning the necklace over in his hand. "It was his mother's bridal piece. Considering that she has since passed on to the afterworld, it must hold even more value for him."

"Then I mustn't take it. I shall return it to him at once."

"No." Studying her face, he handed the necklace back, causing a strange sensation in her chest as his fingers brushed hers. "Be assured, if Tadrick didn't wish you to have the necklace, he would not have made the gift. You saved his life, and tried to save his pride."

"But you saved both of us, and as for his pride . . . well, it just seems excessive for what I've actually done."

"He is at the age where everything is done in excess." Wolf's expression gentled, as did his tone. "It's plain that the boy admires you greatly. Wear his token and he shall be your champion forever."

But she didn't want Tad as her champion. She wanted someone tall, and strong and powerful.

Coloring, she looked away from this stranger who was her husband, denying she wished aught from him. She'd long ago decided she would love a knight from Arthur's court, a Briton trained in the art of chivalry, a gallant with sweet flatteries who lavished her with constant, frivolous gifts. Not some brutish Saxon farmer.

Yet looking at Wolf in his elegant Latin tunic, she realized that she'd long since ceased thinking of him as a savage. He might not own the qualities she'd expect in a British husband, but Wolf did hold a certain charm all his own.

And an undeniable skill in the bedroom.

Her gaze stole to the bed, remembering what they'd done there. She felt the now familiar quickening, the languid heat pulsing through her veins.

Wolf's gaze followed hers. "I, too, find much to admire," he said suddenly, his voice slightly hoarse. "Your work with the crop, your kindness toward Tadrick, your courage in jumping in to save him from drowning—these are all qualities I value greatly in a wife." His hand went to his side, reaching not for the sword, but rather the sack. "This might not be valuable jewelry," he said as he presented it to her, "but Greta tells me you are partial to them. I hope this gift will serve as my own token."

Meeting his gaze, she had the sudden overwhelming urge to reach up and caress his face, to touch his lips with her own. Afraid of such feelings, she merely took the sack, hiding her yearning by lowering her gaze.

He took her hand, and for an exhilarating moment, she feared—and hoped—he would take her to the bed and force her to give vent to the emotions raging inside her.

He merely brushed her fingers with his lips. "I may never measure up to Tadrick's youthful enthusiasm," he said, even as he drew away, "but from this day on, I hope you will consider me your champion as well."

He swept from the room as he had entered it, leaving it to seem doubly huge and twice as empty.

Clutching the sack to her chest, she struggled to regain her bearings. He *had* brought her a gift, she thought in wonder. Something to which he knew she was partial.

She felt like a child on her birthing day, all eager and burning with curiosity. Going to the bed, she plopped down against its army of cushions to shake out the contents of the sack with trembling fingers.

Tears formed in her eyes as she stared at the pile of the sweet little nutmeats. Walnuts, all shelled and ready for consumption.

Yet while she had always craved walnuts, and been unable to get her fill, she found herself oddly reluctant to eat these. Biting into even one would diminish Wolf's gift, she decided. She would save them instead.

Gazing at the pile, touching each nut one by one, she admitted that perhaps she'd judged the man unfairly. She'd been too anxious to consider him evil, to find reasons to hate him, even while he seemed always to be there when she needed rescue. As she thought of how he sent her home to get warmed today, she realized there was more to chivalry than strutting about in armor and prancing across the tournament field.

Walnuts. Picking up the sweetmeats one by one, she returned them to their sack and drew the string tight.

"Damn him," she whispered as she held her prize close to her breast. Trust that Saxon brute to find the one sure way to her heart.

Wolf took the stairs outside Riana's room two at a time, knowing he must fast put distance between them or lose his resolve. More than all else, he longed to storm back into her room, sweep her up into his arms, and show her the joys they could share on that bed.

But he'd sworn he would not take her without her request, an invitation that must issue from her lips and not those expressive eyes. It had nearly unmanned him, the desire he'd seen in the golden depths. Had he kissed her, they'd both have been lost to their physical cravings, but when the insanity cleared, would she feel tender and loving, or just resentful and angry instead?

It was too late in the hunt to spook his quarry by being over-eager. He must stay true to his course and continue to exercise patience.

Though the gods alone knew how much longer he could hold out.

It was with a light step that Riana walked across the field to Greta, the sack of walnuts swinging at her waist. In the seven days since Wolf had given it to her, she'd carried the sack with her always, affixed to her belt, or on a string tied at her neck. She'd come to think of it as her good luck talisman, knowing no harm could possibly befall her with a warrior like Wolf as her champion. It put her in a strange mood, the feel of his token, bumping against her hips. It made her feel giddy and breathless and at charity with the rest of the world.

"That's quite a smile you're wearing," Greta said as Riana joined her for the noonday meal. "Keep on being so cheery and helpful, and maybe even Helga will be unable to find fault with you."

A short time ago, Riana would have bristled, but today she merely chuckled. "You were right. I've found it diffuses her anger when I fail to rise to her barbs. She seems to have lost interest in baiting me." Riana had also discovered that since she'd ceased sparring with Helga, the tension had lessened with the other women as well. A few actually spoke to her now—via Greta—offering helpful suggestions to make her work easier. And because of it, planting no longer seemed such an onerous chore. Often of late, she left the fields with an air of contentment.

"Will you go to the training field this afternoon?" Greta asked, handing her a slice of bread and cheese. "I am told you've grown quite proficient with your bow and arrow."

Riana nodded, trying to hide her rush of pleasure. "Did your brother offer that praise?" she asked. Though Wolf did not conduct her lessons himself, he often watched from a distance. She liked to think that his nods were gestures of approval.

Greta glanced up, clearly surprised by her hopeful note. "Ranulf told me. But I'm certain Wolf agrees with him," she added quickly as the smile faded from her friend's face.

"I wish I could be as certain." Distractedly, Riana played with the sack at her waist. "More and more lately, your brother seems to seize any excuse to avoid me."

"Oh, but Wolf is a busy man, Riana. He's been training his warriors for Cerdric's inspection at the yearly council."

"So busy he cannot come visit me at night?" She hated her wistful tone, but it was lonely at the villa and she was tired of planning out all the things she would say to him, only to face disappointment each time he failed to make an appearance.

Greta gestured for them both to sit. "You've had a change of heart, then? You wish to be his wife, become one of us?"

"No," Riana blurted out, then paused in confusion, realizing that she no longer knew what she wanted. "Even so, what I wish has nothing to do with it. Like Wolf, I have responsibilities to my tribe, obligations to my king. One day, I shall be called back to Camelot and when that day dawns, I must answer the summons. It is my duty. Your brother must understand that."

"Have you spoken of this with him?"

"It's hard to make a point when he rarely comes within hearing distance."

Greta reached out to place a comforting hand on her arm. "Take heart. My brother is a reasonable man. Granted, he can be stubborn and it may take time to convince him, but if you hold tight to your patience, and offer your own concessions, I'm certain you two can find some way to meet both your needs."

Compromise. A foreign concept for one raised without a family. Working together for a common good. Riana rather liked the sound of it.

"Indeed," Greta said suddenly, pointing to the far end of the fields. "Here comes Wolf now."

Heart hammering, Riana glanced up and saw her husband approaching on his great beast of a horse. There was no denying his direction; he was riding straight for her, looking more splendid than ever.

Unconsciously, she rose to her feet. The giddy sensation was back with a vengeance. How could she feel so suddenly shy and yet eager at the same time?

His gaze remained fixed on her as he reined in his horse. "I hope I am not too late," he said as he slipped to the ground before her. "It won't be much of a picnic if you've already eaten. I'd hoped you and I might betake of the noonday meal together."

"I would like that." Both flustered and pleased, Riana grew slowly aware of Greta, still standing beside her. "We'd be honored to have you join us. Greta and I were about to begin."

"Somehow, I do not think my brother is extending his invitation to me." Greta looked from her brother to the horse. "He would not bring Zeus if he meant to sit tamely here in the fields."

"How astute, little sister. If you will excuse us, I have a special place I would like to share with my wife."

At his words, a strange thrill shot through Riana. He uttered them softly, like a caress, as if the two of them stood there alone. "Will you come with me?" he added, extending his hands to her.

She went to him, for it seemed the right thing—the only thing—to do.

His large capable hands encircled her waist, causing her breathing to catch for a moment. Too well, she remembered his touch on her naked skin, bringing parts of her to life she hadn't known existed. Parts that now throbbed alarmingly.

He did not take advantage of the grasp, but rather hoisted her up to the saddle, before swinging up behind her. Cradled in his arms as he grabbed for the reins, she couldn't help but smile at Helga's startled expression as they rode past. "This should put an end to the woman's malicious gossip," Wolf said in her ear, as if sensing her thoughts. "Seeing us together thus, not even Helga can believe I'm estranged from my wife."

So he had staged this merely to quell Helga's nastiness. It was a kind gesture, but Riana felt nonetheless cheated. She had hoped he'd sought her company for the sheer pleasure of being alone with her.

What is wrong with you? she chided herself. *What makes you like a moonsick yearling?*

But she could feel the answer in the strong, firm chest at her back, the powerful arms surrounding her. Even the horse's rhythm, trotting along beneath them, beat home the inescapable message.

She wanted this man, wanted him badly.

Oblivious to her feelings, Wolf's actions tortured her in many small ways, the way he brushed his arm across her breast as he pointed out a passing sight, or breathed low and huskily in her ear as he spoke of their destination. It was an island in the river, he explained, and in summer, it was a favored spot among the younger villagers. Quiet and secluded, it was the ideal spot for courting.

Blushing fiercely, she wondered if he was as oblivious as she'd first thought. He seemed to have an uncanny ability to know her thoughts.

He pulled on the reins as they reached the riverbank, tightening his hold beneath her breasts as he did so. Scarce able to breathe, even when he released her, she willed her heart to slow. A man who could hear her thoughts must surely hear its mad thundering.

Slipping from the saddle, he reached up to help her alight. For a panicked instant, she thought to refuse him, but Wolf would not be denied. Giving her no opportunity to make even a token protest, he swung her down to her feet and turned to tether his horse to a nearby tree.

He returned to her, carrying a blanket and a bulging sack, both of which he thrust in her hands while he went to the bank of the river. Curious, she watched him dig through the undergrowth to pull out a smaller version of the Saxon longboat, big enough to fit three adults. "I made this vessel myself," he said with a proud grin as he placed it in the water. "As children, Ranulf and I had many a great adventure in it. We used to boast that it was the sturdiest craft on the river." He held out a hand to her. "Come, let me show you our special island."

Once more, she could not imagine refusing him. As he settled her in the boat and stowed the sack and blanket, she wondered again why he'd sought her company. It had to be more than quelling gossip, for that could have been accomplished back at the fields. Watching him cast off with cool efficiency, and sit opposite her in the boat, she found herself hoping he merely wished to be alone with her.

"It seems odd to be off on an outing with the great chieftain," she said, hoping to pry an admission out of him. "I thought you were far too busy training your warriors to spare an afternoon for anyone."

"Where is the use in being chief if I cannot declare a holiday?" he said as he turned the boat into the stream, his arm muscles bulging as he rowed. The boat, obeying him, gave no ground to the swift current.

"Is that what this is, a holiday?"

"It is whatever we choose to make of it."

His grin turned boyish and all at once, it was just the two of them, embarking on a great adventure. With a delicious sense of conspiracy, Riana helped him dock the boat and carry their things through the undergrowth to the center of the island. From the copse at the top of the hill, Wolf told her, they could view the river in all directions.

What he didn't tell her, and no doubt meant as her surprise, was what sort of trees covered the hill. "Walnuts," she cried as she stood beneath them. "A whole grove of walnuts."

He smiled in obvious pleasure as she twirled beneath the limbs. "My mother had them planted," he said quietly. "She had a yearning for their fruit, as well."

"Your voice always gentles when you speak of her. She must have been a remarkable woman."

He frowned, busying himself in helping her lay down the blanket and arrange the food upon it. "My father would say Cassandra brought out the softness in everyone, something he deemed a less than admirable trait."

"And you?"

He shrugged. "Once, I'd have agreed with him, but I've come to learn we need the tender, quiet moments of existence, as well as the challenge and strife. It's the contrast that makes life interesting."

"You sound as wise as Greta."

He laughed at her assessment. "I could but wish that wisdom was a gift the gods gave me," he said as he poured a flask of ale and held it out to her. "But it, and patience, are far from my strongest suits."

"Sela oft complains that I lack those traits also." She took the flask and sat beside him, curious about this man who was her husband. "Were you a mischievous child? Did you, too, find trouble before it could find you?"

"My father left me no opportunity for mischief. I would be chieftain one day, he'd harp, and must learn to live accordingly. One false step and I would be instantly punished."

She had the vision of a younger Wolf, wanting badly to please a father who saw him more as his heir than a son. It saddened her, that he had led a youth so harsh and unbending, but it helped her to understand why he demanded obedience. He'd been trained so.

Yet she'd evolved from a different background, and she wanted him to understand this. "I had no restraints," she told him. "I was left at the castle steps as a babe. I grew up in the kitchens, left mostly on my own."

"You never knew your parents?" He handed her a gooseberry tart, his gaze focused on her face, as if he were truly interested.

"I had only Sela. She was one of the cooks then, and too busy to do more than see that I was fed and bathed and put to sleep. She had no time to keep up with my pranks, as she called them, much less punish me. Indeed, she claims I am responsible for most of the gray in her hair."

Reaching for his own tart, Wolf grinned. "She must have been well on in years, even then. It can't have been easy for her."

No, it couldn't have been, but Riana had never before stopped to consider the hardships Sela had borne. The old woman had just been there, ready to serve and scold. "I know. And she will happily relate my many crimes, given the chance. Her favorite story involves walnuts."

"Let me guess. You stole them from a pie she was baking."

"Far worse. I stole them from the king himself."

"Pray, continue." He stretched out on his side, leaning on an elbow, his face alight with humor. "I can't wait to hear the rest."

She sat on her knees, holding her flask in her lap. "Keep in mind, I was young then, barely above my seventh year, and such treats were a rarity to an urchin like me. When I saw that bowl of walnuts, dripping with honey, I didn't stop to think. I followed it straight to the royal chambers."

"You stole inside Arthur's rooms and no one saw you?"

"The servants were harried, for the king was that day returned from battle and everyone was scurrying like mad little hens to make the castle ready. It was easy to hide behind the screen until the maid left and a simple enough matter to remove the nuts from the tray. I found it not nearly as easy to get out the door with my prize before Arthur strode in the room."

"Hence, trouble found you."

She nodded. "Darkly scowling, he appeared so tall and menacing, standing there with his arms across his chest. I began to envision dank dungeons and horrible tortures. When he leaned down to take the bowl from my hands, I knew I would never live to see the next morning."

"Yet quite obviously you did."

"Yes," she said with a sheepish grin. "All at once, Arthur smiled. From then on, the encounter became magical. I'd never been so near a king before, and I was too young to realize I should be in awe, so when he offered me one of his walnuts, I thought it no more than a special feast between two new friends. He must have seen the sheer pleasure of my face as I savored that first sweet taste, for he offered another. And as he did, he warned that all things in life carry a price."

"Ah, the punishment."

She shook her head. "He told me that if I wanted more, I'd have to entertain him. Back then, I knew nothing of singing or dancing, but I did have a wild imagination and a knack for dreaming up stories. I cannot recall what tale I told him, but I remember Arthur smiling. And me, leaving his quarters with a plate full of walnuts."

Wolf smiled. "I can see now why they are special to you." He leaned over to pour more ale in her flask. "I am told your Arthur is an extraordinary man. To have his ear, for an entire afternoon, must have been a heady experience for one so young."

"It should have been, I suppose, but one of the first things he told me, no doubt to put me at ease, was that he, too, had been a foundling. Had Merlin not seen his worth and fostered it, he claims, Arthur might this day be some aging squire, begging crumbs from his good knight's table."

"So he decided to be your Merlin?"

She nodded. "In a way. Arthur looked at me, long and hard, and decreed that it was time I was 'civilized.' Before I could blink, I was off to the royal nursery to be schooled with the other court brats. I admit, I sometimes chafed at the restrictions, but I never again felt neglected. I'd become an important part of the huge Camelot family. Thanks to Arthur."

"Now it is *your* voice that softens."

She slid off her knees to sit with them hugged to her chest. "You cannot know what it was to me, a foundling, being summoned to the king's chambers to entertain him. He and Queen Guinivere would smile at me as if I were the most clever thing imaginable, and after every story, every song or dance, they'd offer some treat." She sighed, remembering. "It was through Arthur that I came to know his sisters, Queens Morgan and Morgause. They were . . ." She paused, recalling his dislike of anything to do with the magical arts. "They were wise and beautiful, and kind to me also. With each visit, they taught me more about the path I hoped to take."

"And what path was that?"

He was too observant, this man, and far too clever. The last thing she wanted was to spoil their outing by arguing about what he would term "witchery." Rising abruptly to her feet, she paced about the grove near the blanket. "I wanted to help my king, in whatever capacity he needed. His sisters were grooming me to one day serve the Lady Guinivere."

"I see. What happened for you to be exiled to that remote village?"

"Who told you I was exiled?" Her pacing quickened. "No, do not answer. This bears Sela's mark. She'd have me think the queens were at fault, or even Merlin, but the truth is, she doesn't know what happened. Nor do I."

Wolf rose to his feet, reaching down to clasp her hands. "I hadn't meant to agitate you. This was meant to be a holiday."

For a breathless moment, she thought he might kiss her, but he merely smiled tightly and tugged at her hands. "Come, if you are done eating, I have other things I would show you."

Taking the diversion he offered gratefully, for his question had stirred up questions and old hurts, she joined him on an exploration of the island.

As he showed her his childhood haunts—the sunken cave, the abandoned tree fortress he and Ranulf constructed—she saw the vast differences between them. Even in play, his life had revolved around the land. How secure he must have felt, able to trace his roots, knowing his place in the scheme of things. In contrast, her own youth had a far less anchored base. While Wolf had trained for the chieftain he'd one day be, she'd sung and danced with no care for the future.

Nor had much changed with adulthood, she realized painfully. Wolf spoke of planting crops and begetting heirs, while she spun vague dreams of somehow becoming an enchantress.

"What fun Ranulf and I had here," he said quietly beside her. "One day, I hope, our sons shall come and reconquer this island."

"Do you think only of males?" she asked, half teasingly. "What if I bear you only daughters?"

He looked at her sharply, causing her to blush and realize that she'd spoken easily of the children they would raise together.

"Then females shall have to lay claim to it," he said with a sudden, dazzling smile. "As you would say yourself, what should their sex matter, as long as we have children aplenty to follow in our steps?"

Staring at his chiselled features, she felt a sudden need to be the wife he wanted, a strong, dependable woman who could bear him an army of children that looked just like their sire.

But in her heart, she feared that dream was as rootless as her past. "Is it so important to have such a brood? After all, your parents had only Greta and you."

He tilted his head, as if surprised by her question. "And we were lonely growing up. I want my household filled with the sounds of childish laughter. I want their smiling faces gathered about us on holidays and special occasions, I want to see our boys, *and* girls, walking tall and proud through the waves of grain in our fields. What use is life, after all, unless we can pass what we've gained on to our loved ones?"

All at once, she realized she could never live up to his expectations. The picture he painted filled her with deep longing, but as she'd told Greta, it was not her fate. She could give him no dynasty, for when the summons came, she'd still have to return to Camelot.

Fortunately, she was spared answering by a sudden clap of thunder.

"Rain," Wolf stated, eyeing the clouds overhead. "We'd best gather our things and return to our boat. We must cross the river before it swells."

Hurrying along behind him to the blanket, Riana resisted the urge to reach out and touch him. He had offered her a glimpse of another life, but that was all it had been, a glimpse. Today's idyll was good and truly over.

With concern, Wolf watched his wife stare off wistfully down the river as he rowed them to the opposite shore. How beautiful she seemed, her cheeks flushed from the day's adventure, her golden hair blowing in the breeze, yet she seemed suddenly as unattainable as ever.

Racing back to the villa in tense silence, he wondered what had upset her. He had to assume it had something to do with having his child. Many young women feared childbirth, being ignorant about it, and perhaps Riana was one of them. He must make certain Sela spoke to her, reassured her, for he felt certain this could be the key to unlocking Riana's emotions. If she could but have a babe of her own, a family of her own, she'd have no need to go running off again.

But for now, he wished to see her smile. She'd seemed so happy and carefree today and he longed for more of that between them.

Helping her alight in front of the villa, he brought her to the shelter of the doorway and reached down to push the sodden hair from her face. "I seem to be making a habit of getting you cold and wet," he told her with a wry grin. "I had no idea it would rain today."

"At least the fields will be watered."

"We all will be."

There was the smile he'd wanted, brief but gratifying. "I had a good time today," she told him, sobering far too quickly.

So had he. He'd meant the outing as a treat for her, but he couldn't remember ever enjoying himself more. Yes, he wanted much more of this between them.

He looked inside the villa, warm and snug, and sighed with regret, knowing Ranulf and his warriors would be waiting in the grand hall for him. "If I promise not to get you wet, do you think we might do this again?" he asked with a grin.

She blinked, unconsciously moistening her lips with her tongue. "I hope so," she told him softly, leaning closer.

Hope, that's what her warm smile gave him, as did the way she held onto his sleeve even after he'd kissed her gently. She was not nearly as immune to him as she might wish to be, his young wife, and though he longed to stay with her, he could see how he might benefit by leaving her yearning for more.

Riding back to the village, he consoled himself with the conviction that one day soon, she would be bearing him both sons and daughters.

A process he could scarce wait to begin.

Eleven

"Not like that, my lady." Gandolfo, a boy from the village, wagged a chubby finger at Riana. "The ball must go *in* the basket. Like this."

Sela watched the boy arc the palm-sized orb at the bushel basket, marvelling at how easily Riana had convinced these boys to let her play. Of late, she seemed to be charming a great deal of River Ford. Every evening, these boys and their sisters gathered here at the square to hear her stories, and many a parent strolled past to listen, as well. No one seemed to mind that she often chose the wrong word in Saxon; the fact that she was learning their language was enough.

Smiling triumphantly as he retrieved the ball, Gandolfo handed it back to Riana, who shook her head as if befuddled. "It seems so simple when you do it," she said to him. "Please, show me again."

"It's my turn," another lad protested. "We never get the ball when Gandolfo plays."

This was seconded by a chorus of voices, all in a high youthful pitch. Laughing, Riana tossed the ball into the crowd. "I think I should just watch you play," she told them. "I can learn more that way."

"As if you need to learn the game," Sela clucked in Briton as Riana joined her. "You've been playing it since you could walk."

"You and I know that, but do not tell them. How else can I practice my Saxon?"

Sela knew that Riana had no real need to practice with these boys, not when she received daily instruction from her husband. Amazing, what the girl could accomplish in a few short weeks when she finally set her mind to it. "I thought Wolf was teaching you," Sela teased. "Given how often he visits your villa, I'd think you'd now be speaking Latin as well. Or can I instead look forward to soon seeing a babe growing within you?"

"Oh, Sela." Sela expected the girl to snap back at her, not look so stricken. "Do you think we might talk?" Riana asked in a troubled tone.

"Of course. Come, sit beside me."

"Not here, not where we can be overheard. I've something of a personal nature I wish to discuss. It's . . . more a favor."

Curiosity prompted Sela's compliance, but so did affection. It had been a long while since she and Riana had shared a chat. "Then tell the boys you must leave now to walk this old woman to her hut. There, we can sit down to a cup of herbal tea."

Smiling wanly, Riana followed her to the hut. They spoke of this and that—the crowd of boys, the burgeoning crop, the spate of rain that blessed the village of late—and they continued in this vein as they went inside to gather the herbs for the tea.

"Isn't it odd, so much rain after such a long dry Spring?" Riana paused with the cup in her hand, giving a sidelong glance at Sela. "Why, it's almost as if someone cast a spell."

"And why would you look to me?" Sela snorted as she took the boiling kettle from the fire. "Had I so broad a talent, I'd have called for the rain during the planting. And by now," she added, glancing pointedly at Riana's midsection, "I would see a child sprouting in that womb."

Flustered, the girl looked away. "Then it would be rare magic indeed," she said, her voice strained. "It is not that way with Wolf and me. He comes to teach me his language each night. Nothing more."

"Is that a wistful note I hear?" Sela teased as she set their cups of tea on the table. "Can it be you now wish for more from him?"

Riana sat, taking her cup in her hands but not drinking it. "Quite frankly, I no longer know what I want."

"Ah, you are in love."

"No!" The girl bit her lip, as if sensing she'd betrayed too much with her vehemence. "I've merely become obsessed. Ever since the night of the Beltane fire, I'm haunted by what Wolf and I did together. The memory is like a fever, thickening my blood, clouding my judgment, leaving me sick with hopeless yearning. I am certain, if just once I could lie with him again, I can cure this illness. I can be free of it. Of him."

Sela, who knew better, merely nodded as she sat opposite her at the table. Riana might fight hard and valiantly, but she would lose the battle. Like it or not, she was falling in love with her husband.

Riana leaned forward, her voice low and coaxing. "I thought that since you brewed that potion for me, you could concoct something similar with which I might lace his wine."

Sela had to stifle a chuckle. "As I recall, you thought it a heinous act when done to you. You'd consider tricking your husband this way?"

Riana looked away, clearly troubled. "I know, but I'm desperate. I don't know what else I can do."

"Riana, my child, have you never looked at yourself? Or at him, when he watches you? If he holds back, it's because he vowed never to take you without invitation. Ask, and he'll be in your bed in an instant."

"Never. I couldn't ask him. No lady would ever be so bold."

Sela snorted. "You talk like the Christians. Perhaps you've lived too long among them. With our people, it's a woman's right to be bold, to select her mate. Not the other way around."

"But Queen Morgan said we must learn to adapt to the standards our conquerors exert upon us. My proud husband is very much the conqueror. He would never give way to my demand that he take me to bed."

If Riana believed that, then she had much to learn about men. "Your protests ring false," Sela said as she sipped at her tea. "I think your hesitance stems less from your sense of propriety, and more from fear."

"And what would I be afraid of?"

"You sense there is more to making love than relieving some itch. Each time you join with your husband, you surrender a part of yourself."

"Never!"

Sela set down her cup. "Live as long as I have, and you'll understand that life is a series of compromises, a constant tide of give and take."

"The Saxon takes. He does not know how to give back."

"No?" Sela stared intently at the girl. "Then teach him. Remember the magician's credo—whatever you send out returns to you threefold."

"The credo deals with casting spells, not teaching barbarians to be civilized. It certainly has little to do with the act of making love."

"Riana, my child, what is magic, if not the art of love?" Sela rose to her feet, knowing this was the most important advice she would ever give this girl. "All creation beats with a heart of its own. No magician, however gifted, can succeed long without its ebb and flow of emotion. Master love, know when to give and when to take it, and one day, you shall become every bit the enchantress you dream of."

Riana again leaned forward eagerly. "Are you saying I do have magical talent?"

"The Goddess gives us all the talent. It is what we choose to do with it that decides our fate." Sela sighed, afraid that the poor girl was as yet too young, too inexperienced to understand. "Ah Riana, do you think it a coincidence that my powers remain limited? Had I taken the opportunity you now scoff at, had I risked all for love, I would not now be buried here in this hut. I could be settled at Camelot, giving this same advice to the king."

Setting down her cup firmly, Riana stood, hands at her sides. "You talk of love and sacrifice, but what of duty? Queens Morgan and Morgause, even Merlin himself, said that to serve the king best, I must learn and train and nurture my talent. That if I hope to become a great magician, I must stay aloof, apart from lesser mortals."

"Bah!" Sela nearly spat out the word. "Magic created without love can only spawn evil. Perhaps your idols at Camelot gave you such advice because they fear your power might far exceed their own."

"You are jealous of them. You always have been." Eyes flashing, Riana went to the door. "I made a mistake, confiding in you. You don't understand anything."

Sela sat, suddenly weary. The girl was young and resistant; nothing anyone could say now would sway her. Riana must learn in her own way, in her own time. "I understand *you*," Sela said to her back. "And I know love can be your salvation. Pride will only bring your doom."

Riana paused at the door, and for a moment, Sela hoped she might turn and listen. The girl spoke, low and bitterly, to the door instead. "I do not love Wolf. I cannot. What I feel for him is lust and once it is out of my system, I can meet my true destiny without regrets." She lifted her chin, her voice now clear and loud. "I shall dance naked for him, like that first night amidst the juniper bushes. If the summoning chant brought Wolf to me then, it can do so again." She strode out of the hut, satisfied with her declaration.

Juniper, Sela remembered uneasily. In all that had happened since coming here, she'd forgotten how Riana summoned Wolf that night. Recalling her fears that the girl might have inadvertently trapped the Saxon warrior for life, she wondered if all her hopes and dreams for Riana could be based on mere delusion.

For what Riana wrought in an impulsive moment, she could undo as rashly in another. Her enchantment might seem strong and binding now but it could yet be broken. Would Wolf then feel desire for his lovely prisoner, his people's enemy, or would he turn on her once he learned the truth? What would become of Riana, especially if what Sela suspected were true, and the girl had developed soft feelings for this man who was her husband?

Trembling, Sela reached for her holy candle, fearing there was little she could—or should—do for the pair. She was but a small player in the enfolding drama, powerless to stem the tragedy brewing about them. She could only follow her own advice, offering her love as a talisman to protect them.

Lighting the candle, she began to pray.

Riana hurried about her room, preparing it and herself for the night ahead. Strategically placing the candles to bathe the room in a warm golden glow, she thought of her conversation with Sela. The woman could be right. Considering Wolf's stiff pride, he could well be waiting only for his wife's invitation. If so, until she issued it, Riana would sleep alone in that bed.

But Sela had been way off the mark when she spoke of love. What Riana felt for Wolf was a physical craving, a need much like drinking and eating, nothing more. If making love to him could free her from this yearning, then she owed it to her peace of mind to seduce him. And if somehow it made her a finer enchantress, all the better.

But she'd never relinquish her heart. It wasn't in Riana to surrender, nor did she have that right, anyway. She couldn't tie herself to Wolf, not with her duty to King Arthur to consider.

Yet why did it cause a pang, the thought of leaving her husband?

Determined not to chase that thought, she went to set another log on the fire. It was warm on this late summer night, but a heated atmosphere suited her plans. Smiling, she eyed the flagon of wine and two glasses waiting on the bedside table. Everything was set in place for seduction.

She felt a qualm, wondering if she had it in her to step up to him and ask for a kiss. It wasn't in her nature to plead, and she could not bear to think he might one day throw such weakness back in her face.

She wandered to the window, staring out at the night, her gaze snared by the moon, so bright in an almost starless black sky.

How huge it seemed tonight, how golden. It seemed to call to her, just as it had on the night of the Beltane fire, urging her to throw off her clothing and dance.

The dance! Of course. She must call upon the Goddess to help summon Wolf, just as she had that first night. Muttering to herself, trying to recapture the right words, she turned back to the room and began rearranging it, moving the table and chairs to the side to make ample space for her movements. Next, she looked about her for the four key elements. She had fire in the hearth and the candles, and air in the breeze soughing through the open window, but what could she do for earth?

Spying her sandals, coated with dried mud from the fields, she slapped them together, creating a small pile of dirt in the center of the room. Now, all she needed was water.

She reached for her ewer and impulsively tossed its contents down the front of her. Tad must have recently filled it, for there was far more water than she'd anticipated, and its coolness made her gasp with shock.

Yet it was not unpleasant, the way her linen shift now clung to her belly and breasts, nor would it matter if it were. She must lose no time in starting her dance.

She began slowly, stepping first on the pile of earth, then circling out to the cool, stone floor, spreading her arms as her mind and spirit took flight. Spinning, dipping, twirling on her toes within the confines of the room, she gazed through the window at the moon as she called upon the Goddess to bless this night, to bless her union with Wolf, to make their coming together bring peace to them both.

And as always when she danced, she lost touch with the here and now, her mind giving way to the soft pulsing world of the Goddess.

Wolf stood at the doorway, watching Riana weave about the room like a graceful swan. Drinking in the sight of her wet shift plastered so revealingly against her flesh, feeling the same awe he'd known the first time he'd seen her dance, he knew she touched far more than his physical being. Then, as now, he was being swept up and out of himself, offered a glimpse of a magical, mystical place most men only dream of.

This time, he would not be left aching for more.

His yearnings hardened into resolve. Tonight he would take her, own her, and they would conquer her mystical world together.

In three long strides, he was across the room, but when he would take her in his arms, some unseen force reached out to stay him. *Patience* he could almost hear the breeze caution. If he wished to enter Riana's world, he sensed, he must let her continue her dance.

So he stood, still and silent, as she dipped and swayed, her soft, floral fragrance trailing in her wake like a web she spun about him. Watching her lips as she muttered in some ancient, indecipherable tongue, he felt his heart grow lighter, more certain. They might not touch in the physical sense—indeed, he doubted she even knew he stood so near to her—yet they linked on some other, higher level.

When she began to inch her tunic up her legs, he felt as if he himself had willed it, even as she silently commanded him to watch with unmoving fascination. With his mind, he caressed each crevice and curve she revealed as his body grew tight and hard with hunger. He did not reach out to grab her, though he longed to with all his being. Instinctively, he knew she must be left free to work her magic.

He remained immobile, even when she slipped her tunic over her head and flung it aside. Watching her dance before him in wanton, naked glory, he held himself in check. Whether or not she was consciously aware of it, Riana offered far more than her body. She was weaving him into her prayers, laying her fragile, vulnerable spirit in his hands.

Knowing this, he battled the lust building inside him as her chanting picked up tempo, her movements grew more and more provocative. Circling him like a hawk would its prey, she held his gaze as she dipped closer, only to swirl off, then hover closer yet. He felt her fingers brush his leg, then his own tunic sliding upward, the cool breeze from the window stealing across his bared flesh. Hot, hard, and painfully ready, he held tight to his resolve as she wound behind him, still chanting her seductive prayer as she inched the tunic up to his arms. With a low guttural oath of his own, he yanked the material up and over his head.

She darted off. For a tense moment, he thought his rash movement might have frightened her off, but she continued circling him with a pleased, dreamy smile. He forced himself not to move, to barely breathe, as she edged closer, pausing long enough for her thigh to brush his, a breast to graze his arm, before twirling off seductively, again out of reach.

As if drawn against her will, she moved in ever narrowing circles until her breasts glanced his chest, causing them both to suck in a sibilant breath. Clearly stunned, as if she too had felt that intimate touch shoot straight to her core, she stopped before him, catching his gaze and holding it captive. He could see her bewilderment and fright, yet resolve glittered in the golden depths. Like himself, she was determined to see this through to the end.

Swaying, chanting softly, she moved closer yet, planting her leg between his thighs. Like a snake, she writhed up against him, rubbing her body against his, driving the blood through his veins like a raging torrent. He kept his arms at his sides by sheer force of will, letting her slide around him, chafing hip against hip, back against back in wildly erotic fashion. As she moved, he could feel her heat radiate into him, melting them both, fusing them together. Soon the dance would be over, he thought with a leap of excitement. Then it would be his turn to weave an enchantment.

She wheeled to face him again, her eyes wide and open as she pressed against him, her lips parting invitingly as she uttered the last, hurried chants. Feeling her building urgency as she rubbed against him, Wolf's brain reeled. He had the dizzying sensation they were soaring upward together, in tempo with her strange rhythmic chanting, caught in some mystic parody of the act of mating.

She cried out suddenly, thrusting back her head and leaving her throat exposed to him. Clutching her by the arms, he rained kisses on the soft, white skin she offered. He could feel her trembling, could feel his own, and he revelled in the moment of shared triumph.

Their souls had joined; it was time now to link their bodies.

Holding her tight to him, Wolf let his passion free. He kissed her throat, the cleft between her breasts, his need for her overwhelming him. Sweeping her up with an arm beneath her knees, he carried her to the bed. They'd started this her way, but they'd finish it the way he knew best.

Riana seemed dazed as he laid her upon the furs. For a moment, he thought she might deny him, but her features cleared with a dazzling smile and she reached out for him with an eagerness to match his own.

Silently, reverently, he took her face in his hands as he lay beside her. This would be nothing like their past two joinings. Tonight, she would come to him well aware of what she was doing. "Are you certain?" he asked her, watching her eyes for the slightest misgivings. "Tell me you want this joining as much as I."

She nodded eagerly.

Dipping down, he took her lips and laid his claim upon her. By night's end, he swore, she'd be crying his name in complete surrender. She would be his woman, now and forever.

Stroking her sides, cupping her breasts, he felt his passion swell within him. "You are so beautiful," he told her as he trailed down her chin, kissing her throat, easing down to the soft swelling breast. He could hear Riana groan, arching up for his touch, but his attention was focused on the blossoming nipple captured by his mouth. Licking it, his tongue swirled around it, sucking it to throbbing erection as he paid homage to the incredible beauty that was his wife.

Nor was he content to remain at her breasts. He touched and

kissed her everywhere, adoring her, hungering for her. She dug her fingers in his hair, his back, whimpering, moaning, and at long last, chanting his name. When he felt her body begin to quiver, when he could hold himself back no longer, he parted her thighs and kneeled between them. "Say it," he rasped out, staring down at her. "By the gods, Riana, say that you want this. That you want me."

She tried to look away, but he held her face immobile. "Tell me," he insisted more gently, rubbing her cheeks with his thumbs. "Just say you want this as desperately as I."

"Yes!" she cried, as if the words had been wrenched from her. "Yes, damn you, I want it. Now."

He felt suddenly as if the world was his, as if nothing on this earth could now ever stop him. Kissing her greedily, sliding into her sweet, welcoming warmth, all he could think of was that she was his, at long last. From this moment on, they would face life together as one.

Rolling over, he lay on his back, holding her waist as she rode him. He watched her face with a building triumph, seeing her pleasure as he swelled within her, his hips driving upward with a life of their own, thrusting harder and deeper with every stroke. Her breathing quickened and she reached for his chest, squeezing the flesh there, chafing his own budding nipples. "Oh, sweet Goddess," she cried out, thrusting her head back, twisting it back and forth in wild abandon.

He could feel her tighten around him, quivering for release, but he slowed his thrusts, determined to prolong their mating. Sliding his hands up to her breasts, kneading them with his hands, he raised himself up to sit beneath her, even while maintaining his slow, rhythmic thrusts. Brought close to his face, she stared at him in breathless bewilderment.

"Call out my name, not your goddess," he told her hoarsely. "I, not she, am the one who makes you feel this magic."

To press his point, he lifted her up by the waist until his shaft barely penetrated her, even as he sucked her nipple into his mouth. Twirling his tongue around it, he slowly released her breast as he let her down, delving even deeper within her. It drove him mad with lust, slowly repeating the pull and thrust as he suckled both breasts, but his patience was rewarded by the low groan in her throat. "More," she moaned, sliding up and down as he bucked against her. "Oh Wolf, yes. More."

With a growl, he rolled over again so she once more lay beneath him, open and eager. Losing what little control he had left, he drove into her like a man possessed, seeking his sanity at the core of her being. She urged him on, chanting his name as she'd once prayed to her goddess, until with a blazing, wondrous shattering, he felt them both explode together. "Wolf," she cried out, one last glorious time, as she shuddered all around him.

Still thrusting, he poured his seed inside her, poured his soul inside her.

Long after he was done, they lay clutched together, silent and awed by what had just transpired between them. This time, Wolf knew the link had been forged, and try as she might, Riana could never now break it, having uttered his name at the brink of supreme passion. He'd made certain she could never forget that moment; she would be his woman forever.

He leaned up on his elbow, looking down on her lovely face. She seemed so peaceful, lying there with her eyes closed, her mouth curved upward in a smile. "It is done," he told her tenderly, brushing her petal-soft cheek with a finger. "We are joined, man to woman, Moriana. You and I are one."

Her lashes fluttered opened and her entire body went stiff. Wolf saw the helplessness in her eyes as she gazed up at him. "Wolf, you don't underst—"

"Hush." He set his finger on her lip. "Your denials are meaningless now. You have shown me far too much with your body and your spirit."

She shook her head, twisting away from him. "What happened between us . . ." She sucked in a deep breath, as if to gain strength from it, before gazing back at him with a far more tender expression. "Oh Wolf, I cannot begin to fathom what it might mean, not yet while it is still so new, but I cannot commit myself to any man. Not even you. Don't you see! I must first fulfill the purpose for which I was born."

It was his turn to withdraw. "A woman's purpose is to serve her husband."

"That is the Saxon in you talking." He'd angered her. He could see it glittering in her eyes, in every taut line of her body as she rose to sit beside him. "You worship Mother Nature. You must sense that each living creature has its own destiny, apart from all others. Even we lowly females. I am destined to be an enchantress, Wolf, and I must serve my king. Nothing I might want or need can change that."

"I have changed it. Tonight proves you belong with me."

She sighed, moving over to sit on her knees before him, her long blond hair like a cloak about her shoulders. "You speak as if I am your property. Tell me, if I asked you to give up your kingdom to follow *my* dream, would you listen?"

"I cannot abandon my people—"

She nodded. "Yet you expect thus of me? It is my essence, this destiny. It is who I am."

"You belong to me now," he repeated stubbornly.

She took his hands in hers. "I have tried to explain what Arthur means to me. If ever he has need of my services, I must be there at his side. Is it that different from the duty you feel toward Cerdric?"

"It's not the same. The gods brought you to me for a purpose."

She shook her head. "It was a mistake, that night. I was trying to summon an escort to take me back to Camelot, but you got in the way. You kept me from going home."

He resented how her face softened when she spoke of Camelot. She should save such yearnings for himself. "You talk of this kingdom as if it were paradise," he said bitterly.

She sat forward, her face eager. "If you could but see it, you would understand. It's an incredibly grand palace, with its tall commanding towers, its gay banners fluttering on every parapet. And people everywhere you turn, warriors training, merchants at the gate, dignitaries arriving from around the world in colorful caravans to bring extravagant gifts. You should see the Round

Table, with all those knights dressed in their finest, gathering to pay homage to the king. They must be among the most noble and self-sacrificing of all creation. There is not a man among them that does not strive to give Arthur his best, who will not give his life for the betterment of the kingdom."

Wolf stifled a snort, for from experience, he knew better than to heed such glowing praise. No one man could be that noble, that good, and put together in one room, even the most honorable tended to give way to petty squabbles. "It sounds far too good to be true," he told her. "I have found that fondness often taints the memory with rosy hues."

She tilted her head, reacting to his skeptical tone. "I was someone there, Wolf. Here, I'm just some useless female, a scorned foreigner, but at Camelot, people listened when I spoke, the king himself gave me audience. I felt important."

Her voice broke on that last. Watching her bite her lip, Wolf realized that a good part of her yearning for Camelot had to do with a sense of belonging. "Ah, Riana, can't you see that I can offer you more than fame and position?" Reaching out, he pulled her back in his arms. "As my woman, you can have the hearth and home, the family that's always been denied you."

She searched his eyes, clearly torn. "I know, but—"

"I have but a small village to offer, I know, but we will make it grow and prosper, become something to one day rival your precious Camelot. You are my wife, my lover, my lifelong mate. Look long and hard at our kingdom, and see that it's worth believing in, well worth fighting for."

He kissed her then, a gentle salutation of the lips that drew a faint whimper from her throat. When he pulled back, surprised by her reaction, she reached out for him desperately.

"Oh Wolf," was all she said as she fell into his arms and sank to the bed with him. But for Wolf, hearing his name on her lips, feeling the eagerness of her body as he took her again, it was more than enough.

He had claimed her and she had surrendered, and they would build on the future from that.

* * *

Hours later, feeling wonderfully replete, Riana lay watching Wolf sleep and thinking of what he had told her. Her hands went to her belly as she imagined a tiny replica of her husband, sprouting to life inside her. It brought a smile to her lips, the thought of a little boy dancing at their heels as they brought him to discover Wolf's island together. He'd have his father's looks and steady disposition, but from her, he would gain curiosity and imagination.

Sighing, she looked about the room, picturing it filled to bursting with children, giggling and darting to and fro as she and their father played with them. Wolf was right. It could be a good life, sharing joy with this man.

Yet it differed so vastly from how she'd always imagined her future.

Wolf stirred suddenly in his sleep, reaching out for her, but he calmed instantly once she nestled back into his chest. Warmed by the security his touch aroused in her, Riana realized she could do far worse than waiting out the days here in his arms. Was it wrong to enjoy every last moment she could spend with him?

After all, her summons might be years in the future. It might never even come at all. Perhaps Wolf was right and she could yet help him build their own little kingdom in this faraway corner of the world.

One thing was certain, she thought as she leaned into his rock solid warmth. Her dancing had done the trick; the Goddess had answered her prayers. Wolf had shown her a most effective means for relieving her physical cravings, and for the time being, at least, they had both found the way to peace and contentment.

Surely it would be foolish not to make the most of this time, to take full advantage of what else her husband might teach her.

And the future, well, it would have to take care of itself.

* * *

On the outskirts of Camelot, a chill wind blew through a cavern, making the candle flames dance. "Troublesome spirits fly tonight," the leader told the group gathered around her. "It is up to us to harness their mischief, to set it swirling in our cauldron of unrest."

"And the old one?" someone asked. "The wizard Merlin, what of him?"

The leader laughed, a long, none-too-pleasant sound. "We need have no more worries on that score. Silly old fool. A good chant, the proper potion, and he is gone forever. It would seem not even the Grand Enchanter is immune to romance."

The others joined in her laughter, but the leader now sobered. "It is but the beginning," she said harshly, drawing her arm over the crystal before her. "If we wish to end Arthur's reign, we must not pause in triumph until his throne has been toppled."

Silence again blanketed the dank cave, each in the coven looking nervously at one another. Treason was a high crime, punishable by burning at the stake, and not one to be entered into lightly.

"What then?" came the querulous question. "What are we to do next?"

"The girl," the leader said with a slow, secretive smile. "She must be brought forth at once."

Twelve

Months later, Riana gathered her cloak against her, feeling the nip of the wind on her bare toes. How chilly it seemed without Wolf beside her, but he was off to Cedric's yearly council, seeking formal royal blessing for their marriage.

Harvest would soon be upon them, she thought, gazing up at the filling moon. Life would grow hectic in the excitement of reaping and storing their crop, and there would be no time for barefoot, midnight strolls with her husband, nor would they be making love beneath the glittering stars in the colder nights of winter.

She sighed, missing Wolf more than she cared to admit. How had it happened, she wondered, that in the waning weeks of summer, she should grow so accustomed to his warm, solid frame beside her each night? So used to him, in fact, that she would miss him enough to steal out at the stroke of twelve, trying to find some essence of the man in their favorite trysting spot, the cliff where they'd once watched the Beltane fire.

At least there was no guard to elude, she thought as she hurried to the path through the woods. Wolf had taken Tad with him, leaving Riana, with Greta's help, to oversee the doings at the village.

She smiled, proud of what she'd accomplished. Helga would likely dislike her forever, but now that Riana could speak their language, most of her coworkers in the fields included her in their noonday discussions, exchanging household hints, as well as the latest gossip. With their help, she'd tried to master the womanly crafts of baking, weaving, and pottery, though her rock-hard bread and hole-ridden blanket brought her nothing but teasing laughter from her husband. To give him credit, he'd tried hard to keep a straight face when eyeing the lopsided pot she'd labored over at the wheel. Maintaining that she had other skills in which she excelled, he'd then swept her up and off to his bedchamber.

Wrapping her arms around her, Riana tried to quell the yearnings now infecting her body. Wolf had been gone barely a week and would return in a day at most, so this hungering for him was impractical at best, and at worst, unseemly. She'd let herself grow dependent on his strong arms and skillful kisses—perhaps even *too* dependent. He'd built a trap, her lusty Saxon, lulling her with his honeyed words and tender caresses. Each night as she lay beside him, he'd stroke and soothe her as he painted glorious pictures in her mind of the kingdom they would build together.

Indeed, the only cloud on the horizon was the odd manner in which Sela watched her. Her worried frowns puzzled Riana. It made her wonder if Sela knew something the rest of them did not, some dire knowledge she refused to impart.

Heading up the path, Riana wished again that Wolf was with her, for the forest encroached often on the path, leaving large sections of it dark and shadowed. As she hurried through one of these patches, she heard a strange murmuring She paused, listening, with the eerie sensation that the stream called to her.

Shivering, she shook off the notion, for the noise had been a hushed, secretive sound, the sort whispered in dark corners and narrow alleys, not the gay, rippling gurgles the stream usually produced in daylight. She felt the flesh rise on her arms, and her stomach, which had been somewhat unsettled of late, pitched in an unpleasant manner.

Determined to ignore the vague, insistent murmuring, she pushed on to her destination, but the higher she climbed, the more the sound tugged at her subconscious like some forgotten dream of childhood. She sensed, rather than heard the summons. Its urgency proved hard to resist.

Torn, she stood on the path. She'd promised Wolf she would avoid the tranquil pool while he was gone, would refrain from all magic, but the thrumming in her veins called her, lured her, made it impossible to think of anything else.

Walking as though in her sleep, she stepped through the undergrowth blindly, her mind focused on the stream ahead.

She found the glade far from peaceful tonight. Taking in every ray of moonlight, the pool's surface shone like a beacon as she approached it, more metal than liquid, a smooth, reflective looking glass with untold depths. Excitement bubbling inside her, she stepped up to its edge, reaching out with an arm in wonder. As if she'd issued a command, the water sprang to life.

All at once, she was surrounded by the sights and sounds of Camelot. Trumpets blared, knights charged by on their huge, snorting steeds, while Arthur waited, tall, silent and regal at the castle gate.

Her heart lurched when she saw his weathered face. How the king had aged greatly in the intervening years. Where once he'd looked bold and determined, worry lines etched uncertainties onto his handsome features.

"Have you word?" Arthur called out suddenly, and a darkly handsome knight, one she had never seen before, stepped forward with a dramatic flourish. "No word," the knight answered sadly, his sure voice colored by a trace of the Breton accent. "I fear, sire, that your magician has vanished."

Magician? Riana asked herself, wondering if he referred to her, if she were the one her king missed so sorely. She reached out with her hand, wanting to touch Arthur, to ease the worry from his features, but the water rippled, erasing his image. In the king's place, a hazy parade of gossamer threads danced, floating, twisting, gathering form like the strings of a web. In their midst, she at last saw, a man lay sleeping.

No, not just any man. A magician. The Great Merlin himself.

She gasped, not knowing the meaning of this vision, yet sensing the peril it represented.

"Go to him," she could hear the Great Enchanter whisper from inside his enchanted cage. "Go now. Arthur needs you more than ever."

And with that, the image faded, as if the energy needed to sustain it had drained away. The pool went still and dark, an ordinary cove once more, with not even a glint of moonlight to lighten its inky silence. Unnerved, Riana backed away, feeling suddenly unsafe in this eerie setting.

Stumbling through the undergrowth, groping her way back to the path, she was stung by a sense of urgency. Never before had she known so vivid a vision. Arthur must be in grave danger.

Not even Sela could dismiss this as her imagination at work. This vision was no silly yearning, no girlish dream of being more than she was. It had come, the summons she had been preparing all her life for.

Go, Merlin had commanded. *Go now.*

"Wolf, wait. Where do you go, this late at night?"

"Is that you, Ranulf?" Reaching up to quiet his jittery mount, Wolf peered through the dark at his friend. "I left word with Yarrick. I'm going home." He smiled at the sound of the word. Home, to his wife.

Ranulf neared, his face drawn in a frown. "Have you the king's leave? It would not do to anger Cerdric now."

"I have spoken with him, yes." Wolf lowered his voice, speaking confidentially. "Between you and I, there's naught the king will deny me tonight. He's too in need of my loyalty, and the warriors who follow me."

"It is true then, that the Britons are swaggering at the borders?"

Wolf nodded. "According to Vangarth. With his bent for trouble, it could be merely his warmongering, but the results would still be the same. To battle the Britons, Cerdric needs an army, and his need could not have come at a better time for me."

Ranulf clasped him on the back. "You did well this evening. For yourself and River Ford."

Wolf had done well, indeed. In formally blessing his marriage, the king had offered to provide Riana's dowry, since she'd been a royal prisoner with no riches of her own. No fool he, Cerdric knew he must ensure loyalty among his thanes, and if granting a few hides of river land—and a share of the loot from the last raid—kept Penawulf aligned behind him, then the king was prepared to be magnanimous. Indeed, he'd even tossed in ten of his finest furs as a royal gift.

It was those furs Wolf wanted to show Riana tonight. He could not wait to see them, draped over her soft, naked body.

"This is the new start we needed," Ranulf was saying beside him. "There is much our village can build on with Cerdric's grant. You did well, Wolf. Your father would be proud."

No, Exar would scorn that his son had achieved all this through a woman, a woman Wolf even now could not banish from his mind. All through the feasting, his hopes for the future had bubbled and churned in his gut. That was why he felt such restlessness, such a driving need to be home. He had to share the good news with Riana, else it would surely explode inside him.

"I must go," he said impatiently to Ranulf as he turned to his horse. "I have this urge to be sleeping this night in my own bed."

Ranulf grinned, as if knowing it was far more than a warm bed Wolf sought. "Take care, then," he called up to him as Wolf mounted Zeus. "The way the clouds now cover the moon, the way will be dark and dangerous."

Glancing up at the sky, Wolf was overtaken by a sudden, strange chill, as if the amassing clouds presaged far more than a change in weather. Urging Zeus out of the pen, his need to get home sharpened, became acute.

"Do not tarry long," he called back to Ranulf, breaking into a gallop.

Riana paused outside Sela's hut, looking about the village at the square where she played with the children, at the grand hall where she conducted the daily council in Wolf's absence, the tower where she'd just left old Enoch guarding the settlement. How ironic, that now when her summons finally came, she would find herself reluctant to heed it.

Inhaling deeply, she turned her back on the village, letting herself in the old woman's hut. She had no choice, she'd been called to Camelot, and she must make her final arrangements before setting out on her journey.

Sela sat before a candle, the sole light in the room, her attention focused on its wavering flame. A prayer-trance, Riana thought with dismay. Sela could be occupied thus for hours.

Yet she stood at the doorway, unable to leave without bidding the old woman farewell.

As if sensing her urgency, Sela suddenly blinked, her gaze lifting to meet Riana's. Recognition flickered in her deep, dark eyes, the knowledge that what she feared most had come to pass. Riana had no need to tell Sela about her vision; the old woman knew already.

"I have been praying for you," Sela said solemnly. "I had hoped you would choose wisely, but I see you are determined to go." She nodded at the sack of belongings Riana carried over her shoulder.

"I must." Riana set the sack on the floor at her feet for the moment. "The vision came from Merlin himself, Sela. He commanded me to hurry."

"It could be a trick." Shadows from the candlelight played across her face, lending her features an air of mystery, perhaps even danger.

Riana shivered. "What is it, Sela? What are you *not* telling me?"

Rising slowly, grimacing as she did so, the old woman took the candle to light several others, filling the room with a golden glow. "You may find Camelot is not as you remember it, child. That beneath all that splendor thrives a sickness, eating at its core."

Riana shook her head, not wanting to believe her. "I shall never believe there is anything evil about Arthur and Guinivere."

"Perhaps not the king and queen, but can you truly vouch for those surrounding them?"

"No," Riana said hesitantly, mentally judging all those she'd known at court. She trusted the king's sisters, Morgan and Morgause, of course, but with so many dwelling at Camelot, it was impossible to determine evil without going there. "If you are right," she told Sela, "then Arthur shall only need me all the more."

"And what of this village?" Crossing the room to her hearth, Sela reached for the pot to brew tea. "Greta and Tad, the women and children, don't you think they have need of you, too?"

Riana winced. Given the circumstances, she'd done her best for them, making certain old Enoch was posted in the guard towers and prepared to sound an attack. His penchant for ale made her uneasy, but he was the only male remaining in the village and he'd promised not to touch a drop until the chieftain's return. "I am leaving them in your care, Sela. You and Greta can take care of these people far better than I."

Sela turned, her gaze boring into Riana. "You mean to travel alone?"

Riana shared the old woman's pain. They'd been together ever since she could remember, and while they'd badgered each other the entire time, it was no pleasant thing contemplating the future without Sela.

Yet as much as she might crave her guardian's company on her journey, Sela had grown too old and feeble for such a trek and Riana would not risk her life. "River Ford depends on you," she said, her voice tight with strain. "Where would they be without your herbs and remedies, your sloeberry wine? I'm counting on you to take care of Myra with her birthing so near. And young Gandolfo—he's so embarrassed by his warts."

"And your husband? What of him?"

Wolf. Riana had tried hard not to think of Wolf, knowing such thoughts would only undermine her resolve, but trust Sela to cut to the heart of the matter. In her mind, Riana could see her husband, his eyes alight as he spoke of the future, so certain she shared his conviction, unwilling to hear that she had prior, deeper obligations that would one day pull her away.

Her leaving would hurt him deeply, she knew.

Her determination wavered. Perhaps she could wait for Wolf's return. If she discussed her vision with him, they might yet reach a compromise, and if not, well, the matter would be taken from her hands.

"You cannot leave him as he is now," Sela said sharply, desperately.

"What are you talking about?" Frowning, Riana crossed the room, coming to a stop before Sela. She noticed the woman's hands trembled as she set the herbs in the water. "There's nothing wrong with Wolf."

"Would that it were true," Sela said, even her voice shaking, "but I fear your husband is under a spell."

"What is this?" Riana reached for the woman's shoulder, urging Sela to look up at her.

Sela stared at her unblinking. "Think, child," she said quietly. "Your dancing that night. The juniper at your feet. You conjured a love enchantment."

"No!" Yet even as she denied it, Riana remembered his strange intensity, his obsession to have her, despite the threats posed to him and his village. All this time, it hadn't been love, or even lust driving him, just some mistaken enchantment meant for another.

She felt cold inside, lost. This changed everything, made a mockery of their nights together, their future together. In truth, it left her with no real reason to stay.

She released Sela's hand, going for her sack at the door. "If I did put a spell on him," she said, hoisting the bundle back up to her shoulder, "then pray, for his sake and mine, say the words that will free Wolf of it. I would not have him suffering needlessly when I am gone."

"You know I have no talent for spells."

"Try, Sela. For me. For this village. He must not desert his people to come charging after me." She reached for the door. "He must not hunger for what is naught but an illusion."

"Don't go." The words seemed wrenched out of the old woman.

Riana sighed heavily. "I shall miss you more than you can ever know, Sela, but we both knew it would one day come to this. The Goddess has called me and I must answer."

"But Riana, I sense great heartache on the path you've chosen."

"So do I, Sela" she said sadly, walking out the door. "So do I."

From the shadows, Helga watched the chieftain's wife leave the old healer's hut. She smiled at the bundle tossed over the foolish girl's shoulder. It had come at last, the moment she'd been waiting for, and it was all Helga could do not to shout out in triumph.

Her suspicions had been raised after hearing Riana talk with Enoch, but seeing the female now, striking out through the gates and off to the river, Helga's hopes had been confirmed. The young fool was leaving them, and in so doing, would spring her own trap.

Helga had long since sent word to Lord Vangarth, whose strange interest in the girl had supplied Helga with handsome rewards. He could not know—nor was she inclined to tell him— but Helga would have gladly played his spy for free, if it meant ridding their village of the hated Briton.

But just in case some quirk of fate brought Riana back to them, Helga meant to make certain the girl would not be welcomed with opened arms. Lifting up the jug of ale, she eyed the guard tower. It was none too soon, she decided, to pay a visit to Enoch.

Facing the dark fields, Riana fought the lurch in her gut. Tears pricked at her eyes as she thought of the women who expected her to join them in the morning. Back in the village, the children would wait for the ending to her latest story tomorrow evening, Ranulf would expect her for her lesson in the afternoon, and sweet, patient Greta would need help with Wolf's homecoming celebration.

Wolf.

Riana hesitated, swamped by a great emptiness. No more trysts in the meadow, no laughing over her household ineptitude, no dreams for the future. Thinking of the children she would now never bear for him, she felt the knot inside her tighten.

All this time, they'd been living an illusion. Herself most of all.

How foolish she felt for not realizing he'd been under a spell, for believing Wolf could desire her for herself alone. Once Sela said the words to undo the spell, he would come to his senses and feel nothing but disdain for her. She was a foundling, whose own parents had abandoned her. When had anyone truly cared about her, needed her?

Save Arthur, of course.

Stiffening her spine, she reminded herself of her duty to her king. Serving Arthur was the one true constant in her life, the only thing giving her purpose and meaning. Her life with Wolf, as wonderful and idyllic as it had been, was merely a dream. Camelot was her reality, and it was long since time she went there.

Clasping her sack, she struck out for the river, determined to find the bank where Wolf left the boat he'd used to ferry them to the island. From there, she reasoned, she could float down-stream and eventually find a major river. Having been summoned by magical force, she could trust the Goddess to guide her way.

Still, she had cause to doubt her deity's interest in her in the hours ahead when she found herself wandering lost on River Ford land. The weather had taken a nasty shift, bringing harsh, heavy storm clouds to pelt the land with rain. Even when the black night gave way to a gray, battered morning, she found it impossible to see more than a few steps ahead of her.

Plagued by nausea, she felt light-headed and feeble. Increasingly, she stumbled, now and then falling in the mud, leaving herself and her belongings a damp, sodden mess.

Her doubts mushroomed. If she were meant to reach Camelot, why couldn't she find the plague-ridden boat? How could it be, that after carefully picking her way, she should find that she had circled back and was once again standing here on the very same cliff overlooking the river?

Hearing a distant rumble, she looked back over her shoulder. Through the mist, she could see what appeared to be horsemen. An army of them, from the sound of it, all heading toward the village.

At first, she feared it was her husband and his warriors, but when she saw these men wore metal helmets, not leather ones, she realized they were British. Had it come at last, her long-awaited escort to Camelot?

As she tried to call out, the ground beneath her slipped. She hadn't time to draw in a breath before the hillside gave way, taking her with it, sending her sack flying. Frantically, she reached out for the nearest solid form, a branch on a rooted pricker bush, and uttered prayers of thanksgiving when it held, preventing her headlong flight.

Her nausea deepening, she heard the sack land with a thud on the bank below. If not for this bush, she thought as she clutched it tighter, she too would fall, to be buried under an avalanche of mud.

She held on, dangling, as the earth continued to slide beneath her. Prickers dug into her hands but a keen sense of survival kept her clinging to the narrow limb. How much longer she could do so she couldn't guess. An ominous sucking noise warned that the bush was none too firmly anchored.

The moment the mud slowed its movement, she groped gingerly about for a toehold, hoping to find some viable way to solid ground, but her feet kept slipping on the slick and oozing surface. Her grip tightened on the branch, wincing as the thorns bit into her skin, her heart thumping madly at the sound of faint little snaps. What good would it do to cling to the limb if within moments it cracked, sending the half to which she clung flying, to join its brothers at the bottom of the cliff?

Tenaciously, she held to the branch, and to the faith that the Goddess would never allow her to die in so useless a fashion.

The snaps became slurps, the sound of roots loosening. Feeling the bush slip, Riana wondered desperately what to do. Oddly enough, it was not to the Goddess that she prayed for help, but to her husband instead. Wolf would know what to do. Wolf would save her.

But the bush gave way, relinquishing its hold on the hillside with a feeble protest. Crying out in alarm, Riana tumbled downward.

Fear, chill and paralyzing, rose up with the scream in her throat. With a hard jolt, her body hit the ground, splattering the mud below. All the air left her lungs in a painful gush.

And with it went her grip on consciousness.

Wolf smelled smoke long before he reached his village. The acrid scent curled in his nostrils, making him ill with dread. He worried about the village, about his sister, but his deepest concern centered around his wife. *Let her be all right,* he found himself chanting, as if his thoughts could keep her from harm.

He rode straight to the villa, overwhelmed with relief to find it still standing. Climbing the stairs to her chambers two at a time, he willed Riana to be in her bed, safely sleeping. It came as a dagger to the heart to find the chamber cold and empty.

But of course she would not be here. She knew her duty. As the chieftain's wife, she must rush to the village at the first sign of trouble. Praying that she had used her lessons from Ranulf well, Wolf flew down the stairs, leaping back on his horse to race to the village.

He found the women and children in the square, buckets in hand, having just doused the flames that had consumed most of the grand hall. Greta was leading them, he noticed. He saw no sign of his wife.

"Riana?" he asked, dropping from his horse.

The women exchanged worried glances, as if no one wished to be the one to break the news. The imaginary dagger twisted in his chest.

"No one has seen her," Greta said in a small voice, refusing to meet his gaze. "We think she may have been taken."

"Which way did the monsters go?" Wolf growled, his hands already tightening to fists.

"You cannot mean to go after them?" Greta reached out to detain him, clasping his arm. "You talk suicide, Wolf. If you wait, the raiders will soon send their ransom demands. You can deal with them then, when you have your warriors riding behind you."

He shook off her arm. "And in the meantime, what will become of Riana? I cannot sit idly by. I must act, and act now."

"No!" Helga stepped forward, her voice ringing with authority. "She is right. There's no use chasing anyone. The Lady Riana is not with them."

The other women again exchanged glances, their expressions frozen with shock. They hadn't expected Helga to speak out, Wolf sensed, an impression strengthened by their gasps at her next remark. "If you wish to find your wife, head out through the fields, instead."

"The fields?"

Helga smirked. "Is that not the route she usually takes when running away?"

Riana woke slowly, painfully, the world one huge pulsating blur. In her mind, she thought she heard someone call out her name, but she could hear little but the blood pounding in her veins.

Or was it out of her veins? She could taste its coppery tinge in her mouth, could feel its chill stickiness between her thighs.

Forcing her eyes open, she tried to focus on her surroundings, to remember who and where she was, but she could see little in the dreary gray of the rain. The strain of focusing proved too much, and as her eyes again closed, two facts registered. One was that she must get up, for the scent of her blood could draw predators, and the other was that it could already be too late.

As she drifted out of consciousness, she recognized the significance of the feral gray eyes surrounding her.

Wolves, wild and ravenous, waiting to pounce.

Gazing down the broken hillside at his wife, Wolf knew desperation. Shouting her name had earned no response; Riana continued to lie immobile. If she were not dead already, he knew, she soon would be from the damp and chill. They had no hope of dragging her back up the mud-soaked hill, but perhaps they could bring a boat to the bank below and retrieve her. He turned, barking orders to the search party he'd assembled.

"Sire, look," Tad shouted suddenly, pointing downward.

Wolf turned, his heart going to his throat as he noticed the pack of wolves lurking below, circling nearer to Riana. "Get the boat here quickly," he commanded, reaching for his sword. "I'll go down and stand guard."

"Sire?"

"Quickly, Tadrick. And bring the healer, Sela. My lady's life might depend on it."

Even as he spoke, he was already making his way down the hill, executing more a hurried, muddy slide than a controlled descent. He found benefit, though, in waving his arms to maintain balance—hearing his undignified approach, the wolves apparently assumed him to be a force of more than one. When he reached solid ground, there was no need to brandish his sword; the animals had already retreated into the bushes.

Dropping his sword, he rushed to kneel down beside Riana to inspect her injuries. He saw at once what drew the wolves. Even in all this mud, the stain of blood was unmistakable.

Frightened by Riana's deep pallor, he gathered her into his arms. She was so cold. He wished he had Cerdric's furs now to wrap her in, but all he had to offer was his own body warmth. Sitting there on the bank, praying Tad would hurry with the boat, he clung to Riana's life as if it were his own, glaring at the wolves as one by one, the pack slinked closer.

Wolf could protect himself, but to use his sword, left a few paces away, he must first lay Riana down in the mud, and that he was loath to do. The few moments she must spend in the chill and damp could drain off what little life remained in her. He hated feeling so helpless, so powerless, but still he held her, shielding his wife as the wolves crept closer. His deep growls and shooing motions scared them back temporarily, but the wolf was not a stupid creature. The pack would not be fended off by such tactics for long, not when he and Riana meant their evening's sustenance.

Indeed, the animals grew swiftly bolder, baring their teeth as if noticing that while this human might posture, he did not attack. Snarling threats, Wolf watched each animal keenly for signs of attack. Most remained wary, almost skittish, looking to their leader. Wolf eyed his sword, weighing his chances of reaching it. Where in the name of Thunor was Tad and that boat?

The boy's frenzied shouts could not have come at a more opportune moment, for the leader was poised and preparing to strike when Wolf called out in answer. Stiffening, the proud animal directed its gaze down river to where the longboat was fast approaching.

None too fast for Wolf. Rising with Riana in his arms, he shouted at the rescue party to hurry. He had to hope the pack again scattered, for he paid little heed to them, intent upon getting Riana to the healer as quickly as possible. Taking long strides along the bank, he shortened the distance between them and the boat, directing them to pull into shore. Sela, he noted with relief, was among them.

He waded into the stream, not waiting for them to dock before depositing his unmoving wife in the boat before the old woman.

Jumping in beside them, he ordered his men to row quickly back to the village.

"How bad is she?" he asked Sela once they were under way.

She frowned as she brought a vial to Riana's lips. "She's banged her head, and the chill could yet bring on the fever, but she's a strong one, and a fighter, and I'd say you reached her in time."

"Then she will live?" May the gods help him but he could not keep the relief from his voice.

"Aye, that *she* will. But I must warn," she added, frowning at the blood on Riana's legs. "We haven't a prayer of saving the baby."

Thirteen

Riana sat up slowly, dizziness and nausea threatening. Squinting, she found she was home, safe in her bed, with pale, filtered sunlight streaming through the windows to light the room. Had it been a dream, then, her fall from the cliff?

No. All too well, she could feel the dull, persistent ache in her belly.

"Look, she is waking," Greta said, rising from her chair beside the bed. "Is that not a good sign, Sela?"

"Fear not, she will survive." The old woman appeared on the other side of the bed, holding out a vial. "Here, drink this," she told Riana. "It will help restore you."

As much as Riana might recoil from the foul smelling potion, she'd seen the power of Sela's restoratives. Gulping it down, trying not to gag, she wondered how she had gotten from the river to this warm, snug room.

Looking up, she had her answer.

Wolf leaned against the far wall, watching her much as he had the first time she'd woken in this bed. He *had* come to save her, she thought gratefully, just as she'd known he would.

But even as the joy leapt to life in her heart, she noticed the tightness of his jaw, the stiffness of the arms crossed at his chest. She found neither love *nor* lust in the cold, silver depths of his eyes; the way he looked at her, he could as well be gazing at a stranger.

How drawn and haggard he seemed, his clothes stained with blood, the stubble of his beard growing in rough and dark. She wanted to go to him, to chide him to eat and sleep, but with a pang, she realized she'd forfeited that right by running away.

"Leave us," he said sharply to the other women. "I would speak to the Lady Moriana alone."

Moriana, he'd said. Not *Riana,* nor even, *my wife.* Over the bed, Sela and Greta exchanged worried glances.

"Be gentle with her," Greta said softly, moving over to him. "Hasn't she suffered enough?"

"Enough?" he asked, pushing off from the wall. "Has she suffered at all, lying in her big, comfortable bed?"

Unnerved by his bitter tone, Riana watched Greta reach out to lay a gentle hand on his arm. "You can at least talk to her, my brother. Act in anger and you will only turn her against you, as Exar did our mother."

Clearly, it was a poor choice of words, for he looked down at his sister with a fearsome scowl. "Talking accomplishes nothing. I tried it your way, Greta, but the moment my back was turned, she repaid my patience by running away. Go now, leave us. It is time my wife learned that she, too, must pay the consequences for her actions."

Watching Greta and Sela file out of the room, Riana longed to call out to them, to beg them to stay, but she held tight to her dignity, fearing it might be all that she had left.

From the way Wolf glared at her, it would seem Sela had found the right spell to lift the enchantment.

When they were alone, Wolf strode about the room, saying nothing, taking pains not to look at her. It hurt to think that such a short time ago, they'd lain together in this bed, making love and laughing at life together. Gone were the tender glances, the gentle moments. Without the enchantment, she realized painfully, it would be like this forever.

She wrapped her arms around her, trying to find warmth.

Wolf went to the table, lifting up the misshapen clay pot. No teasing jibes came from his taut lips now, nor did he laugh at the silly way the pot tilted. He merely fingered its many imperfections with a preoccupied frown.

"What I don't understand," he said suddenly, his voice as tight and controlled as the muscles of his jaw, "is why you would feel the need to creep off in the dead of night. Did I make your life so miserable, you would feel compelled to humiliate me in front of my people?"

Each word was like a slap. Her throat felt so tight, she could only shake her head in denial.

"That was what my mother claimed," he went on, as if her answer mattered little to him. "Cassandra maintained she had to run away because Exar did not return her devotion. Is that the excuse you would use, too?"

"Wolf, I—"

"I could have understood," he interrupted as if Riana hadn't spoken, "had Cassandra gone home to her family, but she lived out her days in the village of my father's sworn enemy, the Briton chief, Eckwid. The thought of my mother in that monster's hands drove Exar so mad with rage, he went raiding without sense or reason. Forty good warriors were lost in the attack, with my father himself mortally wounded. Though he did not die of his wounds right away, of course. He survived long enough to lose the king's favor, and with it, most of the tribe's riches."

Throat tightening, she watched him set the bowl down with deliberate care and move to the table, toying with the tiny sack in which she kept her walnuts. "In the end, Cassandra got her wish," he said in that same emotionless tone. "Exar destroyed himself trying to win her back, and in so doing, destroyed his village. Because of my mother's infidelity, we are now the poor, struggling settlement you scorn."

"I do not scorn River Ford."

He raised a brow. "No? How have you shown any more regard for this village than my mother did in running away?"

"You're not being fair. To me or your mother. Clearly Cassandra, too, had her reasons for leaving. Your father neglected her. He acted without logic or reason."

He spun, betraying his emotion only by the glint in his eyes. "Exar gave her his name and position. Her place was with her husband and children. What would you have the chieftain do when she abandoned us so callously? Sit by and mourn like a woman while his wife bedded another?"

"You speak as if he owned her," she said quietly, knowing she spoke of far more than Exar and Cassandra. "As if your mother were some slave he could hold against her wishes. You men would deny it, but we women have needs, too. Dreams, and destinies of our own."

"She, too, spoke of dreams and spells and other Druid nonsense. She, like you, used her magic as an excuse to avoid her duty to her husband."

"No man can possess another's heart and soul," she said fiercely. "Or direct them to his will."

He gazed into her eyes for a long moment, then turned away with a frown. "I do not tell this sordid tale so we can argue." He pushed away from the table, staring at her coldly. "My point is this. Cassandra did much damage to this tribe and never atoned for it. Ever since, the gods have directed the suffering onto my people. I cannot let that happen again, Riana. I will not allow this village to endure more hardship while the guilty goes unpunished."

The silence that stretched between them was far more painful than any bruise she'd suffered from her fall. She had to find some way to reach him, to make him understand. "If it means aught to you, I did not leave this village lightly. I went because I had to, Wolf. I was summoned."

He tensed, his gaze narrowing. "Indeed? I was told of no messenger."

"It's not as you think," she said, uneasy under his scrutiny. "I had a vision."

"A vision."

Impossible to ignore his contempt. "Yes, a vision," she said determinedly. "I saw an image, shimmering in the river pool. It was the Great Enchanter himself, Merlin, calling me to come to the aid of my king."

"This is your defense? You would tell my people you abandoned us for some image you saw in the water?"

"No one blames you for answering Cerdric's call," she countered. "Why can't you understand that I, too, have no choice? My king needs me as well."

"Tell me, just what did you think you could do for the great Arthur? Summon snakes for him?"

"I cannot know what I am meant to do," she answered evenly, though stung by that remark. "But I know that my Goddess called me to Camelot. Indeed, she even sent my escort. Or can you think it mere coincidence that British soldiers would come just then?"

"No, no coincidence." He tossed the sack to the table, anger glinting in the silver of his eyes. "Those soldiers came to raid the village, knowing our warriors had gone to Cerdric's council. Their motive could have been retaliation for Eckwid's death, or perhaps another attempt to stir unrest along the borders, but let me assure you, Riana, not once in their torching and looting did they mention your name."

"Torching and looting?" Shocked, Riana clutched the blanket as if it could give her warmth. She thought of the children she'd played with, the women from the fields, even Helga.

"The grand hall lies in ashes," he went on flatly, "most of the sheep are slaughtered, and Enoch is not expected to survive the clubbing he took to the head."

Not poor Enoch, Riana thought, horrified. "What of the defenses?" she asked Wolf. "Where were the archers?"

"You might better ask the whereabouts of the chieftain's wife. They looked for you to give the orders, to oversee the defenses. With you gone, the village never stood a chance."

But she'd left careful instructions. Enoch should have had ample time to sound the alarm, to gather the women to fight off the raiders . . .

Unless he had gotten into the ale.

"You don't know . . ." she began to protest, only to realize that it didn't matter. Wolf had left her to lead his village, not some old drunk, and in his eyes, she had betrayed his trust.

"I don't know *what?*" he asked bitterly. "That half my village lies in ashes? That my child is no more than a stain on the river-bank?"

"Child?" she asked, her fingers creeping unconsciously to touch her aching abdomen. An insidious cold crept through Riana, a far greater chill than any she'd suffered that night. So this was the reason for the dull aching, all that blood. "A baby?"

"It had just begun its life." He looked away, his voice tight with strain. "A sprouting seed displanted in the fall, but it could well have been the next chieftain."

"We could have had a daughter," she said distractedly, feeling a stinging in her eyes. Overwhelmed by the loss, she imagined her baby, a tiny precious life she would have guarded with her own. She, who had been abandoned by her parents, would have done all in her power to make certain her child was kept forever safe and sheltered and loved.

But her baby was gone, ripped from her before she could know of its existence, left to become—as Wolf put it—no more than a stain on the rocks.

She could not look at Wolf, knowing his pain, knowing he blamed her for it. More than all else, she ached for his warm, comforting arms, but that door was shut to her, and after this, she feared, it would remain closed forever.

He planted himself before the bed, legs akimbo, arms again folded at his chest. "The law is clear and must be followed," he said stiffly. "Even if I wished it, I cannot spare you."

Even if I wished it.

"The council will convene in the morning," he went on ruthlessly. "As chieftain, it is my duty to recommend that you be tied in the central square, and left there for three days and nights for the village to publicly scorn you."

"I am to be tied to some stake?" she gasped.

"You have broken the law, even as you've broken faith with my people. It is the least they will demand. Not even the chieftain's wife can escape the consequences of her actions."

No, that she could not. Until the day she died, she would be haunted by the specter of her unborn baby.

"I will leave you now to get your rest," he said flatly, "but I suggest you prepare yourself to face the council as soon as you are well."

"Wolf, wait." Though he paused at the door, he would not face her. "I wish . . . I meant . . ." She swallowed again, for her throat ached with strain. "For what it is worth, I am sorry."

For an instant, his shoulders sagged, but he did not turn around. Watching him walk off, numbed with pain as she cradled her empty womb, Riana knew that she would indeed suffer the consequences for her actions, and for a long time to come.

Wolf sat in the town square, his chair positioned on a platform, enabling him to look down upon the proceedings. To his right, a blaze had been lit, partly for light and partly to dispel the predawn chill, but the darkness suited his mood better. Let the others stand amidst the torches, displaying their anger and horror and grief over what had happened; Wolf would stay in the shadows, alone and isolated, giving nothing away of his inner torment.

Riana stood on the other side of the square, as far from him as possible, likewise displaying no emotion. Braided and coiled about her head, her golden hair appeared as lank and lifeless as Riana herself. Not moving, barely even blinking, she seemed lost in her own world as Helga leveled accusations against her before the council.

Wolf wondered at the older woman's fervor, finding it hard to accept her version of ruthless treachery. The Riana he knew might have run away, but she would never have crept off to arrange the British attack, or worse, encouraged their sole guard to drink himself into a stupor.

Nor was he alone in his doubts. When Helga provided witnesses who had seen his wife wandering off nightly to the woods, and others who had watched her that night deep in conversation with Enoch, some in the village stepped forward in Riana's defense. Sela, of course, but also Tadrick and Ranulf, and many of the women, all insisted Riana was incapable of such treason. The most vehement, and best received of these was his sister. In her soft, clear tones, Greta painted a nobler, kinder version of the chieftain's wife, reminding the village of all Riana had done for them, including acts of kindness Wolf himself had not known. By the time Greta was done speaking, the village was aligned in two separate factions, those behind Helga and those supporting his wife.

And through it all, Riana said nothing, did nothing, giving Wolf nowhere to go with his own tortured emotions. If she would fight, he could lash out in anger. If she cried, he could vent his grief. But Riana continued to stare off into space, seemingly untouched by the furor that went on around her.

What of our child? he wanted to cry out to her. For all appearances, she had forgotten their plans, their hopes for the future, or surely, she would be weeping at their loss. If she were not guilty, why then did she so studiously avoid his gaze? It seemed unnatural, her stillness, lending credence to Helga's claim that Riana was a cold and calculating traitor.

"Then perhaps we should take two votes," Helga said suddenly, holding up an arm to stop the arguments. "One to judge the crime of treason, the other for the act of desertion."

She looked to Wolf then to make the decision. Torn, he debated what to do. Part of him wanted to spare his wife, to draw her aside where they might talk and work through this tragedy together, but he was chieftain, and he knew he could not set such an example. Separating the two charges made sense, for they were two very different crimes, but he sensed Helga wanted to make sure that Riana would suffer punishment, one way or another. There was not a soul among them, Riana included, to dispute that she had indeed deserted the village the night in question.

Conscious of his people watching him, Wolf nodded, gesturing at Riana. "Take the prisoner away," he said evenly. "It is time to judge her on both crimes."

* * *

At dawn the next morning, Greta brushed Riana's long golden hair as they waited for the warriors to come for her. "I tried to make them see reason," Greta explained, trying to prepare her friend for the ordeal ahead, "but Helga kept stirring the council, insisting we must set an example. She said your suffering was the only thing that would help this village recover."

"It's all right," Riana said feebly. "It doesn't matter."

"Doesn't matter? Do you understand what will be done to you? In a few moments, you'll be led out to the square where you shall be tied like a cur to a stake, where every villager will be expected—nay, required—to toss insults and garbage at you. Everyone, Riana. Myself included."

Riana nodded, still seemingly untouched by her words. "You'll do what you must. Nor will I blame you. I know you tried hard to save me."

Greta heard the slight emphasis on the word, *you.* "You must not blame Wolf, either. His hands are tied. He is chieftain."

"He's no helpless pawn, if that's what you imply," Riana said softly. "Wolf knows what I will suffer with this punishment and he is glad of it."

"Riana, no," Greta protested, sick at heart. "This is tearing my brother in two. He loves you."

"Is it love to ignore that I lost that child, too? To set me aside as if I no longer existed?" Disturbing, how calm she sounded. "All Wolf feels for me is cold disdain. He won't be happy until he sees me humiliated."

As she finished speaking, the guards came to the door. Riana smiled faintly, stiffening her spine. "You've been a good friend," she said quietly to Greta as she was led from the room. "I will never forget it."

Watching her leave, head held high, Greta's unease merely deepened. Her words rang like a farewell, as if Riana didn't expect to see her again. Did she think she would die from the town's abuse, or more likely, did she plan to run off once more?

Riana must know Wolf would never allow it. It frightened Greta, how cold and unyielding he'd become, and in her own way, Riana could be no less so. What hope had love to flourish, when pride met implacable pride?

They had all better hope that Riana was indeed an enchantress, Greta thought unhappily. If they ever hoped to be happy, the two would need nothing short of magic.

Three nights later, Wolf stood in the gate tower, heartsore and weary, looking out over his village as it slept. Exar would insist that Wolf should feel pride and satisfaction—he'd found the guilty and seen justice served—so why instead did he feel empty and alone? And how, by all that made sense, could he still yearn for his wife?

Where had it all gone, the simple joy, those blissful days of light and laughter? Like a wondrous child, he'd reached out for the fey, fascinating creature that was Riana, only to have her slip through his hands, his hold on her no more substantial than the shimmering visions that called her to Camelot. He knew now how his father must have felt, faced with the hard knowledge that he'd been bewitched by a woman's smile.

Against his will, his gaze went to the stake in the town square. He winced at the sight of Riana, curled up like a child, knees drawn to her chest, head resting at an uncomfortable angle upon them. Four torches had been lit around her to keep her humiliation forever in the public eye, making her seem a sad, lonely figure. She must be exhausted, he thought, well aware of how throughout her punishment, she'd sat there unflinching, taking the insults and table scraps his people threw at her with a stiff, quiet dignity. Too, she must be shivering, for the nights had grown chill and she had naught but her ragged brown dress to shield her from the night.

He tried to tell himself that such hardship was no more than she deserved, that her heartless acts required retribution, but he found himself lifting up one of the furs Cerdric had granted as their wedding gift and making his way to the square.

She was sleeping when he came upon her, making soft little whimpers that tore at his heart. Sick inside, he peeled the offal from her once beautiful hair, knowing he went against tribal law—and his own good judgment—to do so. As he laid the fur over her frail shoulders, her lashes fluttered on her cheeks. "Wolf?" she called out drowsily.

Something twisted deep in his gut, for he could well remember the nights she'd called for him in her sleep. Each time, he'd gathered her close, calming her dreams as he sheltered her in his arms. It struck him, too forcefully, how he missed having this woman sharing his bed. His life.

She will destroy you, logic insisted, yet he leaned down to brush a hand against her cheek. "Hush, the dream has fled," he crooned softly, tucking the fur around her chin.

She nestled into his touch, calming at once, her simple act of trust tugging at his heartstrings. More than all else, he longed to gather her up in his arms and make the nightmare go away for them both, yet he knew they must first resolve the past before they could have any hope for the future.

Sighing heavily, he pulled away.

She opened her eyes then, staring up at him blankly, until a slow smile came to her lips. "Wolf," she repeated quietly. "You have come."

Hope blossomed in her gaze, and a softness he had difficulty resisting. Moving back, forcing himself to concentrate on the burnt structures around them, he held tight to the memory of what could happen when he lost his head to his emotions. Wolf, the man, could let himself fall under this female's spell, but the chieftain must look out for the needs of his people.

He watched the light go out of her eyes, her body sag against the stake. "Why *are* you here?" she asked, her tone as dull as her expression.

Wolf wished now that he hadn't come at all. "It is soon morning," he said wearily. "The first part of your punishment is nearly done—"

"The *first* part?"

He looked away, steeling himself against her. "A storage hut outside the gates has been made ready for you. Sela shall take you to it, and there you shall stay, shunned by the rest of the village, until your period of atonement is done."

"I see. And this period, how long is it to be?"

"Until the council feels you are ready to take your place among us again."

"How smug and complacent you sound." Despite the words, there was no bitterness in her tone, no emotion at all. "In truth, Wolf, the council has nothing to do with it, do they? We both know that ultimately, it is you who will decide my fate."

He eyed her, wondering where she meant to go with this. Leaning back up against the stake, staring off into space, she seemed suddenly a stranger to him.

"It's the child, isn't it?" she asked in that same, flat manner. "That is what you cannot forgive. I will not be released from my isolation until I provide an heir."

Stunned that she could speak so calmly of the death of their baby, he spoke without first weighing his words. "One babe can scarce be enough. Considering your lack of regard for their well-being and safety, I would think several healthy children would be the least I should require."

He had the satisfaction of seeing her flinch, but like a warrior poking through the rubble in the aftermath of battle for some trophy of triumph, she probed deeper into his wound. "Don't you mean several healthy *male* children? Admit it, it's the loss of your heir that concerns you."

He clenched his fists, holding his anger inside him. Not for the world would he admit the depths of his pain. "You will do your duty to this tribe, Riana," he said sternly. "If I must beat you into submission, you will act the part of the chieftain's wife."

She looked up at him, her golden eyes dull and lifeless. "Do you truly think it that easy? You cannot mold me into the image you want your wife to be. You must leave me to be who I truly am, or I shall only shrivel and die inside."

She would tell *him* what he must or must not do? "You doom us, Riana. Until you can make these concessions, we can never live peaceably as man and woman."

"Then let me go, Wolf. You cannot want me, so leave me to make my own way."

"To Camelot?" he asked bitterly. "I pity you, if this is how you mean to go on, for life does not treat kindly those who would live in dreams. Life is hard work and dedication, not some shimmering illusion in a pool."

"Magic exists, Wolf, whether you choose to believe in it or not, and one day, I will prove it to you."

He could see the flame in her eyes now and it enraged him. How could she care more about her dangerous witchery than the loss of their child? Was she so blind, so selfish, she could not see the grief her dabbling in magic had caused?

"We are joined, you and I," he said coldly, "and whatever else we might wish, the bond can never be broken. You will stay in your hut, isolated but well guarded, until you either die, or accept the life the gods have given you."

He could hear her sigh, heavy and sad, and she laid her head back against the stake.

He stared at her, losing the will to argue. "The old woman will come for you in the morning," he told her bleakly, turning to walk away. "How we go on from there is now in your hands."

For Riana, waiting through the predawn hours for Sela, it mattered little if she were tied to a stake or taken to a distant hut. Wherever she went, she knew, she'd remain locked in her pain.

She winced as she thought of her joy when she'd first seen Wolf. In the haze of sleep, she'd forgotten his cold stares as his people condemned her, how he'd not ceased his vigil, watching from above as the village abused her, loath to miss even an instant of her humiliation. For a brief wonderful moment, she had felt his love and thought he'd at long last come to set her free.

But then she had woken to the harsh glare of reality.

One good glance and she'd known that he hadn't forgiven her, that he most likely could not until his children filled his halls with joy and laughter. *"How we go on is in your hands,"* he'd said, making it sound as if she could yet earn her way back into his good graces by giving up her dreams and bearing him children.

And oh, how tempted she was to abandon everything, even her calling, just to hold their newborn baby in her arms. Hearing it cry, watching it suckle at her breasts—then, and only then, could she could fill up this emptiness yawning inside her.

Sela came as the sun was rising over the distant fields, looking older and more haggard than Riana had remembered. Walking to the hut in pained silence, sensing the old woman's heartache, it struck Riana that she was not alone in her suffering. The situation reminded her of something the woman once told her. By running away, Riana had indeed tossed a stone into the water, causing ripple upon ripple of grief.

Reaching the hut in which she would be exiled, she noticed Yarrick scowling at the door. Was the choice deliberate? she wondered. Wolf knew Yarrick sided with Helga and had done his best to make her life miserable, those early days planting in the fields.

Sela ushered her into the tiny one room of the hut. "I found flowers and yon coverlet in an attempt to brighten such mean accommodations," she said, "but I fear there was nothing I could do for the chill and damp."

Riana could detect the odor of mildew, could see it growing on the stone-slab table that formed the focus of the room. A bed of straw in the corner had been covered with the plain blue coverlet Sela mentioned, but aside for two simple wooden chairs at the table, no other furnishings littered the room. There was not even a hearth, she noticed with dismay.

"Your meals will be brought to you," Sela explained, "but should you need to heat them, you must build your fire outside."

"It has been so long," she said, feeling overwhelmed. "I might need your help in getting the fire started."

Sela shook her head slowly. "Alas, but you must realize, child, that I cannot come visit you. Forgive me, but I, too, am bound by tribal law."

Riana sat slowly in one of the chairs. "Wolf, then," she said distractedly. "He will visit often, I am sure. He is so anxious for me to bear him his heir."

The silence that ensued was not the companionable sort, shared between friends. It seemed rife with meaning as it hovered there between them. "What is it?" Riana asked, her gaze pinned to the old woman. "Is even the chieftain forbidden to visit?"

Sela refused to look at her. "There will be no heir," she said quietly. "The fever set in before I could treat you. The damage had been done and your womb will never recover. You are now barren, I fear."

Barren. The word rang between them, stark and ugly. Riana had a sudden urge to run from the hut screaming.

But in truth, where could she go? She could not run fast or far enough away to escape the cruelty of this sentence. Gingerly touching her abdomen, she knew she would now always feel an aching there. She would always be alone.

"Does Wolf know? she asked, not recognizing the strained voice as her own.

"Not yet. The telling, I thought, should be your decision."

Riana shook her head vehemently. "Me, tell him such awful news? Now that you've unwoven the enchantment, he can scarce bear to look at me." Caught up in her misery, she ignored the strange glance Sela gave her. "Don't you see?" she cried out, rising from the chair to pace the room. "I will find no more sympathy from him, or understanding for my grief, than I have already. He'll merely sneer and say that I have brought such anguish upon myself."

"And haven't you?"

She whirled to face Sela, unable to believe the woman had said such a thing to her. "Are you saying I deserve this? To live out my days as an outcast from the village, useless and barren? And all because I answered the call from the Goddess?"

Sela shook her head sadly. "Child, how can you still cling to such a belief after all that has happened? Surely, if the Goddess wanted you leaving River Ford, she would not have brought that cliff down around you."

If so, it seemed a cruel stroke to then take away her ability to bear children. Why keep her in a place where she could only be reviled? A wife who could not conceive an heir was of no use to Wolf, or his village. Once Wolf learned the truth, he would cast her off, setting her loose in a world that cared even less about her.

No, she'd rather believe that the Goddess, knowing Riana's resolve would weaken, had removed the one obstacle in the way of her answering her calling. She was never meant to be with Wolf, to bear his children. The love they'd shared had been but an illusion, lasting only long enough to trick her into hoping this time it would be different, that at long last she'd found someone who would never desert her. Their time together had been a grand dream, but one she must now abandon. All she would ever truly have, her one remaining constant, was her duty to her king.

From the start, she'd been destined to go to Arthur.

A numbing cold curled into her, infecting her. She had to leave this place, as soon as she could arrange it. If Wolf had been angry before, if she'd felt deserted and shunned by his people, how worse it would be once they all learned the truth. She would spend her dying days in isolation, feeling more reviled and abandoned than she had ever felt as a child.

She could not suffer such a life. She would not be a drain on the village resources, on her husband. In truth, her only use in life now was as an enchantress. Arthur's enchantress, in Camelot.

"Come child," Sela said, putting her arm around her. "Let us get you cleaned so you can rest."

She shook off Sela's arm. "No, from now on, I shall take care of myself."

She steeled herself against the hurt she saw on the old woman's face, but to survive, she must learn to rely on no one but herself.

Ordering Sela from the hut, Riana welcomed the chill, letting it stiffen her resolve. Already distancing herself from this place and its people, she began making her plans to escape.

Fourteen

Greta carried the cup of steaming broth to the cot where Sela rested fitfully. In the weeks since Riana's exile, Sela's health had deteriorated. To Greta, it seemed that the old woman was suffering from a broken heart.

"Let me speak with Riana," Greta again begged as she sat beside the cot to offer the broth. "She should know you're unwell. Then maybe she won't be so angry with you."

"You cannot dissuade her." Sela waved the broth away with a feeble hand, sighing as if both the sentiment and the physical effort had cost her. "She's a stubborn one, that girl. Perhaps it is why the Goddess chose her."

Greta sat back on her heels, putting the broth to the side. "Then you believe her? You think Riana truly has been called to Camelot?"

"It is well known that the work of our Goddess is not always apparent and often mysterious. I ask you, what could be more mystifying than sending someone like Riana to do her bidding?"

Greta smiled, glad to see the woman had not lost her wit, along with her strength. "But I'm confused. I thought you believed the Goddess wanted her here at River Ford."

Closing her eyes, Sela spoke softly. "Last night, I had a dream that changed all that. It might even have been a vision."

Unnerved by the woman's shudder, Greta leaned closer. "What is it? What did you see?"

"The past, trying to repeat itself." Opening her eyes, Sela

stared at Greta, her expression as solemn as her voice. "Listen, my child, to what I should have told you at the start. Though born in a Druid college, I was taken by the Romans at a young age. As their slave, I served a gentle, loving girl much like you, Greta, with a zest for life and knowledge her ignorant father could not tamp down. Indeed, it was while we were out on the plains, exploring the mysteries of the ancient stones, that she and I were captured by a band of Saxons. Later, we were separated—I being bartered to Camelot while she stayed on in the enemy camp—but I was here at your birth, Greta. I took you myself from Cassandra's womb."

"You served my mother?" Greta felt less astonishment than a sense of rightness. It was why she'd always felt drawn to Sela. "Wolf knew, didn't he? That's why he allowed you so many liberties?"

Sela reached out to stroke Greta's hair. "Yes, he knew, but since I, too, was kept at the villa and the villagers had no reason to remember me, he preferred not to mention my connection to your mother. He feared it would merely stir up bad feelings and old troubles."

"But how strange, your coming back here."

"Yes," Sela said with a faint smile. "The night your brother captured her, Riana was conjuring a spell and inadvertently bound Wolf to her in a love enchantment. She would have me dissolve that spell but I've come to believe that Wolf is part of some grand plan. Some might say that his god, Wyrd, is using us all like threads to weave his intricate destiny."

"You would have us keep my brother trapped in this spell?"

Sela sat up, reaching for Greta's hand. "We must. In my dream last night, I saw the day when Riana will again try to escape. This time, we must do nothing to stop her."

"But Sela—"

"Hush, there is more." She spoke in strange, compelling tones. "When Riana leaves, you must go with her."

Silence blanketed the room. What Sela asked—nay, demanded—would cost Greta dearly. Her village's respect, her brother's admiration, her home.

"It's a stiff burden to place upon your shoulders, I know." Sela sighed as she released her hand. "I would go myself but what use would I be to Riana, weak as I am and she not speaking to me?"

"Why must anyone go?" Greta pleaded. In her mind, she could see Wolf, his features harsh and unforgiving as he accused her of betrayal. "If your Goddess has called her, surely she will look after Riana herself."

"My child, it is not for me to divine the will of the Goddess, but I do perceive a great peril awaiting Riana. An evil I can sense, yet not quite identify. I know only that there was reason for her to be sent from Camelot. There are those who would see her as a threat."

Greta had the sensation that she was swimming in deep, turbulent waters. "Shouldn't you warn Riana of this? Perhaps she will be less eager to go, knowing the dangers she will face."

Sela shook her head sadly. "I have tried, but you know Riana. She needs to believe she's loved and wanted at Arthur's court, that she will be welcomed with loving arms. She'd be devastated to learn her own mother sent her away."

"But I thought no one knew her mother's identity."

"Nor can they." Clearly distressed, Sela again gripped her hand. "I gave my blood oath never to speak of these matters, nor must you. More is at stake here than either you or she can imagine."

These were turbulent waters, indeed.

Breathing heavily, plainly spent, Sela put her remaining energy into her grip. "Will you do it, child? Will you act out your part in Wyrd's grand scheme and accompany Riana to Camelot?"

Greta nodded solemnly, knowing she agreed to far more than a casual journey. She'd be diving into that churning, perilous sea she'd imagined—she who could not swim a stroke.

"Good," the old woman said on a sigh, falling back on the cushions. "We must begin planning at once. We haven't a moment to lose."

* * *

"There was another raid last night," Tad said between mouthfuls of the thin mutton stew. "But this time, the village was waiting and we were able to snare a prisoner. British dog," he sneered. "It took but five lashes with the whip for him to be singing his tales of treachery."

"Was it the same raiding party that burned the village?" Riana felt no real interest in such matters; she merely wanted to keep the boy talking while she watched him. His eyes were often larger than his stomach, she'd learned in the few weeks she'd been stranded in this hut, and when Tad was over-sated, he had a tendency to grow drowsy and reluctant to move.

Nodding, he took the refill she offered, smiling thinly as he gulped down his food. She found it endearing, how he tried to keep her apprised of the village's doings, but she'd trained herself to remain immune to softer feelings. She must care for nothing but her own escape.

"The raiders were led by Batar, son of Eckwid," Tad explained, reaching for a chunk of hard bread. "Would that I could be with Penawulf now as he rides out with his army to patrol our borders. Glory will come to the warriors who avenge our village, but am I to be given that chance? No, I am left here alone to guard the chieftain's wife."

Riana hardened her heart to his plight, pleased to learn that he was indeed, alone. Tonight was it, the opportunity she'd been waiting for, and she must seize it before Wolf and his warriors returned.

Forcing herself to walk slowly so as not to alert the boy to her urgency, she crossed to her cupboard to lift out the sweetbread Greta had baked for her, a treat she'd been saving for just such an occasion. She set it before Tad, gratified by how his eyes widened appreciatively. Needing no encouragement, he was gobbling up his dessert before she could sit opposite him at the table.

Smiling sweetly, she began to talk of inconsequentials, gradually toning her voice to a quiet, dreamy quality. She knew the ever polite Tad would never interrupt, so she spoke nonstop about her tedious daily routine and the less interesting details of her childhood at Camelot, while the boy finished off the sweetbread.

Watching his gaze drift, his posture slumping in the chair, she waited patiently. Part of her hated tricking the boy thus, but the fates had given her little choice. To answer her summons, she had to escape, and poor, trusting Tad stood in her way.

She continued with her monologue as his eyelids drooped, even after his arms fell to his sides and his head sagged on his shoulder. As it lolled, then settled on his chest, she painstakingly rose from her chair. Her destination was the bed, under which lay the bundle Helga had foolishly left behind earlier today.

Riana frowned as she thought of the hateful woman's visit. How smugly Helga had stood in the doorway, her gaze poking and prying into every nook and corner, clearing hoping to ferret out yet another crime with which to charge Riana. Without invitation, she'd stepped into the room as if she owned it, setting the bundle she carried on the floor by the table as she paced imperiously before Riana.

She had come to inform the prisoner that in the chieftain's absence, she had delegated herself as Riana's warden. It was time, she announced, for the pampering to come to an end, for the prisoner to be punished as she deserved. Starting tomorrow, Riana would work from dawn to dusk as a slave, performing whatever menial task was put before her. Kicking the bundle on the floor, Helga had smiled, saying these were the shackles she'd wear as she worked, a badge of her guilt and shame.

The smile had turned vicious as Helga stepped up to Riana to grab her hair. Enjoy these golden tresses, she'd warned, for come morning, they would be shorn. Indeed, bit by bit, she meant to strip away every part of their prisoner's pride until the Briton begged to be one of them.

When Riana had protested, insisting that the chieftain would have her head for this, Helga had merely sneered. Did she truly believe this would earn Penawulf's disapproval? The man cared naught what happened to his wayward wife; indeed, he'd come to rue their union and would be happy to be relieved of it.

Satisfied by Riana's tight, pale features, the awful female had strode from the room, forgetting, in her complacency, that she'd left her bundle on the floor.

But Riana had not. Staring at those iron cuffs and chains, she'd known how she could put them to use. She would not act as Helga's slave while Wolf looked on, unaffected. Now, while she still could, she would make her escape.

Slowly, keeping her voice even, she continued her prattle as she carried the heavy bundle to Tad's chair. She had a nasty moment, hearing the metal clank as she lifted the shackles from the sack, but Tad slept on, oblivious. Refusing to look upon his young, vulnerable face, she slipped the chain around the legs of the stone slab table, then slowly, painstakingly, slipped it around Tad's waist. He stirred slightly, but she kept on in her singsong tone until she clapped the cuffs around his wrists.

He woke then, gazing at her first with confusion, then dawning dismay. Backing away as he struggled against the chain, she went for the weapons he'd stowed just outside the door. When she returned, Tad had subsided, and now gazed at her with a wounded expression.

Setting his short, flat sword and simple ash bow beside her meager sack of belongings, she crossed the room to fetch and don her cloak. His eyes followed her, more bewildered than accusing, as if he could not believe her capable of such a thing.

She would not respond to his hurt—she must not. Circumstance, not any conscious desire on her part, had led her to this.

Still, she could not bring herself to leave him without explanation. "I'm sorry," she said as she gathered up the small pile of treasures she kept by her bed. "I would not have done this to you, Tad, had there been any other way, but my husband has left me no choice. I need to take your weapons if I am to survive, but I will leave behind your mother's necklace." Trying not to wince, she set his gift before him on the table.

"My lady—"

"No, Tad, I am not your lady. Nor am I Wolf's. I am an enchantress, called forth by forces of magic, and my place is at Camelot."

The boy shook his head stubbornly. "You belong here, in this village, and you shall always be my lady to me."

Riana paused, hands tightening on the bag of walnuts she held in her hands. Swamped by a wave of longing, she nearly faltered, but she summoned the more painful memories—Wolf's anger, Helga's plans for her, the loss of her sweet, innocent babe.

"Do not go, Lady Riana," Tad pleaded. "Wait at least to speak to the chieftain. You cannot leave him without word again."

Stiffening, Riana tied the bag to the rope belt at her waist. "Very well, I'll leave word then," she told him quietly as she reached for the quiver of arrows and flung them over her shoulder. "Deliver these words to your chief. Tell him that he has to understand that my duty is every bit as commanding as his, that I must go to Camelot to serve my king. Tell him I must . . ." Again, she faltered, "I must go home."

"Then I know you will return to us," Tad said stubbornly, looking her straight in the eye. "Like it or not, my lady, your home is now River Ford."

"Farewell," she told him, fearing the tenderness erupting inside her. "I hope this doesn't land you in too much trouble."

He flashed a reluctant grin. "My mother always said my stomach would be my undoing." Sobering, he eyed the pile at her feet. "Take care and be wary, Lady Riana. I shall miss you. We all shall."

Riana nodded, unable to speak. She must not let herself feel, or give way to tears. Straightening her shoulders, she picked up the weapons, and shifting the bag of her belongings to her other shoulder, left the hut.

Outside, she turned at once for the stream, for she meant to follow its banks all the way until she found Wolf's boat. This time, she must not lose her way and fall down a cliff. There was no rain tonight, but the bite of autumn chilled the air, and the wealth of clouds stealing toward the moon warned that the current dry spell could be of short duration.

But then, no one ever said it would be an easy journey.

A heavy weight seem to press on her chest as she headed toward the stream, as if her heart sensed that she could never truly escape this village. In leaving River Ford, she would feel less free than ever, for she would go carrying the burden of a thousand warm memories.

She touched the bag of walnuts at her waist, the sole reminder of her stay here, her last remaining link with Wolf. She should toss it, make a clean break and start afresh, yet each time she told her hands to untie the bag from her belt, her heart made a hundred excuses. Her fingers were stiff and frozen on this dreary autumn evening, she had no time to waste with something she could as easily accomplish later, she might need the bag for something else . . .

"Riana, wait!"

At the voice behind her, she whirled, raising the sword. "Are you mad, coming up upon me like that?" she cried, recognizing Greta. "You startled me so, I could have killed you."

Greta laughed weakly. "I must grow accustomed to such dangers, I suppose, if I'm to accompany you on your quest." She held up her own sack. "I'll wager you forgot to pack food."

Riana uttered an oath. "What of it? I've a bow with arrows aplenty, and this blade, as well. Why be weighted down with supplies when I can always catch my meal as I go?" Sliding the sword in its scabbard, she turned her back on Greta and continued on her way.

"Ah, but you need not worry about meals at all if I go with you." Stubbornly, Greta trailed behind her. "I have ample supplies and my cooking is superior to your own. Be truthful, Riana. You can't tell me you won't be glad of the company, with the days growing shorter and the threat of winter coming on. See, I brought furs, to cover us as we sleep."

How typical, that the girl had thought this out better than she.

Yet how could that be, when Riana had told no one of her plans? She halted and her unwanted tagalong nearly ran into her back.

"Why do you stop, Riana? Shouldn't we hurry?"

"How it is you come to be here waiting, prepared for flight," she said, turning to face Greta. "How could you anticipate I would choose this night to escape?"

"Sela told me."

"Sela!" Throwing up her hands in disgust, Riana marched off.

"Riana, wait." Greta again scrambled along behind her. "You don't understand. She too had a vision."

Riana shivered, though her chill had nothing to do with the evening air. "I want no more of her interference. Hasn't she meddled enough in my life as it is?"

"Sela's a wise woman, who can see things the rest of us don't." Greta's voice held a certain breathlessness, no doubt from trying to keep up with Riana's determined pace. "She had a deeper reason for keeping you here, Riana. She knows more than you what awaits at Camelot."

The chill had crept under Riana's skin. She tried to deny she felt fear, telling herself this warning was but another of Sela's ploys to keep her buried in this isolated village, but nevertheless, she drew her cloak tighter about her. "And so she would send a girl no stronger, older or wiser than I to accompany me on this perilous journey? If Sela is so worried, why does she not come with me instead?"

"In her vision, the Goddess charged me with the task. Someone must remain behind to care for the people of River Ford. To watch over Wolf."

Hearing the girl's voice break on that last, Riana saw what this journey would cost her friend. "Ah Greta, if you come with me now, you can never go home. You will be no more immune to tribal law than I and those you love will revile you as a pariah. Can you bear to have even your brother shun you?"

Her shudder proved that Greta was well aware of the seriousness of her decision, but she did not falter. "Fate has made us sisters. Your battles are my battles."

Feeling a tightness in her throat, Riana remembered this girl facing the council, speaking out in her defense. *Sisters.* Odd, how the notion warmed her. "You are quite insane, you know," she said, shaking her head. "And outrageously persistent."

Greta grinned. "I would say that makes two of us."

Riana didn't want to grin back, but she found it an uplifting sensation, the knowledge that she need not be alone. "Very well," she said, trying to remain stern and focused. "I have one stipulation. If you accompany me, you must never again speak of River Ford, or of anyone in this village."

"But—"

Riana held up a hand to stop her. "This is my rule. Swear to obey it, or we will not take another step together."

"You are wrong about this, Riana. You need to talk about what happened. Else how can you learn to forget and forgive?"

"And why would I forgive? So they can again reject and abandon me?" Embarrassed by her outburst, she spoke quickly. "I mean it, Greta. From this moment on, swear that we will not again speak of this place."

"Very well, but I must wonder what we will talk about then. This looks to be a long and difficult journey."

"I suggest we begin it at once." Riana now allowed herself to smile, partly because of Greta's half-hearted compliance, but primarily because they'd at last come upon the boat. "Here," she said, nodding at the craft as she hitched her skirt up and tucked the hem in her belt. "You can stow your things in the front."

"But this belongs to Wolf—" Greta broke off, biting her lip. "I suppose it doesn't truly matter at this point, but Riana, do you know anything about navigating these rivers?"

Riana refused to be daunted. "I can learn."

"So I'm to dive into turbulent waters, indeed."

"I beg your pardon?"

"Never mind." Sighing, Greta cast a fearful glance back the way they had come, as if seeking a last glimpse of the village where she had lived her entire life.

Watching her, Riana was struck again by what this journey would cost Greta. "You don't really have to leave with me," she said softly. "No one will think any less of you if you stay here where you belong."

Visibly shaking herself, Greta hurled her bundle into the boat and then climbed in behind it. "Let's go. If we wait much longer, my br . . . I mean, the warriors will return and start breathing down our necks."

Riana could not stop the sigh of relief. She'd never admit it, but she hadn't relished the prospect of making this journey alone. Pushing the boat from the bank, she scrambled in beside Greta, wet skirts and all. "Here we go then," she said brightly, reaching for the oars. "Next stop, Camelot."

Wolf strode into the king's tent, annoyed to find Vangarth perched at Cerdric's side. From the man's smirk, it would seem Vangarth was behind this summons, no doubt a chastisement for retaliating against Batar's raid without royal permission. Not for the first time, Wolf wondered how his nemesis seemed always to know his actions even as he committed them.

As was his manner, Cerdric wasted no time with chatter. "My sources tell me that you have slain the British chieftain, Batar. This disappoints me greatly, Penawulf, for I'd hoped you would not show your father's rash and uncontrollable thirst for vengeance."

"My actions had naught to do with Exar and Cassandra," Wolf said tightly, his gaze never leaving Vangarth. "It would seem *your sources* failed to inform you that Batar and his men raided my village while I and my warriors were attending your council, razing half the structures and taking the life of the sole male left behind."

Cerdric looked instantly to Vangarth, whose shrug proved that he was indeed the source of the information. "Interesting," Vangarth said in his unctuous tone, "but still, we must wonder how you could feel justified in taking the law into your own

hands. You could have done your king the courtesy of informing him of your plans. You have jeopardized our uneasy truce
with the Britons by killing first your mother's lover, and now
his son."

"Eckwid was slain by royal decree," Wolf said calmly, refusing
to let Vangarth goad him. "In vengeance for his attack on the
king's stronghold. As for Batar, I did not seek royal permission
since he was still on River Ford land and it is my right to execute
justice within my borders. Still, I did send word to the king of
my intent. I, more than anyone, understand the need to keep good
relations with Camelot."

"I received no such message."

Wolf turned his attention to the king. "No, sire, you did not.
I was on my way to visit you, even before your summons, after
finding my unfortunate messenger left on the road for the scav-
engers, his throat slit."

"How convenient," Vangarth drawled quietly.

"Convenient?" Wolf asked, outraged. "The man had a wife
and seven children. I doubt they would share your view."

"Come, Penawulf. Even you must see how his death makes it
now impossible to disprove your claim."

"Do you call me a liar?" Wolf's hand went to the sword at his
waist.

"Enough!" Cerdric rose to his feet, his eyes glittering in the
lamp light. "The last thing I need now is my warriors squabbling.
Vangarth, leave us. I would talk to Penawulf alone."

"But sire—"

"Go. You and I will talk later."

Vangarth looked from Cerdric to Wolf, his resentment plain.
Turning on a heel, he quit the tent, his dark looks presaging
further trouble.

"It was never my intent to undermine your authority," Wolf
told the king stiffly when Vangarth was gone.

Cerdric nodded, clasping Wolf's shoulder with a worried
frown. "Forgive me for doubting you, but I have much weighing

upon my mind. I should have known Batar would attempt to avenge his father's death."

"Forgive me, sire, but I disagree. Batar had no love for Eckwid. Had we not slain his father, he'd have done so himself eventually. Besides, if revenge were his motive, he'd have come after me and my warriors, not innocent women and children."

"Good point. Nor was it his first act of cowardice. Batar and several other lesser chieftains have been raiding our borders for some time, seeking the weaker villages."

"You think it part of some larger plan?"

Squeezing his shoulder, Cerdric left him to pour them both a flagon of ale. "What I think is of no import. I must *know* what these Britons mean to do. I cannot make ungrounded charges, but neither can I sit idly by while they pick away at my kingdom bit by vulnerable bit."

Taking the flagon from his king's hand, Wolf sensed that Cerdric was leading to something. He did not wait long to find out what it was.

"These chieftains would not act in defiance of the treaty without approval from those who hold greater power. They are mere puppets, Penawulf, and I would know who is pulling their strings."

"Camelot?"

Cerdric's gaze hardened. "Over the years, I have found much to respect in their king, but if Arthur is behind this threat to my people, I must act accordingly. I need you to go to Camelot, Penawulf. I must rely on you to gather the information I need."

A spy? Wolf recoiled, uncomfortable with the role. He was a warrior, a man of bold and honest strokes and the thought of hiding and lying, abusing the trust of others, made him feel unclean. "I am pledged to your service, sire, but I can't see where I can help. Despite our current peace, Camelot is not known to welcome Saxons within their midst."

"Yes, but you are wed to one of them. Your wife, I am told, was once well favored by Arthur and his queen. They would not deny her entry, nor her husband were he with her." Draining his ale, Cerdric slammed the flagon down on the table. "Do you think I don't understand how distasteful this is? Drastic times call for drastic measures, Penawulf. I must turn to you for help. I can turn nowhere else."

Put like that, Wolf had no choice and he knew it.

Finishing his ale, making hasty plans with Cerdric, he quit the tent with a troubled spirit. He told himself he must forget the dishonesty of the role he must play—the cause was just and in truth, that was what mattered.

And selfishly enough, he saw how this mission could work to his personal advantage. By being forced to take Riana away from his village, he would gain time to talk to her, reason with her, perhaps even come to an understanding. Nor did it escape his notice how pleased she'd be that he was at long last taking her to Camelot.

Despairing that she would ever reach Arthur's kingdom, Riana sat in the boat opposite Greta several days later, bouncing along the river to nowhere. With both tempers frayed and unraveling, the two girls had begun to hurl accusations.

"What do you mean we are lost?" Greta asked, incredulous. "You can't cook, you can't row, but I'd think you could at least know where we were going."

Stung, even though she'd been castigating herself for this, Riana snapped back. "I don't see you taking a hand with the oars. You sit there shouting orders and whining complaints, but I'm the one with sore shoulders."

"And I'm to blame? You insisted upon setting off on an insane quest in a vehicle you cannot master. What of your claims to be such a great enchantress? Why not just chant some spell and let magic steer the blasted boat?"

"You do the conjuring," Riana said angrily. "I'm not the one who received training from Sela." She did not like how much it hurt that after all the years of begging for lessons, the old woman would turn around and teach Greta instead. "Surely you learned something worthwhile."

"I thought we were not supposed to speak of her." Greta thrust out her chin, a gesture Riana had begun to despise. "But then, as I've learned, you are fond of changing the rules to suit yourself as we go along."

"If I truly wanted to suit myself, I would have told you no at the start. I rue the day I ever said you could accompany me."

"Moriana, the magnanimous. Everything must be your way, or no way. I swear . . ." She stopped midcomplaint, no doubt seeing the sudden pallor on Riana's face. "What is it? What's wrong?"

"The current is increasing." Riana tightened her grip on the oars lest the force of the water wrench them from her hands. "I'm finding it harder and harder to steer."

Greta turned in the boat, peering ahead. "The river forks up ahead. You should steer to the right, for the left fork is quite narrow and appears to be littered with stones and fallen limbs."

In an attempt to control their direction, Riana stuck an oar deep in the water. The craft veered right, striking a submerged rock, jolting the oar from her grasp. "Greta, quick!" she cried out. "Catch the paddle."

But it was too late. They watched it go bouncing down the river without them. They also watched the boat being pulled toward the fork to the left.

Stabbing the remaining oar in the water, then paddling frantically with it on both sides of the boat, Riana worked to battle the current, but her arms, weakened from all her rowing, proved her efforts too feeble and late. Paddle though she might, they were sucked into the narrow opening.

Bouncing and slipping through river debris, Riana prayed aloud for a miracle. Silently, she blessed Wolf for building the craft so sturdily, for its hull held firm as they scraped against limbs and rocks littering the riverbed. Indeed, she'd even begun to think her prayers would be answered, that they might yet brush through this unscathed, when they hit a log hiding beneath the water.

Unprepared for the collision, Riana watched both Greta and their bag of supplies be jolted upward. She grabbed for the girl, managing to keep her in the vessel, but she was not as quick in saving their food and dry clothing. Nor, in the terror of the moment, had she given thought to their sole remaining oar.

It was not until they burst out of the narrow section and were floating through calmer water that she had time to consider what the loss of the items might mean. Glancing about, she noticed it was quite some distance to either bank, a distance that widened with every moment they were pulled inexorably along. She dipped her hands in the river, her instincts screaming that they must set ashore at once, but the water was even colder here and she soon had to stop paddling.

Not that she'd accomplished much, she thought as she brought her hands to her mouth to blow warmth back into them. Smelling the briny scent, she recognized why the river was so rapidly widening, why the current proved too strong for her puny efforts. "By the Goddess," she cried out to her companion. "We're being pulled out to sea!"

Greta gazed at her with wide, frightened eyes. "Is this the work of your Goddess? Will she now punish me for the awful things I said to you?"

"Then I would think she'd be punishing us both."

Greta gave her a feeble smile. "Oh Riana, I didn't mean any of it. I was tired and worried and feeling resentful."

"I know. So was I."

Greta looked ahead at the widening expanse of water. "We didn't need to reach Camelot to find grave peril, did we?"

"We'll be all right," Riana hastened to assure her, though she felt far from reassured herself. "The Goddess shall watch over us."

"But the sea, Riana. I never told you, for I feared you'd send me back, but I cannot swim a stroke."

Riana tried not to gulp, knowing this was no time to give way to fear. "Do not fret," she told Greta, forcing her voice to remain calm. "I can swim for us both."

Greta eyed her, tilting her head. "After the horrid things I said, you would still save me?"

Riana looked at the near empty boat and tallied up their chances with no food, no clothes, and no paddles. "Let us just pray it need never come to that."

Fifteen

Drenched from the drizzle, Riana was feeling very much in need of divine protection as she peered through the chill gray haze for sight of a shoreline—any shoreline.

The way their boat rocked in the bouncing sea, she'd be in danger of losing the contents of her stomach, were there anything in it. Poor Greta had succumbed long ago to alternately retching up bile over the side of the boat, and moaning for deliverance. The girl did not say it, but they both knew who was to blame for their predicament. For all her boasts and good intentions, Riana had yet again failed to manage a decent escape.

In this gloom, she had no way of knowing how long they'd been drifting at sea, though a darkening in the haze might indicate that they'd spent two nights so beleaguered. She now felt foolish, and ever more humble, over her claims of being an enchantress. Each moment, it grew more clear that she had no real powers, for if she did, her prayers would have called forth a rescue. Before it proved too late.

Too late. Glancing at Greta, trying so valiantly to smile when she looked like death itself, Riana feared her friend might not last through another stormy night.

Concentrating harder, she sifted through her mind, seeking the right incantation, knowing she must not let anything happen to the girl who had gently and patiently eased her through those early days at River Ford, who stood staunchly beside her there at the end. Desperately, Riana chanted the words she prayed would summon help.

Take me, if it's a sacrifice you want, she added silently, *but in your divine wisdom, Mother-Of-Us-All, please see fit to spare Greta.*

All that happened was that it seemed to rain harder.

Eventually, Greta fell off into a fitful sleep. Riana paused in her praying to settle her own cloak around her friend's shivering body. That Greta did not protest Riana's sacrifice, that she did not even wake, was a bad sign indeed. Swallowing hard, Riana increased her chanting.

Exhausted, she too eventually succumbed to a troubled sleep in which she again saw King Arthur waiting at the gate to Camelot, whispering her name. In her dream, it was as if she had journeyed a lifetime, sacrificing all but her soul for this miraculous moment. She felt such a sense of rightness, of inevitability, she marvelled at ever having doubted it would happen. Approaching her beloved king, holding out her hand, she was startled when he suddenly called out, "You there. Are you alive?"

She opened her eyes when she felt the jolt. Reliving the moment their boat hit the log, she grabbed for Greta. They were still out at sea, she noticed as her wits slowly returned to her. But they were no longer alone.

A long rope tied them to a larger vessel, and the voice she'd heard came from a man dangling from the ladder attached to its side. Something in his pale features seemed familiar, but Riana's main concern was the girl she held in her arms. "My friend is ill," she said. "She needs food, and shelter from the rain."

A second man, darkly handsome and dressed in the ornately decorated tunic of a knight, looked down from the side of boat. "Come then," he said with a broad, welcoming smile. "Let's get you both to safety."

With their help, she managed to hoist Greta up into the larger boat, then climb the rope herself. "We owe you our lives," she told the knight when she reached the deck, even while trying to remember why he too should seem so familiar.

He bowed low, a surprisingly courtly gesture for a tall and powerfully built male. "Ah, but it is our duty to rescue damsels in distress. We shall be only too pleased to escort you ladies to where you need to go."

"Would you know the way to Camelot?"

The paler man eyed her curiously, while the knight broadened his smile. "What a fortunate coincidence. Camelot happens to be our own destination. You have business with the king?"

The paler man laughed, sneering at her ragged, homespun wool.

Riana drew herself up, behaving with quiet dignity as she'd once been trained to do. "I grew up in the royal nursery," she stated simply. "There was a time when King Arthur summoned me most evenings to entertain him and his queen. I am called Moriana, but I was known at court as Riana, the waif Arthur rescued from the kitchens."

She relaxed under the knight's generous smile, liking the way he ignored her rags and focused on her face instead. "Indeed, Arthur has spoken to me of you often. He tells me his court misses your songs and stories." His features clouded. "But pray, how came you to be in such dire straits, drifting out to sea like this?"

"It's a long story," Riana said, smiling feebly. She saw no sense in telling them she'd been kept prisoner in a Saxon village. Not when it meant explaining who Greta was and why she'd accompanied her. "It is perhaps something I should first relate to the king."

The paler man smiled thinly. "Then by all means, we must make haste to get you to Camelot." He took her hand, bowing over it, gazing up at her in a most unsettling manner. "Allow me to present ourselves. My traveling companion is Arthur's right hand, Sir Lancelot of the Lake."

All at once, Riana recalled where she'd seen this tall, splendid-looking knight—in her vision, delivering bad news about Merlin to the king.

"And I . . ." the other man went on, grinning with no real humor, "I am Mordred, Arthur's son and heir."

* * *

"Soon, mademoiselle." Fennick, Mordred's chief squire, gestured ahead of them. "At the next crest, we shall see Camelot at last."

Greta smiled, hoping to appear enthusiastic, but even though she'd recovered from their ordeal in the boat, she'd found nothing to revive her spirits since landing on British soil. Missing the lush green of River Ford's fields, she felt small and lost amidst the rocky crags surrounding them. Even the untamed expanse of the Saxon forests had been less intimidating than the frozen landscape through which they now traveled. She could see why Arthur's fortress was considered impenetrable. Who in his right mind would wish to lay siege in this rough, bleak landscape?

"Of course, it is winter now," Fennick went on, seeing her frown. "In Spring, with the hills green and the wind less fearsome, you will find no finer place on earth."

As his tone so closely echoed Riana's, those long ago days when she spoke so yearningly of her homeland, Greta looked to her friend, riding between the two knights who had rescued them. She would have expected Riana to be joyful, or at least relieved to be nearing Camelot at last, but she retained the same sorrowful expression. *Let's go home,* Greta wanted to plead with her. Unless this king of hers could provide some miracle to help Riana conceive, her friend would find no more peace here than she had in River Ford.

But in her heart, Greta knew it would be a useless request, for Riana was nothing if not stubborn, and determined to answer what she saw as her calling. No amount of homesickness or suffering could sway her from her mission to help Arthur. All Greta could do was be her friend's eyes and ears, watching and listening to all those with whom Riana came in contact, staying ever alert to the danger Sela predicted would eventually find them.

As was often the case in the past few days, Greta studied the two very different men riding beside her sister-in-law. She'd come to appreciate Sir Lancelot's rare, yet generous smile. Unlike the other boisterous knights who had joined them once they landed on British soil, Lancelot was not given to lavish displays of emotion. Yet when he focused his attention on a person, he did so completely, making them feel as if they alone mattered.

In contrast, Mordred was lavish with his flatteries, and not nearly so genuine with his smiles. Though he, too, was handsome and exceptionally well mannered, his humor was often at the expense of another, and the intent way he watched everyone left Greta feeling confused and disturbed.

"Voila, Camelot!"

Summoned by Fennick's excited yell, Greta's attention turned to the view ahead. She could not stifle her gasp, for here, at last, she saw why the bards spoke long and often about this kingdom.

In the valley below stretched a settlement a good twenty times the size of their humble village, ringed by a sizable moat and a twelve foot high wall of wood and stone. Huts, villas, and myriad storage sheds were arranged in tiered fashion, bordered by narrow lanes leading to the center. In each of the many watchtowers along the wall, bowmen stood at the ready, one watching the hordes of people inside the gates, one to survey the countryside beyond, and another to supervise the line of petitioners clamoring at the gate.

But the sight drawing Greta's gaze was the graceful castle on the rise in the center. It seemed to shimmer, its stone walls taking on the silver of the frozen winter sunshine. Even for a king's fortress, it seemed impossibly immense, spreading in all directions over the hill, its many pointed turrets reaching for the sky. For all its vastness, it seemed such a light and airy thing, as if with an enchantment, it could as easily disappear. To Greta, accustomed to drab wood fortresses, Arthur's sparkling castle seemed more a fairy dwelling than the stronghold of a mortal king.

To reinforce this feeling, bright banners fluttered gaily from the corner towers, dancing on the wind. Watching them furl and unfurl, Greta could make out the form of a blood red dragon and a dark, slithering serpent.

This surprised her, since both were pagan symbols and Camelot was said to be firmly Christian. The dragon she could understand, since Arthur descended from the Pendragon line, but the snake was of the primitive older religions, long since banned by British royalty. They followed the Christ and his symbol was the cross—not the serpentine messenger of Mother Earth.

As the breeze played with the banners, both snake and dragon seemed to leer at Greta. If only Sela were here, she found herself wishing yet again. Staring at those symbols, filled with both awe and unease, Greta sensed their display was somehow significant. Though not a fanciful person, she had the sudden strange sensation that the castle had been watching and waiting for them, that it now sighed with contentment as they neared the gates.

With a forced smile for Fennick, Greta nudged her mount forward, knowing she too, like Riana, must ride toward her destiny. Though unfortunately, her fate would be the far less desirable task of watching out for them both.

Riana noticed the petitioners outside, then their fellows inside as she passed over the drawbridge and through the iron gate. Most wore rags and looked ill or malnourished. So many people, with so many problems. This was not the Camelot she remembered.

Riding behind Lancelot and Mordred on the main road to the castle, she glanced back to Greta. She too looked uneasy, though in her case, it was likely more a case of missing her home.

With an unexpected pang, Riana thought of River Ford. Had they harvested the crop before the first snows, she wondered? Did Tad lose status for what she had done to him, and did Wolf . . .

Realizing her hand had unconsciously strayed to the bag of walnuts at her waist, she yanked it away, gripping the reins as tightly as she held onto her emotions. She would not think of Wolf—she could not. She'd been called to Camelot by divine will, and she must not let old hurts and regrets stand in the way of helping her king.

As they rode through the castle gate, a trumpet blared from the tower. Emerging from doors scattered about the huge inner courtyard, grooms and servants chattered noisily as they formed a line to greet and assist the arriving party. All hushed, leaving only the sound of the horses' hooves hitting the cobblestones, as Arthur himself strode through the castle's main doorway.

He stood on the steps before it, hands clasped behind his back, keen eyes missing nothing as he looked down on each member of their party. Riana held her breath as his gaze came to rest on her, her tentative smile disappearing when his attention quickly moved on to another. Her breath returned, albeit slowly, as she grappled with the realization that the man she'd idolized so long hadn't even recognized her.

Biting her lip, she told herself it had been a while, and judging by the hordes of petitioners streaming through his gates, a busy man like Arthur could not be expected to remember every waif he'd ever rescued. Gazing upon his tense, drawn features, she could see the years had not been overly kind in her absence. As in her vision, his hair had gone gray beyond the temples, and worry lines dug into the planes of his weathered face.

Her escorts dismounted with a swift, fluid motion, handing their horses to the grooms to lead away, while she and Greta alighted a good deal less efficiently. Arthur greeted Mordred with a brief, fleeting smile, turning to search Lancelot's eyes. "Any word?" Riana heard the king ask,

"He is gone," Lancelot answered quietly as he climbed the steps to Arthur. "I'm told the faeries have ensnared him."

In her mind, Riana again saw Merlin, trapped in the twisting, snarling threads of her vision.

Arthur nodded. "He warned me this was how it would end." With a sigh, he clapped Lancelot on the back. "But we must discuss this later. I take care not to speak about the faerie folk around my priests. It makes the good fathers uneasy whenever magic is mentioned."

Lancelot smiled grimly. "They shall be happy indeed at this news. The Great Enchanter was never much in their favor."

"More's the pity. Imagine what miracles we could have fashioned blending Merlin's magic with their own."

So Merlin was gone, Riana thought uneasily as she and Greta made their way up the steps to the castle door. Somehow, she'd expected that when she got here, the Great Enchanter would explain what he wished her to do. To learn she was alone, that Arthur's safety and well-being might fall on her shoulders alone, loomed as an awesome responsibility.

As if her fears were audible, Arthur stopped speaking to turn his attention to her. Again her breath held as he tilted his head, studying her. "And who is this young beauty you've brought to us?"

"I could not find Merlin for you, sire," Mordred said quickly, before the more cautious Lancelot could speak, "but I've unearthed perhaps the next best thing. Behold, the long lost Lady Moriana."

Throughout their journey together, she'd repeatedly told Mordred she had no right to the title, yet here he was, using it before the king, making it seem as if she meant to make a false claim. Riana wanted to correct him, but her tongue felt suddenly tied, trapped as she was under the king's intense scrutiny. She could be a child again, caught stealing his walnuts.

All at once, Arthur smiled, his broad, boyish grin subtracting years from his features. "Little Riana? Is that truly you?" Striding closer, he clasped her shoulders and stared into her eyes. "I cannot tell you what good it does this weary old warrior's heart to see you alive and so well. We'd despaired of ever seeing you again."

"It was not by choice that I stayed away," she told him solemnly. "I'd have moved the very heavens to return to you."

"Ah, but this cannot be our Riana, so stiff and grim." Chucking her under the chin, he erased the intervening years, bringing her back to the days they'd sang and laughed together, when she'd wished him to be the father she'd never known. This was why she'd fought so hard and long to return to Camelot. When Arthur smiled at her like this, she knew a strong, sure sense of belonging.

Yet all too swiftly, the smile vanished as he turned to call out orders to the grooms, becoming the distant king once more, and forcing Riana to also remember how it could feel to be suddenly alone and forgotten.

"Come, all of you," Arthur said to the others. "I've kept you standing too long when you must be eager to rest from your travels."

The poor man was ever busy and much in demand, Riana chided herself as she followed him into the castle. It would be childish and unforgivably selfish to expect him to drop his grave concerns to concentrate on her petty problems. She had come to be of help to the king, not a further drain on him.

Arthur came to a stop in the center of the grand entrance hall, the rest of them gathering around him. Calling his servants, informing them of what accommodations and treatment each newcomer would require, Arthur paused when he again noticed Riana. "Hmm, where shall we put you?" he asked, shaking his head. "You've grown too old for the nursery, yet there's no place for you or your companion among the queen's retinue. I'm afraid my lady already has more maids-in-waiting than she can deal with."

"But I did not come to wait on Lady Guinivere," Riana blurted out. "I am here to be of service to you, milord."

"Not much has changed, I see," Mordred muttered behind them. "It's said the younger Moriana didn't know her place either."

Riana stiffened. She found Mordred odd, and wondered often how Arthur could have sired such a pale, brooding malcontent, though looking at them now, she could see a resemblance between father and son in a faint, disturbing way. The features were the same, yet while on Arthur, they painted a picture of strength and nobility, on his son, they blurred into an ever-shifting sense of uncertainty. She could not like Mordred, with his veiled gazes and snide insinuations, and she knew the sentiment was returned threefold.

Riana was about to tell Arthur about her vision when she noticed everyone else now gazed at the stairway to their left. Three ladies glided down it, as silent and graceful as wraiths, as different from each other as birth, life and death. They stared at Riana, their reactions as varied as their appearances. Queen Guinivere smiled with obvious pleasure, Morgause wore an air of amusement, while Morgan was either angry or very scared.

Though the king's sisters, Riana realized, could as easily be reacting to the priest trailing at their heels. Neither Morgause nor Morgan, she remembered, had much use for the new religion.

"My love, come look," Arthur called out to his wife. "Our little Riana has been returned to us." Smiling tenderly, he held out a hand to his wife as she approached. Guinivere beamed at her king, yet somehow managed to include every newcomer in her welcoming smile. Riana had forgotten how beautiful she was, how kind and generous and full of love. To many, she was considered the softer side of Arthur.

As Guinivere moved on to greet Lancelot and the other knights, Riana's gaze slid to Arthur's sisters, waiting quietly beside the priest. As dark as Guinivere was fair, Queen Morgan was a composed, secretive person, who gave away little of her inner workings. Riana could remember feeling unsure of herself in this mysterious woman's presence, and as a result, she'd always enjoyed Morgan's sister more. Morgause was much like herself, often apt to act on impulse and regret it later. Many was the time Morgause had been banished back to her husband's kingdom of Orkney after some scrape or mischief—an exile the woman detested, insisting that all she had waiting in faraway Scotland was a cold, damp pile of rocks and five raucous, brawling sons.

Morgan had been banished too, Riana now remembered, though she couldn't recall being told why, or to where. All she knew for certain was that she was glad to find all three queens in residence. Together, she felt certain, they could form a solid wall of protection against whatever danger Arthur might face.

As if to support this feeling, Guinivere stepped up to link hands. "Welcome home, Riana. I cannot tell you how the king and I have missed your tales and music. We must have you brought at once to my chambers to be cleaned and pampered and dressed as befitting your station."

Remembering what that station truly was, Riana curtsied low. "I expect no such treatment, milady. I came only to serve your husband, the king, having been summoned by his magician, Mer—"

"We can talk of this later," Guinivere said abruptly, her eyes flashing a warning before she turned to face the priest. "Father Ignacious, come bless these weary travelers. We need to get them settled in their chambers, now that they are back home where they belong."

Dour-faced, garbed in unrelieved black, the priest muttered off a string of monotonous Latin. Riana knew little of the tongue, but from the few words she could decipher, and the way Greta rolled her eyes, she could assume the message was far from uplifting.

Knowing Greta had even less liking for the Christian clergy than the queens did, Riana moved closer, in case her friend might feel the urge to speak her mind aloud. Greta did, but ever tactful, she kept it to a whisper in Riana's ear. "That was a blessing? Why then do I now feel doomed?"

"It is their way to be grim," Riana hissed back.

"Then we must avoid this priest, else his ill humor infects us."

Stifling a giggle, Riana looked up to notice Morgause smiling enigmatically at them. Stepping between them and the priest, she offered to show the newcomers to their quarters. "There is an empty room in my wing," Morgause added with a wink to Riana. "I'm certain they'll be most comfortable there."

Arthur agreed with a distracted nod, clearly relieved to have the matter dealt with so he could concentrate on hearing about his knights' travels. With the same air of preoccupation, he promised that he and Riana could talk tomorrow, to decide what role she'd play in the future.

She found it hard to hide her disappointment. Riana didn't know exactly what she'd expected from her return to Camelot, but it certainly wasn't this anticlimactic let down. How unsettling, to be home at last, only to find it was not quite the home she remembered.

Following behind Morgause, passing through halls richly decorated with tapestries and statuary, Riana fought a vague, growing uneasiness. She had been raised here, had known every nook and cranny of the castle, yet it felt as though she viewed these stone walls for the first time. Why had she never noticed how drafty the corridors were, how cold the uncarpeted stone could feel through the thin soles of her shoes?

Indeed, only Queen Morgause appeared to be as she recalled. Staring at the queen as they entered the small room she and Greta would share, Riana's mind drifted back in time to the happy, lazy afternoons she'd spent with Morgause, talking about the world of image and magic. Unlike Arthur, Morgause hadn't aged a moment, her red-gold hair as bright and shimmering as a girl's, her skin as soft and rosy as the petal of an unfolding rose. When she spoke, she still had a way of making each breathy word seem so fascinating, so vital, Riana found herself leaning forward to catch every syllable.

Greta didn't lean, she couldn't help but notice. Clearly distracted, her friend could have been a thousand miles away. Concerned, Riana asked what was wrong the instant Morgause left them.

Greta shook her head as if to shake herself out of her doldrums. "I cannot say," she said in her calm, quiet fashion. "I merely have this queasy feeling, nothing I can pinpoint or elaborate upon."

As this coincided too closely with her own current mood, Riana tried to divert her. "Perhaps you miss River Ford."

"Perhaps." Greta's frown indicated that more than homesickness bothered her. "But I think we might be wise to keep our eyes and ears open, to trust nothing and no one until I can get to the root of my unease."

Riana wanted to insist that nothing was wrong, but the more she thought of how she'd been greeted, the more it bothered her that nothing had been mentioned of her banishment. Or of the reason for it. Everyone behaved as if Riana had chosen to flit off

on her own, and now that she'd come to her senses, they were
happy to welcome her back.

Yet someone had sent the guards that long ago night to drag
her from the nursery and into the night. And until she learned
who, and why, she would watch and listen as Greta suggested.

Unconsciously, her hand went to the bag of walnuts at her
waist, stroking its familiar shape for comfort.

Unlike his warriors, Wolf did not go straight from the longboats to the village. His destination was the villa, having sent
word home weeks ago that Riana should return there, that her
banishment could be ended. He hoped to find her thus more
inclined to accompany him to Camelot.

After receiving his orders from Cerdric, he'd meant to return
home for her immediately, but no sooner had they left the king's
camp than he and his warriors were met by stragglers from
Batar's raiding party. After a brief, futile skirmish, the devious
Britons had fled, leading Wolf's troops on a merry chase through
both kingdoms, before they could again engage in battle. Routing
the enemy had been quick work, but highly unpleasant. Throughout the journey home, Wolf had longed for the peace and quiet
of hearth and home.

Standing before the villa, he paused, knowing such dreams
were most likely futile. So much ugliness had happened between
them, he and Riana might never bring things back to the way
they were. Yet how he ached to hold her, to feel her warm, sweet
body melted against his own. At times, his hunger for her cut so
deep, he felt half mad with the yearning. He had to find some
way to break through the barriers separating them, to find the
key to unlock the joy and laughter.

Perhaps they could make a start on their journey to Camelot.

But that hope faded as he entered the deathly still villa, and it
died completely when he strode into their empty bedchamber.
Looking about him, seeing the healthy layer of dust covering
everything, he knew Riana's absence was no temporary matter.

"She's not here," said a voice from the doorway, hammering home the obvious.

Whirling, Wolf found Helga there, her face drawn with concern but her dark eyes gleaming. "She ran away again," she added far too smugly.

"When?" he ground out, as if the time of her departure would make a difference. Riana was gone, leaving his life as dramatically as she'd entered it, and she would never return. She'd gone too far this time; after this, neither he nor the village could ever forgive her.

"She left soon after you did," Helga was saying. "She tricked the boy, Tadrick, and chained him to her table."

"She was alone in that hut. Where in the name of Wodin did she get chains?"

Helga shrugged, shaking her head. "Perhaps the boy was careless. There's more, milord. Your wife didn't escape alone. Your sister went with her."

"Greta?" Stunned, Wolf tried to imagine his delicate sister agreeing to undertake such a trek. Greta knew her responsibility to this village and it was not like her to so impulsively leave it.

"The prisoner took Tadrick's weapons," Helga added. "Perhaps she used them to force your sister."

Unwillingly, Wolf thought of the long hours of lessons, teaching Riana to shoot an arrow and wield a sword. "Greta was her friend," he protested, as much to himself as Helga. "It makes no sense that Riana would so risk her life."

"Unless . . ." Helga sighed, then shook her head. "No, I will not suggest it."

"Suggest what, woman?"

"I find it hard to say this, knowing how little you wish to hear ill of your wife, but the iron of the chains *was* forged in a British smithy."

Wolf clenched his fists at his sides. "Go on."

"Perhaps your wife was not always alone in that hut. She could have had help from a fellow countryman, a Briton grateful for the information she's been feeding him about the absence of our warriors from the village. I still say it was too great a coincidence that she ran off the same night as the raid."

"What would be her motive?" Riana had run away, it was true, but Wolf did not like this woman's eagerness to blacken his wife's name. "What possible benefit could she derive from destroying this poor village?"

"Do not underrate yourself, milord. It is well known that you have Cerdric's favor, that to destroy Penawulf means removing a major force in the king's defenses. Once your wife found she could not destroy you, she had to flee, taking your sister as a hostage for her safe passage."

Related thus, it sounded plausible, yet he could not credit Riana with such deviousness. "Before I will judge my wife, I will hear what the old woman, Sela, has to say."

Helga shook her head sadly. "She has slipped into the sleep of the dead. Some think it's an enchantment your wife put upon her, for the old woman has been thus since the night she ran away."

Riana wouldn't hurt Sela, Wolf protested silently. "An enchantment?" he asked. "I thought you scoffed at my wife's magical talent."

"I did once, sire. After seeing poor Sela, I do not anymore." Her eyes narrowed, commanding his attention. "Indeed, I now fear your wife has used her witchery on the entire village. Our chieftain, most of all."

"What nonsense is this?"

"Why else would you all remain blind to the evidence, refusing to see her crimes? She has everyone bewitched, I tell you."

Wolf denied the twinge of uneasiness the accusation provoked. "You have made no secret of your antipathy for anything British," he said coldly. "How can I be certain this so-called evidence isn't your bitterness interpreting the facts to fit your hatred?"

Helga inhaled deeply, as if struggling against her own anger. "I am curious to hear my chieftain's interpretation of this fact, then," she said, unable to keep the sharp edge from her tone. "Is it also a coincidence that the night your wife left, the chest containing the village's gold vanished with her? I will wager my last breath that River Ford's livelihood and future not only now rests in the coffers of Camelot, but that the Lady Riana had an armed escort to bring it there."

Wolf felt a slow rage build within him. Riana would know what that gold meant to this village, how its loss threatened their survival. Was she that gone in her ambition to serve Arthur, she could be so cruel and selfish?

"It is my opinion that this is why she took Greta hostage," Helga added. "She knew you would never do anything to risk your sister's life."

"Enough!" Wolf exploded, fighting the sick feeling inside him. "I will hear no more of your vile accusations. Come to me when you have concrete proof of my wife's crimes."

"Proof?" Helga threw up her hands in exasperation. "Hearing all this, you can still claim she has not bewitched you? Forgive me, milord, but I fear your poor father must be turning over in his grave."

She stomped off, leaving Wolf alone with his thoughts as he paced the room he'd once shared with Riana. Could there be a grain of truth in Helga's accusations? Had he let his lust blind him to the true Riana?

He paused before the table, his gaze resting on the misshapen bowl his wife had fashioned for him. Lifting it up, his fingers curling around the baked clay, he could hear her laughter, smell her very scent. He gazed about the room in which they'd once been so happy, remembering the night she'd danced for him, the dreams they'd shared on that big, empty bed. The thought that she might have been plotting and planning his destruction all that time clawed at his mind like talons. It would explain why she did not cry at the death of their child. Given her knowledge of herbs, and the fact that she would not want such a reminder of her stay here, she might well have killed the baby herself.

"Damn you!" he shouted, hurling the clay pot and sending it crashing against the wall.

It burst into a hundred pieces, raining bit by bit to the floor.

Gazing at the splintered shards, feeling as if a bit of himself lay there broken and shattered, he turned on a heel to quit the room.

Nothing could be gained through grief and regret. What was done, was done, and as chieftain, he must now make reparations. He had duties to fulfill, jobs to perform, for both his king and his village.

His path was clear, and it led straight to Camelot.

Sixteen

Riana waited several days for her interview with the king. She might know that Arthur was busy with affairs of state, but the longer he delayed in sending for her, the less secure she felt about the future. If she could have been banished once, it could happen again, only this time, she would have nowhere to go. Greta could return to River Ford, but Riana had burned that bridge behind her. In twice leaving the village, she had made certain that all their doors would remain closed to her.

It was with great relief that she greeted Arthur's summons, and great speed with which she donned the blue underdress and cream-colored tunic Morgause had given her for special occasions. Seeing the bag of walnuts she'd tossed on the bed, she decided to wear her rope belt under her tunic. Though it was foolish and too sentimental, it somehow gave her comfort to carry Wolf's gift around, and she felt in great need of confidence now.

Reaching the large, rambling garden built along Camelot's rear wall, she found Arthur standing beside a fountain, staring pensively into the water as she approached. He has bad news, she thought, suddenly convinced that he again meant to send her away.

But then he turned to greet her, his handsome face breaking into a wide, welcoming smile. "Come, my child," he said, gesturing to a table set under the shade of an oak. "I'm about to partake of my midday refreshment and I hope you will join me."

She smiled at the bowl of walnuts, touched that he'd remembered. "Sugared walnuts, milord?" she asked. "As I recall, you never offered them without wanting something in return. It was how you convinced me to do sums, play the harp, and perform all the other onerous tasks a child must learn. I must wonder what it is you expect of me now."

He grinned as they both sat. "We've missed you, child. My court had grown grim in your absence."

"And no wonder, milord, with that dour-faced priest chanting of doom and destruction."

He tried to hide another grin, unsuccessfully. "Take care you're not overheard, for it's no small crime to be accused of blasphemy. Father Ignacious has many talents, but a sense of humor is not one of them."

"But why tolerate him and his harsh laws? I can't remember you being a follower of the Christian teachings, not when Merlin was at court."

He sighed, more an impatient sound than a weary one. "Merlin is gone. He himself would say that times change, and the wise change with them. If we cannot stop the Christian tide, it is better to ride their wave."

"Compromise, milord?"

"It is often the wise policy, especially when my queen favors their ways. The priest has promised Guinivere that if she prays to the Virgin Mother, she will yet bear a child. And, as they would both point out, it is my sacred duty to beget an heir for England."

Though he spoke lightly, this was a real concern. Ever since Mordred had made his existence known, Riana knew, all Camelot had been praying for the blessed event that would prevent the unlikable prince from taking the throne. But Guinivere's infertility reminded Riana too forcefully of her own problems, and she was happy when Arthur changed the subject.

"We are not here to discuss religion," he said, suddenly solemn. "Let us talk about you. The queen and I can't help but notice that you're not the same joyful girl we remember. Tell me, Riana, what has happened to put such sadness on your features?"

Facing his direct gaze, she could not bear to tell the truth, knowing he, like Wolf, would be disappointed in how she'd behaved. "If I am sad," she half-lied instead, "it is at the loss of the magician, Merlin. I have admired him greatly and hoped to study at his side. I've reason to think I have talents, if nurtured and trained, that can one day be of great use to you."

"So my sisters tell me."

"They do?"

Hard to feel a spurt of hope, of vindication that her pain and grief had not been for naught—that she was meant to serve her king through magic.

"Both Morgan and Morgause request that you apprentice with them. I've suggested that you work with each, alternating your days between the two. If this meets with your favor, of course."

"Oh, but it does. Wonderfully."

"There, a smile at last. That's more like our Riana. Tell me, child, if only for my own peace of mind, is this why you ran away from us? Were you unhappy because Merlin forbade my sisters to teach you magic?"

The Great Enchanter forbade her lessons? Daunted by this, Riana nearly lost sight of the first part of his question. "Oh, but I did not run off," she blurted out in confusion as its implications sunk in. "I was sent away, taken from the nursery by an armed guard."

Arthur sat back in his chair, still staring at her. "Indeed? And just where were you taken?"

"I was left at the outpost hamlet of Milford, where I stayed with the cook, Sela, until . . ."

Conscious of treading on unsteady ground, she wanted to change the subject, but trust Arthur to pounce at once. "Until what, Riana?"

She took a deep breath. "I was captured by Saxons and brought to the village of River Ford."

"Is that not the home of Penawulf, son of Exar?"

It unnerved her that the king should know of Wolf. She looked away, not wanting him to see how the very mention of the man's name could affect her. "Yes, but I did not stay long. At first opportunity, I made my escape." Conscious of the wealth of information she'd omitted, she finished off with a defiant, "I was not meant to live and die a Saxon slave."

She turned to gauge his reaction and saw his stern expression. "I can hear your anger and sympathize with it, but if it's vengeance you seek, I cannot help you. Peace with the Saxons must be maintained. A warrior like Penawulf makes a finer ally than enemy."

This, she'd known already. Nor did she wish to inflict more suffering on River Ford. "In truth, sire, I'd as soon put the past behind me," she told him honestly. "I'm here now, returned to my home, and I wish only to serve you."

He reached across the table, frowning as he clasped his strong, large hands over hers. "Yes, well, you'll find much has changed in your absence. As such, I must ask that you be discreet about your lessons with my sisters. With the climate at court being what it is, it might be best if it's assumed that you've returned to serve as my bard, nothing more."

She wanted to ask, *what climate?* But he was the king, and this was his home, and Riana had no wish to confirm that she did indeed sense an undercurrent of something not quite right here at Camelot. Better to pretend it was all in her imagination.

Arthur offered his hand, gallantly helping her to her feet. "I must leave to deal with other matters," he said with an apologetic smile, "but I do hope you'll come to our chambers this evening to sing and tell your stories."

She nodded, pleased by the invitation, yet saddened by the memories it evoked. In her mind, she could see the children of River Ford gathered around her, listening avidly as she taught them songs, or entertained them with tales of dragons and monsters.

Arthur brushed a knuckle over her cheek. "Such sadness in one so young. Talk with the queen about what causes your heavy sighs and wistful expressions. She has great wisdom in matters of the heart."

Riana would have asked which queen, Guinivere or one of his sisters, but Arthur was already striding away, and in truth, did it matter? Wanting to forget she'd ever seen River Ford, Riana was not about to discuss her stay there with anyone.

As she'd told Arthur, the past was past. Tomorrow, she would begin her lessons and take the first step toward the future.

At long last, she would become an enchantress.

The next day, watching Riana hurry off to meet with Arthur's sisters, Greta fought the urge to follow after her. Part of her felt uneasy at the thought of Riana facing unknown dangers alone, but another small part felt envy. Working beside Sela as she'd brewed her herbs into potions, Greta had caught a glimpse into the mystical world of healing and magic. More than she cared to admit, she wanted to delve deeper into that world, to see if she too had the talent to become an enchantress.

But she'd been charged to look after Riana, to keep her from harm, not lose herself in a selfish, impossible dream. Shaking free of such thoughts, she decided she might better go offer her services again to Guinivere's maids-in-waiting. It was not in her nature to sit idle, and too, much information could be gained from the gossip the women engaged in.

As Greta turned to head in the other direction from Riana, she found King Arthur standing in the hallway, blocking her path.

"Nothing bad will befall her, you know," he said pleasantly, as if they spoke every day. "I shall not allow it."

Greta knew instantly that he spoke of Riana. "Nor shall I, milord," she told him with a stiffening in her shoulders.

He smiled broadly. "I'm glad we are of one mind. Indeed, I would speak more on this with you. Shall we stroll?"

She blinked, startled and dismayed to be thus singled out by the king. "Like all in Camelot," she told him softly, "I am yours to command." She lowered her gaze, partly in respect, but more to avoid his penetrating stare.

"For the moment," he said conversationally as they walked

down the hall, "let us forget that I am the king. After all, you are not truly one of my subjects. You owe your loyalty to your own liege lord, King Cerdric."

"Did Riana tell you I was a Saxon?" she asked, alarmed and wondering what he meant to do with this information.

"No, your face did. I met Exar on the battlefield long ago and you share many of your father's features."

Greta blushed, not at all pleased. She would much prefer to have inherited Cassandra's classic Roman beauty.

"A more valiant man I've never faced," Arthur went on, "nor a more stubborn one." He paused to open a wooden door leading out to a walled parapet. "I've heard," he said, standing aside as she brushed past into the cool, breezy air, "that your brother's inherited these traits from your father."

"If so, I would say he puts them to better use."

Arthur nodded, as if her words pleased him. Joining her at the wall, he gazed out over the city. "Tell me, what do you think of my Camelot?"

She chose her words with care. "It's incredibly beautiful. So vast and luxurious. I am certain there is nothing quite like it in the entire world."

"Perhaps, but you've skillfully evaded my question. I've supplicants aplenty to tell me what they think I wish to hear. From you, little Saxon, I want the same honesty I always received from your father."

"In that case . . ." She swallowed, then plunged in. "I find the beauty cold, the luxury tenuous. I see a danger in too much wealth and power, for it brings out the envy and greed in others. River Ford might be crude and rough by Camelot's standards, but no one there secretly strives to depose the other. We work together for the good of the tribe. Such honest simplicity is a luxury the people in this castle will never again know."

She braced herself for his anger, refusing to regret her words. She felt better for having released her pent-up emotion.

Arthur surprised her by smiling. "Well put, milady. You have a fine grasp of life for one so young. Your brother must miss your presence sorely. Tell me, why did Penawulf send you here?"

He was a wily one, this king. "I am no spy," she told him quietly. "If he had need of one, Wolf would come himself before sending a woman."

"Wolf?"

"Riana gave him the name. It suited so well, we've all taken to using it. Though I daresay Wolf will seem more a bear when he learns I am here."

"Which brings us back to my question. Just why *are* you here?"

Gazing up at his strong profile, Greta felt the urge to unburden herself, to tell him that Riana was her brother's wife, her sister, whom she would guard with her life, but Riana had charged her to say nothing of these things. "Riana is my friend," she said instead, though no less vehemently, "and I would not let her venture out on her own."

Arthur stared at her for a long moment, taking her measure, before pushing off from the wall. "Come, you must be chilled." He opened the door, ushering her back inside. "I apologize if I seem to interrogate you, but despite its faults, this city and its people are as dear to me as River Ford is to you." Inhaling deeply, he spoke in a commanding tone. "Since you share my concern for Riana, I've decided my sisters must include you in her training. You shall be at her side when she goes to her lessons."

Greta could not stop the leap of her heart, but neither could she forget her loyalty. "Riana has waited a lifetime to train as a magician. I am a stranger, and a Saxon at that. My presence could well interfere with what the queens will choose to teach her."

"Spoken like a true friend. Still, Riana tends to live by her emotions, and I'd like to think you'll be there to serve as a calming influence should she need it."

He held her gaze for a long moment, making his message plain. Arthur was telling her that he saw something to trust in her, something he might not find in his own sisters. Meeting his gaze, she made it equally plain that she would not betray such trust lightly.

"Very well, but you might wait a few days before implementing your decision," she told him. "Much has altered in Riana's absence and this change disturbs her. I would not add to the difficulty of her adjustment."

Arthur smiled, taking her hand to place a kiss on it. "Our Riana is lucky to have you, I think. Good friends are rare indeed." Walking off, he turned the corner to vanish as quickly as he'd appeared.

Feeling as if she'd just been swept up by a gale, Greta settled back down to earth with a smile. So she too would receive lessons in magic. And she need not feel guilt, for she'd been given no choice in the matter. The king himself had decreed it.

As Riana would say, the future was in the hands of the Goddess.

Dressed in the simple brown robes of an apprentice, Riana knocked on the door to Queen Morgan's chambers, hoping she'd chosen right. In her nervousness, she'd forgotten which queen had summoned her today.

The door seemed to open of its own volition until Riana stepped into the dark room and noticed the gnome-like servant. "Milady," the woman called out in a reedy tone as the door slid eerily shut, "the girl has come."

Riana sighed in relief. Clearly she'd been expected.

"Have her warm herself by the fire," came a voice from the shadows.

Ushered to one of two padded chairs, Riana took in her surroundings. It wasn't easy to discern details, since the sole light came from the gentle blaze in the large stone hearth, but aside from dark, heavy tapestries at the windows, and the fur on the bed, the furnishings were sparse and simple, more the chambers of a monk than the sister to the king.

"Forgive me if I kept you waiting," Morgan said, materializing behind Riana. She too wore the voluminous brown robe, with the cowl pulled over her black plaited hair. She seemed much like her chambers, dark and deceptively simple. "I was deep in prayer when you arrived."

"You were praying?"

"Not the prayers Father Ignacious might encourage, I fear." With a surprisingly girlish grin, she gestured Riana to sit as she poured tea. "It's the nature of my praying, I suspect, that brings you to visit me today."

"I believe I'm meant to become an enchantress," Riana stated simply as she sat. "And since I have much to learn, I would start at once."

Frowning, Morgan paused in her pouring. "The first rule of sorcery—nay, of all life—is to cultivate patience. You can't hope to achieve in one day what it take years to accomplish. Magic, handled poorly, can be a plague upon the land."

"But you will teach me? You won't send me away?"

Morgan refused to look at her as she handed Riana a cup, then sat beside her. "First, I wish you to tell me about your life outside Camelot."

Confused, Riana sipped the tea. "What does my past have to do with learning the powers of enchantment?"

"There is no *power* in enchantment." Rising to her feet, Morgan seemed suddenly to tower over her, though her voice remained as quiet and controlled as ever. "Only the fool approaches the path of magic with blind ambition. Do you mean to be a fool?"

"No, I—"

"Good. You were right about having much to learn. From now on, if you wish me to tutor you, you will speak no more in my presence. Answer my questions with a nod or a shake of your head. Is that understood?"

Riana did not understand, but she nodded anyway, not wishing to upset this woman who would be her teacher further.

Morgan sighed, turning to stare into the fire. "Ah, Moriana, how much you remind me of myself at your age. So eager to make my mark on the world, and so tragically unaware of the path ahead. I didn't realize then how many a pure spirit has been lost wandering amongst the dark arts. But I do now, child. Far too well."

"But—"

"No talking!" Morgan spun, her dark eyes glinting despite the lack of light in the room. "Have you no idea what is at stake here?"

Riana shook her head, unnerved by the woman's intensity.

"No, of course not, you are too young. Life is too often an illusion, child, a gilded reflection of what others wish us to see." Sighing heavily, Morgan pointed to the door. "Go now, for you have taxed me already."

"But my lessons . . ." Too late, Riana remembered she was not allowed to speak.

"We can try again tomorrow," Morgan said wearily, "but heed this well. In this room, if you wish to learn from me, you will keep faith with your vow of silence."

Nodding, Riana stood, feeling vastly uneasy as she left the room.

"And heed this always," Morgan called out as Riana reached the door. "Here at Camelot, nothing is as it seems."

Riana left the room, grateful to leave its stifling atmosphere, its sense of unreality. Yet before she could completely recover, she was met by a young, smiling servant in the hallway beyond.

"Queen Morgause has been waiting for you," the girl said with a curtsy. "You were expected to join her in breaking her fast."

Riana cast a glance back at Morgan's door. Apparently, she wasn't meant to be here until tomorrow, yet both the queen and her servant acted as though they'd known she would come.

Nothing is as it seems.

Blinking fast, sensing that she'd just been given her first important lesson, she followed after the servant to the chambers of Queen Morgause.

Entering the room, Riana felt again as if she'd moved into a different world. Resplendent in a blue and silver gown, her hair floating like a red-gold cloud on her shoulders, Morgause welcomed her with a wide, beaming smile. As she led Riana to a small table in the center of the room, the filmy fabric of her gown shimmered with a life of its own. Her surroundings held the same, magical glow, more dream than substance, as different from Morgan's cubicle as the women themselves. Everywhere Riana looked, she found silk and furs, treasure piled upon treasure.

"I like to surround myself with beautiful things," Morgause explained in her light, tinkling voice. "Some think it extravagant, but I find I'm better able to pray and think when the world surrounding me is beautiful and gay."

Watching Morgause drift about the table directing the maid to arrange a kingly feast, Riana compared the two sisters, finding marked differences she hadn't noticed as a child. She saw now how Morgan must feel at a disadvantage to be so dark and quiet and solemn, compared to a sister who glittered like sunshine and stole the attention of everyone she met.

Morgause led the conversation as they ate, urging Riana to speak of inconsequentials as she refilled her cup and heaped food on her plate. Charmed by such attentiveness, Riana understood why men considered her fascinating, why Morgause was said to have a rare magic indeed.

After Riana had eaten more than her fill, Morgause asked if she'd like to take a short walk. "Come," the queen said, rising to her feet and holding out her hands. "I have something I wish to show my new apprentice."

Tugging Riana to the far corner of the room, Morgause pressed a carved gargoyle on the wall until a heretofore invisible door swung open. She flashed her secretive smile, urging Riana to follow her into the tiny vestibule. Snatching up the wall sconce, Morgause went to a narrow stairway curving downward, its steps swallowed up by the darkness below.

Not wishing to be left behind, Riana hurried behind her down the staircase, winding down and down until she felt certain they must be in the very bowels of the earth. When they reached the bottom, she found it even darker and unpleasantly dank, like at the base of a well. Following Morgause down a long, stone passageway, Riana knew she should be frightened, or at least cautious, but it was hard not to catch the woman's excitement. Something important was about to happen; Riana could feel it brewing in the chill, damp air.

And then suddenly they left the castle depths, emerging deep in the forest beyond the great wall of Camelot. It seemed impossible that they could have covered such a large distance in so short a time, but the gnarled limbs overhead, entwining like locked fingers to keep out the light, proved they could be nowhere else.

Taking a narrow, winding path through the hushed forest, Riana knew this was an area rarely frequented by mortal men. Indeed, it had the feel of the divine, the snow melted here as if a deity reigned over these environs.

With a heightened sense of unreality, she followed Morgause until they came upon a small glade, a silent, special place where silvery sunlight filtered down to a crystalline pool of still water. Its glassy surface could be a looking glass, so clear was her reflection.

"It's a secret spot, known only to the chosen," Morgause crooned, her voice hypnotic. "I come here to think and reflect when the cares of the castle press upon me. Here, I have my finest inspirations. At times, I can actually hear the soft, clear voice of the Goddess."

She went on, saying more of the same. Unable to take her gaze from her reflection, Riana heard the voice fade into a thin whisper, then a breeze. Filled with a sudden chill and a swirling vertigo, Riana was startled to find Morgause's cool hands on her shoulders, easing her back from the pool.

"What happened?" she asked, blinking rapidly.

"Nothing." Gone was the bright, tinkling voice, the air of shimmering silver; Morgause seemed suddenly drained of life. Frowning, the queen turned back for the passageway into the castle. "Perhaps I was wrong to bring you here. Gazing into the pool affects people different ways. It helps me see visions, but perhaps you were not made for such work."

"Oh, but I am." Scrambling behind Morgause, realizing she'd disappointed this woman, Riana tried to find a way back into her good graces. "Indeed, it was a vision that brought me to Camelot. In a pool much like this one, I saw the great Merlin bidding me come help the king."

"Truly?" Raising a brow, Morgause made it clear what little credit she gave to Riana's claims.

"No, it's true." Riana was at a loss to know what she'd done wrong. It was as if the sun had vanished behind a cloud, so dark and stormy did the queen now appear. Like her sister, she too forbade Riana to speak as they climbed the stairs and returned to her quarters. Even that room, once so gay and cheerful, seemed to have taken on a far more somber tone.

Given the queen's current mood, Riana expected to be dismissed forever, but as she went to the door to leave, Morgause called out for her to return at dawn on the day after tomorrow. "We shall see," she added cryptically, "what happens then."

Relief warred with weariness as Riana hurried to her room. Passing by a window, she saw it was dark, that a full day had elapsed since she'd first set off from her quarters. Yet to her, it felt like midday at the most. What happened in that secret glade? She couldn't help but wonder.

All she knew for certain, after this first day of her very confusing training, was that Queen Morgan had been right.

Nothing was as it seemed.

Life at Camelot grew no simpler for Riana as the days wore on. Her lessons continued with both queens, but now, by royal decree, Greta was included. Arthur stated this was because he had no other position to offer her, but his sisters viewed the edict with resentment and suspicion.

Not that they could argue his decision, for the king had ridden off to the eastern borders to investigate the rash of skirmishes there.

Rumor had it that the Saxons had grown greedy, and meant now to gobble up more than their agreed allotment of British soil.

When the lessons seemed to stall, with neither queen imparting any information she and Greta hadn't already learned, Riana tried to be patient, but with no more visits to the shimmering pool, nor any whispered secrets, more and more, she had the sense of time running out. How was she to help Arthur when she knew so little of the magical arts?

One morning, when Greta was off fetching flax and Riana was preparing the queen's kettle of boiled oats, she was surprised to feel Morgan's gentle touch on her shoulder. "Patience, child. The drama will yet unfold, and you shall play your part in it."

Riana whirled, questions churning inside her. She wanted to ask what drama, and above all, what would be her part, but she was bound by her vow and had to keep silent.

Morgan smiled in approval. "See, you *are* learning." She sighed at Riana's astonishment. "No, I can't read your thoughts. I don't need to, your every emotion is there in your features. To achieve the skills you seek, you must learn to control your outward reactions, even as you are now learning to control your tongue. I would not have it so, for subduing you thus is like clipping the wings and voice of a song bird, but if you truly wish to be an enchantress . . ."

Riana nodded eagerly.

"Then use these days wisely. Stop fretting about what you're being taught, and concentrate on learning about what's happening around you. Watch others, learn to judge human nature by comparing what they say to what they actually do. Use more than your eyes to see. Use your ears, your instincts and experiences, and most of all, think with your heart."

Riana stiffened. Morgan might expect her to hear and feel and sense, but her heart was dead to her, frozen in place the day she left River Ford.

"This makes you unhappy," Morgan had gone on to add, "but remember, even grief has its own lesson to impart."

She had glided off then, leaving Riana haunted by memories

she could not banish. Wolf, rising from the stream. Wolf, charging up with Zeus and taking her to the walnut grove on the island. Wolf, the last time she'd seen him, so angry, so in pain at the death of his child.

This was what her mentor wished her to experience? What lesson, she wondered, could be learned from being offered such a glimpse of happiness, only to have it snatched away? Had she never known Wolf, never lain in his arms and dreamed with him about the future, she would not now be tortured by such a yawning emptiness as she faced the lonely years ahead. Try as she might to banish him from her mind, she ached for her husband, and for the precious little baby she would now never know.

To keep her composure, to continue on, Riana must forget she'd ever met her Saxon lover.

Over the weeks, she fell into a pattern, her days filled with lessons, her evenings devoted to entertaining the royal pair, with no room for more than a casual nod to the young swains that began hounding her. Though she offered no encouragement, they seemed attracted by her aloofness, her sadness, as if her inaccessibility were lure enough.

One fine Spring morning, as all Camelot had gathered in the courtyard to welcome the king and his warriors home from the skirmishes at the border, two such would-be suitors, Gwidion and Francis, started arguing over who had the right to seek her hand. Tossing their gloves before her, they demanded she choose between them.

Alarmed, fearing their antics would capture Arthur's attention, she told them that since she had no wish to marry, they must stop such nonsense at once. They ignored her, vowing to fight to the death to win her, and before her horrified eyes, began throwing punches.

Arthur noticed. Striding over, his armor clanking, he towered over both men with a stern frown. "What is this nonsense at my front door?" he growled. "You, Lady Greta. What has happened here?"

Unaware that she'd joined them, Riana turned to her, stunned that Arthur would recall Greta's name, much less ask her for an explanation.

Before anyone could speak, Gwidion fell to a knee before the appalled Riana. "I wish to offer my name to her in marriage," he declared loudly.

"Nay!" Francis kneeled on her other side. "Tell him, milady. Tell this knave it is I you will choose."

"Enough!" Arthur shouted at the two fools. "Get up, both of you. What can you be thinking of, behaving thus on a day meant to honor the valiant men who accompanied me into battle? I will not have you spoil their homecoming with this public display. *If* there is to be a marriage, it will be decided quietly, not out here brawling in my courtyard. Go, leave my sight. Retire to your quarters until I can decide what to do with you."

He turned then to face Riana, and her heart lodged in her throat. "Did you encourage them?" he asked quietly.

"She did not," Greta said firmly.

The king nodded at Greta before turning to Riana. "Then I am to assume you have no wish to wed either rambunctious pup?"

It was on the tip of her tongue to detail the many, specific reasons why she would *never* wed either knight, but given the king's present mood, the less said the better. "No, sire, I do not."

Arthur stepped closer, gazing at her face. "Ah child, what am I to do with you? You've grown too lovely to be left on your own. It is time, it appears, that we find you a husband."

Dismayed by the prospect, Riana tried to protest. "But milord—"

"You must soon make up your mind or I shall decide for you," Arthur interrupted. "And in the meantime, I want no more incidents like this last."

Riana had barely completed her perfunctory curtsy when Greta hissed at her. "What can you be thinking of, Riana? I've respected your wishes to keep silent, but surely you must now tell your king you're already married."

"Take care," Riana whispered back, drawing her friend out of earshot of the others. "The last thing I need now is for him to learn I was once wed to a Saxon."

"Once?"

"I was forced into the marriage, Greta, and our courts don't recognize any pact made under duress. Besides, you know Wolf wants naught to do with me. He's likely forgotten my existence." She winced, dismayed at how much the thought hurt her. "I bet he's already found himself a new wife."

"How you underestimate my brother." Greta shook with emotion, mostly outrage. "When Wolf gives his word, he keeps it to his grave."

"But he cannot in this case, can he? According to tribal law, the chieftain must have an heir. How long do you think your brother shall keep me, Greta, once he discovers I'm barren?"

The words hung between them, as stark and empty as her womb. Disconcerted by the tightness behind her eyes, Riana worked to keep her voice low and even. "My time in your village is like a dream from which I have woken. A wisp of memory, nothing more."

"You are wrong about that," Greta said quietly. "I must leave you now, for I promised Queen Morgan to help dye her new linen, but heed this warning well. It is not yet over with Wolf," she said in a deep, disturbing voice unlike her own. "Your paths are destined to cross again."

Riana watched Greta hurry off, unsettled by the words she'd uttered. Part of her felt a fluttering hope, yet the saner part knew how Wolf would rage when next he saw her. Did she truly want such a confrontation?

Even as she thought this, she heard someone shout "Prisoner!" outside the gate. All in the courtyard came to stiff and silent attention.

At Arthur's nod, the gate creaked open and a contingent of warriors marched forward, dragging a man, kicking and fighting all the way. Though his body was bruised and battered, his features swollen and bloodied, Riana could see at a glance who it was.

Greta was right; it was not yet over.

With a sinking heart, Riana stared into the cold gray eyes of her husband.

Seventeen

Wolf raged against his bindings, furious at having been captured. He'd made his camp in plain sight, with an emissary flag posted in the forefront, so at most, Arthur's knights should have ordered him off Camelot land. To be kicked and beaten and dragged here in chains was the ultimate humiliation.

And for this, he grew more and more certain, he must blame his wife. Knowing he'd be coming, Riana had sent these men to lie in wait for him. Was he meant to be killed like the two poor souls who accompanied him?

Against his will, his gaze sought and found Riana. She stood by herself in the busy courtyard, watching his less than graceful approach, and his heart constricted for a painful instant at the sight of her. How unjust that she must appear so incredibly beautiful in her fine blue wool and silver jewelry—expensive ornaments her husband could never provide for her.

How was he to maintain his resolve when every inch of him still ached to touch her, to hold her, to hear her soft lilting voice? He knew a sudden strong urge to rush to her side, to sweep her up and carry her off, to kiss her and make love to her until they could both again see reason.

It was as well that his bindings prevented this, as did the return of his sanity. His feelings for this woman already carried too great a price. As chieftain of River Ford, he could afford to pay no more.

He had come to gain useful information for his king, to protect his sister, and with luck, recapture the village's gold. Once these feats had been accomplished, he meant to drag his reluctant wife back to River Ford, where she would answer for crimes against his people.

Though he had no intention of revealing his true plans to anyone—least of all to Riana.

Deliberately looking away from her, he turned his attention to her king, the fabled Arthur she'd traveled so far to serve. Tall and imposing in his battle armor, Arthur returned his measuring gaze, leaving Wolf to wonder if the king had witnessed the long moments he'd stared at Riana. At a glance, Wolf saw that it would be no easy thing battling this man. Arthur was strong and decisive and held all the advantages, while Wolf had only his wits and pride and stubborn determination. Still, he had come seeking justice and he would not leave without it.

"We found this Saxon brute prowling outside the city walls," drawled the man who led the raid on his camp and ordered Wolf bound and gagged. "The Great God alone knows what mischief he was about."

Arthur raised a brow. "Perhaps he can tell us himself if you remove that gag from his mouth."

"But sire—"

"Remove it!" the king barked at the warrior nearest Wolf.

As the man hastened to obey—albeit none too gently—Wolf eyed the man who would have kept him silent. Standing close to Arthur, he seemed a pale replica of the king, shorter and thinner and far less commanding. The man wished him dead, Wolf sensed, and would have long since run him through with the slightest excuse, had an older knight not ridden up to demand that the intruder be brought, alive, to the castle. When the man had ridden off again, Wolf had remained quiet and relatively submissive, determined he would fight his battle with Arthur, not this pale, weak substitute.

"Tell us," Arthur said, drawing Wolf's attention back to him. "What cause had you to lurk outside my city?"

"I was neither lurking, nor prowling," Wolf stated calmly. "I and my men were asleep in our tents, under the mistaken impression that visitors to Camelot received fair treatment. Especially those flying an emissary flag at their camp's entrance."

"We saw no flag." Glaring at Wolf, his captor spat at the ground.

"And did you also fail to notice, when you hacked down my two companions, that neither man bore arms against you?"

Awesome in his anger, Arthur turned to the paler version of himself. "Mordred, is this true?"

Wolf was not surprised by the name. He'd heard much of the bastard prince, and none of it had been flattering.

Nor did his opinion improve when Mordred went suddenly petulant. "How were we to know they were unarmed? We saw Saxons, running and shouting from their tents, and in light of the raids plaguing our country, we thought it wise to act first and ask questions later. You were not yet returned, sire, and we dared not leave any threat to Camelot unchallenged."

Arthur's hand went to rest upon the hilt of his sword, as if he sought comfort from the cold, hard metal. A glint in his eyes as he gazed at his son led Wolf to believe the king had his own doubts about that version. "I offered no resistance," Wolf said quietly, hoping to foster those doubts. "So why was I bound and gagged, given no chance to state my business?"

"You shall have your chance," Arthur told him, "but not here in my courtyard. I and my men must remove our battle gear and partake of some sustenance, but when we're refreshed, we can convene in the grand hall to decide this matter." Turning on a heel, Arthur strode off.

As this left his son to deal with the prisoner, Wolf was not surprised to find himself being jostled and poked as he was dragged into the castle.

Turning to look back at Riana, he found she was gone. Damn her for being the heartless witch Helga called her. Having seen to his humiliation, no doubt she was either making plans to once more elude him, or have him murdered in his bed.

* * *

Nothing could be further from the truth. Riana had gone racing through the castle halls, trying to catch up with the king. Somehow, she had to convince Arthur that Wolf didn't deserve to be treated like an animal.

Unfortunately, by the time she reached his chambers, the king and queen were locked inside with strict instructions not to be disturbed. Haughtily, the guard informed her she must wait in the grand hall, like everyone else.

Knowing better than to appeal to Mordred for help, she went to find Greta, who would want to know at once that her brother had come to Camelot. Then too, Riana realized that the plea for leniency might better come from his sister. She had good reason to fear what emotions she'd betray if the king questioned her too closely about the newcomer.

Even now, she still trembled from the wonderful, terrible moment she'd looked into her husband's eyes. She had found it all, the love, the hope, the home she yearned for—only to have Wolf deliberately look away, as if he meant to keep these things locked inside him, just beyond reach.

She told herself it hardly mattered. Too much had changed, herself most of all. She had a new life now, a duty and destiny to fulfill. She would not have Wolf's life on her hands, yet neither could she let him serve as a distraction. Somehow, Greta must prove to Arthur that Wolf posed no threat, and at the same time, convince her brother to leave at once. Greta must make it clear to Wolf that Riana had no intention of going anywhere with him, that she meant to deny he was ever her husband.

He did not need to know how painful that would be for her.

Unnervingly, Greta was not in Queen Morgan's chambers, nor in the room they shared. Conscious of the moments ticking away, Riana decided not to waste time searching for the girl. She might better go to the grand hall and defend Wolf herself.

She was thus in a rare state of nerves when she entered the lady's gallery overlooking the hall—and none too pleased to find Greta seated there already, leaning over the railing as if ready to leap down to her brother's aid should he need it. The girl glanced up when Riana shuffled into the seat beside her, Greta's eyes glinting with a I-told-you-so expression, but she swiftly turned her attention back to the scene unfolding below.

Seated on his throne with Prince Mordred standing behind him, Arthur gestured for the guard to bring in the prisoner. Glaring with distrust and suspicion, his knights lined up to form a path through which Wolf must proceed on his route to the king. Each held a hand on the hilt of his sword, prepared with just a blink of the king's eye to slay the intruder. As Wolf was shoved along that ever-narrowing tunnel of human animosity, Riana could not help but compare the scene below to her own presentation to King Cerdric.

Where the Saxon thanes had filled the halls with bawdy jokes and raucous laughter, Arthur's knights remained quiet and solemn, almost grim, yet she could see little difference between them. Whether left to run rampant or cloaked beneath a veneer of civilization, bloodlust reigned in both halls, its urgings as deep and compelling—and dangerous.

Riana's heart pounded painfully as she watched Wolf walk with his head held high, unaffected by the hostility burning around him. Despite the welts on his body and the ropes at his wrists, he strode with the same controlled poise with which he'd approached Cerdric. There were some who would respect such self-assurance, she knew, but most would deem it insolence, using the excuse to run him through with their blades.

Mordred appeared to be one of the latter. Hand clasped at his sword, he kept one eye on Wolf as he leaned down to whisper in his father's ear. Arthur instantly frowned.

Greta gripped Riana's arm, her gaze riveted on the scene below, as Wolf was forced to his knees before the king.

"State your name and your business," Arthur commanded, his voice booming across the hall.

"I am Penawulf of River Ford," Wolf said, his own tones no less regal. "I am here as an emissary for the Saxon nation."

A low, discontented rumbling curled about the room. Arthur

held up a hand to halt it. "Arise, Penawulf, and tell this court what word you bring from Cerdric."

"If you will, your highness," Wolf said as he rose slowly to his feet, "my king would have me deliver his message in private, and there is a matter of my own I would discuss with you."

"Saxon dog!" Mordred cried out. "Can you truly believe we would leave our liege lord alone and unprotected with the man who has slain too many of our brethren already?"

Again Arthur held up a hand, his gaze focused on Wolf. "I would know, Penawulf, if the rumors are true. On your word, did you slay my vassal, Batar, in cold blood?"

Greta's grip tightened. Riana, remembering how Tad had spoken about the routing of Batar's troops, realized her friend had good cause to be alarmed. She stood, meaning to speak up in Wolf's behalf, but he forestalled this by offering his own defense.

"Batar was slain, my lord, but not in cold blood. Ask your rumor-mongers where he and his men died. They will tell you, if *they* are honest, that it was well within my borders."

Arthur turned to his son. It was Mordred's turn to frown.

"There has always been bad blood between his tribe and mine," Wolf went on, "but a truce was made and River Ford honored it."

"Yet you killed Batar."

"Innocent women and children were attacked in that raid." Wolf glared at Mordred. "My village still bears the hardship it caused. I sought only justice."

Arthur nodded. "But you have taken your vengeance. What more can you want that you would ask a private audience with me?"

"Someone I hold dear." He paused, turning to look up at the woman's gallery.

Meeting his gaze, Riana felt her heart trip madly. She could tell herself she had a new life now, a duty to perform, but deep down, she knew that her heart belonged to her husband. More than she believed possible, she longed to be his wife once more.

"If you will, sire," Wolf went on, his gaze moving past dismissively, "I would ask that my sister Greta be returned to River Ford."

Riana sat, her brain as cold and numb as if her heart had stopped entirely. The cut had been deliberate, a blatant message. Riana need not bother renouncing him; he meant to pretend that she'd never existed.

She bit her lip to keep it from trembling. For all her brave words to Greta, Riana had not been prepared for this. She had not known how it would kill her to look on him while Wolf so pointedly looked away.

Holding herself stiff and proud, determined that no one see her anguish, she watched Greta rise and smile down with great joy at her brother. She saw the girl glance at her, then her brother's almost imperceptible shake of his head, and then Greta's consternation. She, like Riana, thought Wolf had come seeking his wife. That he would ignore her—nay, deny her—confused his sister greatly.

"Lady Greta," Arthur called out. "Do you acknowledge this man as your brother?"

"I do, my lord."

"Then perhaps, after our talk, you would care to visit with him?"

"I would indeed, my lord, but first," she said, smiling prettily, "I would ask that the ropes be removed from his wrists."

"At once." Waving his hand, Arthur summoned a knight to slit through Wolf's bindings.

"Sire—" Mordred started to protest.

Again, Arthur forestalled him. "It is my decree. Lady Greta, you can wait for your brother outside the council room. Prince Mordred, I'm certain, has his own business to deal with, as do you others. Go, be about your day, and leave Penawulf and myself to discuss this message from his king."

Clasping Wolf on the back, Arthur led him away, even as Greta hurried off to the council room. Everyone else scattered, leaving Riana sitting in the grand hall, feeling as alone and empty as the cavernous room around her. Biting her lip, she tried again to tell herself that all had turned out as she'd wanted, that she was now free to pursue her calling, but gazing about her, she felt merely abandoned.

Feeling the sting at her eyes, she jumped to her feet and hurried from the room with her head held high. She had not succumbed to the silly weakness of weeping thus far, and she was not about to do so now.

In truth, she should be grateful Wolf had made the break cleanly, a swift, slashing wound that might scar, but would heal with time and patience. Only a fool would wallow in regret and self-pity, and as she'd told Morgan, she had no intention of playing the fool.

She would lose not a moment. She would go to Queen Morgause and from this day on, she would bury herself in her lessons.

Wolf watched Arthur circle around the huge oak table in the center of the cavernous stone-walled room. "This is it," the king said, wearing his pride like a badge. "The famed table around which I gather my knights. Rather ordinary looking, isn't it?"

Wolf eyed the wood, stained and dented and darkened by many years' good use. Perhaps it was the setting, with all light directed upon it, but standing before this table, Wolf could feel the weight of the decisions made in this room. "I have heard of your Round Table," he told Arthur, "as indeed, who in all England has not, but I hadn't expected to find it so impressive. It gives off an aura of hard choices and costly triumphs. Of unity and strength."

Well pleased by his words, Arthur urged him to take the seat opposite him. "Some men walk in here and see a table, nothing more. Those men rarely last long at Camelot."

"Nor will I," Wolf took care to point out as they both sat. "I do not mean to stay in your kingdom any longer than necessary."

Arthur laughed. "How blunt, but how like your father. Though Exar and I fought on opposite ends of the battlefield, there was always respect and honesty between us. I hope it can be thus between you and me."

Wolf thought of his mission and steeled himself against the charm of this man. He was here to serve the interests of his king first, and his own second, and that would leave little room for truth or admiration.

"Tell me, Penawulf," Arthur went on. "What is this message you would deliver?"

Wolf chose his words with care. "My lord Cerdric is concerned with the raids across the border. He would know, from Arthur's own lips, if Camelot is behind them."

"Camelot?" Arthur's outrage could be feigned, but Wolf didn't believe so. "I could as well ask why Cerdric feels entitled to be pillaging my southern outposts."

That gave Wolf pause. Arthur believed Saxons were raiding British villages? More than ever, he had cause to suspect that someone hovered behind the scenes, stirring up trouble. "Cerdric is not behind these attacks," Wolf swore to him. "I would stake my life on it."

Arthur studied him speculatively. "He sent you here to poke and pry, didn't he? He knew that your fine Roman manners and regal bearing would appeal to me, that I'd be charmed by your mastery of our language. No, don't bother to protest. I'd have done the same in his place."

Yes, Wolf thought. No doubt this king would.

"Very well," Arthur continued, "I suggest a stay of a minimum of a fortnight, Penawulf. Poke and pry to your heart's content, as long as you adhere to Camelot's basic tenets. Here, blood is spilled only as a last resort, after grievances have been brought before the council. A knight of my realm fights for justice, not for pride or greed."

"Are your warriors to conform to such laws?"

His smile turned rueful. "You spoke of hard choices and costly triumphs. Some, I suppose, will always think it weak and womanish to settle differences with words rather than swords."

"But you do not?"

"Having fought more battles than any man should, I've learned it's hard enough killing for a cause, like freedom or protecting loved ones, but to enter into a blood feud, to fight a man merely because he hails from a rival tribe or worships a different god is a waste. To kill for greed is a tragedy."

Against his will, Wolf felt the stirrings of the respect Arthur had asked for. He struggled against it, reminding himself that because of his wife, he had much to resent about this king. Too, only a fool would take what the man said at face value. Wolf would stay the fortnight, watching and listening, before making his judgment. "I shall follow your laws and give you no cause to regret my stay here," he told Arthur solemnly, giving nothing away of his true thoughts.

"Splendid." Arthur rose, extending his hand for Wolf to clasp. "My good friend, Sir Kay, will show you about and help you get settled."

Sir Kay, Wolf realized, was the name of the knight who had stopped Mordred from killing him. If he must have a watchdog, it was fortunate it would be a man he could respect.

Shaking the king's hand, Wolf could not stop the question he'd been burning to ask. "One thing more, my lord, I would know, what has the girl, Riana, told you about her stay in our village?"

Arthur raised a brow, and Wolf cursed his own impatience. He could ill afford to stir this man's curiosity in this arena.

"Riana says little." Arthur continued to watch him as he spoke. "Only that she was captured and enslaved. If you wish to learn more, talk to Lancelot or Mordred. They brought her home.

So her escort had been Arthur's son and second-in-command? *Where is my village's gold?* Wolf wanted to demand, but it was too soon in his stay for making accusations. He still needed information for Cerdric.

"Riana is now under my protection," Arthur warned. "I will not allow you to take her from Camelot against her will."

That she had said nothing of their marriage added to her crimes. "I understand," Wolf told Arthur, even while silently vowing not to leave without her.

* * *

That night, a feast was laid in the newcomer's honor. This did not sit well with many in the castle, Riana especially. She'd have pleaded some illness, but Morgause had been adamant that she could not win Arthur's favor by hiding in her room. And without the king's nod, Riana would go nowhere in her ambitions to become an enchantress.

Her head still spun from all she'd learned today, for Morgause had brought out her book of runes and spells for Riana's perusal. She felt bad for Greta, who by visiting with her brother had missed the important lesson. For the first time, Riana had felt the power surging within her, a heady, seductive feeling—and tomorrow, Morgause had promised, they would return to the sacred pool.

Riana had returned to her room, certain she was well on her way to accomplishing what she was meant to do, only to learn that the husband who did not even want her remained determined to block her path. Listening to Greta chatter on about how Wolf would not be leaving in the morning as Riana supposed, but would rather stay on as a royal guest roaming the halls at will, made the blood in her veins go cold and still. How could Riana concentrate on her studies if at any moment, she might bump into Wolf, or in her agitation, inadvertently say the wrong thing?

Forced to sit at the far end of the long banquet table, watching Wolf talk and laugh with the royal family and unable to hear a word they uttered, Riana wondered how she'd survive the coming fortnight. While she might withstand the strain on her nerves, her poor heart was likely to crack under the pressure.

She could scarce bear to gaze at him. He seemed so incredibly handsome, garbed in the deep blue and silver livery of Arthur's armed guard. His graceful, casual gait as he'd strode into the room brought back too many painful memories of the walks they'd taken together. As if it had been only today, she could see him again as he'd emerged from the river, godlike and heroic after saving her life.

Was there nothing this man could not do? His tunic might not sport the silver cross in the center, yet he seemed every inch the

royal knight, gallant and charming and far too confident as he
moved easily about the room like a skilled diplomat. Under other
circumstances, Riana might have swelled with pride to see Wolf
so well received, but tonight, given his scowls and the past shared
between them, she could feel only trepidation.

Nor did it help to be seated so near those great pests, Francis
and Gwidion, who spent a good part of the meal arguing over
whom had the right to talk to her. Morgause would point out how
flirting with them could make Wolf jealous, but Riana found the
prospect distasteful. She had no wish to encourage any man,
especially not her husband. She wanted Wolf gone, and as soon
as possible, so her life could return to normal.

Ignoring her swains, she stole another glance at Wolf, finding
him deep in conversation with Morgause, whose arm rested pos-
sessively on his wrist. Feeling literally ill at the sight of her mentor flirting with her husband, she realized she would never
survive a fortnight of this.

Indeed, she had very real doubts she would last the night.

Wolf wanted to yank his hand away from the woman's cloying
grasp, but Morgause was Arthur's sister, and from all reports,
Riana's mentor, and he could not risk alienating her until he had
the information he sought.

Having spoken to his sister, he was more confused than ever.
Helga would have him believe his wife was an evil traitor, yet
Greta swore that Riana had used no force against her, unless it
was in forcing Greta to beg to be taken along. Nor had any chests
accompanied them, filled with gold or otherwise. According to
Greta, Riana had neglected to take even food.

Yet her escape had been well executed and the chains had
indeed been British, so how could he dismiss Helga's accusations? After all, Greta was known to have a soft heart and be far
too trusting; she was no match for a cold, calculating liar.

She's bewitched you.

Even as Helga's warning flitted through his mind, his gaze

drifted back to Riana. She hardly looked the part of a spy. Nor would it seem she'd gained much with her efforts if she must be relegated to the lower end of the table. Try as he might, Wolf could not ignore the slight sag to her shoulders, her listlessness as she ate, or the way she held herself apart from those around her. He would not have thought Riana had it in her to act so defeated, nor did he like how much her behavior disturbed him.

"You haven't heard a word I've said, have you?" Morgause asked petulantly, breaking his preoccupation. "What, I wonder, draws your attention to the far end of the room?"

Wolf distrusted this female and would not have her guessing his thoughts. "I was thinking of home," he lied. "All those I left behind."

Smiling seductively, Morgause leaned closer until her sweet, heady scent wafted around him. "Ah, but you have no need for homesickness tonight," she said in her soft, breathy voice. "Not when you have me to help you forget."

Under the table, he felt her leg rub against his own. Annoyed, for this was one complication he'd as soon avoid, he spoke more sharply than he intended. "Save the seduction, my lady, for the face that haunts me most belongs to my wife." Uncomfortably, he realized how true that was.

From her narrowed gaze, he saw he'd displeased Morgause, but when she withdrew her leg, all he felt was relief. Pulling his arm free, he turned his back to the woman and concentrated on the argument in which Arthur and his son were now engaged.

"You will set this savage loose in Camelot?" Mordred was saying, two spots of color appearing on his pallid cheeks. "He could be a spy, sent by Cerdric to learn our weaknesses."

Arthur shrugged. "Then we must show no weakness, and he'll have naught to report."

"He's a Saxon," Mordred sputtered. "Our enemy!"

"You are overeager to brand a man your foe. Do you forget the pact of peace we keep with his people?"

"Does he?"

"That will be enough, Mordred." Arthur clenched the stem of

his goblet. "I will not have you stirring up mischief where there is no cause. In all our dealings, Cerdric has never once given me reason to doubt his word, and if he now sends his emissary, I am happy to entertain him. It has long been my contention that our tribes must learn to live together. What better way to start than by exchanging ideas and learning each other's ways?"

Listening to them, Wolf couldn't help but compare Arthur and his son to Cerdric and Vangarth. Both kings were immensely wise, while their underlings were dangerously ambitious.

"We will make this a pleasant evening," Arthur added, gulping down his wine. "Let's send this Saxon home with tales of our fine hospitality, not of how we bicker and complain at the table. You there," he called to the hovering servant. "More wine for everyone."

As his own goblet was refilled, Wolf noticed the woman on his left, Arthur's other sister, Morgan. Though quiet and subdued, she seemed to watch everything. At the moment, her alert gaze focused on the far end of the table.

Glancing there, Wolf found that Riana had risen to her feet and was trying to break free of the two knaves clasping either arm as if to pull her in separate directions. More agitated by the moment, Riana cast a frightened glance up at the king, then at Wolf. He'd seen that expression before, the night he'd first captured her. She was scared to death and didn't want him to know it.

Then, like now, he acted without thinking. Pushing back his chair, he rose to his feet and strode to her side.

"Is there a problem?" he asked quietly, folding his arms across his chest as he surveyed the two pups who detained her. "I could be wrong, but from where I sit, it does not seem the young lady welcomes your attentions. I suggest you release her at once."

They did, but it was already too late. "Riana?" Arthur called out, rising to his feet. "What is the cause of this disturbance?"

"Nothing, sire." Face pale, she eyed the door with longing.

"A mere misunderstanding," Wolf offered, even while wondering why he did so. He should be pleased if Riana fell into disfavor with her beloved king. "No harm done."

"On the contrary!" The knave to his right jumped suddenly to his feet. "The only misunderstanding is on Gwidion's part. He cannot get it into his thick head that Riana shall marry me."

Even as Wolf stiffened, enraged that anyone would consider he had a right to *his* woman, the other young fool leaped up, knocking over his goblet in the process. "Francis will never have her without killing me first."

"Stop it!" Riana cried out. "Both of you. How many times must I say I cannot, and will not marry anyone?"

"How deliciously melodramatic," Mordred drawled at the king's side. "I daresay, sire, I can see now why you chose her as your bard. Is she always this entertaining?"

Seeing Riana's quick flush, Wolf fought the urge to put an arm around her shoulders. She'd made it more than clear that she neither wanted, nor needed his protection.

Staring down at her, Arthur sighed heavily. "The only way to stop this nonsense is to find you a husband at once."

Wolf waited. If she spoke out now, if she claimed him in front of her king and all her people, there might yet be hope for them.

"Choose me," Gwidion shouted.

"Nay, I am the man for Riana," Francis argued.

Wolf couldn't stop himself. "You've barely begun to shave. You're not even half the man she requires. Either of you."

"Is that a challenge?" Though Francis spoke, both knaves stepped forward belligerently.

"Enough, I tell you!" Arthur pounded his fist on the table and the two pups edged back toward their seats. "Here at Camelot, we do not brawl at the table. We air our differences in a civilized manner."

"At the Round Table, sire?" Mordred asked, pretending to concentrate on his food. "I thought that was for settling grave matters of state, not the love life of the current court bard."

Arthur stared at Wolf. "Such issues are more often settled in the training grounds. It occurs to me that it has been an age or more since Camelot has staged a tournament. Perhaps we can hold a joust, open to all challengers, and the victor can claim Riana. What say you to that challenge Penawulf?"

Riana gasped, turning to face Wolf with wide, frightened eyes. "Refuse. You can't compete. You know nothing of tournament play."

"Alas, she is right." Trust Mordred to overhear and pounce at once. "The Saxon fights from the ground with a club. What would he know of the intricacies of unseating a man from his horse?"

"He can train. Sir Kay, will you see to his instruction?"

The burly knight stood, his florid face darkened by a frown. "As you wish, milord, but it takes years for these boys to attain knighthood. I can't promise much in a fortnight."

"You can't be serious," Mordred sneered. "What madness is this that you would put a Saxon on Camelot's training fields?"

"It is not I who would put him there, but rather our guest himself." Arthur smiled at Wolf. "Penawulf?"

Mordred was right. It was insanity, yet likewise tempting. Training with Arthur's warriors, Wolf could learn much about British life and warfare, but more importantly, here was one way he could legally take Riana from Camelot.

Inhaling deeply, he nodded.

"Splendid. Bailiff, make the arrangements. Kay, you can begin his training in the morning. As for you, Penawulf, I suggest you join us for your last celebrations. Knowing Kay, come tomorrow, your diet and drink shall be severely restricted."

"Sire, may I take my leave now?" Riana asked in a small voice. "I find I am not feeling well."

At Arthur's nod, Wolf kept his arms at his chest, fighting the urge to reach out and detain her. He wanted to ask why she wanted him to refuse the challenge, why she told no one he was her husband, why she felt the need to again and again betray him, but he doubted he'd be comfortable with her answers. Arthur was right. Better to spend this night drinking and forgetting.

Tomorrow, he could begin both his training, and his quest for the truth.

Eighteen

All that night and into the next morning, Riana struggled with what to do. Wolf's decision to enter this joust made no sense. Though skilled on the battlefield, he must know that British military arts differed from Saxon methods. He was liable to get himself killed.

Dressing for their lesson today with Morgan, she grew desperate enough to broach the subject with Greta. "You spoke with Wolf," Riana said. "Why has he come?"

Greta looked up from braiding her hair, clearly surprised. "Why, for you, of course."

"Me? Then why barely acknowledge my existence? Why does he not tell Arthur we are already married?"

Greta raised a brow. "Why don't you?"

Riana chose to ignore that. "It is madness, this tournament. He will be killed, and for what? For a woman who angers him so, he cannot bring himself to gaze upon her? He hates me, anyone can see that, yet he persists as if he has no choice in the matter. I'm beginning to wonder if Sela never did unweave that enchantment." Too upset to guard her words, she didn't realize she'd spoken that thought aloud until Greta began shaking her head.

"She didn't. Before we left, Sela spoke of your love spell. She did nothing to reverse it because she considers it part of some divine plan. She, like I, believe that you and Wolf are meant to be together."

Riana sat on the bed, her emotions tangled. Last night, facing Wolf as he rescued her from those two pests, she'd felt the pull between them, that overwhelming need to touch and hold him, and she'd begun to think that beneath all the anger and hurt and pain, Wolf might feel similar needs. To learn that he could not, that it was that plagued enchantment that drove him, stripped away any last fantasy she might have been dreaming.

Better to know the truth, she tried to tell herself, than to delude herself further with hope.

"Your brother will not be pleased to learn he's been bewitched," she told Greta, her tone flat and lifeless. "Especially if I do nothing to free him."

Nodding wisely, Greta sat beside her. "Men like to rage at that which they can't control, but mark my words. Even if we find some way to undo your enchantment, it won't change how he feels inside. Wolf loves you, Riana."

"How can you know this? Did he say so? Did he ask of me at all?"

Greta refused to look at her. "He loves you, I tell you. And spell or no, he always will."

Poor Greta was worse than herself, Riana thought, both of them dreaming fantasies that could never be. "The fact remains, I must break the enchantment. Perhaps I can ask Morgan today to help us . . . a pox on that oath of silence," she said angrily. "How can I ask if I cannot talk?"

"I can ask for you." Greta smiled faintly. "I am not bound by the same oath."

Riana nodded, knowing Morgan was more likely to respond to Greta, to whom she spoke freely and treated like a daughter. Around Riana, the queen retained her stilted manner, holding herself aloof, as if fearful of revealing too much. Morgan's unwavering gaze as she watched them, constantly studying and judging her, left Riana fearing she might never earn the woman's affection and trust.

Making plans on how best to introduce the subject, they made their way to Morgan's chambers and were promptly put to work sorting herbs. Since Morgan sat across from her, Riana was able to watch the queen's face when Greta posed her question.

Predictably surprised, Morgan glanced up, her gaze sliding instantly to Riana. "There is such a spell, yes," Morgan said thoughtfully, "but it must never be used without caution. The results can be disastrous."

She knows, Riana thought uneasily.

"But surely there's a way to counteract such a spell," Greta pressed.

"For every force, there is a counter force. That is the law of Nature." Morgan sighed heavily. "But much harm can be done by both. Why do you ask, child?"

Riana, wriggling under the queen's scrutiny, breathed a sigh of relief when Morgan turned to Greta. Perhaps the woman merely suspected something amiss and was using her dark gaze to probe out the truth.

"Come now," the queen coaxed with a half-grin. "Don't tell me you've found some young gentleman you wish to hold captive?"

"No, of course not." Greta concentrated hard on her sorting. "I heard some flirts about the court, talking and teasing. I was merely curious to learn if what they said was true."

Again, Morgan's enigmatic gaze went to Riana. "The young should not tamper with such spells. You'll find that while weaving them is easy enough, undoing such mischief is quite beyond your current skills."

Riana pretended to study the herb leaves, avoiding Morgan's unflinching regard. It couldn't be true, she thought unhappily. If indeed she'd trapped Wolf in a spell, there must be some way to release him, to send him home where he belonged.

She had a lesson with Queen Morgause tomorrow, she thought, brightening. Perhaps she could ask her other mentor, instead.

The opportunity came sooner than she'd expected. That evening, after another awkward dinner where she must watch Wolf flirt with Morgause from across the hall, she was called to the woman's chambers—the message seeming less an invitation and more a summons.

On her way there, Riana prepared in her mind how she would ask for help, only to be stunned into silence when Morgause herself opened the door, clad in the brown robe of an apprentice. Everything about the woman seemed subdued, from the cowl covering her braided red-gold hair to her somber expression. Indeed, Morgause seemed suddenly as dark and mysterious as her sister.

The room behind her, once so bright and shimmering, would now be as black as the night outside if not for a sole, flickering candle. Riana imagined she could hear whispering in the shadows, a slithering, rustling sound not quite mortal. Intellectually, she might know it was illusion, but the hows and whys left her uneasy. She needed help and guidance, yet both queens seemed determined to remain mystifying and unpredictable.

"I must know," Morgause demanded suddenly, pulling her into the room and sitting her before the table. "What is there between you and this Saxon brute?"

Staring at the candle flame, a flustered Riana forgot everything she'd meant to say. She'd meant to be clever, to wheedle out the unweaving spell without revealing too much about herself, but the more the flame danced, the less she could remember about how she'd meant to do this.

"Tell me," Morgause whispered again into her ear. "What is there between you and Penawulf?"

Watching the candle, persuaded by the queen's insistent urging, Riana felt the need to unburden herself grow stronger until it seemed she could not stop the words from spilling off her lips.

She told Morgause everything, from the night she first danced for Wolf, to the ugly dawn when she'd lost his baby. "Help me," she finished off, fighting the tears. "Help me find a way to break this enchantment."

"Of course."

The matter-of-fact tone drew Riana's gaze from the flame. She blinked rapidly, feeling as if she'd just woken from a deep, troubled sleep.

Morgause paced before her, her long, fluid stride like that of a sleek, powerful cat. "But to find the right spell will take great concentration and sacrifice. It might be wise, I think, to rid ourselves of the Saxon's sister."

"Greta?" Dizzy with confusion, Riana's hand went to her throat. "No, she is a friend to me. I will allow no harm to her."

"We mean her no harm, goose," Morgause said with a warm smile as she began to circle Riana. "But do you truly wish her to witness what I next mean to show you? No matter what claims she might make, the girl's first loyalty will be always to her brother. We cannot have such a disturbing presence when seeking our answers in the secret pool."

Riana heard a ripple, as if she gazed now into those still, reflective waters, but perhaps it was the strange, mysterious rustling in the shadows.

"Speak to Guinivere," Morgause urged, her voice melding with the sweet, mesmerizing tone of a distant chanting. "Make the queen believe she needs Greta's help with her tapestry, for at least one day each week."

Yes, she could do that, Riana thought, and Greta would understand. She too wanted Wolf set free.

Morgause smiled as she circled, edging ever closer, the low, rhythmic chanting moving with her, until both were at Riana's ear, stirring up the scent of long buried secrets, shrouded by time and need. "If you truly wish to reverse that spell," Morgause whispered with the sibilance of a hundred voices, "I alone can help you. Place your trust in my hands, Riana. Greta can take her lessons with Morgan, while you come here to me alone."

Riana gripped the arms of her chair as the room seemed to spin about her. It made sense. Morgan preferred Greta; they'd probably never miss her. So why this tiny persistent niggling that something was wrong?

"Go to Guinivere," Morgause coaxed, now crooning into her

other ear. "Convince her to use her influence with her husband. Use your powers to make certain this tournament never happens."

"Tournament?" The word caught Riana unprepared. She had to think hard to remember the contest that would choose her husband.

"Do you want a man who will rule you, who will keep you from your magic?"

"No," Riana whispered with no real conviction, tortured by bittersweet memories of her days and nights with Wolf.

"There is but one path for you, child," Morgause went on, her voice ringing with conviction enough for them both. "You have been called by the Goddess. You are meant to serve Arthur as his Great Enchantress."

My destiny, Riana thought in a daze, reminded suddenly of the twisting, twining threads around Merlin. She must let nothing stand in the way of what she'd been called to do.

"Prove you are worthy." The voice in her ear deepened, stern and commanding, no longer the soft, breathy tones of Morgause. "Answer this first test of your dedication. Go to Arthur's queen. Make her see reason."

A test? Riana thought, a host of voices mingling in her head, goading her into proving her dedication to Arthur, pressing her to justify Merlin's summons, demanding that she send the Saxon away. If she did not soon free him of the enchantment, and Wolf should endanger himself with his meddling, his blood would be on her hands.

"I'll do it," she cried out, desperate to spare him.

The voices stilled at once, the swirling shadows retreating abruptly to the corners of the room.

All that remained was the smiling Morgause, pointing to the door.

On the far reaches of River Ford, Helga waited in the dark for the longboat to row closer. This stretch might be isolated, but she dared not call out. She would not risk being heard by her fellow villagers, for no one must guess that she, with Lord Vangarth's help, was the source of their woes. Bewitched by the Briton, they would never understand that Riana had been like a diseased limb, that sometimes, the body must suffer the pains of amputation to be rid of a damaged part.

Watching Vangarth land and alight from his boat, Helga braced herself for the upcoming interview. Now that the Briton was gone, and Penawulf had denounced her, Vangarth had no need to retain the village's chest of gold. Returning it had no doubt slipped his mind, with all he had to think about, but she did not relish the task of reminding him. He was not an easy man when angered, their Lord Vangarth, nor a pleasant one.

"Any word?" he barked at her as he strode closer. "Has Penawulf returned?"

"Not yet, milord. Ranulf still leads the village, and he keeps it on full alert." Not exactly true, but she saw no reason for Vangarth to know their weaknesses. He'd been useful to her in getting rid of the Briton, but she knew this man wouldn't hesitate to harm her chieftain and people if they got in the way of his ambitions.

"Time grows short. Have Ranulf send a messenger to Camelot telling Penawulf that he must not tarry in Arthur's court. War is imminent. A chieftain should be here with his people."

"War?"

"The Britons are amassing on the borders, ready to attack at a word. You can thank your chieftain's wife for this, I'll wager. She wasted no time in telling Arthur all she could about our defenses. One wonders, in fact, if the lack of word from Penawulf is more ominous than we first supposed. If I were Ranulf, I'd go myself to Camelot to make certain he is unharmed."

"Damn her!" Helga hissed. "I will go to Camelot and kill the British bitch myself."

Vangarth reached out to clasp her arm. "I have told you before, Moriana is clever, and she no doubt hopes to goad us into such rash actions. We must keep our wits clear and remain one step ahead of her. Talk to Ranulf. He is the one who must go to Camelot to save your chieftain. I will meet you here at week's end to hear of your progress."

He turned then, and would have left, had Helga not called out to him. "My lord, wait. Perhaps you have forgotten, but you gave your word that at first opportunity, you would return River Ford's chest of gold."

He stopped, spinning to face her. "Do you doubt me?"

Helga fought the urge to recoil from his fury. "No, of course not. It is just we have dire need of that gold."

"I said you will have it and you shall. Now, have you any other complaints before I take my leave?"

"No, milord."

"Good. Then might I suggest you worry about what you must do, and leave me to deal with my own concerns? Week's end, woman. Right here, in this spot. And make certain you have good news for me."

He marched off then, leaving Helga alone in the dark, wondering how in the name of all the great gods she was to convince Ranulf that their chieftain was in danger and Ranulf too needed to go to Camelot.

Several days later on her way to her lessons with Morgause, Riana saw Queen Guinivere walking through the palace garden. "Milady, might I have a moment of your time?" she called out, unaware of why she did so.

Guinivere stopped on the path, smiling warmly. "Of course, my child. I was just on my way to the chapel to light a candle, but I always have time to spare for you." She gestured to a small bench, indicating that they both sit. "What is on your mind?"

What indeed? Riana's brain seemed dulled, foggy and swarming with whispers. Why *had* she felt the sudden strong need to talk to Guinivere?

The tournament, she thought in an instant of clarity, as if someone had spoken the word in her ear. She needed the queen's help in stopping the competition.

"I've heard you're having difficulty finding the right shades of red and black for your tapestry," she said instead, surprising herself yet again. "Greta is a master at mixing dyes. She'd gladly help, should you wish it."

"Do you think so?" Guinivere asked eagerly. "I've exhausted my own paltry knowledge and I'd leap at the chance to . . . but no, Greta seems quite happy and certainly busy enough, working with my brother's sisters."

"I'm certain no one will mind if you steal her services for a mere day a week." Even as she uttered the words, Riana was aware of having heard them before. The other night, she thought hazily, in Morgause's chambers.

"I would be grateful for her help." To stress this, Guinivere took and squeezed her hand. "Tell her, if she wishes, I'd be happy to have her visit me this morning."

If Greta went to Guinivere today, she would miss their lesson. But then, Riana realized uneasily, wasn't this what Morgause wanted?

"What is it?" Guinivere asked softly, again applying pressure to her hand. "Something is plainly troubling you."

Could she tell this kind and gentle woman that her mind no longer seemed to be her own, that the words she spoke seemed to come from elsewhere? "It is the tournament," she said instead. "I cannot bear being offered up this way. What if I must be given over to that Saxon?"

Guinivere gave a girlish grin. "To me, it seems no real hardship. This Penawulf is an exceptionally fine looking man."

"You don't know . . ."

Too late, Riana knew she shouldn't have spoken. Pulling her hand free, she looked away to avoid Guinivere's soft brown penetrating gaze.

"Is he the one?" the queen probed softly. "Did Penawulf put such sadness in your eyes?"

As tempted as she was to confide in this gentle woman, Riana had vowed never to speak of her life with Wolf.

But she had, she realized slowly. That same night, staring into the candle. Morgause now knew all there was to know about her.

Uncomfortable with such thoughts, Riana concentrated instead on what the Goddess had called her to do. And the first step, she realized hazily, was in sending Wolf away. "It's not sadness, milady," she told Guinivere firmly, "but rather apprehension. I do not wish such a man for my husband. Please intervene with the king. Make him see reason."

"But I've already tried. I questioned his wisdom in finding you a husband in what is merely a game, but Arthur is surprisingly adamant. He insists your future must be settled before you land in more mischief and sees much of value in this Saxon." Rising with a sigh, Guinivere held out her hands to help Riana to her feet.

Strolling beside her along the path, Guinivere spoke gently. "It is frightening, I know, to consider wedding a stranger, but Arthur loves you as he would his own daughter, and he'd give you to no man he wasn't certain you can come to love in time. Oh Riana, there is so much only a husband can provide. Do you not want a home and children?"

Again, Riana couldn't look at her, lest she reveal what must remain a private pain. "I have other interests," she said stiffly.

Guinivere stopped, taking her by the shoulders. "Do not make your choice impulsively, Riana. You are young, and think you have your life ahead of you, but all too soon you'll be like me, growing old and frightened at the emptiness of your womb. Each time I hear a baby cry, or hold another's child in my arms, I die a bit more inside."

Dismayed to see such anguish in this woman who had been so kind to her, Riana cast about in her mind for words of comfort. "Milady, I am sorry," she offered helplessly.

Guinivere released her grip to continue walking. "I don't tell you this to gain sympathy, but more to offer a warning. It's no easy life, being childless. Everywhere I go, I hear the whispers of concern, of pity, even scorn. And though he tries to hide it, I see the disappointment on my husband's face. This is why I go each day to the chapel, praying to the Virgin for a miracle. I would give anything to bear Arthur a son. A true heir, so he need not be forced to acknowledge his bastard, Mordred."

Riana ached for the queen, even as her hand touched her own belly. She knew about whispers, about emptiness, and the disappointment on her husband's face. And she, too, prayed every day for a miracle.

Yet unwilling to speak of such things, Riana placed a comforting hand on the queen's arm. "I shall think on what you've said, milady," she promised, wanting to see the smile return to Guinivere's gentle face.

Taking her in her arms, Guinivere embraced her. "I would not have you suffer as I have," she told Riana as they broke apart.

"Nor would I have you endure any more misery, either."

Leaving the queen on the path, Riana swallowed to ease the tightness in her throat. How selfish she felt, worrying so about her own problems that she'd been blind to Arthur and Guinivere's misery. If she thought it would help, she, too, would pray to this Virgin to end their pain.

Then again, she saw on a flash of inspiration, she might better appeal to the Goddess.

Magic, she thought, realizing that this must be the reason she'd been called to help Arthur. In all those potions and incantations she would learn from Morgause, surely she would find a cure for infertility. Imagine the joy on Arthur's face if his queen at long last presented him with a wriggling, bawling heir.

But it was not Arthur's face she saw, nor even Guinivere's. It was herself she envisioned, beside Wolf as he cradled his newborn son.

Dismayed that she could let herself be so easily distracted from her duty, she hurried back into the castle to inform Greta of the change of plans. It was best that her friend not be with them if it meant Morgause would be more willing to help her. Odd, how it had worked out. Greta, working with Morgan, while her destiny drew Riana more and more to Morgause.

She denied a sudden qualm, the sense again of something

being not quite right. Hastening her step, she told herself she had work to do, important work, and she must not dally.

Wolf stalked through the forest, alert for the sound of snapping twigs, a branch being pushed aside. The others in his party remained behind in the clearing, sharing a jug of ale, while Wolf alone kept to the hunt.

In the week he'd been at Camelot, he'd made few friends among the Britons and he relished this chance to walk free through the forest where the rules were simple and honest, unlike at court. Always on edge, watching and listening for secrets, he'd sensed that all was not well in Arthur's kingdom. A disease had sprouted in some dark, hidden corner, and there were those who would see it grow and prosper.

At first, like Helga, he'd believed Riana must be involved in the conspiracy, but watching from afar, seeing her affection for the king and his queen, her kindness to Greta, Wolf had cause to wonder. Last night, he'd come upon his wife telling stories to the castle children, much as she'd done with the young ones in River Ford. Inside the grand hall, the ladies of the court danced and flirted with the knights at yet another celebration in Wolf's honor, while Riana sat in the courtyard with the children gathered around her, their young, eager faces raised to hers in complete adoration.

The sight left Wolf wondering who was the real Moriana. The cold, calculating witch who robbed his village, or the sweet, loving angel he'd held in his arms?

At a sudden sound behind him, he whirled, noticing a female clad in a dark brown robe, winding through the trees in the distance. He knew that flowing hair, had felt the golden strands slide through his fingers. At first, he thought Riana must be a vision, conjured up by his yearnings, but then he noticed Morgause behind her, and knew he'd never dream up that unsettling female.

Considering the queen's intent manner as she nudged Riana along, they must be in a great hurry. The furtive manner with which Morgause glanced over her shoulder fueled his suspicions that she was up to no good. *Where could they go,* Wolf wondered, *in the midst of such a dense forest?*

Determined to find out, he followed silently, keeping low and out of sight. Must his wife appear to be a different person each time he saw her? That first night in the dining hall, he'd been lured to her side by a frightened, helpless Riana, but this woman creeping through the woods, her features blank and expressionless, seemed a virtual stranger. He sensed he could step up right before her and she'd see nothing but the path ahead.

Even as he hastened his step, thinking to test this theory, he heard a strange, sizzling sound, before both females vanished before his eyes.

He stopped where he stood, puzzled. One moment they'd been walking along the path ahead of him, and in the blink of an eye, all that remained was a weird shimmering, like the air rising from the fields on a hot, humid day.

Crouching down, touching the earth and going still, he listened to the forest. Through the usual rhythms, he could feel a steady thud of footsteps ahead, yet could see no trace of his wife when he looked in that direction. Indeed, it stung his eyes each time he tried.

Still, he kept on the trail, alternately feeling the earth and following his instincts, growing more baffled by the moment, until he touched the ground and felt nothing but the earth's natural rhythms. Clearly, both women had stopped.

Hand gripping the knife at his belt, he circled the area where he'd last heard them. Softly, so faintly he could well have imagined it, he caught a snatch of what seemed to be singing.

He heard it again, and just as quickly, it vanished on the breeze. Tuning in on the sound as it faded in and out, Wolf came upon a glade surrounding a small pond of crystalline water. Staying well within the cover of the trees, he searched the pond's perimeter, until Riana's image wavered into his vision. Perched at the lip on the far side of the pond, she spoke in a singsong chant as she gazed sightlessly into the water. Morgause, watching from a distance, smiled in satisfaction.

Magic.

Wolf battled his anger. He'd told Riana he would tolerate no more witchery, yet here she was, defying him once more. He wanted to march over and demand she cease at once, but reason prevailed. He would learn far more about his wife by watching silently.

Edging back to blend with the trees, he saw Morgause stiffen, her cool, green gaze scanning the shoreline, then the woods surrounding it. Before she reached his hiding place, the chanting stopped and Morgause turned her attention back to Riana.

With one last furtive glance behind them, the queen took Riana by the arm and pulled her back onto the barely discernible path through the trees.

Vowing not to lose sight of his wife this time, Wolf tracked Riana with all his senses, not just his vision. Straining, he caught her floral scent, heard her rapid breathing, as the witch hurried her back the way they had come. When once more they seemed to vanish, Wolf used Riana's lingering fragrance to find the narrow opening, well-hidden in a mound of stones.

Stepping through the doorway some moments after the two women, he found himself in a dark, damp tunnel. He followed the light bouncing in the distance as it wound its way beneath the earth, taking care to make no sound, for the women did not speak. He found their silence strange, but then all Riana's behavior today had been out of character. Though her body was there, her mind seemed to be elsewhere.

At long last, the light came to a stop, before winding slowly upward. Hearing the sound of shuffling footsteps, he realized Morgause and Riana were climbing a freestanding staircase. He thought at first to follow, but in truth, he had no need. His keen sense of direction told him he stood in the bowels of Camelot, and he'd wager his last weapon that the stairway led to a little-known doorway into the queen's chambers.

Again, he wondered at the need for such secrecy.

As a door slammed above, he knew he would find no more answers today. Waiting for his eyes to adjust to the dark, he made his way back, needing all his senses to grope through the tunnel. It felt unclean, that fetid darkness, and it was with great relief that he finally emerged into the sunlight. Breathing deeply of the fresh, forest air, he struggled to make sense of what had just happened.

He was still puzzling over Riana's strange behavior when he came upon Sir Kay, stumbling about looking for him. "Where have you been, boy?" the man huffed, his aging, rounding body not meant for such exercise. "I'd begun to fear you'd decided to leave us."

Wolf glanced over his shoulder, still troubled. "Tell me, Kay. You would know of such things. Can a witch make herself disappear?"

Kay tilted his head, clearly curious. "Merlin vanished all the time. He told us it was a simple enough illusion. Why do you ask?"

Wolf took in another gulp of air. "I saw Morgause just now, walking through the forest, and then I saw nothing but shimmering air."

Nodding, Kay started back toward the others. "That shimmering, it makes you uneasy, no? Like there's something not quite natural about it."

Unnatural. Falling into step beside his trainer, Wolf decided that everything about the afternoon defied the natural order. "I wonder, for her to vanish like that, do you think she saw me watching?"

"Hard to say, not being there. These witches, sometimes they merely sense another presence, and they're known to guard their secrets well. But whatever the case, you'd be wise to steer clear of that Morgause. Many is the eager young swain who thought to tame her, and found instead that her kisses are poison. Ask Arthur. He knows better than to place his heart in the hands of a witch, yet look how he let her weave her spell around him. And see what that unholy union has wrought." He spat on the ground as he added, "Mordred."

Falling into step beside Kay, Wolf smiled, for it was not the first time his trainer had told the tale of incest with such disgust. "The girl, Riana," Wolf had to ask, "is she cut of the same mold?"

"I would not think so." Plainly surprised, Kay paused as if to consider this. "Unlike her mentor, Riana shuns all male company and stays mostly to herself. But then, she does spend much of her day with the woman."

"She was with Morgause in the forest today."

"Hmm." Kay eyed him curiously. "This is not about the witch, then. Your concern is for the girl, isn't it?"

The man might seem a bumbling fool to some, but Wolf had firsthand knowledge of how astute Kay could be. "My concern is for what is going on here," he said sharply, not wanting his trainer to guess the truth.

"Now, don't go prickling. I have no wish to pry, but you can't fool this old warrior. I might not have known you long, but I know enough to realize that you wouldn't be entering that tournament without good reason."

She is my wife and no other man shall ever have her, Wolf thought stubbornly. For him, that was reason enough.

"At the risk of meddling," Kay went on, "let me offer this. Morgause is known more for her promiscuity than her generous spirit. For her to take the court foundling under her wing, she must have some secret, selfish motive. If you care aught for the girl, remove her from the woman's influence before much harm is done."

Unconsciously, Wolf's hand went to the knife at his belt. He would kill the witch gladly, before he let her hurt one hair on Riana's head.

The strength of his emotion stunned him. So it had not died, his need to protect his young wife. Indeed, it left him wondering how many other feelings still breathed within him.

Only one thing was certain. After today, he knew less than ever about the true nature of his wife's heart or motivations. He would need to dig deeper to find the truth.

And the best place to start would be with Riana herself.

Nineteen

Reeling with confusion, Riana woke in a chair in the queen's chambers, wondering how it had gotten to be so late that a fire would be set and candles would light the room. The last thing she could remember was sipping a sickeningly sweet mulled wine.

As she slowly focused, she realized Morgause knelt before her, her feline eyes glittering like twin emeralds. "You spoke, Moriana," the woman said breathlessly. "This time when you gazed into the crystal pool, you spoke aloud of a vision."

Riana searched her brain to remember, but all she found was a yawning gap in her memory, and a dull throbbing in the back of her head.

"Merlin himself must have spoken through you," Morgause said in a conspiratorial tone. "Most was of a military nature, the sort of information the magician would want to relate to his king."

"Military?" Riana asked with a long, involuntary shiver.

"You spoke of a war council, convening to plot an attack on the Saxon Shores. King Cerdric himself sat at the council, Riana. Merlin wants us to warn Arthur to move his troops to the southeast border."

An attack? Thinking of Tad and Ranulf and even the odious Helga, Riana found it hard to imagine any Saxon threat.

But then she remembered Cerdric's grand hall with Vangarth, and of course, that severed head.

"You feel torn because of your Saxon," Morgause commiserated, seeing her indecision. "Yet if you don't report what you've seen, where will the fingers point when Camelot is attacked and the king is left unprepared? The Round Table will say you brought the Saxon spy here, and then sat back to let your husband's armies destroy us."

Riana shook her head, still uncertain. "But how can I tell the king what I've seen when I can't remember even seeing it?"

"I can remind you, prompt you. Is it not wiser to be cautious, to err on the side of safety? If your vision is true, our warriors will be ready. And if not, the army has merely been inconvenienced for a brief time."

As always, everything Morgause said made sense, yet Riana felt vaguely uncomfortable. "I saw nothing else in the pool?" she asked, hoping there might have been some mention of the cure for Guinivere's infertility.

"Poor Riana," Morgause said with a quirk of her lips. "No, you said nothing about your enchantment, nor the cure for your barrenness either."

Reminded of how much Morgause now knew about her, Riana felt suddenly hemmed in by the woman, as if there were too little air for them to breathe.

Morgause seemed to sense this also. Sighing, she rose and moved away to the kettle, intent upon brewing.

"I must go," Riana said, suddenly desperate to leave this ever-shifting room. "I must rest and rid myself of this headache."

"Nonsense. My herbal tea is what you need." Setting the kettle on the fire, Morgause hurried over to fuss like a doting mother. "Poor lamb," she crooned, massaging Riana's taut shoulders. "How disappointing it must be to have your first real vision and be unable to remember it."

Riana didn't bother to correct her. She knew Morgause did not like hearing about that other vision in River Ford, the one with Merlin that had summoned her to Camelot.

"You'll remember more next time," Morgause insisted, "provided your Saxon doesn't stumble along and ruin everything.

He's a lusty one, I'll grant you that, but you'll discover that sex and magic rarely mix."

"I have no intention of mixing them." Her mentor's repeated mention of Wolf's physical appeal annoyed Riana; it reminded her of how Morgause pawed him each night in the dining hall. "I've told you, before he will go, I must find some way to unweave my enchantment."

"And so you shall, with my help, but we might be too late. What good will it do to reverse the spell if he's already won the tournament?" Her fingers paused their rubbing as Morgause thought aloud. "Of course, we could make certain he does not win by finding ourselves a champion, the one undefeated knight at court guaranteed to defeat your Saxon."

Riana spun in her chair to face her. "You can't mean Sir Lancelot?"

Smiling, Morgause took her shoulders and began kneading them once more. "Lancelot is highly susceptible to a lady in distress, and his skill is unsurpassed. If he can't best your Saxon, no one can."

Turning back to face the fire, Riana shook her head, feeling ugly inside. "You're asking me to plot against my husband."

"For his own best interests. Think, Riana. Camelot fears and resents the Saxon already, but once his countrymen begin attacking British settlements, what do you think our knights will do to him?"

It made sense to send Wolf away, Riana knew, yet she could imagine his fury when he learned of her choice. "You don't know Wolf. He'll feel betrayed if I choose against him."

"And this matters? Is it his feelings you wish to protect, or his life?"

Morgause was right; here was the one, sure way to ensure his safety.

"It's not always easy to do what is right, is it?" Morgause said softly. "But this man means to stop your forays into the magical realm. He will prevent you from fulfilling your duty to our king. Is that what you want?"

Riana stood, the pain in her head worsening by the moment. "I'm not sure what I want, only that I must rest. We can talk tomorrow . . ." She hesitated, remembering. "No, I must go to my lesson with Morgan."

Morgause went still. "I thought we'd agreed you would learn your magic from me."

"Greta says Morgan asks each day for me. It will raise suspicion if I do not visit her."

"Considering the rumors about what my sister did to Merlin, it might raise more than suspicion if you don't avoid Morgan."

"What rumors?"

Morgause sighed unhappily. "My sister has made no secret of her hatred for Merlin, not after he convinced Arthur to revive Roman law. A defender of the old pagan religion, she feels his policies have done more damage to England than the Romans. And while I might agree with her in principle, I can't condone her methods. After all, now that she's rid him of his magician, what will her greed and ambition do to my poor brother?"

Morgan, plotting against the king? "No, she'd never hurt Arthur."

"And on what do you base this defense? Fact? Experience?"

No, Riana simply *felt* Morgan must be innocent.

"Do you think I wish to believe such evil of my own sister?" the woman cried out. "But I see her surrounding herself with darkness and shadow, seeing a select, secret few, and I must wonder. She killed her own husband when he tried to stop her plotting. Why balk now at ridding herself of the one man who stands in the way of her mad quest for power?"

Riana shook her head to clear it, more confused than ever. Morgan did seem shrouded in mystery, and had every logical appearance of guilt, yet deep in her heart, Riana kept hearing the words, *Nothing is as it seems.*

Morgause placed a comforting hand on her shoulder. "Forgive me if I've upset you, but I worry about you, child. What mother would not?"

Riana froze, shaken to the core. The woman couldn't possibly mean what her words implied. She looked up for an explanation, but Morgause turned away, twisting her hands as she paced across the room. "My poor, sweet baby," she said in obvious anguish. "I hadn't wanted to tell you, not like this, but the business with your husband has me rattled. Your arrogant Saxon is so very far from what a mother would wish for her only daughter."

Her *mother?* All her life, Riana had longed for this moment, so why did she feel such shock. Such a vague, vast uneasiness?

Morgause turned to her then, her expression regretful. "How clumsy of me. You must hate me for keeping my secret all these years."

"Why did you? I mean, even while working together, you've given not even the slightest hint."

Tears glistened in her emerald eyes. "I wanted to tell you, more than you can imagine, but long ago, I gave my word to Arthur. He will despise me now for breaking it. One impulsive, emotional outburst, and I've ruined the trust he and I have built between us."

Morgause seemed so young, so contrite, Riana was moved to pity. "I will say nothing to him, to anyone, but it seems unfair that he demand your silence. Surely he'd understand why you now broke your vow."

Morgause shook her head sadly. "He would not have the world know he was your father."

Arthur, her *father?* It was too much suddenly—too overwhelmingly much.

"His kingdom could forgive Mordred, for every youth makes his mistakes," Morgause went on, her voice strained, "but to learn that he'd twice lain with his sister, and at a time when he was already married . . ." She took a deep breath, sniffing back tears. "It was no easy thing for me, leaving you at the castle doorstep with only my brother's promise that he'd care for you. Arthur kept his word, Riana. So too should have I."

Riana gripped her hands in her lap. For so long, she'd yearned for answers, but hearing them now, she felt sick inside. "I don't understand. If Arthur did care for me, why then was I sent away?"

Morgause shook her head. "I've lain awake many a night pondering that question. I can't see how anyone could have guessed the truth, else you'd be dead, not exiled. I've come to think it might have been Merlin, or perhaps even my sister, grown jealous of your emerging talent. They would not want a mere girl usurping their influence on my brother."

Shocked and numbed, Riana could feel no sense of kinship with this woman. And Arthur, her father? It made sense, she supposed, the way he'd watched out for her, but it hurt that he would remain so anxious to deny his daughter. She could see his keeping the secret from others, but why not admit their relation to her?

Morgause came to a stop before her, tears sparkling like diamonds on her cheeks. "My precious child, I know I've lost all right to meddle in your life, but loving you so, I want only the very best for you. Do you think I can bear to watch you sacrifice your true calling for that . . . that barbarian? He would keep you his plaything, his slave, and never let you serve your father, the king, as you were born to do."

Typically, Morgause had overexaggerated, but in essence, what she said was true. Now, more than ever, Riana could see where her destiny lay. Helping Arthur, her father, beget his heir.

Unconsciously, her hand went to her belly. Even now, she could feel the ache there, the constant reminder of the child she would never bear. Oh Wolf, she thought on a wave of grief. How clear it all was now. Long ago, the fates had decreed that their marriage would never survive.

"Trust in your mother's knowledge and experience," Morgause purred. "I urge you, send your Saxon back to his village, and I shall do anything else you would ask of me."

Anything? Cold and numb inside, Riana wondered if Morgause would help find the cure to remove her son Mordred from the throne. "Guinivere is desperate for a child," Riana said, testing her. "Help me brew a potion to help her conceive and I shall do whatever *you* wish."

"No!" As if startled by her outburst, Morgause looked hurriedly away. "That is . . . you must understand . . . Merlin worked for years to cure her infertility. What can we possibly hope to achieve?"

"We must try." Riana drew herself up, determined to make her intentions clear to this stranger who had birthed her. "As you said yourself, I've been brought here to serve my king and I shall, with or without your support. Now, will you help me, or must I seek my husband's aid instead?"

It was an idle threat, and they both knew it, but Morgause eyed her approvingly. "Very well, my child," she said, stepping up to clasp Riana's hands. "From this day on, we shall work together, mother and daughter, enchantress helping enchantress, finding our answers in the sacred pool. And when we are done, we shall grant your father what he so richly deserves."

Deep down, Riana knew this was a triumph, that she'd taken a strong step toward her destiny, yet all she could feel was the increasing throb in her head and a desperate need to flee. "Tomorrow," she told Morgause distractedly, removing her hands from the woman's grasp. "We shall begin our search then."

Morgause paced across her chambers in a dither of excitement. Today, at the sacred pool, the girl had proved she owned more talent than any of them had ever dreamed. Properly managed, young Moriana could prove a treasure indeed.

But first, Morgause thought with a frown, they must rid themselves of those who would sway the girl from what they wanted of her—primary of whom was her virile Saxon husband. Morgause did not like Riana's reluctance to send the handsome brute away.

Nor, in truth, could she blame the girl. Were Penawulf less observant and clever, Morgause would be tempted to try him in bed herself, for the mere sight of his virile form set her body throbbing. But any man who would track down his woman the length of England was that most boring of male animals, the faithful mate, else he would not have spurned her three times already.

They could not wait for Lancelot to unseat him in the tournament. Lifting up a vial of noxious smelling potions, she decided she might better deal with the handsome Lord Penawulf herself.

Since his return from the forest, Wolf had spent the entire evening tracking Riana through the castle, only to discover she'd yet to emerge from the chambers of Queen Morgause. It did little to enhance her innocence that his wife would choose to remain closeted with that witch all this time.

His impulse was to pound upon the door and drag her from the room, but once again, he knew he'd learn more from the less direct approach.

His patience was rewarded moments later when Riana stepped through the door. Though he stood in plain sight, she failed to notice him, her glazed eyes staring sightlessly ahead, much as they had in the forest. With that same distracted air, she hurried down the hall, wrapping her arms around her as if to gain warmth. Wolf found nothing furtive in her actions; she seemed more tortured and frightened and in a great haste to flee that room.

Concerned, worried about what Morgause might have done to her, Wolf followed, ready to offer his protection should Riana need it. While he took no care to muffle his footsteps, never once did she turn to confront him as they descended a flight of stone steps. With the same air of driven preoccupation, she passed through the oak door to the walled garden courtyard Arthur had designed for his wife.

Wolf could think of no better place to go when troubled; he came here often late at night when he wished to be alone with his thoughts. A certain tranquility reigned along the shaded paths, an aura of purity and hope rose up from the flower beds— clean emotions that were stifled and corrupted inside the walls of the castle. Coming out here, Wolf always felt as if he could breathe, truly breathe for the first time all day.

The night was warm, with the scent of lilacs wafting on the balmy air. Above, a soft golden moon looked down, bathing the scene with a gentle, forgiving light, making a far different scene from that under full sunlight. It was much like viewing the truth, Wolf realized—one's perception could vary greatly with the illumination.

His mood mellowing by the moment, he gazed at the woman who was his wife, torn between his own perceptions. Villainess or victim, Riana would always be the loveliest female he would ever know. Golden hair stirred by the breeze, she stood gazing up at the moon, holding herself tightly, seemingly lost and alone and ready to weep.

Yet in all the time he had known her, he had never seen Riana actually cry. She'd shed no tears when he'd captured her, when he'd forced her to the fields, or even when his village humiliated her. Instead she'd gone cold and withdrawn, just as she'd done when she lost their baby. It struck him that what he had once perceived as a lack of emotion could be merely an inability to vent it. Given her past, was it any wonder she would fear revealing what she held deep in her heart?

As he stood staring at her, his mind drifted back to the softer moments between them, the unguarded ones when she'd felt free to dance for him, make love with him. That had been *his* Riana, the sweet, loving girl who had brought such joy and laughter into his life. Seeing her now, so sad and unsure, he wanted to unwrap her arms so he could hold her and offer his own warmth instead. Did her guilt or innocence truly matter tonight? The question would still be there in the morning to be decided.

At his approach, she looked up, startled. He thought at first she meant to flee, but as if she too were caught by the lure of memories, she stood motionless before him, her golden eyes searching his.

"I would touch you," he said quietly, holding out his hand. "To see and feel for myself that all is well with you."

Fear and confusion glittered in the golden depths, but she slowly unwrapped her arms to clasp his hand. Would it always be thus, he wondered as their fingers connected—would he always feel the same lightning jolt of awareness?

Gazing down at her, he realized that now that he had her attention, he didn't know what to say. She seemed so frail, the link between them so fragile, and he hadn't the words to break through the barrier that stood between them.

So he tugged her close, pulling her into his embrace, cradling her against his chest like a priceless treasure he must guard for his king.

Nay, he thought, painfully aware of his reluctance to let her go—Riana was one treasure he would guard for himself.

It felt so right, the way she clung to him, as if the two of them, here and now, alone made sense in a world gone mad. *What had gone wrong?* he wondered desperately. *Where had they taken the first ill-fated step that pulled them apart?*

But glancing up at the castle looming before him, he knew the step had been taken long before he had ever met her. In her heart, Riana would always need to belong to this place and its king.

"Little has changed," he said sadly, kissing the top of her head. "It will always be thus, won't it? Me, chasing you. You chasing a dream."

Stiffening, she pulled away, and as she did, Wolf retreated back into his own protective shell. They were what life had made them, and nothing could change it. Whatever comfort they might share was fleeting at best, and for tonight, the tenderness was over.

Painfully aware of the sudden shift in emotion, Riana stared up at Wolf, not knowing whether to be grateful or enraged that he was here, that he'd held her, that he'd again offered hope when in truth there was none.

She clenched her fists at her sides, determined not to show how much she longed to be back in his arms, to lose herself in that sweet, impossible fantasy. "Why are you here?" she ground out, her throat raw with emotion. "You belong with your people in River Ford."

He too stood stiffly, his gray eyes glinting in the moonlight. "You were once one of them, or have you forgotten?"

Did he truly think she could ever forget? There in his village, she'd known what it meant to be part of something, of someone, she who had yearned all her life for a family to call her own.

But she had a family now, she thought in confusion, a mother, and a father, both calling for her help.

"What happened to our dreams?" Wolf probed quietly. "Can't you remember, Riana, the plans we shared for the future?"

What could she tell him? That she had no right to make plans when she had no future to offer? But that would mean relating what she'd just learned from Morgause, something she'd promised never to do.

Staring at Wolf, knowing from the way he'd held her that he must be suffering also, she yearned to forget her obligations and fling herself back in the haven of his arms. Dear Goddess of the Earth and Sky, where would she find the strength to send this man away?

"Everything has changed," she said tightly, reminding herself sternly that his emotions stemmed from that damned enchantment. "You of all people should know that."

"All I know is that we were wed and you are my woman."

He would not make this easy. "Such stubbornness will get you killed. Have you see these knights in action? Can you truly believe an untrained outsider can best them all?"

"I do." Faced with his confidence, his sheer brute presence, she found it hard not to believe him. "Never doubt for an instant that I shall emerge any less than victorious, Riana. I alone know what I am fighting for."

She could scarcely breathe as he stepped up to take her hand, turning it over to trace a slow, lazy line on her palm. Every bone in her seemed to melt, and with it her willpower.

Frantically, she fought it, conscious of how capitulating to him now could endanger Wolf's life. He had to leave before the Saxons attacked, or Morgause was right—Camelot would brand him a spy and demand he die a hideous death.

"It makes no sense, your being here," she said desperately. "You should be home, with Tad and Helga and the others, getting the soil ready for the Spring planting. It is madness, staying here where Arthur's knights will test you beyond endurance. Can anything be worth such sacrifice?"

"You answer me." Without warning, he swooped down and took her again in his arms.

Unlike his earlier embrace, his kiss was no gentle reminder of what had been, but a firm pronouncement of what passion would always be stirred between them. Taking her mouth like a warrior slashing across the battlefield, he brought home the hot, searing nights they'd shared in the villa. Heart thundering in her chest, blood pounding in her brain, she lost herself to the longing. One kiss, she promised her conscience. Was it too much to ask when faced with the long, bleak future ahead?

This time it was Wolf who pulled away, his dark features as tormented as her own as he gazed down at her. "That much, at least, hasn't changed," he said huskily.

Trembling all over, she closed her eyes in an attempt to summon her strength. As Morgause had said, it was for his own welfare that Wolf must leave Camelot, and the sooner the better. "I was foolish to succumb to you," she told him coldly. "It's a mistake I have no intention of repeating. I have a life here, a good life, and I will not let past weaknesses interfere with the work I must do."

"Work?" he sneered. "Is that what you call your witchery?"

"I am no witch. I am an enchantress."

He grabbed her wrist, his fingers digging into the flesh. "I've had enough of this dangerous foolishness. I won't have you tampering with forces you can't understand. Can't you see you're being used, Riana? You've placed your trust in the wrong people. This so-called training is designed to trick you into wrongdoing and evil."

Unwillingly, she wondered if there was truth in his accusation. Where once she'd spoken of Camelot as if it were a castle in the air, she now feared her memories had been hope and illusion.

These days, the castle seemed besieged by the plots and secrets hatching within it, a hundred hungry vultures, waiting for Arthur's dream to die so they could pick the bones clean.

"You ask why I am here?" Wolf asked fiercely, making her achingly aware of how tall and powerful he was, and how her body would always yearn for him. "I came for you, Riana. And I will leave with nothing more and nothing less."

"No!" Riana felt as if the word were ripped from her mouth. "I—I don't want you in my life."

His gaze held her, ensnared her. "You can lie to these people, but I watched you dance for me. I lay beside you and stroked your hair, and I crouched at the bottom of that cliff, holding and protecting you, the night you lost our child. We have too much between us to stop trying now."

He could have wielded a knife, so deeply did his words pierce her. Flooded with pain, by regret, she could not find the words to deny him.

"You are and always will be my woman," Wolf said solemnly. "I will not leave these walls without you."

He turned then to stride away, leaving her to stare after him, longing for him, knowing she would have to hurt them both deeply to save his life.

Two days before the tournament, a desperate Riana decided to visit Queen Morgan. It made her feel guilty and vastly uneasy, but since she and Morgause were no closer to a cure for Guinivere's infertility, or a spell to undo her enchantment, a desperate Riana decided she must put her trust in someone other than her mother.

Welcomed inside, Riana blinked as she stared about Morgan's chambers. Gone were the dark draperies and with them the shadows. Fresh air and sunlight spilled in through the opened windows, showing the room to be far larger than she'd originally supposed.

And far emptier.

Even Morgan seemed different, her dark robes abandoned for a simple yellow tunic. Surprisingly lovely and quite maidenish with the wreath of daisies twined in her dark, flowing hair, Morgan seemed such a stranger, Riana thought at first she had come to the wrong chambers.

"I once thought an enchantress must surround herself with an image, a glamour," Morgan said with a self-deprecating grin. "Of late, I've come to realize it was just a facade I hid behind. I find I've grown mightily tired of hiding."

"I know I am bound by an oath of silence," Riana said in a rush, likewise tired of keeping secrets, "but it is vital that I speak to you."

Studying Riana's face, Morgan sighed. "How ironic, that we should grow beyond the need for silence just as I am leaving."

"You're leaving?" Riana asked, stunned. But how foolish of her. Why else would the room be so empty?

"It is the way of the ancients to leave the land as they found it, and so too shall I leave these chambers." Morgan gestured her to the two chairs by the hearth, all that remained save the simple pine bed in the corner. "I've already packed my things, but I've kept out a bit of raspberry wine for just such an occasion. Please say you'll join me?"

Riana nodded, feeling an overwhelming melancholy, the sense of having waited too long and now it was too late. She knew, even if the words had not been uttered, that Morgan would never return to Camelot.

Pouring the wine, the queen handed her a goblet, then poured her own. Sitting as Morgan did, Riana set her wine on the floor, too upset to drink it.

"Alas, we could have learned much from each other," Morgan said sadly, echoing Riana's own thoughts. "But I fear the time for that is past."

Fear. With all that had been happening lately, Riana had trouble sifting through her myriad emotions, but she knew that more than mere alarm had her wanting to reach out and grab this woman, to beg her to stay. "It doesn't make sense," she said desperately, clutching her hands in her lap. "Why leave now, and in such a hurry?"

Morgan smiled sadly, then looked away. "Never think that I would abandon you here by choice."

Abandoned. Yes, that was exactly how Riana felt. And suddenly very frightened.

"There has been talk," Morgan said flatly. "About attempts made on the Saxon's life."

"Someone has tried to kill Wolf?" Riana's fear escalated to dread, an overwhelming sense of impending doom.

"Thank you for not accusing me," Morgan said softly. "Others are not so kind. They point to the poison found in his wine last night and claim I am the only logical suspect."

"Wolf, poisoned? I must know, is he all right?"

"He has the constitution of a horse, and the will of the most stubborn mule. It will take far more than a few herbs to bring that warrior down."

Studying her, Riana felt certain that this woman hadn't poisoned Wolf. More, the way Morgan smiled at her now, the queen must not only know Riana loved him—she approved of her choice.

"He shall live to fight in the tournament," Morgan went on as if to confirm this, "and given his strength, he'll most likely win. Go with him, Moriana. Go to River Ford and bear his children."

"I cannot," Riana said sadly, wanting her to know the reason. "I will never be the wife he needs. I am barren."

Morgan's expression clouded. Fingers tightening on her goblet, she closed her eyes and raised her face heavenward. "Is it divine will that demands such atonement?" she asked fiercely.

Shaking herself, she opened her eyes, her expression sad. "Ah child, would that I could spare you the suffering, but we've each been given a different path to follow and mine takes me to the Summer Sea. I shall pray long and hard for you, though, in the convent where I'll make my new home."

"A convent? You will pray to the Christian god?"

"I go there for my brother's sake, to appease his priests." Morgan's smile grew conspiratorial. "But between you and me, I chose this particular convent for its proximity to Avalon."

As a child, Riana had oft been held enthralled by tales of the mystical, mist-shrouded island. On its mountain, the Old Ones were said to dwell in a crystal castle, from which they watched and oft ruled the world's triumphs and tragedies. "You will go to Avalon?" she asked, unable to keep the awe from her tone.

Morgan nodded. "If I am called." She sighed, sipping from her glass. "But you, my child, what do you mean to do with your future if you will not go with Penawulf?"

"I will continue to train with your sister. Now, more than ever, it's important that I become an enchantress and serve Arthur." She did not, out of respect for the need for secrecy, explain her reasons for helping the king.

"Has she brought you to the sacred pool?" Morgan demanded, her gaze suddenly, disturbingly intense.

At Riana's nod, Morgan rose from her chair to come clasp her hands and pull her to her feet. "Listen, and heed me well. You are surrounded by forces you are too young and kind and loving to ever fathom, but you must know that there is danger in gazing too long in the crystal. After a time, we are tempted to see only what we wish to see. Or worse, what others would have us imagine."

In her mind, Riana could hear Wolf issuing the same warning. "Who are these others you caution me against?"

Releasing her hands, Morgan shook her head. "All I can offer is advice. Take care in whom you give your trust, for there are those who would betray it, and lead you astray."

A knock sounded at the door and not waiting for it to be opened to them, the royal guard shoved into the room. They were here to escort the queen from Camelot, their leader announced. Morgan must leave at once.

Swallowing the tightness in her throat, Riana reached for her. "It is too soon. There is so much to talk about. You can't leave like this."

With a wistful smile, Morgan took her into her embrace. "Seek love, not power," she whispered into Riana's ear. "And remember, all true magic is born from the goodness in your heart."

Riana clung to her, stunned by the strength of her emotions. "I'm not ready to lose you."

Morgan stood back, smiling enigmatically. "Ah, but we shall see each other again. You and I have yet to play out our roles in this drama."

And with those cryptic words, she glided away, leaving only her distinctive scent behind.

After she was gone, Riana left the empty room to reluctantly make her way to her lessons. Now, she had no choice but to rely upon Morgause, to agree to the plan to use Lancelot as her champion. Given the attempt on his life, Wolf must be forced to leave Camelot.

Even if he must believe she betrayed him.

Twenty

The evening before the tournament, Riana received an urgent summons from Morgause. Heart filled with hope, she hurried to the woman's chambers. This afternoon, they'd stumbled upon an old tome of Merlin's, a rare books of spells from which Morgause had been certain they would soon find the means to undo her enchantment.

None too soon, Riana felt, considering the attempt on Wolf's life.

Morgause waited for her outside her closed bedroom door, her face aglow with excitement. "I've done it!" she cried out the instant she saw Riana. "Here at last is the cure for Guinivere."

Staring at the vial Morgause held up, Riana had to remind herself why this too was important. Worrying so about Wolf, she'd forgotten the need for a cure, and what it would mean for her father, the king.

"Bring the potion to the queen," Morgause instructed with a proud, satisfied smile. "Tell her to take five drops tonight, in anticipation for the king's return from his overnight hunting trip. If this does not put the rightful heir on the throne of England, we can no longer believe in magic."

Riana took the vial, feeling troubled. She knew Morgause was at odds with Mordred—their public quarreling kept the tongues wagging all throughout Camelot—but she nonetheless wondered why Morgause would help the queen create the heir who would one day take her son's throne. Riana wanted to believe Morgause acted out of love for her daughter, as the woman insisted, but ever since Morgan had been sent from Camelot, Riana found herself questioning the motives and actions of everyone around her.

"Do hurry," Morgause urged, glancing back at the closed door behind her. "You must bring the cure to Guinivere at once."

"Now?" Riana asked, startled by her abrupt tone. "But it's late evening and the king is not due back until tomorrow. Surely it can wait."

"And miss the optimal time in the queen's cycle? Can this kingdom afford to wait another month, another moment? Considering the unrest brewing about us, the sooner this matter is settled, the better." Morgause lowered her voice, gripping Riana's arm as she spoke. "We are counting on you, child. Do not fail us."

"Us?"

"All England depends upon what you do next." Morgause smiled, her voice softening with her features. "Can you not hear the magical realm calling? Your destiny waits and you must meet it. This is the moment you've waited for all your life."

Riana stared at the amber liquid, torn between what her mind would have her do and the urgings of her heart. "Yes, Mother," she said, giving away nothing of her inner doubts as she turned away down the hall.

But once out of sight, she intended to change direction. She must first go to her room, she decided, where she could think without the charismatic Morgause goading her into action.

"Hurry," she heard Morgause call out behind her. "Prove that you are every bit Arthur's daughter. His enchantress. Make the future unfold as the Goddess decrees."

"Did you get rid of her?"

Morgause stared at her son, lazing on her bed, stuffing his mouth with her sweetmeats. "Riana is gone, if that's what you mean," she snapped. "Perhaps it's time you took your leave as well. Everyone must think I've distanced myself from you. It will not do, at this point in our plans, to let anyone guess how very much we talk to each other."

Mordred merely yawned. "Oh Mother, how droll you are. You really do fancy yourself as the great manipulator. Makes me shudder to think what you shall do to me once I'm crowned king of all England."

"Don't irritate me with your quips, Mordred. You are and shall always be nothing without my magic. Remember that."

"As if you would let me forget." Sighing, he rolled indolently off the bed, sidling up to her, whispering in her ear. "What a pity that they will never allow a female to rise to the throne."

"You have your own work to do," she told him, keeping her voice even and her fury concealed. "Arctemis is on his way here with word that the Saxon raid is a hoax. Truly, Mordred, you must manage better if you hope to stir unrest at the borders."

"Arctemis is a bloody fool."

"He is not alone." Morgause enjoyed seeing her son in a position of discomfort. There were times when she quite despised the weakling she'd birthed. Mordred was right about one thing. Had she any other access to the throne, she'd happily rid herself of this spineless spawn of Arthur. "You've surrounded yourself with dolts. You tell me that this Vangarth, as Cerdric's favorite, can do much for our cause, yet what has he done save drive that Saxon into our midst?"

"Penawulf should have died at the castle gate," Mordred snarled, "had Kay not bumbled onto us. The damned Saxon bastard has more lives than a cat."

Thinking of the failed poisoning, Morgause was inclined to agree. "He certainly poses more danger. We must get rid of him."

"How fierce of you, or should I say vindictive? What happened, Mother? Did he spurn you and you now need to teach him a lesson?"

She wanted to rake her long nails across his eyes. "As ever, you disappoint me," she said coolly enough. "I've explained that Penawulf's death could be the catalyst we need, for Cerdric will be forced to respond to the murder of his emissary. Present this kingdom with a new, more powerful Saxon threat, and eventually, the masses will turn against Arthur. Dolt, do you wish to be king or not?"

He narrowed his eyes as he gazed at her. "Tell me, Mother, when has it ever mattered what *I* wanted?"

She shouldn't have called him a dolt. Now she'd have to appease his vanity, an effort she sorely resented. "Darling, bear with me. I'm so worried about this potion and how it will work, I am taking my anxiety out on you. I know you're doing your best." Too bad his *best* would never be good enough. "Please, you know I hate it when we quarrel."

"Spare me," he drawled, betraying his own disdain. "And spare us both the performance. Not everyone is as gullible and trusting as your precious little apprentice."

"That precious little apprentice is the key to your future, don't forget. Be grateful that Riana's eager to do my bidding."

"Yes, but for how long? She might be naive, but she's not stupid. Sooner or later, she'll see through your machinations."

"And what of it? She has but one more task to perform and after that, I shall have no more use for her."

"Another accident, Mother? Don't you think someone somewhere is going to notice how you've littered the hall with corpses?"

She merely shrugged. By that time, it would be too late. Mordred would be king of England—a regent ruled by the Royal Enchantress.

He shook his head and gave her a nasty grin as he went for the door. "You might get away with your murders, but if I were you, I'd take care to be a bit more discreet about whom you take as a lover. You won't want your husband's sons learning of your last conquest, for treachery does not sit well with the sons of Lot of Orkney. Those ruffians would as soon slit your throat than let you bed the offspring of the man who killed their father."

"Don't fret over me. Worry about the part you must play tonight."

Mordred's mouth curved in a lascivious smile. "I shall take

great pleasure in it, madam. Just make certain you play yours half as well."

Hateful boy, Morgause thought as she slammed her door shut on his back. It would be no easy thing, ruling England beside him.

Then again, once he sired his own heir, she'd have no further need of him.

"Bring the vial to Guinivere," she whispered, mentally urging Riana. "Let the future unfold as *I* decree."

In her chambers, Riana stared at the vial on the table before her, uncertain what to do. On the surface, Morgause had given her no real reason to doubt her motives, yet all Riana's instincts screamed for caution. Before she acted, she must analyze her sudden reluctance to bring the cure to Guinivere. The future of England could well depend on what she did next.

Yet she was a jumble of conflicting emotions, unable to determine if her hesitation stemmed from fear for Guinivere's safety, or an envy that the queen might conceive while she could not. Should she heed some vague, niggling sensation, and ignore the urgings of her mother and needs of her father? And what of her duty, her destiny, divine decree?

Give me a sign, she pleaded with the Goddess. *Show me I am meant to bring this potion to the queen.*

Yet what real hope had she of an answer? Perhaps it was the stifling influence of the grim Christian priests, but the deity seemed unable to reach her within the walls of this castle. Only when gazing in the crystal pool of the forest had Riana felt the touch of the divine, and even then, she could remember merely the sensation, never the actual message, relying each time upon her mother to relay what words she'd spoken.

Yet Morgause could be one of the people Wolf cautioned her against when he'd told her not to place her trust in the wrong people. Wolf, who her mother—and most of Camelot—called their enemy. Wolf, who had nearly been killed by poison.

Looking at the amber liquid, she found herself wondering about the color of the potion in Wolf's drink that night.

But what was she thinking? That her own mother might have tried to kill him? True, Morgause made no secret of her dislike, but everyone else blamed her sister, Morgan. Morgan who had cautioned Riana that nothing was at it seemed.

Approaching the vial, Riana eyed it as if it were some viper loaded with venom. If the potion were indeed poison and she gave it to Guinivere, Riana would be the instrument of her death. Arthur would be devastated, without his beloved queen. He might even lose the will to rule.

Riana could destroy the potion, replacing it with a more innocuous brew, but what if she were wrong? What if this was indeed the cure Morgause promised, and she denied England its heir?

She had but one way to find out, she realized, reaching for the stopper. Riana must test the potion herself.

She paused, unnerved by how badly her hand trembled. This was no light undertaking, no time for an impulsive act. She could well die a hideous death if her fears were not groundless.

Yet could she take the chance that kind, trusting Guinivere would die in her stead?

Taking a deep breath, she dipped her finger in the liquid and brought it to her tongue. She tasted no bitterness, nor could she find an identifiable scent, but it proved little save Sela's claim that she never could detect the difference between one ingredient and another. When it came to mixing herbs, Greta had always far surpassed Riana at their lessons.

For an instant, she considered asking Greta to study the potion's contents, but this would only endanger her friend too, and waste valuable time. Five drops, Morgause had prescribed. Four more and Riana would have the answer.

Bringing the vial to her lips, she closed her eyes as she took the sip. She likely imbibed more than necessary, but if it were poison, the extra amount would make little difference. She'd still be dead in any case.

When the moments ticked by and nothing happened, she began to relax. No gripping pains in her gut, no nausea or vertigo. It struck her then that she might have endured yet another test of her dedication.

As if to confirm this, she heard a knock at the door. Answering it, she found Guinivere's servant, come with word that the queen was lonely tonight and in need of Riana's company.

Was this, then, her sign from the Goddess?

Armed with the hope that divine will was nudging her to Guinivere's chambers, Riana cupped the vial in her hand and followed the servant down the hall.

It wasn't until she'd left the vial with a deliriously happy Guinivere that Riana felt the first strange tingle in the core of her body.

In his chambers, Wolf waited for Sir Kay who was this moment procuring the list of challengers, so they could discuss their last minute strategy. Having trained or fought with most everyone in court, Kay felt confident that he could point out each competitor's strengths and flaws.

Yet it was not the tournament tomorrow that had Wolf pacing, but rather the current rumor circulating about the court, the news that Arthur had received word of a Saxon war council now convening to plan an attack on the Saxon Shores. Some said the prediction came from a magical vision, while others claimed a corroboration had come from the Saxons themselves, with someone close to Cerdric providing information for a price.

Wolf might know better than to pay heed to everything he heard at court, but any fool could put the pieces together. The raids along the border, the rumors of an attack—someone was stirring up trouble for a reason. Knowing that Arthur's strength came from his ability to maintain the peace, this someone, by creating a war and manipulating its outcome from behind the scenes, could yet topple the throne.

But for the conspiracy to work, there must be at least two

high-placed traitors, Briton and Saxon, working together. Wolf had his suspicions, but without proof, he feared neither Arthur nor Cerdric were likely to listen—not when the culprits had to be near and dear to them.

Before he could make accusations, Wolf had to be certain. And his best access to such information was through Riana.

Wolf cursed the god Wyrd for weaving his threads of destiny so intricately. He had to use Riana, his conscience and sense of duty commanded it, but in so doing, he'd add the death blow to the shambles of their marriage. Were she guilty, were she able to thus betray her king, he could never again trust her. Yet if he bullied and coerced her to betray those around her, and she were innocent, she would hate him forever.

Damn that Morgause and her blind, selfish ambition. How many must suffer, so she might put her ill-begotten bastard on England's throne?

Serving as a welcome distraction, Kay appeared at the door. Entering the room, he waved the list with one hand, a jug of ale with the other. "Ten challengers, I'm told," he pronounced as he set himself down at the table. "Eleven in all, with you." Taking a long pull from the jug, he unrolled the list and spread it out before him to study the names.

Wolf tried to show interest, but he could not see where discussing his opponents would make a difference. In his training, he'd acquired the necessary skill, and his resolve would not fail him, so all that remained was to pray for the gods' favor. Yet Kay had been a good friend and this seemed important to him, so Wolf held his tongue as they went through the exercise.

"Lamorak?" Kay said with a frown. "Why would the witch's current lover enter this competition?"

"She has a lover?" Wolf asked, surprised. "The way Morgause fondles half the court, I'd thought her out seeking one."

"She must hide her true lust from her sons, now that those hotheaded Scots are returned to court. Should the princes of Orkney learn she's taken the son of their father's murderer as a lover, they will use the sword first and ask questions later."

So Morgause would send her lover to defeat him? She must feel desperate indeed. "I remember this Lamorak," he said, putting face to the name. "Lots of brawn but little brains."

"That is how the witch likes them."

"Yes, I can well imagine. He was there, you know, drinking with us the night my wine was laced with poison."

Kay's gaze narrowed. "You can bet the witch led him by the nose, for he hasn't the wits to act on his own. Not much of a man, to my way of thinking. Makes my skin crawl, to think of little Riana being his wife."

Kay was not alone in that. "I can best Lamorak," Wolf said firmly. The exercise had gained in appeal, now that he could see the stakes had been raised. What else had the witch done to stack the odds against him? "Tell me, who else is on the list?"

"Well, Gwidion and Francis, of course. Normally, I'd be inclined to dismiss that silly pair, but there's no telling what a man in love will do."

Yes, Wolf thought wryly. *Love was a most unpredictable emotion.*

"Now that's odd," Kay said suddenly, pausing for another swig before peering again at the list. "I wondered why Riana was talking so intently with him last night, but this makes no sense. The man can't intend to marry her. Not with his vow of celibacy."

"Are you telling me Father Ignacious has entered the competition?" Wolf asked with a laugh as he tried to imagine the bony clergyman controlling one of Arthur's powerful steeds.

"I wish it were he," Kay said solemnly, "but we have a far more serious problem. It appears Sir Lancelot has entered the lists."

Lancelot? Wolf felt his first misgivings. Not that he would lose the tournament, for he was determined to do what he must to win, but this was Camelot's champion, their favorite, and the court would not react kindly to his defeat. Even in victory, Wolf could face serious problems.

So concerned was he with this, that he did not at first recall Kay's mentioning that Riana had met with the man the night before. He did so now with a lurch in his gut. "When you saw her with Lancelot," he asked Kay, "did either give any indication of being in love?"

The older man shook his head. "In truth, they seemed more like strangers, Riana speaking the most, Lancelot mostly nodding."

Was it as he suspected then? Had Riana been actively plotting to ensure his defeat?

"Steady, boy. If Lance loves any woman, it would be Guinivere."

Busy exploring his wife's motives, Wolf took some time for that to sink in. "Lancelot and Arthur's queen?" he asked, stunned. "He would betray his king so?"

"Never! Nor would he even tell anyone his true feelings. I doubt the queen guesses, and she's certainly done nothing to encourage him. I only know, having overheard the poor soul confiding to his confessor."

"But as you said, it makes no sense," Wolf pressed. "If Lancelot's heart is indeed pledged elsewhere, why does he compete for Riana's hand?"

Kay grinned. "The man's so accursedly noble, he probably thinks he's rescuing a damsel in distress."

Wolf was far from amused. "In essence, what you're saying is that a cold and calculating Riana is using Lancelot to make certain she needn't marry me?"

"In essence, yes, though I wouldn't say she's cold—"

"Damn her! All her machinations won't change the fact that she's already my wife."

"Your what?" In his surprise, Kay nearly dropped the jug. "Forgive me, boy, but why in the name of creation are we risking your neck with this farce if the two of you are already wed?"

Too late, Wolf realized what he'd revealed in his rash outburst. He could hardy explain all his reasons to a good friend of Arthur's, so he settled for the one Kay could best understand. "I want a wife. She wants to be Arthur's Enchantress. I thought if I came here and fought for her fair and square, using her ways and weapons, she'd remember the passion we've shared and she'd see that we are meant to be together."

"You could have saved yourself a lot of effort and danger by telling the king all this."

"A man must have his pride. I would not have the world knowing my wife disobeys me." That was true enough, as well.

Kay nodded sagely, offering the jug to Wolf. "Aye, women. Who can understand them? But I warn you, Arthur is most observant. Knowing him well, I'll wager he's guessed the truth already. I always wondered why he let a Saxon enter a competition tournament reserved only for his knights. He must approve of you."

"Little good it will do if Riana will go to such lengths to see me defeated."

Sighing heavily, Kay rose awkwardly to his feet. "No one asks this old man's advice in the ways of love, but I'm offering it anyway. Go to her, boy. Talk to your wife and learn her reasons. You could yet find a simple solution for you both."

"Nothing about our marriage has been simple."

"Ah, but you spoke of passion," Kay said with a smile. "I've found it's always a damned fine place to start."

"And how am I to inspire passion when every time I've tried to get near Riana, that witch, Morgause, puts herself in my path?"

Wolf heard his frustration and bitterness, and from his raised brow, so did Kay. They also heard the sudden, sharp raps on the door.

"Enter," Wolf called over his shoulder, assuming it to be one of Kay's drinking cronies, come to share the jug. Seeing Kay's brow raise another notch, he turned to face the newcomer.

Clad in a simple, linen night shift that left little to the imagination, his wife stood at the threshold, her eyes glassy and slightly unfocused, her hands making quick, fidgeting motions. "Are you busy?" she asked, looking everywhere but at his face. "You and I must talk."

Stunned, Wolf turned back to Sir Kay, who stood there grinning from ear to ear.

"I'm sorry," Riana said, her gaze following his to Kay. "I didn't realize you had a visitor."

"I was just leaving." Shuffling past, Kay gave him a sly, little wink. "I assume you know what to do from here."

His teasing was lost on Wolf, who barely noticed his departure, so intent was he upon his wife. What could have happened to send her out roaming the halls at this hour and in such a state? Noticing the dark shadows where her nipples strained against the fabric, he felt that familiar tightening in his groin. It had been so long since he'd made love to her sweet, luscious body, so very, very long. May the gods save him, how was he to stop from taking her here on the spot?

She means to betray you, he tried to tell himself. She'd hired Lancelot to defeat him and was quite likely in league with Morgause, as well. Yet no matter how many crimes he tried to lay at her door, the fact remained. He continued to burn for this woman.

As if oblivious to her effect on him, she paced before his line of vision, her hands moving busily as though she were washing them. "I had to come. To warn you. I didn't want to do this, not to you, but they are my parents. As she said, my destiny is clear."

"You're not making sense."

She laughed, a quick, breathless sound. "Me, flighty, impulsive Riana, make sense?" She stared at him wildly, her laughter now almost a sob. "Leave this place, Wolf. That's the only thing that makes sense."

She tottered slightly, reminding Wolf of Kay after too many pulls at the jug. Still, try as he might, he could not picture her and the queen indulging in a long bout of drinking.

Nor did she have the inability to focus, so prevalent in the drunken. Indeed, her gaze as she halted before him all but riveted him to the spot. "You can't win tomorrow. They won't let you. And I cannot bear to have your blood on my conscience."

He could feel her gaze probe deep within him, stirring up old feelings, old joys, and a healthy dose of the passion he'd told Kay they'd shared.

"I've asked Sir Lancelot to serve as my champion," she said, looking away. "We've made certain you haven't a prayer of winning."

He knew this already, so why did hearing it from her lips make the hurt probe deeper? "Why, Riana? Why betray me thus?"

He half expected her to rant and rave about her abduction, or the abuse she'd suffered at the hands of his village, but she merely flinched at the question instead. "It was the only way I knew to save your life," she said quietly, flatly.

"And to whom here in Camelot does my life—or death—matter?"

"To me." This time, her voice was so small he could barely hear her. "I love you."

It was less the words and more the way she'd uttered them that pierced his heart. He understood the confusion and torment behind them, for he felt it himself. And how else could he respond but by grabbing for her and pulling her tight to his chest.

Taking her head in his hands, sliding his fingers through the cool, sleek strands of her hair, he gave in to the passion flaring within him.

With a tiny whimper, she surrendered any pretense of resistance. Her own hands digging into his hair, she held tight throughout their long, frenzied kiss. When he pulled away to kiss her cheeks, her ears, her throat, it seemed her hands moved everywhere at once, yanking at his clothing, stroking his flesh as she revealed it until he thought he would burst.

"I can't do this," she chanted over and over under her breath, even while proving otherwise by rubbing her eager body against him.

For Wolf, too long denied the pleasures of his wife's passion, her avid demands served as a powerful aphrodisiac. Like a man possessed, he pulled at the shift, trying to yank it from her body, every part of him straining to stake his claim upon her.

When he could take it no more, he backed her up to the wall, unable to wait long enough to properly bed her. Hefting her up on his thighs, with the tattered shift bunched at her waist, he rammed his turgid flesh inside her. Her groan met his as their mouths again sought each other out, tongue stabbing tongue, lips open, wet and greedy.

With every thrust, her nails dug deeper into his back, her groans grew louder. He felt like the stag, rutting in the forest in a glorious celebration of life. Clutching him, riding him like a thing possessed, Riana was his female, his mate, and for them both, this moment, this joining, was all that existed.

Given the choice, he'd have prolonged their coupling forever, but she was so greedy, so hot and demanding, he did indeed burst, spilling his seed inside her as she cried out in the pleasure of her own violent climax.

With a long, sensuous groan, she melted against him, going limp all over as she slid down his legs to stand on her own. Still, Wolf could not release her, holding tight to her sweat-dampened frame as she gazed up at him with glazed eyes.

"More," she whispered, reaching up with her arms to pull his face down to hers, her lips seeking his mouth. The earthy taste of the ale mingled with the tang on her tongue as their tongues intertwined lazily, pleasure building on pleasure. Sliding his hands up beneath her shift, he felt her quicken again beneath his touch, even as his own loins sparked to life.

She pulled away, breathing heavily as she ran her hands through the hair of his chest. Smiling secretively, she traced her tongue along the lines her fingers drew, across his small budding nipples, then down to his belly. He gasped when he realized what she meant to do next, but it was not in him to stop her. Reveling in her touch, groaning with intense pleasure, he was all the more ready to bed her again.

But this time, he would do so properly. Lifting her in his arms, kissing her hungrily, he carried her to the bed in the corner. As he set her upon it, he lifted the torn shift over her head and tossed it to the floor. When she would grab for him, he bade her lie back so he could look at her. "Lie still," he crooned as he yanked off his kilt, "and let me pleasure you."

Leaning down, he ran his hands along her sides, and up her legs to part her thighs. She wriggled beneath his touch as if close to orgasm. Pleased, he stroked her mound of hair, even as he flicked his tongue across her tight, hard nipples, then lapped them with slow, languid pleasure. Joining her on the bed, he pulled each breast in his mouth, making them soft and dusky and impossibly round. As he stroked her, as his fingers slid down into the core of her, Riana writhed and groaned and called out for more. Crying out his name, she trembled around his touch.

"More," she still demanded, and Wolf happily obliged her. Tracing circles with his tongue, he made love to her with his mouth, touching and tasting her everywhere until he again felt her shuddering orgasm.

She reached for him, kissing him with the same blind greediness with which they'd begun. It drove him mad with lust, her great need for him, and more than eager to please her. Parting her thighs with his legs, he again drove inside her, feeling that miraculous surge of power as she climaxed over and over around him.

And still she wanted more.

He took her twice again, once with her straddling him, and once rolling about on the floor, but the time came at last when his seed ran dry. Lying beside her, staring at her beautiful, love-roughed face, he wished for one of her aphrodisiacs, for he'd like nothing better than to make love to his woman all the night long.

"Had I the means, I would do this incessantly," he told her, holding her face in his hands. "But I fear Nature will have her way with me. By the gods, Riana, give me rest and we shall continue our mating in the morning."

"Tomorrow?" Her dreamy expression focused, then went tight with alarm. "No, you must leave before the tournament."

Shaking her head, she rolled away, rising up to a sitting position, arms wrapped around her knees. How lovely she looked to him, her hair tousled and wild about her bare shoulders, the candlelight shining like a halo around it. How beautiful, yet all at once, more inaccessible than ever.

It made him angry that she would yet again deny the link between them. With one breath she spoke of love, with another, she demanded he leave. She was his, damn it. How many times must he prove himself before she would let him claim her?

Moving over to kneel before her, he took her chin in his hands, forcing her to face him. "You want me to leave Camelot. I will go, tonight, but only if you come with me."

"Wolf—"

"Make no mistake, Riana. I do not fear your Lancelot, for all his reputation, for I have the greater motivation to win. I will not lose you to another. I have tried living without you, Riana. Tonight, lying with you again, I know I cannot."

"Oh Wolf, you don't know what drives you. It—"

She was interrupted by a frantic shout in the hall. "Stop the traitor!"

Wolf's first thought was to ignore the resulting commotion, certain that nothing could be more important than this moment with his wife, but the shouts grew louder and more frantic. Hearing Mordred cry out, "Get him! Kill the French bastard!" he realized this was far more than some casual castle brawl. The prince would not call for the death of his father's good friend unless something were very wrong.

"I must go," he told Riana, reaching for his sword and his kilt. He donned the kilt as he went for the door; the sword he held primed and ready in his hand.

"Wolf?" Riana had risen, standing naked and dazed and far too vulnerable in the center of the room. "What is happening?"

"Get dressed," he said gently. "I'll be back as soon as I find out."

Outside in the hall, all was confusion. Knights scrambled past, brandishing a varied assortment of weapons, all screaming for blood. They seemed to be coming from the general direction of the queen's chambers.

Wolf saw the trail of blood long before he found the corpses. Recognizing several of the dead knights as companions of Mordred, he wondered who could be responsible for the carnage. He said a silent prayer of thanks that Riana could vouch for his whereabouts. Were no other culprit found, he knew, Camelot would be happy to blame the Saxon.

Guinivere seemed safe enough, standing in the center of her chamber, though her pale, haunted features held less life than the corpses in the hallway. Prince Mordred stood beside her, wincing as he rubbed his cheek.

Looking up, the prince's gaze turned cold and hard as he saw Wolf march into the room. "Penawulf, how ironic. Do you two always chase after the same women?"

Impatient with the sly innuendoes that Mordred alone seemed to fathom, Wolf ignored the taunt, focusing instead on the reddening mark on the prince's cheek. It had all the appearance of a slap. "Milady, are you all right?" he asked Guinivere, his hand clasping his sword. The queen need but raise a finger and Wolf would gladly to run her toad of a stepson through the gut.

She merely shook her head, warning him to do nothing.

Turning back to Mordred, Wolf saw the man break into a wide, beaming smile. "Ah, Sir Kay, just the man I require," he said brightly, and Wolf spun to find his trainer at the door behind him.

"What is this madness?" Kay demanded. "What mischief are you up to now, Mordred?"

"In the name of my father, the king, I command that you arrest the queen at once."

A stunned, appalled silence fell over the room.

"Arrest my Lady Guinivere?" Kay gasped. "On what charge?"

Smiling coldly, Mordred turned to the queen. "Shall I tell them, madam, or shall you?"

Guinivere stood as still and pale as the stone of the walls around her.

Mordred merely laughed. "Our lady, the queen, has betrayed the king. And the charge of treason, I do believe, is punishable by burning at the stake."

Twenty-one

Pushing her way into the queen's chambers, a dazed and horrified Riana struggled to take in the scene before her. All the blood and death in the hallway, Guinivere by the window, ashen and visibly trembling, the angry guards now leading an unarmed Wolf away.

"This man's done nothing," she blurted out without thinking. "He has been with me all night."

"How interesting." Emerging from behind the queen in the window alcove, Prince Mordred laughed, a dry, hollow sound. "But as yet, Penawulf stands accused of no crime. I merely thought it best he be removed to avoid further mischief." He glanced meaningfully at the clothing she'd donned. "None too soon, it would seem."

Blushing, she realized Wolf's blue and silver tunic had obviously been made for his proportions, not hers. She could no doubt fit two of her inside it, but in her haste, it had seemed more appropriate for wandering about the castle than her torn night shift. Now, facing Mordred's leer, she saw how it might get both her and Wolf into trouble.

"Leave her alone, Mordred," Wolf growled, struggling with the four guards holding him. "I swear, I will tear you limb from limb if you touch one hair on her head."

"How positively touching. Do tell me the truth," Mordred drawled, turning to Riana. "Are you absolutely certain this lusty Saxon has done *nothing* to displease the king?"

"I am more than certain," she told him defiantly. "And I shall tell the king so, the instant he arrives."

"We shall await the moment breathlessly. Between you and your Saxon, and the queen with her lover, I daresay Camelot has never seen such high drama. The trials could go on for days."

Lover? Trials? Riana looked again to Wolf, hoping he could explain what was going on here, but his glare remained on Mordred. "Riana is not some mouse you can capture and take pleasure in torturing. Leave her alone, Mordred, or I shall—"

"Shall what, Saxon? What do you think will happen to you once my father learns you've been defiling his pet, right here beneath his very nose?"

"Save your explanations for the king," Wolf cautioned her when Riana would speak out in his defense. "Nothing you can say to his son will make the slightest difference."

"How right you are there, Penawulf," Mordred snarled. "Take him away," he ordered the guard, laughing again as it took all four to subdue their prisoner and drag him off.

Frightened by what Mordred meant to do to him, Riana could not keep the trembling from her tone. "Take care in how you treat him. Remember, he is Cerdric's emissary. The king will punish severely anyone who abuses him."

"How very melodramatic," Mordred laughed. "Sorry to disappoint you, my dear, but I merely mean to set your Saxon free outside the gates. If he has any sense, he shall go home where he belongs."

"He won't leave," she thought aloud. "Not without me."

"You always have had a high opinion of yourself. Only a fool would risk Arthur's wrath for the sake of a foolish lover."

"I am more than his lover. I am his wife!"

For an instant, Mordred looked so furious she thought he might strike her, but his anger cooled into a sarcastic smile. "How droll. I'm sure this tale will entertain my father for hours, but I haven't the time for it now." Impatiently, he turned to the queen, still standing motionless by the window. "Make yourself useful," he barked at Riana. "See to the queen's needs until the king returns to the castle."

Watching the prince march off, so pompous and full of himself, Riana felt sick inside. She wanted to ask Guinivere what could have happened to cause so much death, but the queen had withdrawn into herself, murmuring "It was a mistake, just a mistake," over and over again to the shadows outside the window.

Not knowing what else to do, Riana strode over to stand beside her, placing a supporting hand on her shoulder. "Soon the king will be home and he will see it all straightened out," she said soothingly. In truth, she didn't know how this could be, not when she couldn't guess how any of it had even happened. Arthur's loving queen, with the celibate Lancelot? It made no sense.

"It is all my fault," Guinivere said flatly, speaking to the night air as much as to Riana. "Poor Lance . . ."

Her voice trailed off on a sob. "It's all right," Riana said, speaking as though to a child. "You needn't talk about it if you don't want."

Guinivere shook her head, distracted and confused. "Even now, I can't grasp what came over me. One moment I was sane and lucid, over there working on my tapestry, and all at once, I felt a strange tingling . . ." She bit her lip, turning to gaze back at the door. "Lance came to report on the day's events, as he does every night, and when I saw him standing before me, a haze came over my vision, over all my senses. A lurid, commanding haze, and looking through it, I thought Lance suddenly the most incredibly beautiful creature I'd ever seen. I had to have him. Nothing would stop me from knowing his touch, his love."

Uneasily, Riana thought of her own torrid evening, how upon gazing at Wolf, she'd been overcome by the same desperate yearning.

"Poor Lance, ever the gentleman," Guinivere went on as if the words were wrenched from deep within her. "He tried to withdraw, to politely bring me to my senses, but he was no match for the fire raging inside me. He surrendered like a man drowning, and even then I demanded more."

More, Riana thought. *How often had she repeated the word tonight?*

Guinivere shook her head. "It was sheer madness, the way we came together. And sheer horror, when Mordred came upon us. My stepson had no choice but to defend his father's honor, just as poor Lance had to kill to escape." She tilted her head, as if realizing something odd. "How swiftly his knights rushed to Mordred's aide. How could they know he would—"

As she spoke, a trumpet blared, loud and long in the tower below. "The king," Guinivere said, clutching at Riana's arm. "Oh child, this will kill Arthur. How shall I ever face him?"

"We shall face him together." Though Riana felt the same, sick panic, she willed her voice to remain calm. "Never fear, my lady. Come what may, I shall stay at your side."

Greta managed to get inside the royal chambers moments before the king. Wild rumors were flying about the castle, and the bloody corpses confirmed them. Gazing at Riana and the queen, clutching each other's hands as if their lives depended on it, Greta felt as if her heart had lodged in her throat. *It had come,* she thought to herself, *the crisis Morgan warned her about.*

Noticing her, Riana broke away from the queen to draw Greta to the far side of the room, her features harried and frightened. "Go, before the king arrives. You have no part in this and must not take any blame."

"Where is Wolf?" Greta blurted out, her brother's safety being her foremost concern. Nor was her mind eased when Riana told her that Mordred had banished Wolf outside the gates. Greta did not trust the prince, and after hearing Riana's hurried rendition of tonight's events, she had even less reason to do so.

"Come with me," Greta begged her friend. "We can find my brother and then leave tonight for River Ford."

Riana merely cast a sad, worried glance back at the queen. "I cannot leave her. It will be horrible for her, facing the king, and she has no one else."

"What of all her maids-in-waiting?"

Riana gestured about the empty room. "Do you see them here? Everyone has scattered, fearing Arthur's wrath."

"And you do not?"

"I have more reason than anyone." Riana shuddered. "Oh Greta, it's my fault this happened. I brought her the potion." She gave a hasty account about the cure she'd given the queen and its effects on them both.

"Morgause," Greta said with disgust. "I should have known she'd have a hand in this."

"You are wrong about her, Greta." Riana's face tightened. "You must be. I cannot live with the knowledge that my own mother could be so evil."

Mother? Greta felt the dread build inside her. She knew how deeply Riana had longed for maternal love; this must be why she'd followed the woman so blindly. Acknowledging the truth would well kill her.

Though Riana's troubled features indicated that doubt was already sifting in.

Before Greta could press home her conviction that Morgause must not be trusted, they heard the clatter of armor, accompanied by thudding footsteps in the hallway. Turning her head in that direction, Riana hissed, "Say nothing. I must have the facts before I say aught to the king."

"But Riana—"

"Promise me, Greta. It will only make everything worse if we make accusations without proof."

Greta could not see how the situation could worsen but neither did she make the promise. She knew Morgause was behind this, that the woman preyed upon Riana's loving heart and need for family, but her friend would be hard to convince. Greta must find evidence that they might bring before the king.

"Go, quickly," Riana urged. "Before Arthur singles you out."

"I will find Wolf," Greta promised. "He will help us."

To herself, she added, *and I shall find the proof.*

* * *

Riana paced outside the royal chambers. Hearing Arthur's angry shouts, she longed to rush to Guinivere's defense, but the queen herself had ordered her from the room. She would be grateful for her support later, Guinivere had told Riana, but for now, she must talk to her husband alone.

How could everything have gone so horribly wrong? Riana wondered. She'd come here to help Arthur, not add to his burdens. Surely this was some nightmare from which she would soon awaken.

Rubbing her arms, feeling the silver trim of Wolf's tunic, she remembered back to the wild, exhilarating hours she'd spent with him. Perhaps she'd been wrong, comparing her own bizarre behavior to the queen's, for unlike Guinivere, Riana did not regret a single instant. Rubbing the tunic, finding his scent still on it, she wished with all her heart that she could be holding Wolf, lost in the sheer joy of joining with him, forgetting that the rest of the world—and its problems—even existed. For those few blissful hours, it seemed like nothing could ever come between them.

Instead, here she was, trapped in a nightmare, while Wolf was out there somewhere in the night, no doubt once more believing the worst of her. Her heart might yearn that Greta would indeed find him, but her rational mind clung to the past few hours, fearing it would be the last she'd ever see of her husband. She tried to tell herself it was all for the best, for Wolf would be safer thus, but every part of her longed to feel his arms around her, to stand in the shelter of his rock solid strength.

"Riana, my child, what have you done?"

Hearing her mother's voice, Riana looked up to find Morgause standing behind her, her features reflecting Riana's own sorrow and pain. Sighing heavily, the woman closed the distance between them, gently taking Riana into her arms. "I must know. The potion. Did you take it to the queen as I instructed?"

Hearing her urgency, reminded of Greta's accusation, Riana tensed. Morgause, feeling this, held her by the arms so she could search her daughter's face. "What is it? You did take it to the queen immediately? No delay?"

Riana looked away. How could she tell her mother she'd tasted it first?

"You tried it, didn't you?" Morgause pressed. Hard to mistake the disappointment in her voice. "You saw a cure for your own infertility and could not resist the temptation."

Riana's first instinct was to deny this, but knowing that for Morgause, her greed would be more palatable than her distrust, she merely nodded.

"I feared as much." The woman now gazed at her with pity. "Don't you know better than to tamper with another's magic? The spell was for Guinivere. You tainted it, by tasting it first."

"It was not like that. I . . . I . . ."

"My poor, misguided child, you seem doomed to forever take the wrong step. Bad enough to enslave your Saxon with your impulsive actions, but this? May the Goddess spare us, can't you see what calamity you've caused?"

Riana could see all too painfully. "I must tell the king," she said, breaking away from Morgause to go to the door.

"No!" Morgause grabbed her arm. "Let me break this unpleasant news to my brother. We must be careful, after all, lest he lash out in anger. You would not want your Saxon or his sister bearing the brunt of his rage."

Riana paused, torn between her conscience and her fear for Wolf's welfare. Until she knew he was safely gone, until Greta too was on her way to River Ford, how could she risk endangering more innocent lives?

"Let someone older and wiser deal with this delicate situation," Morgause went on. "For once, let reason, and not impulse, govern your actions."

The words struck a chord. However pure her intentions had been, the results of Riana's impetuousness had caused enough harm already.

"Trust me," Morgause finished off with a tender smile, taking Riana once more in her arms. "After all, am I not your mother?"

* * *

It was no easy thing, holding onto that trust as Riana watched her beloved queen be tried for the crime of treason. Only once in the proceedings did Morgause speak out, with the vague mention that some force other than the queen's treachery might be at fault, but Mordred silenced his mother with a demand for proof. When Riana herself would have spoken, Morgause shot her a warning glance, mouthing the words, "not now."

Not yet, her mother continued to caution, even as the verdict of guilty was read, even when the queen was hastily sentenced to burn at the stake at dawn. *Trust me,* Morgause chanted, reminding Riana that they must not act until they were certain Wolf and Greta were safe. Assuring her daughter that she was this moment working to provide both Saxons safe passage out of Camelot, Morgause urged Riana to go to her room to wait, remaining quiet and out of sight.

But mindful of her promise to Guinivere, Riana had instead come to the royal chambers to wait with the queen.

Standing at the window in the predawn darkness, staring down at the kindling piled high about the scaffold below, Riana had never been more frightened. She'd done her best to be patient, to let her older and wiser mother lead the way, but as hour after precious hour ticked away, she thought more of Wolf's warning not to place her trust in the hands of the wrong people.

Turning to face Guinivere, sitting quiet and still and far too resigned to her fate, Riana could bear to keep silent no more. "Milady, I'm so, so very sorry," she said in a rush, telling the queen everything that had happened since she'd first seen the need for the potion.

When Riana was done, Guinivere rose slowly, coming over to take her hands with trembling fingers. Her grasp was cold, Riana noticed, as if the very life had gone out of her limbs. "I'm grateful that you've confided in me, my dear, but please, do not fret on my account. Lancelot will not let me burn at the stake. His sense of honor will never allow it."

Riana shook her head, confused. "I don't understand."

"The code of chivalry. Even Arthur, for all his ranting and raging, is counting on his old friend to come to my rescue. Do you notice any guard out there, any impediment at all? My husband knows no true knight would let a lady suffer for what he considers his own misdeed, Lancelot least of all."

"Then this execution is staged?"

Guinivere squeezed her hands gently. "The king is torn between his love for me and the cry for justice. To judge his wife any less severely than he would another subject would make a mockery of all he has ever stood for. I had to be tried, and then sentenced, but in his heart, Arthur still prays I'll be saved."

"And what if Lancelot does not come? What if something has happened to him and he cannot?"

"I shall bow to God's will. But in truth, I think He means a far harder atonement for me."

"Why must you atone? I am the one who—"

Guinivere reached up to place a chilled finger to her lips. "Even if the potion was tainted, as you claim, I'm told magic merely enhances what is already there. I can't deny that I found much about Lance to attract me, nor can I swear that I'd never again react the same."

"You would condemn yourself on supposition? And what of the king? Surely he deserves to know there was a potion."

Guinivere shook her head sadly. "What good will it do, when I cannot swear that I did not betray him, if only in my heart? And what if there is indeed a babe? How will he feel to know his heir came from another man's loins? No, I will not add to his misery. Leave him his rage, Riana. With all the treachery and strife surrounding him, Arthur needs the strength his anger will lend him."

"But I can't bear to watch you go to the stake while I and Morgause go free."

"My child, no one goes free. We all must eventually make our own atonement."

Wolf had called it living with the consequences of her actions, but in essence, the message was the same. She, like Guinivere, must live with her guilt forever. "I never meant to cause such heartache," she said, her voice breaking. "I wanted to help. Both you and the king. In my heart, I have always wished you were my mother."

Something softened in Guinivere's gaze. "It is not the blood, but how two people act that forms the bond. In *my* heart, you always *have* been a daughter, Riana. And as such, I charge you to watch over the king in my absence. He shall need all the love you can give him in the days ahead."

And at that, the door slammed open, five armed guards and a smug Mordred bursting through it. To Riana, it was a measure of how low Guinivere had fallen that the prince saw no reason to first announce his presence. He bowed before them, though more with insolence than respect. "I've brought the guard, mi-lady, to escort you to your execution."

"You coldhearted—"

"Riana!" Guinivere reached again for her hand, squeezing it. "Save your anger for more worthy causes." She brushed a cool, tender hand against her cheek. "I shall always remember how you alone stood by me, but now it is over. Go to bed, child. Get your rest."

Drifting away, the queen nodded at the guards, who stood aside as she passed by them and out into the hall. Smiling grimly, Mordred followed at her heels.

It was *not* over, Riana thought fiercely. She would go down there and stand by the scaffold and if Lancelot never appeared, she would tell all Camelot the truth, no matter what the queen asked of her. She would not let this valiant, noble woman burn, while Mordred stood by gloating.

Hurrying behind them quietly, she heard the prince speak low and urgently to Guinivere, even as he tugged at her arm. Riana had heard only "before it's too late," when the queen swung her hand to strike Mordred's face.

"Once more, I shall forget you suggested such a vile thing, but if you do not unhand me this instant, I shall shout from the rooftops what you have just proposed to me."

"Arthur *will* lose the throne, madam," he hissed back. "With me, you can still be queen."

"I'd rather die!"

"And so you shall, like the witch you are."

Horrified, Riana rushed up to yank his hand away. "Take your filthy hands off the queen," she cried out. "You're not fit to touch the kindest, noblest—"

"The word you're searching for, I believe, is trollop."

"How dare you!"

"I dare because the woman has been tried and convicted of lifting her skirts to the wrong man. As too shall you be, if you're not careful. I think the king might be interested in what information you've been giving your Saxon lover. But no, he is your husband, didn't you say? The king might be interested in learning to whom you owe the greater loyalty."

"Riana, leave us," the queen commanded. "Please."

"But—"

"Nothing can be served now by endangering yourself further. Let me face my punishment, knowing you at least are safe."

Riana looked from Guinivere to the grinning Mordred, wishing she could scratch out his hateful eyes, yet reluctant to disobey a royal command. Hanging back as the guard accompanied Guinivere to the courtyard, Riana did not go to her chambers, but rather followed silently behind them outside to the courtyard. She stood beside the scaffold, to be ready if the need arose to speak out and stop the execution.

A cold wind stirred across the dark, moonless sky as the guards led the proud and silent Guinivere up to the scaffold. Shivering, Riana eyed the wood and kindling piled around it, fuel enough to raze a town, much less a single frail female. What madness drove the king to do this? she couldn't help wonder. For that matter, where was Arthur on this chill, ugly morning he would burn his wife?

No one had come to the courtyard to witness this act of judgment, she realized, as if all in Camelot would spare their queen the humiliation. Glancing back over her shoulder, she found the king watching from an upper window, though his gaze was not on the prisoner being tied to the stake. He peered through the dark in the distance, as if anticipating a messenger, or a visitor to the castle.

It was not for some stranger that Arthur waited, Riana realized. He, like them all, was hoping for Lancelot.

A host of flaming torches ringed the scaffold, showing Guinivere's solitary form, her white gown and pale hair fluttering in the breeze. How alone she seemed, and yet so brave as she faced her fate. It brought Riana back to the night she'd stood facing Helga's accusations in River Ford, and she could not forget how her spirits had been lifted to hear sweet, gentle Greta raise her voice in her defense.

How could she now do any less for her queen?

Glancing up at the castle window, she saw Arthur had turned his gaze to the courtyard. Noticing how his fingers gripped the sill, she followed his gaze to the dark figure taking one of the torches and raising it with his hand. Mordred, Riana realized with a clutch of fear. He was pacing the steps to the kindling at Guinivere's feet.

"No!" she cried out, running over to grasp his arm. "You must stop this execution at once. The queen is innocent. I am the one to blame."

Mordred merely laughed, pushing her to the side. Lifting the torch once more, he hesitated. "One last chance," he said quietly, looking up with naked longing into the queen's ashen face. "Say the word and I shall stop this."

"I beg you," Riana shouted up to the window. "My king, you must listen to me and stop this, before it's too late. Burn me, not Guinivere."

Whatever Arthur might have said was lost in the roar of distant hoofbeats, thundering down the road to the castle. "Guards, to action!" Mordred shouted, but his voice too was drowned by the stampede of charging horsemen.

Lancelot, Riana thought, scrambling up to move out of the

way, both from the rescuing troops and the guards now rushing into the courtyard, brandishing swords.

Metal clanked against metal, horse collided with human, and through the din and bloodshed, Riana watched Mordred set the torch to the timber. "No!" she screamed, but it was already too late. Stirred by the wind, the flames leaped from branch to branch, gaining force, licking at the hem of Guinivere's gown. Riana ran for the stairs to the scaffold, blinded by desperation. She had to save the queen.

Hands grabbed her from behind, beating at her, and too late, she saw her dress had caught on fire. Looking into the cold, gray eyes of Mordred, she struggled to break free. "Let me go to her," she railed at him. "You cold-hearted beast, how can you let an innocent woman die?"

He said nothing, nodding back at the scaffold. Following his gaze, Riana watched Lancelot carrying Guinivere to his horse while his warriors cleared a path around them. Within moments, they were all mounted and thundering back out the gate to vanish into the night.

"How remarkably brave and noble," Mordred said quietly, when the din had died down.

Shaking free of his grasp, Riana glanced about her at the death and destruction, at the flames now consuming the scaffold, and shuddered. "He could have come sooner."

"Not Lancelot, you." Mordred shook his head. "But however valiant your attempt, it was remarkably foolish. You risked your life needlessly, and for what? They'd have ridden off to their doom, no matter what you did."

"And who is to blame for that?" Looking down at her charred gown, the burned skin of her arm, Riana needed an outlet for her pain and frustration and rage. "You've doomed us all with your heartless cruelty."

He frowned, as if disappointed in her. "How little you know me."

Riana gestured around them. "You think I can't see the pleasure you take from this, or the greed in your eyes as you gazed upon the queen? How sick you are, lusting after your father's wife. I'm ashamed to admit we come from the same mother."

He tilted his head, regarding her as he would a heretofore unseen oddity. "Is that what Morgause told you?"

"You deny it?"

"Let me put it this way. After my birth, my devoted parent developed a healthy disdain for pregnancy. She tinkered with her herbs and chants to make certain she need never suffer such a nasty condition again."

"But she said . . ." She trailed off, trying to remember just what Morgause had told her. She'd hugged her, spoken of her love and a deep-seated wish to protect her daughter. "She said," Riana tried again, "that I was her sole hope for the future. That she was glad to have an offspring who could at long last carry on her work."

She saw genuine pity in his smile. "Trusting soul, have you not yet learned that the woman will say whatever she must to get her way?"

"If so, it's a trait that runs rampant in the family."

He laughed, as if truly amused. "Ah, Riana bites. It would seem you are not quite the mouse my mother thinks you. You shall bear watching, I think, but now, if you will excuse me, I have much to do to prepare for the king's departure."

"Departure?"

He looked back to the castle gates with a sigh. "What choice does he have now, but to drag his armies across England tracking down the two misguided lovers?"

Glancing up at the castle window, seeing Arthur staring after the departing rescuers, she saw the king's relief—and defeat—in each line of his slumped body. She had to go to him, talk to him, before Morgause could taunt and goad him into action. Not knowing the truth about the portion, he would feel compelled to chase after his wife. His pride would demand it.

"Why do you do this?" she asked Mordred, feeling more ill with every moment. "What can you possibly hope to gain by making the king and queen suffer?"

"Ah, now you've disappointed me again, mouse. Isn't it perfectly obvious what I stand to gain?"

Of course it was. If she hadn't been so upset, she'd have known it at once. "You will never get the throne. I'll bet my life on that."

"Your life, mouse?" He smiled, chilling her with its cold calculation. "Yes, I suppose it might yet come to that."

Twenty-two

Riana had no need to go to the king's chambers. He was waiting for her in the entrance hall, the instant she entered the castle. Still shaken by Mordred's implied threat, she found it hard to face this man for whom she'd caused such grief.

Her father.

Arthur had dark shadows beneath his eyes, as if he hadn't slept in days and the tension in his jaw showed how tightly he held himself in check. She wanted to run up to him, to hold and comfort him, but he was the king, and she his lowly subject, and such liberties could never be taken.

He was also very angry. "What did you mean just now?" he barked at her. "You would protest the queen's guilt?"

Riana merely nodded.

"What can you say that was not already offered at the trial?"

She flinched at the force of his voice, knowing the anger and pain behind it, but she did not lose her resolve. Holding her head high, she explained how she'd tainted what she'd hoped would have been the cure for Guinivere's sterility.

"And from where did you get this potion?" he asked sharply once she was done.

She faltered, the question catching her unaware. It seemed a strange one to ask, especially when Arthur's expression indicated he'd already formed an answer. "From Queen Morgause," she said quietly.

Arthur muttered a low oath. "Logically, I suspected her, but I preferred to look the other way, loath to believe my own sister could wish such ill for me."

Riana found it unpleasant, hearing the king put her own doubts and motivations into words. She hadn't wanted to think Morgause had been manipulating her, not if she were her mother. Only now, Mordred claimed that this too had been a lie, a clever ploy to bend Riana to her will.

"If she's guilty," Arthur said, thinking aloud, "what vile genius to use my queen to destroy me, taking my greatest strength and making it my greatest weakness." Swearing again, he ran a harried hand through his graying hair. "She started months ago with the sly insinuations, planting that niggling doubt and nurturing it until it grew into a monster. I was primed for my reaction. In my rage, I judged my wife and lover of so many years without once considering, or asking, her version of what happened. The single most important person in my life, and just like that, I condemned both her life and our love to death."

Riana felt his anguish. "The queen begged me to say nothing, for she would not have all this betrayal break your spirit. She wanted to leave you your anger. She said it would lend you strength."

"How well she knows me." He looked away, but not before Riana saw the torment burning in his eyes. "Would that I had trusted her more."

"She understood, milord. And her love for you never wavered. She asked me to stand by you, to guard you from those who wish you harm."

"Thank you for that." He said the words so softly, she nearly didn't hear them. Taking in a deep breath, he turned to face her. "But I would feel better knowing you are away from Camelot, too. It is no longer safe for you here, and I would hate to see anything happen to you in my absence."

"You're going away?"

"I must go after Guinivere, to apologize, and to make certain she, too, is well situated and safe from my sister's machinations."

"But what of Camelot?" Riana blurted out, suddenly fright-

ened of the uncertain future. "You shall give your enemies the
opportunity to destroy it should you leave now."

He looked at her long and hard, sighing as he gazed about the
empty hall. "What in truth is left of my court? Too many fine
knights have died already in this tragedy, others have left to follow Lancelot. My dream is dying and I cannot stop its passing,
but I shall have justice, Riana. I cannot allow the innocent to
suffer while the guilty go unpunished, or my Round Table will
have stood for naught."

Watching him march away, his boot heels sounding a dirge
across the stone tile floor, Riana realized she had seen this king
at his finest moment. Faced with betrayals that would break another man's spirit, Arthur would continue on, tall, proud and
alone, fighting for what he believed in to his last dying breath.

Gazing at his retreating figure, feeling the sting behind her
eyes, she realized how very much this man reminded her of her
husband.

Wolf, she thought in a sudden panic. In the hysteria of the last
few days, she'd lost track of him. Morgause swore she was taking
care of his welfare and Greta's, but if the woman had plotted
such evil against her own brother, what was to stop her from
lying to Riana, over and over again?

She wanted to appeal to the king for help, but Arthur was
already shouting for his bailiff and captain-at-arms, and she realized she could not tax him further, not with all that he faced
ahead.

Nor must she rely upon anyone else for help. As distasteful as
it was, she had to confront the woman who most likely held the
key to Wolf's location, Morgause herself.

Excited by what she'd unearthed, Greta was just coming out
of Morgause's bedchamber when Riana marched up. Hard to tell
which girl was the most surprised, but Riana recovered first.
"What are you doing here?" she asked, her voice barely above
a whisper.

How telling, that Riana, too, should feel a need for stealth, but caught up in her own intrigue, Greta cast a furtive glance down the hallway. "I came seeking proof of the woman's guilt."

"Here, in her own bedchamber? What if she caught you?"

"She is busy with her lover. I knew, from watching her pattern, that she would not return for an hour or so."

Riana looked suddenly worried. "Is Wolf helping you? Do you know where he is?"

"No," Greta said, knowing she betrayed her own fears. "I can't find him. From talking to the guards, I know only that he never left the castle. I'm hoping this evidence will convince the king to investigate on my behalf."

"You found it? Your proof of Morgause's guilt?"

Greta held out the book in her hands. "It's all here, the recipe for the potion, complete with notes in her own handwriting. I even have a second potion in this vial. In case something went wrong with the first attempt, I imagine she wanted to be ready to try again."

"It was all a lie then?" Riana asked flatly.

She nodded, sorry to add to Riana's heartache. "It was merely a powerful aphrodisiac. Clearly, Morgause planned for the queen to be caught betraying her husband."

"With Mordred," Riana said as if thinking aloud. "That poor Lancelot should appear at that moment was apparently an unfortunate mistake."

Greta shuddered, appalled that anyone would go to such lengths to steal a throne. "All the more reason I must go to the king with my proof," she said fiercely.

"But can you trust this information? After all, if it could so condemn her, why would she leave this book where anyone could find it?"

"She put a glamour on it, hiding it from the naked eye." Seeing her friend's startled expression, Greta felt suddenly sheepish. "It's a fairly simple spell to do and undo." She murmured something, then waved her hands, and both book and vial vanished from view.

Riana shook her head, visibly struggling to take it all in. "All this time, you've been learning true magic from Morgan, while I foolishly let Morgause use me to hatch her plots."

Greta refrained from saying, *I warned you*. She reasoned Riana was miserable enough. "Come with me, while I offer this proof to the king. Together we can convince him to help us find Wolf."

Riana shook her head. "Perhaps I can join you later but I think I might better stay and keep Morgause distracted. We won't want her finding her notes are missing before you have your audience with Arthur. But do not delay, Greta. The king is even now making his plans to ride out after Guinivere."

"But that's madness. In whose hands shall he leave his kingdom now that Lancelot is gone?"

Greta didn't need Riana's answer; her grim expression said it all. And they both knew Mordred would lose no time in abusing the power. They had to make certain Wolf was safely away, and the sooner the better.

Riana did not wait long for Morgause. Hair tousled and lips red and bruised, she looked as if she and her lover had enjoyed themselves immensely. That this woman could be taking her pleasure so casually while the innocent Guinivere walked to the stake, made Riana stiff with anger.

She struggled to control it, though. She must not lose her head when dealing with this female.

She waited long enough for Morgause to get inside her bedchamber before knocking on the door. Morgause greeted her with a woeful expression. "I've been grieving," the woman said, tears glittering in her green eyes as she led Riana into the room. "Guinivere was such a dear, dear sister to me."

"The queen is still alive," Riana told her, unable to keep the coolness from her tone. "Lancelot rode up and saved her."

"I know," Morgause said, surprising her yet again with disarming tenderness. "I saw it just now in the crystal."

She pointed to the glowing globe on the table by the fire

Opalescent pastels swirled within its center, every now and then taking on a vague, almost recognizable form. "Come, look for yourself."

Riana had a sudden aversion to the crystal, but she was far too conscious of the worktable, tucked back in its dark corner, and the need to keep Morgause as far away from it as possible.

As she approached the globe, the swirling images gathered force, then substance. Deep within its depths, she could see a battlefield, Arthur's banners lying trampled and unheeded in the mud. Everywhere she looked, she saw bloodshed and death, the British army all but destroyed.

She turned away, horrified.

"What did you see?" Morgause leaned closer, her green eyes glinting in the candle flame.

Riana refused to look at her, lest she fall again under her spell. "Guinivere's near-execution," she lied. "I did not enjoy reliving that horror."

"Splendid! You are making great progress, my child."

"Am I?"

"But of course you are. Why, as little ago as yesterday, you could not recall what you saw when you gazed in the pool."

"No, I meant, am I truly your child?"

Morgause went still, tight and coiled for action. "What nonsense is this?"

"Mordred tells me that you, too, are barren. That you saw to your sterility yourself, taking the proper herbs right after giving birth to him."

Shaking her head sadly, the woman stepped up to put a comforting arm around Riana. "And you believed him? He is my son, and I try to love him, but Mordred is a notorious liar. Riana, my precious, what have I ever done to make you doubt me?"

Morgause was so good, so slick at her persuasion, that even knowing the truth, Riana was tempted to surrender to the woman's soothing tones. Instead, she shrugged away, reminding herself what happened each time she fell victim to her mentor's selfish influence. "You ask what you have done? Everything you've ever told me has been a lie, calculated to bend me to your will. You aren't my mother. You told me that to separate me from your sister Morgan, to keep me from learning worthwhile magic. What was it, milady? Were you afraid my powers would one day outshine your own?"

Morgause dropped the pose of concerned parent with a nasty laugh. "Afraid of *you?* Silly child, even your Saxon friend Greta has a thousand times more talent and skill."

"Perhaps, but I have the king's favor. That's what frightens you most."

Morgause took care not to meet her eyes, proving she was not as poised as she'd have Riana believe. *"Had* his favor, don't you mean? Once Arthur learns you tainted the potion, you will be less than nothing to him."

"He knows. I told him just now."

Morgause visibly burned. For the first time, Riana could see her true age, the lines of dissipation about her mouth and eyes, the cold disdain the woman worked so hard to keep hidden. "You stupid bitch," Morgause hissed. "What have you done?"

"I didn't tell Arthur your part in it, if that's what worries you." Riana could have added that she hadn't needed to, but perhaps it was best for them all for Morgause to learn that from Arthur herself.

"You don't have to tell him. My brother's no fool. He can put two and two together."

"Just what is that two and two, and why should you fear it? You who have done nothing wrong?"

"I'm not afraid," Morgause said, tossing back her red-gold mane. "I have no reason to be."

"Ah, but sooner or later, the king will discover that you deliberately altered the potion, not me." Riana knew she shouldn't have offered that warning, but ever since seeing Greta's proof, a terrible rage had been building within her and she could no longer take what this woman would do to her.

Morgause waved a dismissive hand. "Tell him what you will

I know my way around my brother. When I'm done with him, he will believe my word over that of a silly, grasping child."

With conscious effort, Riana kept herself from blurting out that they had proof to offer Arthur. Silently, she urged Greta to hurry.

"That's all you've ever been, you know, a foolish, greedy girl," Morgause continued to taunt. "Camelot laughed at your attempts, and some even pitied you. As if you—*you*—would ever become an enchantress."

Riana drew herself up. "You can belittle my talent if you want, but never forget, I was called here by the Great Enchanter himself."

"Go to him," Morgause chanted in a perfect imitation of Merlin's voice. *"Arthur needs you now more than ever."*

Riana stared at her, aghast. How could Morgause possibly know the exact words of her vision unless . . .

"Close your mouth, goose," the woman sneered. "Your gaping is most unattractive."

"You sent that vision?"

"What conceit to think otherwise. Did you truly believe one of your limited skill could be of any use to a king? You were summoned here to bring about his downfall, which, in all candor, is the only arena in which you've shown any real talent. You should continue to do as I say, for without me, you are nothing. Certainly never an enchantress."

Inside, Riana felt lashed to the bone, but she refused to let this woman see it. She forced a smile. "What a generous offer, letting me continue as your apprentice when I'm so inept, but I fear I must refuse. I could never live with myself if I knowingly followed your evil path. Indeed, I'm ashamed to ever have been part of it. I thank the Goddess that you're *not* truly my mother."

Morgause laughed again, a nasty sound. "Come now, did I treat you that badly? At least I gave you the *illusion* that someone cared about you."

"If you're trying to make me feel bad that my father denied me, don't bother. I—"

"Your father?" Morgause pounced. "What makes you believe I did not lie about that too?"

Riana felt suddenly, dreadfully cold. So she was to be robbed of even this dream? There seemed no end to the woman's cruelty.

"Poor silly Riana," Morgause went on, not content with the pain she'd already wrought. "Did you truly think the king's affection runs any deeper than that of your Saxon lover? Or do you still believe your husband's devotion is caused by anything other than your mistaken enchantment?"

"You lied about Wolf, too," Riana lashed out, hating Morgause more than she thought possible. "You never meant to help me undo that spell. Nor did you ever intend to help him or Greta escape Camelot. Where is he now, milady? Is he buried in the castle dungeons, or have you hidden him in some dark corner with your foul magic?"

Morgause gave her enigmatic smile. "Now why would I give you that information? As long as you don't know what I am doing with your Saxon, you will have no choice but to behave."

Never had she hated anyone more. "If anything happens to Wolf," she bit out, "you shall be the one to pay."

"Are you threatening me? My dear girl, how can you possibly hope to prevail when you have so little power? I shall destroy you and your lusty Saxon three times over."

Three times. Whatever we do returns to us threefold, Sela had often preached. As if the old woman whispered the words in her ear now, Riana looked into those soulless green eyes and knew that Morgause would pay for her crimes. "I have no need to use my power against you," she said quietly. "In the end, it is your own actions that will destroy you."

This time, the woman's laughter was forced. "Or so you wish."

Riana shrugged, gazing back at the swirling globe. "Someday, you must remind me to tell you what I *truly* saw in the crystal."

A misleading untruth, perhaps, but at least she had the satisfaction of seeing the woman's ashen features as she left the room.

* * *

Later that day, Mordred sat on the king's throne, uneasy with the sensation. He should feel more invincible, more in power, but he felt merely like a boy trying to fill his father's much larger shoes.

No matter, he told himself angrily. When he was king, he'd have the damned seat removed and his own installed. He'd want no memories of the arrogant lout who had sired him littering *his* hall. Why should Mordred waste time remembering the man who had spent most of his life ignoring that his only son even existed?

"You've got to shut her up," Morgause demanded, pacing before him like an irate cat. "That little bitch will ruin everything."

"As usual, you are overreacting, Mother. What can Riana do, with the king gone after his wife, and his Round Table now in shambles? I would think you'd be celebrating that how admirably everything is proceeding according to our plans."

"She is right now scouring this castle for her precious Saxon. I shudder to think of your chances should he see himself her guardian."

"I've done nothing to the girl. She has no score to settle with *me.*" Not quite true, not after the way he'd treated her beloved queen, but Morgause didn't know that.

Gaze narrowing, she betrayed her scorn. "She knows about the potion, you fool. How long will it be before word gets to my brother?"

"I did warn you what would come of all your games."

"Ungrateful whelp. What I did, I did for you."

Mordred stifled a yawn, knowing better. Indeed, a good part of the appeal Guinivere held for him was that she had always been kinder and more caring than his mother.

Typically, Morgause didn't notice his derision. Sidling up to him, she all but purred in his ear. "But now that you shall be ruling Camelot in Arthur's absence, you can make certain Riana talks to no one, ever again."

"And what would I stand to gain from her death?"

He'd enraged her—he could see the glints of anger in her feline eyes—but she kept her tone soft and clear. "I would not think you'd want your father knowing about your own part in the plot against his wife. The girl will soon guess that you tried to trap Guinivere into serving as your queen."

Mordred might have panicked, had he not recognized that this was his mother's intention. Sick to death of the woman's manipulations, he betrayed his disdain. "I need merely say you tricked me, too. I will claim to be an innocent victim of my mother's wiles."

"You think because you're his heir, he'll keep a blind spot where you are concerned," she went on, "but I promise, nothing will save you when I'm done talking to him. Stand by me now, or I shall see you destroyed."

He was done with her threats. All his life, she'd maneuvered him into doing her will, dangling her affection and approval as bait. If he no longer cared about love, if greed and ambition now overtook all maternal ties and made him a monster, she had no one but herself to blame.

No doubt seeing his unconcern, she dug her nails into his wrist. "Do not forget, I have the coven behind me."

He didn't bother to correct her. He'd long since made certain that her group of frightened bitches would do whatever he commanded. Morgause had no real power over him, and it was time she learned it.

"You bore me," he announced, shaking off her grip. "I'm a busy king with no time to watch you stir up mischief. You'll retire to your chambers, madam, and there you shall remain until I decide what to do with you."

"You vicious, conniving—"

"Lamorak!" Mordred called out, interrupting her tirade. "Take the queen my mother to her chambers and see that she stays there."

As expected, Morgause silenced immediately when she saw who her guard was to be.

Taking care to keep his features blank, Mordred dismissed them, almost pitying the poor female, for she'd learn soon enough that her lover offered little advantage. Mordred, drinking with

Lot's sons tonight, would warn them that their mother slept with the son of their father's murderer.

They'd probably kill her. But then, he decided with a shrug, this too she had brought upon herself.

And at the moment, he had more vital issues occupying his mind. Primary of which was the Saxon prisoner, rotting in the castle dungeons. Mordred had no real quarrel with Penawulf, only that the man had chosen the wrong girl to marry. United against him, he and Riana presented too great a danger.

Summoning Fennick, his squire, and one other guard, Mordred made them swear to secrecy, warning that the kingdom's welfare relied upon their discretion. They were to remove the Saxon from his cell and take him outside the gate to the woods with no one being the wiser.

"You mean to let him go, after all?" Fennick asked, clearly surprised.

"Not at all," Mordred told him with a smile. "On the outskirts of the woods, you'll meet a small band of Saxons. Hand the prisoner to them. I do believe our good friend, Lord Vangarth, has his own plans for him."

Wolf prowled the cramped confines of his cell like a caged animal, sick with worry and frustration. He knew nothing about what went on in the castle overhead, save that he'd been forced to leave his wife and sister in the thick of it.

It ate at him, the not knowing, as did his powerlessness to act on it. He'd investigated every nook of the windowless pit in which they'd thrown him and had yet to discover even a remote hope of escape. Convinced that he'd been tossed in this dark, dank hole and left here to rot forever, he rattled the bars of his cage.

To his surprise, his protest for once met with a response. Two guards hurried down the stone steps toward him, their lantern giving off far more light than the sole torch on the wall. Indeed, it was so bright, Wolf had to look away from it.

Opening the cage door, they grabbed him roughly, one tying

his hands behind his back, while the other held a sword to his chest. "What is this?" he asked, taking care to flex his wrists to ensure the maximum laxity in his bindings. "Where are you taking me?" he tried again when they pushed and prodded him out of the cell.

"Silence!" was his only answer, but their quiet and stealth was answer enough. His would be no public hearing—their clandestine behavior indicated that his fate had already been decided behind closed doors. An emissary of Cerdric's could not be found dead inside the walls of Camelot, but there was nothing to stop them from dumping his corpse in the woods.

Stumbling between his captors as they led him through a dank tunnel leading out of the dungeons, he pretended to be dazed from his imprisonment, but all the while he worked at the ropes at his wrists, grateful that in their haste to get him out of the dungeons, his captors had been careless in tying them. By the time they broke out of the tunnel and into the night air, he had chafed his wrists raw, but he was free.

He picked his moment carefully, waiting until they were far enough away from the castle to be out of sight. With the element of surprise on his side, it was easy enough to swing his arm up and knock down the youth holding the sword, but the second guard, older and tougher, recovered before Wolf could manage a second swing.

He took a nasty punch to the gut, robbing him of his breath, but he was trained in hand-to-hand combat and his instincts for survival rushed to the fore. Seeing the man grab for the knife at his waist, Wolf brought his fist up and smashed it into his jaw. His opponent went reeling backward, but with a snarl, recovered and came charging, knife in hand.

Coiled and ready to strike, Wolf met his attack, reaching for the man's wrist at the last possible moment and twisting his arm until his captor yelped in pain. The knife dropped with a thud to the ground.

They brawled in earnest, a quiet, grunting match, wrestling and landing punches, but Wolf did so with a desperate edge. If he lost, he'd die, and end all hope of saving Riana and Greta, so he fought with inspired strength until his fist connected with the bridge of the man's nose. This time when his foe staggered backward, he went down and didn't get up.

Winded and bruised, Wolf could have used a rest, but he wasted no time in using his bindings to tie his captors' arms behind them. He saw no need to kill them, since he would be long gone when they awoke and they'd never find him in the cover of the forest. Grabbing their weapons, he took one last glance back at Camelot, dark and brooding on this moonless night. He would need to rest—between his imprisonment and this battle, he was exhausted—but he would be back.

And this time, when he left, he'd be taking Riana with him.

Riana found Greta later that evening, hurrying down the hall. She pulled her into the alcove where she'd been hiding, cautioning her friend to be quiet. "Mordred is looking for me," Riana explained, letting her worry steal into her tone. "He's even posted a guard at our bedroom door."

"Where have you been all day? I've been all over the castle, searching for you, worried sick. Merciful heavens, Riana, what has happened to your arm?"

In her worry, Riana had forgotten that she'd burned it. "I hope you can deal with my injury later, but for now, we have more serious concerns. I've spent the day looking for Wolf. He's been languishing all this time in the dungeons but before I could have him released, Mordred had him taken outside the gate. The tower guard told me he saw him heading toward the forest with Fennick and another of the prince's guards."

"Fennick has returned. None too happily, I might add. He and the man with him were bruised and bloodied."

Riana smiled. "I pray to the Goddess that means Wolf got away. We must do the same. Arthur was right. It's no longer safe for us here."

Greta looked suddenly grim. "I must warn you, I never did

have my audience with the king. I had to leave the book with Sir Kay, in hopes that he can get the evidence to Arthur."

Not exactly good news, but they had no time to rue that which they couldn't change. "It won't be easy for even Sir Kay to leave Camelot. Mordred has sealed off all the doors to the castle."

"Then we are trapped here?"

Faced with this possibility all evening, Riana had spent the last few hours in her hiding place trying to devise a way out of Camelot. Hers was far from an ideal plan, but it was the only exit she knew of that Mordred would not be watching. "I hope not," she told Greta. "I have an idea but it could involve some risk. I don't suppose Morgan taught you a spell for making us invisible?"

Greta's eyes were round and wide as she shook her head. "She wanted my magic to be open and honest."

More than ever, Riana regretted that she had not stayed with Morgan and learned the craft from her. "The Goddess willing, we won't need such magic," she said with more hope than conviction. "I know of a secret passage. It will mean getting past Morgause, but she should be preoccupied with her guard tonight."

Greta, bless her quick wit, understood at once. "Lamorak. The entire castle has been buzzing with the news that Mordred had assigned his mother's lover to keep Morgause confined to her room."

"And knowing Morgause, she will make good use of him. At this late hour, they might be asleep, but if not, I'm certain they shall be too busy to notice us slipping through the room."

"What if we are seen?"

Riana tried not to shudder. "It's a risk, but where is our option? Mordred will find us soon in any case, and I would rather take the chance at escape than to sit here like cornered mice waiting for a large, vicious cat to pounce."

Greta took in a deep breath. "Then let's go. The sooner the better."

Riana couldn't resist hugging her, being so very, very glad to have such a friend beside her. This was no easy undertaking, nor would it get easier once outside the castle.

Yet whatever transpired, she vowed, she would see Wolf's sister safely away.

Silently, they made their way to Morgause's chambers. Smiling when they found no guard in the hall, Riana held a finger to her lips as she gingerly eased open the door.

Inside the queen's chambers, they could hear moans and whisperings in the darkness. Having no wish to see what went on within the draperies of the queen's bed, Riana led Greta to the secret doorway. Never had the room seemed so vast, or had time passed so slowly. Each footfall was painstakingly measured, knowing one false step could lead to their doom.

Coming up to the wall at last, she reached out to steady Greta, again making the gesture for silence. She should have warned the secret door to be quiet, for it swung open with a betraying rasp.

"Who goes there?" Morgause called out, and Riana froze to the spot. They were caught. Even were they to run now, Lamorak, with his sword, could be on them before they could reach the curving stairway.

Yet even as she cursed her luck, the hallway door burst open. A band of Scots erupted into the room with a bloodcurdling yell, swinging their swords as they swooped down on the bed. Paralyzed with shock, Riana heard Morgause call out her sons' names, then her screams, mingling with the sound of metal hacking bone. It took Greta, reaching out with a trembling hand, to remind Riana what was at stake here.

"We must hurry, or we could be next," Riana whispered hoarsely after she'd yanked Greta into the secret room and shut the door behind them.

"But it was awful." Greta could not stop trembling. "To die in so hideous a fashion."

Riana, too, was shuddering as she reached for the sconce on the wall. When she'd told Morgause that her evil would be returned to her, she hadn't known it would come so soon, or so

Barbara Benedict

violently. "I know, but there's nothing we could have done to stop it. It is done and we must be gone, lest we wish to share in her fate."

"Where are we going?" Greta asked fearfully as they started down the long winding staircase.

"It's a secret passage Morgause showed me." Riana could hear her voice echo eerily off the dank stone walls around them. "Though I doubt she ever expected it to provide the means for our escape."

"And once we're out of the castle, what then?"

Riana grimaced, for their options were sorely limited. She reasoned that Greta would want to return to River Ford, but with war so imminent, it would not be safe to cross the frontiers. "I thought perhaps we should make our way to the Summer Country. To Queen Morgan."

But after that . . .

She could only pray that Morgan would have the answer.

Twenty-three

The second day of his freedom, Wolf stood within the cover of the forest, staring up at the heavily-armed towers of Camelot, feeling as powerless now as he had in his dungeon cage. He still knew no way to reach Riana and Greta, much less get them to safety.

Having explored the entire wall surrounding the kingdom, he saw much to concern him. Armed guards stood at every entrance and along the ramparts, each grim and ever alert, while inside, activity had ground to a halt. The strong military presence, the absence of normal business, the wary, on-edge aura blanketing the place, indicated the castle was readying itself for a siege.

And his women were trapped inside.

Frustrated, he gripped the sword in his hand, desperate enough to go charging through the gate however hopeless his mission, but he was spared the insanity by the sound of a branch snapping behind him. Keeping out of sight, he peered through the trees to see who was there. The last thing he needed now was to be re-captured by a British scouting party.

He went in the direction of the sound, keeping low as he tracked the presence until he came upon a small troop of Britons, camped in a clearing in the woods. Wolf recognized a few of the knights from his days in the training fields, but only one well enough to trust. Sir Kay sat at the center of the circle, his customary jug of ale in hand.

Preferring to err on the cautious side, Wolf waited until his trainer left the group—and had finished relieving himself—to approach him.

"Wolf!" Sir Kay said, happily surprised. "You're alive!"

"Very much," Wolf said, glancing over his shoulder. "But I'd prefer that your companions don't know I'm here. I don't need Mordred alerted that I mean to return for my women."

"You can trust these men. Indeed, we too are hiding from Mordred, awaiting word from Arthur before joining him in his fight to regain Camelot."

So this was why the castle seemed ready for war. "What happened that Mordred could assume control?"

Kay told him about Guinivere's trial and escape, how the prince had seized his chance when the king went after her. "Of course," he finished off, "I have proof, thanks to your sister, that Morgause created the entire tragedy by giving Guinivere one of her accursed potions."

The woman's guilt did not surprise Wolf, but he had to know, even though he hated having to ask the question. "Does your proof in any way implicate Riana?"

Kay eyed him curiously. "Nay, the notations are in the witch's hand."

"Yes, but you said Riana gave the queen the potion."

Kay shrugged, clearly troubled. "I know not her reasons. For that, you must ask your wife yourself, but we've no more to fear from Morgause in any case. She was killed, night before last, by her sons. I heard Mordred himself, spurring them to action."

"Against his own mother?"

"Unnatural, perhaps, but Morgause was never a natural mother. And now he seeks to place the blame on Riana, since she and your sister vanished the same night Morgause was murdered. He claims they must have used magic to escape, since every door and gate was sealed tight."

Wolf shook his head. "Morgause had a secret entrance through her chambers. Riana knew of it. Damn, had I but remembered it earlier, I could have been here to meet them."

"I don't know what you could do. Mordred has his soldiers scouring the countryside for them and a big Saxon like you would draw their attention at once."

Yes, Mordred wanted him dead, too. Still, Wolf could not leave his women out there stumbling about England, falling into the wily prince's trap. "I must find them. Do you know where they would go?"

Kay shook his head slowly. "I can but guess, mind you. Females in this kingdom go to the convent to be guaranteed safety, but I will warn, there are many holy establishments across the breadth of England."

"Then I shall try each one."

Kay's face clouded. "It could take years. Mordred could still get to them first."

"I know my wife's scent. I shall detect it and track her until I find them both. I will not fail in this. I cannot."

"But they'll be safe enough with the nuns. Wait 'til Arthur gets word to us and if there's no battle, my men and I can accompany you then."

But Wolf was already turning away. He didn't know why he persisted, but as it had been from the first night he'd seen her, he felt compelled to follow his wife, certain something dreadful would happen if he did not. He'd find no peace until he knew both Riana and Greta were safe.

Weeks later, Riana stared at the walls of the convent that served as both her sanctuary and her prison. No one could reach her if she did not wish to see them, but neither could she leave—not as long as Mordred sat on the throne of England.

She and Greta had arrived mere days ago after a long and arduous journey. It had been no easy thing, picking their way over unknown lands, seeking the Summer Country. At first, they couldn't ask for directions, finding Mordred's guards in every village they approached. But this past week, the military presence had suddenly withdrawn. It was said in the villages that Mordred's army had been recalled, that his warriors were even now marching to meet the king's forces in a battle for the crown.

Shuddering, Riana remembered the vision she'd seen in Morgause's crystal. All the blood and death and suffering—was that to be the fate of England? Husband against wife, father fighting son—could the Goddess be so cruel, she would lead Riana here to Arthur, merely to bring about such tragedy and heartache?

Riana moved slowly through each day as if the burden of guilt weighed down her shoulders. Unable to eat, to sleep, she lived every hour laden with worry and regret.

Nor did it help to be stranded here with the Christian holy women. They were kind, these nuns, and clearly meant well, but their ways were strange and their god demanding. Riana needed Greta to talk to, but ever since coming to the convent, her friend had grown increasingly mysterious, sneaking off at dawn each morning and returning after they'd all retired for the night. "I go to the woods to pray," she'd answer vaguely when Riana tried to question her, before disappearing once more into the forest.

Alone with her tortured thoughts, Riana wondered if she'd ever be given the chance to make things right. Over and over, she played out how she could have acted, should have acted, praying she'd find some way yet to make her atonement. With her king and queen, with the kingdom of Camelot, but most of all, with her husband. Above all else, she had to find some way to undo her misbegotten enchantment, to say the words that would set him free.

Yet how she ached to think he might leave her life forever. Morgause was right. Without the spell, what cause did he have to stay with her when all she had ever done was cause him hardship and pain? There were people who were born unlovable, she knew, and clearly she must be one of them. Else, why would everyone always abandon her?

She was happy to learn that Morgause wasn't her mother, but she nonetheless felt bereft, now having no one. She regretted losing Arthur as a father most of all. It had given her purpose, doing what she had for the man who had sired her. Now what was she to do? She wasn't an enchantress, nor could she be a wife and mother—she could go nowhere.

Hearing a noise behind her, she turned to face Queen Morgan, simply garbed in the brown robes of an apprentice, watching her with a gentle, curious expression.

Riana should have been stunned, but it seemed suddenly the most natural thing in the world that Morgan should appear when she most needed her. When the woman held out her arms, it seemed equally inevitable that Riana would fall into her tender grasp.

"I'm sorry," she told Morgan quietly. "Your sister is dead and your brother's kingdom is unraveling, and it's all my fault."

"Come now, *all* your fault?" Laughing softly, Morgan held her at arm's length. "I've heard and seen everything that's happened at Camelot in the crystal. Nothing leads me to suppose you deserve total credit."

Riana listed her crimes, starting with the heartache she'd caused Wolf, down to the potion she'd given the queen. "Morgause implied I was the catalyst," she finished off. "That my pathetic attempts at magic were what caused everything to fall apart."

Morgan sighed. "They were coming apart long before you ever walked upon the scene." Taking Riana by the arm, she led her away from the nuns working so diligently in their garden to the quieter, more secluded area outside the rear gate. "Let me tell you about my sister," she said as they strolled to the lake in the distance. "It was her greatest talent, finding one's needs, one's hopes and dreams, and then using them to further her own ambitions. Tell me, did you ever lose track of time, or your memory of what happened when you were with her? Did you leave her room feeling as if you were in a trance?"

Riana felt suddenly unnerved. "It was always thus when we went to the crystal pool. She would later tell me what I said during my trance. She insisted I must tell the king about these visions."

Morgan nodded. "She put words in your head, convincing you

to thus influence Arthur, while she kept your true visions for her private use."

"She told me she summoned me to Camelot." Thinking aloud, Riana cringed inwardly at the memory. "She imitated Merlin's voice completely."

Morgan gave her arm a reassuring squeeze. "If she lied in other areas, couldn't this also be an untruth? Myself, I believe you were called by Merlin. He always said you would come to Arthur in his final hour of need."

"Me?" If it were true, it would mean her purpose in life had been restored to her. "Are you certain?"

Morgan nodded solemnly. "It's why I said nothing of my sister's misdoings," she said, leading them both to the path that circled the lake. "All my life, I have watched Morgause commit some crime, then cleverly shift the blame to me. She had an art of making me seem mean and spiteful, and I never wanted to appear so in your eyes. I held tight to the faith that you would come to me when the day came to serve my brother."

Riana remembered the sense of rightness she'd felt upon first seeing Morgan. "Now?" she asked aloud. "But what can I do for him? I who ruins everything I touch."

Morgan smiled, even as she shook her head. "When you first came to me for lessons many years ago, I found you too vain and cocky and over-impatient. Now you're too humble and resigned. You must find balance, Riana. Learn from your mistakes, for that is what leads to strength. And now, more than ever, you'll need to be strong. Your uncle needs you."

"Uncle?" Riana's brain reeled with confusion. "Arthur?"

Morgan looked away, her face pained. "I've known this moment would come, but I've put it off, not knowing quite how to prepare for it. It's no easy thing, admitting your weakness to your daughter."

Unlike when Morgause uttered the claim, Riana felt no shock, nor any aversion. Rather, the prospect settled into her, finding a home there. She was filled with an overwhelming relief, and again, that sense of rightness, to realize that here at long last was her mother.

Walking beside Morgan, Riana stared at the woman's profile, seeing the shared features she'd been too preoccupied to notice— the slight curve of the nose, the amber eyes, the same delicate frame. She felt swamped with gratitude to be given this second chance. This time, she would be patient and learn from Morgan—everything the woman had to teach her.

"Years ago," her mother began, still looking away, "I visited Ireland, and one night as I lay wild and restless in my bed, I was called out to the green, rolling hills. A man waited for me, an intensely beautiful creature. Some might call it seduction, but in my heart, I know I went to him gladly, and I wept until my eyes were dry when he vanished at the dawn. Those were the most wonderful moments of my life. Save, perhaps," she paused to gaze fondly at Riana, "for the morning I gave birth to my daughter."

"Did Arthur know my father is from the faerie realm?"

"Not at first. But Merlin, being born of the same realm, knew at once. He told me of your talent, but he, like I, feared those who would exploit it. And worse, I was wed to a man who would happily murder any child he hadn't fathered, so I saw no solution save to leave you at the castle doorstep, knowing you'd find a good home at Camelot."

Riana thought of a much younger Morgan, frightened for the life of her baby and understood why her mother might leave her behind. "But," she said, voicing the doubt aloud, "why then send me away?"

"I returned for a visit and found my little Moriana had become the darling of the royal pair. My clever, impulsive Riana, who likewise drew my sister's watchful gaze. The more the king did for you, the more I feared what Morgause would do to a usurper of his affections. She had her own child, Mordred, stashed away in Scotland until the time was ripe to present him. It was concern for your life, knowing Morgause mustn't guess the tie between us, that prompted me to send you off with the old woman."

Sela. No wonder her guardian had been so against her returning to Camelot. It made Riana feel twice as guilty, knowing she'd behaved so badly to someone who had only wanted to keep her from harm.

"But age and experience have taught me that no one can alter another's fate," Morgan went on, her voice strained. "I should have foreseen your return. I should have realized I had neither the power, nor the right, to make your decisions for you."

"You kept cautioning me to exercise patience. Now I see why."

"You have so many of my sister's traits, I feared you'd be tempted to follow her path. It broke my heart, watching you parrot her words. You were *my* hopes and dreams, Riana. Morgause learned this and used it to force me into a corner." Morgan came to a stop, turning to face Riana. "But even she could not stop what was meant to be. You have a power, an inner strength she could never hope to own. In the end, if you can discover it for yourself, it is what shall save us all."

Riana returned her intense gaze, at a loss for what her mother wanted. "Is this some test? I don't know what is required of me."

"I know," Sighing again, Morgan gestured out over the lake. "Feel it?" she asked in a strange tone. "Around us, a storm is brewing, as if the heavens themselves are gathering force. Tell me, what do you see when you gaze out over the water?"

A haze hovered over the lake, and with it an eerie silence, though Riana too could sense something building in the air around them. Peering in the distance, she could almost make out an island, shimmering in and out of view. "I see what seems to be a crystal castle, rising up out of a hilly island. But the fog weaves in and out, and I can't see it clearly."

"Avalon," Morgan whispered. "Concentrate harder. Now can you see it?'

But the scene shifted into the battlefield she'd seen in the crystal. Riana tensed, hearing the blood cries and clash of metal as if she stood on the field beside the warring factions. It was Arthur's army, she thought with a clutch of fear, searching through the swordplay and fallen bodies for sign of her uncle.

She found him with his son, faced off in arm to arm combat. Arthur's face was sad and beaten; Mordred's more driven. Perhaps determination made up for a lack of skill, for Mordred's sword swung down on Arthur's head, even as the king's spear pierced his son's chest. Riana gasped, horrified. "The king has fallen," she cried out.

"I know," Morgan said quietly.

Pulling her gaze from the lake, focusing on the woman beside her, Riana saw a great sadness in her mother's eyes. "You have seen it, too?"

Morgan nodded. "I wait only for them to bring Arthur here to us."

"But it was such a grave injury. Surely he can't survive the journey."

Morgan gestured out over the lake, to where the island had earlier shimmered. "It is ordained that he shall live to be brought to the Old Ones on the mystical island of Avalon."

"Is that my function? Am I to take him there?"

Again, she saw great sadness in Morgan's eyes. "I can't predict what the fates will decide, but they could well have another task for you."

"Wait," Riana called out when Morgan turned into the forest behind them. "Where do you go? What am I to do now?"

"We both shall wait." Morgan's soft voice echoed eerily through the fog. "I must now pray and you must go back to your convent to think long and hard while you wait. Prepare yourself, child, for Arthur's final hour."

Riana had little time for preparation, for barely had dusk fallen when she heard a loud shouting at the convent gate. "Open in the name of King Arthur!" she heard men cry out. "And send forth your finest healers."

Rushing to the open courtyard, she found Sir Kay and Bedevere, carrying the king on a litter. Both men looked battle-worn and travel weary, but it was Arthur who drew her concern. She ran to him, taking his hand as she surveyed his injuries. Blood caked and drying on his helmet, all color drained from his features, he looked dead already. "Where is Greta?" she cried out, and hearing her voice, Arthur opened his eyes. She could see by the glint in that sunken gaze what effort he exerted, staving off death.

"My sister Morgan, where is she?" he rasped out, clasping her hand so hard it was all she could do not to cry out with the pain.

"She's down by the lake, praying. She knew you would come."

He closed his eyes, loosening his grip. "Take me to her at once."

"But sire, these nuns are healers," Bedevere said in confusion. "Surely we should see to your wounds first."

"Take me to Morgan." Arthur's voice was barely a whisper. "She knows what must be done."

They made a strange party, silently making their way to the lake with huge flaring torches wavering in the light, gathering breeze. Walking beside Sir Kay, remembering how he'd befriended her husband, Riana had to ask if he'd heard word of Wolf. Face clouding, Kay said Wolf had gone looking for them weeks ago and he'd hoped to find him here. That he had not . . .

She did not encourage him to finish the thought. She had no wish to think that her husband might be dead.

Darkness had fallen when they reached the lake, making Morgan's emergence from the forest all the more otherworldly. Behind her, three females, likewise garbed in brown robes, each carried a single, flickering torch, which they too set in the ground to form a circle around the king's litter. The last apprentice, Riana saw with surprise, was her good friend Greta. All this time she'd been with Morgan and said nothing about it?

Morgan went straight to her brother, kneeling beside him with tears on her cheeks. "I have come, as promised," he said to her, his voice weak with strain. "Now it is time for me to die."

"Not yet." Gently laying her hands upon him, she murmured a strange incantation. "That should help ease the pain," she said softly, "and get you through what you must yet accomplish. Remember your vow to the Old Ones, my brother. It is time to return your sword to the lake."

He grimaced, gesturing to his weapon. "Bedevere, bring Excalibur."

Riana watched helplessly, growing more confused. She could see no way she might help her king in this.

His trusted knight knelt beside him, holding out the sword. "Sire, this worries me. She is your sister, I know, but what she is asking . . . I can't forget that she has oft misled you in the past."

"That was Morgause," Riana blurted out, but Morgan silenced her with a look.

Arthur took the sword from Bedevere, smiling wanly, but his features tightened as Excalibur's tip fell to the ground. "My strength has left me," he said hoarsely. "Bedevere, my good friend, do not let me fail even in this. Take my sword and hurl it in the lake."

"Sire, it makes no sense. Excalibur is the symbol of your reign. Without it, you have nothing."

"Untrue," Riana again blurted out. "There is the Round Table. That is the finest symbol of the king's reign."

Once more, Morgan shook her head to call for quiet, but this time, she did so with a tiny smile.

"She is right," Arthur said weakly. "It was never the fighting I stood for, but rather unity under the laws of civility and justice. I beg you one last time, Bedevere, will you answer my request?"

"Sire, please, do not ask it."

Desperately, Arthur looked to Kay. "You, my oldest friend, who was there when I first pulled Excalibur from the stone. Help me send it back to its resting place where it belongs."

Kay glanced from Morgan to Bedevere, clearly torn. "Sire," he said at last, "I've been a fighting man all my life and it goes against the grain to be tossing aside such a fine weapon."

"If your sister is so eager," Bedevere said, glaring at Morgan, "why does she not dispose of it herself?"

Morgan rose to her feet, suddenly taller and more commanding. "My brother knows I am a priestess of the Old Ones, and am forbidden to lay hands upon any mortal weapon."

Arthur looked about him. "Is there no one who will help me in my hour of need?"

"I will." Everyone turned to her, blatantly stunned, but no more surprised than Riana herself. Hearing only the words of Merlin's prediction, she'd given no thought to how she, a tiny, untrained female, would even lift that monstrous blade, much less hurl it such a distance. She braced herself against their laughter.

It never came. Arthur held up a hand, gesturing her closer, smiling as she knelt beside him. "Of those I hold most dear, you, Riana, understand my dream. My life did revolve around my Round Table, but dreams, I've discovered, can grow as old as the men who create them. My vision is dying, as am I, and I no longer have the strength nor the will to fight for it."

"Sire—"

He held up a hand to still her protest. "My people are stubborn and will cling to the old ways, so I leave it to you, all that is left of my blood and dreams, to carry on my hopes for this kingdom. You and your Penawulf will blend the best of both our worlds to forge a finer England, a stronger one. One day, through your children's children, this throne shall again stand tall and proud."

She would have warned that she was barren, but again Morgan silenced her with a look, even as she clasped Riana's shoulder. "Here is the reason you were called, Moriana. Take the sword and send it to the depths of the lake."

"A girl?" Bedevere sputtered. "You must be joking."

Morgan ignored him, helping Riana rise to her feet. "Amazing things can be accomplished with the proper faith. In your heart, Riana, haven't you always believed you were born to carry out the king's last request? Clasp on to that belief, my child, and hold tight to your faith in the future."

Riana reached for Excalibur, trying not to show her dismay at how heavy she found it. It was impossible. She could not lift it

"Have patience," Morgan coaxed beside her. "Breathe deeply

and as you do, think of your love for the king. For your husband. Draw on the force of that love, and with it, all your concentration, until you can visualize yourself throwing the sword in the water."

"But that is magic."

"Yes," Morgan breathed. "That is exactly what it is." Taking Riana by the arms, Morgan looked deeply into her eyes. "And your magic lies in your ability to love without reservation."

Her words sifted into Riana, making sense, and she saw how all her many mistakes had been leading up to this moment. She had found her weaknesses and learned her lessons; it was time to draw on her strength.

Holding tight to Excalibur, gazing down at Arthur, she summoned up memories of this man who had been so kind to her. The walnuts they'd shared, their strolls through the garden—each time, Arthur had breathed his dream to life inside her. She could not let it die with a sad whimper. Throwing this sword would be a symbol of the pact she now made with Arthur. Come what may, she would carry his dream into the future.

And somehow, she would forge that dream with Wolf.

Putting all her mind, body and training to work, she felt a sudden exhilarating lucidity. Every incantation she'd ever heard sorted itself into place until she knew the words she must use. Chanting with growing confidence, she watched the sword begin to glow in her hand. She could feel the power surge up from her core, streaming to the arms she now lifted in the air. Raising the sword over her head, she called out to the heavens to bless this weapon, to take it back into the deity's bosom for safekeeping.

And all at once, it rose out of her hands, soaring through the air in a graceful arc. In awe, she watched it dip down to spear the lake with barely a ripple. A great golden glow spread across the water's surface as Excalibur slowly, silently vanished into the depths.

In the ensuing quiet, feeling completely depleted, Riana grew slowly aware of those around her. Kay and Bedevere seemed almost comical with their slack-jawed countenances, but the king lay back with a contented sigh. "It is done," he said, closing his eyes. "Kay, Bedevere, leave us now and go carry word of my death to what's left of my people."

Watching the knights return to the convent, Riana noticed the distant lightning, arcing across the sky. Morgan's storm, she thought, hearing the muffled rumble of thunder.

Next to her, Morgan smiled with undisguised pride. "You did well, though I doubt few will ever know the truth of this day." She gestured at the departing knights. "When the tale is recounted before the fires, it will be one of them who hurled the sword in the lake."

"It is better thus. No one will believe a mere female could have done it anyway, and I have no need for such notoriety."

Morgan nodded, clearly pleased. "It is those who do their work quietly that do the greatest good. Always look to your own heart for reassurance and recognition. When I am gone . . ."

"Gone?" Riana asked in sudden panic. "Where will you go?"

But she knew, even before Morgan pointed out over the lake. It was time, Riana realized, to bring Arthur to the magical island of Avalon. "Take me with you," she begged, feeling her world slip away. "We've just found each other. Must I lose my mother now after a lifetime of searching?"

Tears welled in Morgan's eyes. "Oh child, how I wish it could be otherwise. But those who cannot see Avalon can never cross its shores."

So it *had* been a test? "I almost saw it." Desperately squinting, Riana peered through the dark. "I will see it. With patience and concentration."

"Perhaps, but the king is dying and we can delay no longer. You must stay and do your uncle's bidding."

"But I can't carry on the ideals of the Round Table without help."

"For help, you must look to another."

Riana's gaze drifted to Greta, the friend who had always stood by her, but even as that hope flared, Morgan dashed it by shaking her head. "She will go with me," she said gently.

"You'll take a Saxon instead of your own daughter?" Riana

heard her own pettiness. "It's wrong, I know, to feel such envy, but I'm frightened. I can't bear the thought of being alone."

Morgan ran gentle fingers along Riana's face. "You needn't be alone. You did your part for your king, now make peace with your husband. Reverse your enchantment and break your unnatural hold on him."

Riana knew a sudden despair. "But then I shall lose him, too."

"All good magic requires sacrifice, and true love is a matter of faith. Trust in your husband and pray that he does not fail you."

"But I don't even know how to undo the enchantment."

"Don't you? It is like raising the sword. Sometimes, magic is less knowing, and more *feeling* what must be done." Smiling, she reached over and tucked the hair behind Riana's ears. "I've every faith in you. But now, I'm being selfish, wasting precious time when I must make arrangements for my brother, and poor Greta is anxious to say her goodbyes."

Thunder rumbled in the heavens as Morgan gestured to the girl. Needing no further encouragement, Greta ran over and threw herself in Riana's arms. "Please don't hate me," she pleaded. "I was called."

Riana clung to her friend, feeling a deep, aching loneliness. "I know. We must each follow the path the Goddess chooses for us. But I shall miss you dreadfully, Greta. You were always my common sense."

"But now you shall have Wolf. Take good care of him, Riana."

Pulling back, Riana smiled ruefully. "Then you'd best pray hard for me over on your island, for your brother will not want me once he learns the truth. There's too much he can never accept, mostly my inability to bear his children."

"This is why Morgan goes to Avalon," Greta told her. "We've been praying, trying to find a true spell to cure your barrenness, but she decided to beseech the Old Ones to do her this favor. If granted, it will mean she can never return to this world, but she's prepared to make the atonement. She says it's her way of proving her love, of showing how much she regrets having abandoned you."

Riana glanced over her shoulder at Morgan, feeling a harsh tightness in her throat. "But you, Greta," she asked, turning back to her friend, "you don't need to turn your back on this world, too."

"But I'm avid to learn what the Old Ones can teach me, Riana. Help my brother understand. Tell him that one day, when my time of service is done, I will return to River Ford. Maybe not in his lifetime, but tell Wolf I shall do my utmost to bring glory to his name and carry on our family's noble tradition."

"Have you had a vision?" Riana had to ask.

Greta smiled enigmatically. "Arthur was right. England shall one day rise from the ashes."

"Greta," Morgan called out. "Come, the barge is pulling into shore. We must go before the storm is upon us."

Greta leaned over to kiss her cheek. "I'm sorry, Riana, but I must go."

Hearing the slap of the oar on water, Riana looked up to see the ghostly form emerge from the darkness. Its canopy draped with black silk, poled by four shadowy boatmen, the vessel seemed as insubstantial as the wisps of fog trailing behind it. No one uttered a word as it banked on the shore, and the boatmen disembarked to carry Arthur's litter aboard.

At Morgan's gesture, Greta and the others filed onto the barge, all with the same eerie silence, broken only by the increasing reverberations from the sky. Watching Morgan follow suit, Riana ached to call out, to beg them not to go, but she willed herself to remain still. It would accomplish little, save to make their parting harder.

"Always remember," Morgan called out over the waters as the barge slipped into the mists, "magic is a gift to be used wisely and sparingly. And always, your magic must come from your heart."

Hugging herself as her mother, uncle and best friend vanished behind the wall of fog surrounding Avalon, Riana fought the encroaching loneliness. As drops of rain fell down around her, she saw with heartbreaking clarity how empty her life could now be. What good was love when those she cared about only left her?

Yet they had left her with a mission, she realized. Arthur and Morgan, even Greta, had all pointed the way to her husband. Wolf was the key to the future.

Yet before there could be any hope for them, she must first break the enchantment.

It wouldn't be easy making him then care for her, but as Morgan said, true love was a matter of faith. She had to trust that her love for Wolf would give her strength. That love would give her power to forge a better future.

Inhaling deeply, she turned back to the convent, taking her first step on this, her new, true path.

And there, standing like an omen before her with only the rain between them, waited Wolf.

Twenty-four

Watching Riana walk to him through the rain, Wolf battled conflicting emotions. Joy and relief, certainly, at seeing her alive and well, but also confusion, even suspicion, over what he'd just seen. Was it witchery that raised that glowing sword from her hands to the lake? Why embrace Queen Morgan, the witch accused of poisoning him, and what had his sister Greta to do with all of it?

Yet the questions stilled in his throat as Riana came to a stop before him, reaching up with a gentle hand to stroke his face. "Whatever befalls us," she said quietly, her gaze drinking him, "know always that I love you."

It was too much for a man who had tracked his woman halfway across England and Wolf's restraint vanished. Grabbing Riana, pulling her close, he swooped down to take possession of her lips. It was foolish to give free rein to his emotions with the storm swirling about them, with the dangers posed by the chaos that now ruled England, but in that moment, Wolf could think only of Riana's soft, white flesh, her warm, eager body, and the fever overtook his good sense.

With a groan, deep in his throat, he surrendered to the passion raging within him.

Riana returned his kiss with her own hungry passion, and with all the love she had in her. Seeing Wolf, she'd known at last what

Morgan had tried to explain, that to reverse the enchantment, to free her beloved Saxon, she must free her own emotions and hold nothing back.

And all was set in place—even a storm, so like the first night she'd entrapped him. Riana needed only the strength and the faith to go through with it.

Wolf kissed her, drawing from her lips as if she were life itself. She gave all she had, saying, "I love you," over and over into his mouth, like some chant meant to keep them always together. As she clung to him, kissing him, Riana fought her desire, knowing how easily she could lose her resolve in the flood of pleasure he inevitably brought her. This act of love must be for Wolf alone. Only by unselfishly giving herself to this man, she now realized, could she hope to grant him his freedom.

Still kissing and caressing her, Wolf moved them back to a bed of leaves. Together, they dropped to their knees, touching each other everywhere at once, the fever burning between them even as the rain, cool and reviving, poured down on their faces. Lowering her onto his cloak, he tore away their clothing in his haste to join together.

As he stroked her, she ran her hands along his rain-soaked flesh and hair, memorizing each line and muscle for the long, lonely days she feared lay ahead. Touching his face, his chest, each tensing, pulsing muscle, she let her love spill out and over him, so it would go with her husband even if she could not, and forever after serve as his protection.

Lightning streaked across the sky, thunder rocked the ground beneath them, but Riana heard only words—ancient, mystical murmurings she now recognized and understood. It was as Morgan had said, she *felt* the magic, the power surging through her, even as she had when lifting the sword.

Parting her thighs, she welcomed him into the heart of her, wrapping her legs and arms protectively around her man as she took him to that special world of hope and redemption, praying for the Goddess to deliver him safe and whole when they returned. And as he drove inside her, moving in the age-old dance of love, she blanketed him with her warmth, giving all that she had to this man she would love for the rest of her existence.

Watching his rain-soaked face as he loved her, she felt the emotion clog in her throat, the tears well in her eyes, as she gave herself unconditionally. She chanted silently at first, but her fervency built with the rising power of his thrusts, her desperation echoed by the force of the storm raging around them. Too soon, she was crying out the words, then shouting them to the warring heavens, screaming out "I love you," even as, with a great shuddering gasp, Wolf exploded his seed inside her.

It is done, she thought with a mixture of relief and sadness. Deep in her core, she knew she had reversed the enchantment.

She clung to him, savoring the joy of holding him, hearing his heart beat so near her own, feeling the warmth of his body covering hers. She was afraid to let go, she realized, afraid of how he would now look at her.

Around them the storm slowly subsided, the lightning stealing off to another kingdom, another sky, while the thunder lost force with every reverberation. Riana tried not to lose heart, not to lose faith, but their passion was now as spent as the storm, and she couldn't help but fear what would be left in its wake.

Trust in your husband, Morgan had told her. And Greta had insisted Wolf would love her, with or without the magic. Riana wanted to believe as she clung to her husband with bittersweet longing, summoning the courage to tell him the truth she had so long denied him.

Above her, Wolf came slowly to his senses. Wariness struck first, the sense of everything being slightly off-kilter. He tensed certain that something was wrong, that something was missing Glancing about him at the rain-soaked forest, he felt suddenly foreign, completely out of his element in what must surely be a Druid holy place.

Uneasily, he remembered his sister going off with those holy women, out over the lake. They had to get out of this place and

back home to River Ford, where they belonged. He and Greta
and . . .

Riana.

Staring down at her, it slammed into him, that sense of his
world falling apart. This was Riana, his wife, but she seemed
suddenly more a stranger than the woman he chased across England. Gone was the greed to possess her, the desperation to see
her safe—he was left with an aching emptiness, as if some vital
part of him had died.

A chasm rife with doubt and distrust.

Riana felt the moment Wolf first tensed, and knew her first
pang of dread. She fought the urge to reach out for him as he
pulled away, sensing it was already too late.

He rose to his feet with the agility of a cat, and far more swiftly
than the situation would warrant. "You must have bewitched
me," he whispered without a trace of tenderness, his gaze searching the lakeside. "Where was my good sense that I gave no
thought to the danger?"

Danger?

"What is it?" she asked, rising up to grab her tunic so she
might hastily cover herself. Logically, she might know Mordred
was dead, but she could not lose the sense of peril.

"I heard a noise," Wolf said distractedly. "Perhaps it was the
raindrops, falling from the leaves." As if he didn't believe the
explanation, he continued to peer through the trees.

Riana listened to the drops, thinking how magical it seemed
in the aftermath of the storm, with a reluctant moon breaking
through the clouds, the silvery wisps of fog curling about the
ground. Too bad she felt so chilled by her dampness, by the dread
building inside her.

Wolf shrugged into his kilt. "Sky-fire could have struck the
tree above us, an enemy could have crept up undetected. Only a
fool would leave himself so open to attack on British soil."

Swallowing hard, Riana knew the time had come to tell him the truth. "I have something I must explain to you."

"Not here," he said curtly, gathering up his cloak and other clothing, wrapping the lot in a big, soggy ball. "We can go to yon convent where it is warm and dry. I saw Sir Kay head in that direction and I must speak with him as well."

She reached out to hold his arm. "I would as soon say what I must, here and now, before we take another step."

"We must get Greta and make our way to safety." As if he hadn't heard her—or had no wish to—he turned to walk back to the lake.

Riana grabbed for him. "Greta will not be coming with us. She has gone to the magical island of Avalon, to learn and train with the Old Ones. It's a great honor, much like the Christians' heaven."

"My sister is dead?" he asked, roughly shaking free of her grasp. "You let those witches take her life?"

He was so angry, she thought with growing hopelessness. "Greta is not dead," she told him firmly, though feeling sick inside. "She's very much alive, following what she sees as her destiny. She hoped you would understand, knowing this is what your mother would have wished for her."

"Druid nonsense."

She winced at the sound of his contempt, but held her head high. "It is far more than nonsense. Indeed, I'd have gone, too, had I been able."

"You'd have left me?" His voice was strange, his gaze commanded by the mists rising off the lake. "Even now, in death you would follow your king?"

"I was not given the chance." Unhappily, she heard the crack in her voice. This was not going well. Wolf's calm exterior didn't deceive her; she knew he was very, very angry. "Only the chosen can cross Avalon's shores," she told him. "My path, I was told, is to offer atonement."

"Atonement?" he asked sharply. "Tell me, wife, what have you done that requires you to make amends?"

She wanted to hold him, to share one another's warmth as she explained, but each moment he withdrew further from her. "You were right," she told him dully. "I did bewitch you."

He looked at her as if she had just slithered out from under a stone.

She fought a rising sense of desperation, of it all slipping through her fingers. "That first night on the hill, when I was dancing, I called for a man who would love me forever. I didn't mean to entrap you. I hadn't even known you were there. It was all a mistake."

The silence was appalling. She could see his rage by the way he balled his fists, the way he refused to look at her. "Was it also a mistake that all this time, you've done nothing about this trap you wove around me?"

Shrinking inside, she pushed herself to go on. "I asked Sela to undo my enchantment before I left River Ford. When I realized she had not, I went to Morgause for help. It was not until now, tonight, that I discovered for myself the right spell to set you free."

"So even this was a trick?" He looked down at the ground where they had just lain. "Is there nothing between us that isn't spawned by witchery?"

Riana felt as if a little bit more of her died each moment she stared at his stiff profile. She wanted to tell him yes, that her love for him was more enduring than anything she had ever known, but she knew he would no longer believe anything she told him.

"Helga tried to warn me," he went on in a dull tone, "but I wouldn't listen. Even there in Camelot, with the evidence of your crimes piling up around me, I clung to the image I'd burned on my brain. It, too, was an illusion, wasn't it? You were no more a wife to me than you were a friend to Arthur and Guinivere. You used me, even as you used everyone else, to further your vile schemes of ambition. Did you enjoy yourself, playing your deceits, jerking me about like some dumb beast on a leash?"

"Wolf, no, it wasn't like that."

But he was beyond listening. "No more lies!" He turned to her then, his features tight with strain. "I'd have given the world to you, Riana. My heart, my home, my life." He took a deep breath, as if to steady himself. "You spoke of atonement. Yours shall be to come with me now."

"You still want me?" Hard to keep the eagerness from her tone.

His gaze narrowed. "You are my wife and I need an heir. The day you bear me a son, I shall set *you* free, casting you out upon the world with gold enough to see you don't starve." He turned then to go, as if expecting she would follow, but she stood her ground, unwilling to believe she had heard him right.

"Are you saying," she said with forced calm to his back, "that you expect me to sell my son for a bag of gold?"

"Remorse? From you, Riana?" He turned to scowl at her. "Where was such regret when you killed our first child?"

Riana shook with emotion, stunned that he could be so deliberately cruel. "Again, you would condemn me?" she lashed out. "How can you be so cold, you who never bothered to notice, much less ask, what I suffered? Always too busy being the great chieftain, maintaining tribal law, you couldn't bother to notice what a mere wife was feeling."

He was so cold, so closed to her.

All at once, it became too much. The words spilled out, dredged up from the long, empty hours of hurt and worry and pain. "Do you truly think a day goes by that I'm not haunted by what I've lost?" she cried. "That I don't hear my baby's cries every night in my dreams? You, Wolf, can find another female to bear you children, but I shall never, ever hold my child in my arms." Hugging herself, she fought the need to lose herself in great, gulping sobs. "As a result of that one, foolish act, I am doomed to be barren for the rest of my life. Useless to you or any other man."

"You are barren?" he asked, each clipped syllable like a slap to the face. "How long have you known?"

"The length of my suffering matters?" she asked, incredulous that he could remain so unfeeling in the face of her pain. "It makes it more a crime that I have had to bear such awful knowledge alone all this time?"

"Yes!" He growled the word. "You could have told me when I first came to Camelot, bloodied and bruised by your treacherous prince. When I held you in the garden, or in my rooms after making love, those were the times to tell me, not in this last minute confession."

That he was right did little to assuage her misery. As swiftly as it had come, her anger left her, leaving her feeling empty once more, and completely defeated.

"What trickery are you up to now, Riana?" Wolf asked. "Is this your revenge, to strip away my last vestige of pride and hope, to leave me with nothing? I will not have it. Keep your lies, your deceits. I want no more to do with you."

"Wolf, wait," she called again, but this time he did not falter. Flinging his bundled cloak over a shoulder, he walked away to be swallowed up by the fog.

She would not chase after him, nor could she bear to watch him walk out of her life. Still hugging herself, she gazed back at the lake, fighting the tears filling her swollen eyes. Despite all her faith, all her prayers, in the end, Wolf had failed her. All he cared about was the children she would never bear him.

She stared at where Avalon should be, thinking of her mother there, sacrificing her human existence on the slight chance she could convince the Old Ones to cure her daughter's infertility. Poor Morgan had made her sacrifice in vain, then, for barren or not, Wolf would have no more to do with her.

Reaching down to touch the bag of walnuts that always gave her comfort, she remembered that in all the emotional upheaval, she'd never attached the rope belt at her waist. Nor could she find the sack after groping about the ground. To Riana, it seemed the last, fatal blow, that she should not have even that tiny bit of her husband to carry around with her.

Crumpling in a heap, she gave into the violent sobs now racking her body.

Hearing the sounds of her weeping drift to him through the eerie fog, Wolf paused in his tracks. Old habits die hard he thought, even as he fought the urge to console her. How many ways must Riana rip out his heart and stomp it into the ground before he learned his lesson? He could no more trust her tears than he could heed her words of love.

His mind still reeled from what she had told him. All this time, her accursed witchery had been leading him into one misery after another. The thought of his little sister, lost to him on that damned, distant island, made the rage well up into his throat. And what of his village, abandoned in his insane quest to possess her? A few weeks more, and it would be too late to start the planting—a few days more and the anarchy that now gripped England could rush in and destroy River Ford before he could get back to save it.

All could be lost and for what? For a witch, whose basic profession was deception? A woman, who by her own admission would have left him yet again to follow her beloved king?

Well, the enchantment was lifted and he for one was glad to be free of it. Inhaling deeply, he told himself it was well past time he was quit of that Druid witch who was his wife. He would go now to Sir Kay before the man left the convent, to see if his old friend could help him in getting home to his village.

Yet Wolf hesitated, Riana's sobs cutting him to the bone.

"Here he is," he heard a man shout in Saxon. Before he could turn, a rope whipped over his head, the noose tightening around his arms. "Hurry," the brute called out, "I can't hold him long by myself."

Enraged, Wolf kicked at his attacker, cursing himself for falling too easily into the trap. He could hear no sobs now, he realized bitterly. Her tears, along with that confession, had been merely another ploy to keep him here long enough for her companions to surround him.

Eyeing the band that rushed up to encircle him, he saw a mixture of Saxons and Britons alike. One he recognized as Mordred's knave, the guard Fennick who would have killed him outside

Camelot's walls. "You led us a merry chase," Fennick sneered as his companions locked Wolf in chains. "But at long last, your uncanny good fortune has run out."

So Riana would steal even his luck? "Where are you taking me?" he asked, unable to keep his rage from his tone.

Fennick smiled. "Home, to River Ford, where you should have stayed in the first place. I fear your village has not fared well in the raids. It is now up to you to see how much they will pay in the long run."

Filled with a blind, helpless rage, Wolf struggled against his bindings. "Bastard, you would use innocents to bend me to your will?"

"Not I, Penawulf. I am but a lowly soldier, offering my services to whoever will pay for them. But if I were you, I'd be grateful we have orders to bring you in one piece. Like my Lord Mordred, I have little love for you and would as soon see you drawn and quartered."

"Who pays your wages? Is it the witch, Moriana, who would thus destroy me?"

Fennick merely laughed as he ordered the Saxons to take him away. "That you will learn in good time, Saxon. All in good time."

Hearing shouts, Riana had gone at once to see what caused them, but she shrank back at the sight of Fennick and the other three who had served Mordred. Too late, she saw they had Wolf trapped in chains between them.

Her first instinct was to rush in to help him, but there were twelve men in all, eight of them fierce Saxon warriors, and one frail girl alone would not stop them. Sir Kay and Sir Bedevere were still at the convent; she would go to them for help.

As she turned to go there, she heard Wolf ask if she were to blame for the attack on him. Appalled that he could think her capable of such treachery, she nearly lost heart. Surely it was pointless, risking her life for a man who would as soon see her dead.

Yet her feelings for her husband were still painfully alive, and loving him as she did, she could not sit idly by while this unknown someone took his life. She had to act; she was Wolf's sole hope of survival.

Thankfully, the Saxons made a great deal of noise as they pushed Wolf before them in the opposite direction, so she was able to skirt around the path to make her way back to the convent. Heart in her throat, she left the cover of the trees to dash across the short clearing to the rear gate of the convent when a hand shot out of the dark to grab her.

"Not so fast, milady," Fennick said with a chuckle. "I have someone who will be very glad to see you."

Twenty-five

Vangarth smiled as he strode through the gate of River Ford, its defenses falling aside at the slightest crook of his finger. He did so enjoy life when all his plans fell neatly into place.

Once he'd learned of the atrocities Penawulf had been committing, he'd been forced to take the good people of this village into protective custody—or at least, that was the version Vangarth planned to tell Cerdric. In truth, he'd set up camp here the moment Ranulf had left for Camelot, determined to be in charge when this fine riverfront holding was granted by the king. As it would be, once Vangarth sprung the trap he'd been building around Penawulf and the king was at last convinced of his rival's lack of worth.

Soon, Vangarth thought gleefully. Any day, his warriors would return with Penawulf, and the final stages of his plan could be put into motion.

"Sire!" the guard called down from the tower. "A small party approaches. It is the Briton, Fennick, and his men."

Vangarth hid his distaste. It had been most unpleasant, working with the weak, foolish Mordred, and he did not relish taking on his underlings now that the prince was dead. Still, Vangarth had not gotten where he was by letting his personal tastes interfere with the profitable and expedient, and it suited his purposes to make use of the Britons. Later, when he had what he wanted, he could as easily dispose of them.

Yet when he saw what cargo they delivered, he could almost

envision sparing them. They could have brought no riper plum than Penawulf's wife.

He'd forgotten how incredibly lovely Moriana was, even with her hair uncombed and her clothing tattered. Indeed, he would take much pleasure from her, after she helped him drive her husband to his knees. His beautiful wife was Penawulf's greatest weakness. The poor, besotted fool would do most anything to save her life.

"You've done well," he told Fennick as they approached him. "Take our new prisoner to the hag, Helga, and see that she's cleaned up. Lady Moriana shall join me for dinner."

The girl answered by spitting at his feet.

He forced a smile. "Did you know that I hold this village hostage? With their men and children locked away, the women will do whatever I command them. Oh, and did I forget to mention I also hold captive a sick old Briton named Sela?"

Gratifyingly, he saw fear leap into her golden eyes. Before he could press her further, the fat cow, Helga, came running up, placing herself between him and his prisoner, her own eyes flashing fire. "I demand you take this witch away at once!" she shrieked. "I have not sacrificed my soul so she can return to haunt this village."

"You make demands of me?" Vangarth asked, incredulous at her audacity.

Dark eyes narrowing, Helga stood with her beefy arms across her chest, sturdy legs planted to bar his way. "You forget, I know what you've done. I can go to Cerdric and tell him how you've taken control of the village in its chieftain's absence and cleverly plotted Penawulf's demise."

"Stupid cow," he said distastefully, lifting his sword to run it through her throat.

Helga dropped, blood gurgling from her neck.

"My power here is absolute," Vangarth told Moriana conversationally as he stepped over the dying woman. "This is what befalls those foolish enough to defy me."

He laughed at his prisoner's shocked expression. He'd known

this venture would be profitable, but not that it could prove so entertaining. Ordering Fennick to take Moriana away, Vangarth sighed with satisfaction. She was a feisty one, Penawulf's great love, but only a female, and he hadn't met one yet he could not maneuver into doing his will.

He could scarce wait for dinner. Tonight would be most entertaining, indeed.

Riana waited in Greta's hut for Vangarth's brutes to fetch her, feeling the lack of her friend's presence amidst the dainty furnishings and missing her warmth more than she'd dreamed possible. She hoped Greta was praying for them on faraway Avalon, for they would all need a world of prayers to get out of this alive.

Riana felt the weight of responsibility. The village's survival could depend on what she did next, yet she had no idea what Vangarth meant her to do. It made her uneasy that he should dress her in such finery. A soft gold, shimmering with luminescent threads, the intricately woven tunic gave her a regal air—or more accurately, a sacrificial one. She might look her best, but she felt like a goose being plumped for the slaughter.

She was startled by a sound behind her, like the hiss of a snake. Turning in that direction, she saw the top half of Tad's grim face in the window. She ran to him at once.

"We must whisper," he cautioned before she could speak. "There are at least three men guarding the doorway."

"I'm so glad to see you. Oh Tad, what is happening here?"

His face hardened, stripping away the last trace of youth. "Helga thinks she's helping River Ford, but Vangarth has merely been using her to spring a trap on our chieftain."

"No more. He killed Helga this afternoon."

Tad shook his head. "She tried to blame you for everything. Because of her coaxing, Ranulf decided to join Penawulf in Camelot. We learned just yesterday that it was a trap when Ranulf and seven of our finest warriors were ambushed on the road."

"Ranulf too is dead?" Riana gripped the sill to steady herself.

Kind, gallant Ranulf, who so patiently taught her to defend herself.

Tad nodded bleakly. "I would have been in their number, but I was hungry and went off to gather berries. Ranulf was dying when I returned, but he lived long enough to name Vangarth his murderer. I came here at once to find the village under his thumb, and you his prisoner."

"His men have your chieftain as well," Riana said, thinking aloud. "I think he means to use me to force Wolf to do what he wants, whatever that might be. Oh Tad, what will happen when Vangarth discovers how little Wolf loves me? The entire village will be at risk. You must go get help."

"But from where?"

She nibbled her lip, thinking. "Cerdric. Convince the king that River Ford and its chieftain stand in grave danger. I shall delay Vangarth as long as I can, but you must hurry. Go now and run as if your life depends on it."

"The lives of everyone," he corrected, smiling sadly as he gazed up at her. "Welcome home, my lady. I always knew you'd return."

Home, she thought as she watched him run off through the fields. Long ago, she had turned her back on this village, and that thoughtless act had been the start of River Ford's troubles. This time, come what may, she meant to stand firm and do all in her power to save it.

Even as she turned with a determined sigh to face the door, it crashed open, revealing three surly guards and Fennick. "Come," Fennick commanded. "Our Lord Vangarth grows impatient."

Swallowing deeply, forcing herself not to glance backward, she followed the guard to the largest hut remaining in the village. It had once been a storage shed, but Vangarth had commandeered it for his use, looting the village to furnish it. Riana recognized Yarrick's fine oak table, Helga's best chairs, the beautiful tapestries Greta had woven.

"Not quite the grandeur I'm accustomed to," Vangarth said, gesturing around him, "but it shall do in a pinch. Though I mus say, your beauty, my lady, is by far the finest adornment this mean hovel has seen."

Riana forced herself to smile, reminding herself that she must stall this man until Tad could return with Cerdric. "I thank you, milord. I did take special care with my appearance."

Returning the smile, he led her to the table. "I am happy to find you more amenable. Amazing, what a bath and fine attire can do for a woman."

Her skin crawled as his hands lingered on her shoulders long after he'd seated her. It took all her resolve not to shrug away, to run screaming from the room. "I find I am curious, milord. The beautiful clothing, this fine feast—it is plain that you must be leading up to something."

His grip tightened on her shoulders before he let go. Crossing to his own seat, he flashed a grin as forced as her own. "I've been told there's nothing more dangerous than an intelligent woman. Would you pose a danger to me, Lady Moriana?"

She made herself face him. "I've no wish to lose my life, not after having done what I must to survive in both Saxon and British camps all this time. I merely want to know what I must do next."

He laughed, as if she truly amused him. "Ah, a woman after my own heart." Lifting his goblet, he saluted her. "Very well, my dear, I shall be equally blunt. If you truly wish to live, you will help me discredit your husband. I want to see him humbled, here before his own village."

She nodded, though inwardly, she wanted to throw her wine in his face. "I, too, would enjoy his humiliation. I have never forgiven him for the punishment he forced upon me."

"Yes, I heard about that sentence. A bit severe, I thought at the time, but that's Penawulf, concerned more with his pride than any human emotions. This is why I wish to bring him down a bit. Play along with me, let him think you have sided with me against him, force him to slink away defeated. Then at last we shall both have our revenge."

He spoke softly, like a man intent upon seduction. Riana

fought the urge to shudder. "My reasons for this are clear enough, but I would know, my lord, what motive have you for this?"

Vangarth gripped the goblet, disdain covering his features. "Have you any idea what it's been like, living in that man's shadow? No matter the misdeed, Penawulf always regains the king's favor. For once, I want this village, the entire kingdom to see him as he truly is. I am gratified to find that you, his beloved wife, want the same."

Raising her goblet to him, she swallowed the bile in her throat. "To his humiliation, then."

Vangarth said nothing, merely smiling as he attacked his meal. It was an incredible feast—roast pheasant and honeyed ham, a treasure trove of fruits and buttered vegetables, with a basket of at least six different sweetbreads. Riana ate, tasting none of it, her stomach too busy roiling with mounting dread to find any pleasure in food, no matter how delicious.

Aside from encouraging her to eat, to drink more wine, Vangarth said little throughout the meal. When they were done, when Riana could not force another bite down her throat, he came to her side to lead her from the table. Once again, his hands lingered overlong, sliding down her arms to rest at her waist, keeping her hard and fast at his side. "Come," he said in that same, seductive tone, "I have something to show you."

He led her to the back of the hut, to a well guarded room, poorly lit and barely ventilated, inside which waited a host of frightened children. The village youths, she noticed with a lurch. As if accustomed to misuse at his hands, they backed away to the walls when they saw it was Vangarth.

Laughing nastily, he took a candle from the guard and led Riana inside the room, his smile seeming maniacal against the flickering flame. "I want to show you that I did not gain my power by leaving anything to chance. To remind you, in case you are tempted to change your mind, that I still hold the power to persuade you."

He held out the candle so that Riana could see the bed in the far corner, and the pale, still figure lying motionless upon it. She sucked in a breath as she recognized Sela.

"The death trance," Vangarth told her quietly. "Curable, I'm told, with the proper potion. I don't think I need to tell you she shall never get that potion if you fail to do as I tell you."

The old Riana would have ranted and railed, only to harm them all further, but like her mother had once advised, she instead kept her features blank, her voice cool and unruffled, giving nothing away of her inner turmoil. "Such melodrama is unnecessary, milord. I've told you already, my need for vengeance matches your own."

He studied her for a long moment. "Poor Penawulf, I almost pity him. There is nothing worse than to love a heartless woman."

Ironically, Riana gained strength from this. Since Wolf didn't love her, nothing she could do or say would hurt him. Vangarth could plot and scheme, but he would learn that he, like Helga, held no real leverage. In the end, Wolf would prevail.

Though of course, he would despise his wife more than ever.

So be it. It killed her to turn her back on the ailing Sela, the cowering children, but everyone's lives depended on Riana successfully maintaining her pose until Tad could return with Cerdric. Following Vangarth from the room, she prayed silently and fervently for divine intervention. It would be best for them all, she told the Goddess, should Wolf arrive on the scene *after* the king came to River Ford.

But once again, the fates conspired against them. Even as she and Vangarth returned to the table, the guards burst into the room, faces grim with purpose. "Forgive the interruption," Fennick said curtly, "but you asked to be informed of his arrival."

"Splendid!" Vangarth said, dragging Riana behind him. "Our guest of honor has come, at last."

Wolf kept his rage banked as he marched, still chained, toward River Ford. He'd long since realized he had Vangarth to thank for his return here, but he'd yet to figure out why, or what part Riana might have played in it.

He'd had time aplenty to ponder that question on the journey here, made longer by a need to evade the warring factions now battling for the kingless England. In his mind, Wolf replayed that long ago day when Vangarth had visited them, looking for some hint that even then, she'd planned to destroy him. Instead, he remembered her fear of the man, even distaste, and her surprising defiance as she stood proudly beside him, claiming Wolf as her husband. No, if there were treachery, he decided, it must be a more recent thing.

If. Grimacing, he acknowledged that he might have misjudged Riana.

He'd been angry that night by the lake, sick at heart to learn the love that had caused so much pain and suffering had been conjured by witchery. In his mind, he could hear his father denouncing his mother's Druid wiles, and like Exar, Wolf had let himself believe only the very worst of his wife.

But now that his rage had the time to cool, he found too much of his father's pride and impatience in his actions that night. Like Exar, he'd lashed out in his pain and anger, giving Riana no opportunity to explain, giving himself no chance to listen.

Throughout his long journey, he could hear her tortured voice like a haunting refrain, charging him with being too absorbed in his chieftain's duties to notice her suffering. Over and over, he saw the tears filling her eyes as she spoke of their lost child and her inability to bear another.

And in his darkest, most truthful moments, he asked himself who he was to pass judgment. Perhaps the enchantment caused his greed to possess her, but even after she'd lifted the spell, he'd been so consumed by his own emotions, he'd left no room for her pain. It was only in hindsight that he'd heard and absorbed her regret, her sorrow.

For it was not until Riana was gone, far beyond any words of explanation or apology, that he found the small sack wrapped up in his bundle of clothing. Recognizing the bag Riana invariably wore at her waist, he'd opened it, dropping its contents in his lap. As he'd stared at the dry, shriveled walnuts, he'd thought long and hard about why she would still have his long ago gift to her.

Such a small thing, yet so like her to show her true emotions in such a quiet, secretive way.

Approaching the gate, Wolf thought of that night in the royal garden when he'd gazed at Riana in the moonlight. Perceptions change, he'd realized then, according to the light shed upon them. With all he'd seen and heard and learned about his wife, wasn't it time he stopped gazing at the outer Riana and focused instead on what was there in her heart?

As if put there to test him, Riana stood inside the gate, a vision designed to steal all his breath. Pure gold, from her flowing hair to the hem of her shimmering tunic, she seemed more dream than substance, a bright, gleaming memory he would take to his grave. Staring into her golden eyes, Wolf acknowledged the truth. Some misguided enchantment might have drawn him to Riana, but somewhere along the way, the girl herself had made him love her.

And may the gods protect them all, he would love her forever.

As if to refute any claim Wolf might make on her, Vangarth put a possessive hand about Riana's waist. "Penawulf, how gracious of you to join us. This lovely morsel and I were just saying how starved we are for entertainment. You're just what we need to stave off our boredom."

Given how he had left her, Wolf should have expected this, but he nonetheless felt staggered by the blow.

He stared at her, noticing the stiffness in her body, the anguish in her gaze. It would seem she was not enjoying herself as much as Vangarth would have him believe. Wolf realized he was at a crossroads. Either he could think the worst and condemn her, as Vangarth no doubt expected, or for once, he could believe in Riana, and trust her. It would kill him if her love proved as false as the man who now held her, but Wolf was sick of lies and misunderstandings. He would rather be dead if he could not hold tight to his faith in his wife.

"If you wish to live," he told Vangarth quietly, though no less threateningly, "you will take your hands off my woman."

"Ah, but she likes being fondled, don't you, my dear?"

Riana didn't move away as Vangarth cupped her breast, but Wolf saw her telltale shudder. "Touch her again and I'll kill you," he growled.

Vangarth eyed his chains. "How emasculating it must feel to watch me paw the woman you love while you must stand there and do nothing."

"You waste your time if you hope to taunt him thus," Riana said so coldly he didn't recognize her voice. "Wolf has no love for me."

"Indeed? His rage seems genuine enough. Perhaps we should test it." Vangarth nodded to the two men next to him. "Fennick, Rolfe, undo his chains."

"Sire, is that wise?"

The fools should have saved their breath, Wolf knew, for Vangarth never took his risks unduly. Unsheathing his knife, the brute held the blade to Riana's throat. "Fear not. Penawulf will do nothing as long as I hold the power of life and death over his woman."

Wolf struggled against the black rage engulfing him, knowing how Vangarth liked to goad him into acting rashly. If he hoped to save Riana, Wolf must remain unruffled and keep all his wits about him. "What would you have me do?" he asked calmly enough when the shackles fell away from his chafed wrists.

"I told you. We seek some sport. My men and I are hungry for a hunt and you, Penawulf, shall be our quarry."

"One against twenty? I hardly see where that is sport."

"Out of respect for our long-standing rivalry, I'll give you a head start. Should you manage to elude us until the morning, you can return here and claim your wife as the prize. If not . . ."

Vangarth let the words trail off, both of them knowing there was no need to finish.

"What of Cerdric's disapproval?" Wolf asked, looking about him for any hope of escape. "Coming here and taking this village is bad enough, but how can you hope to explain away my corpse?"

"I have no intention of leaving your body anywhere near River Ford. Indeed, you'll be found, badly burned, in the village of Watershire. Poor Cerdric will have to conclude that his favored pet was guilty of razing and looting that hamlet, especially when I show him the ill-gotten gains from many other such raids, hidden here in your village. Why, the king will be so pleased with me for stopping your insane quest for power, he'll grant me your holdings, and a good portion of the loot, as well."

"Let me guess," Wolf said, unable to hide his bitterness. "I am also the one who conspired with Mordred to topple Arthur's kingdom."

Vangarth smiled viciously. "How diabolically clever you were to put Mordred on the throne to weaken it and thus leave Britain ripe for invasion."

"And of course, an ambitious Saxon can now carve out an empire for himself with the right resources."

Vangarth smiled nastily. "Too bad you had to die and leave me to take your place. I shall enjoy ruling your village, Penawulf, and even more, I shall enjoy using your wife."

Wolf ached to rip him in two but forced himself merely to shrug. "You'll find the female is more trouble than she's worth."

"Why then do you rage each time I touch her?"

He would kill the fiend, Wolf swore, but outwardly, he remained unruffled. "She is my property, as is this village. And I warn, I have no intention of handing either over to you without a fight."

"How touching. But I ask you, have you ever been known to best me in competition?"

"And I ask you, have you ever been known not to cheat?"

With a hearty laugh, Vangarth thrust Riana at Fennick. "Keep your sword on her. If he takes one step near her, run her through."

Wolf noted Fennick's distaste, but ever the trained soldier, he did as he was bid. Fennick too would die, Wolf vowed, if he hurt one single hair on his wife's beautiful head.

Still laughing, Vangarth called for his horse. "If I were you,

Penawulf, I'd start running. You have until I am mounted to get a jump on me. My men have orders to follow soon, but I reserve the pleasure of having the first go at you for myself."

Every instinct for survival screamed at Wolf to run, knowing that he stood a good chance in the forest, but he knew that if he left now, he would never again see Riana alive. Vangarth had no intention of honoring the terms of this competition. Should Wolf elude them, and return in the morning, he would still kill them both.

So Wolf stood where he was, eyeing Fennick, reasoning that a man who could so easily switch masters must be the weak link in Vangarth's armor. Having trained long and hard with Sir Kay in the art of unseating a man from his horse, Wolf knew that with the proper weapon, he could even the odds. Fennick held such a weapon at his wife's throat.

"Have you been listening to him?" Wolf asked the man, nodding at Vangarth, now striding over to the waiting, prancing horse. "You must see that he has no intention of letting you live, either. He'll kill you along with me, to substantiate his claim that I've sided with the Britons."

Fennick lowered the sword to Riana's waist, but he did not drop it. Eyeing Vangarth grabbing the reins of his steed, Wolf felt the sweat gather on his neck. "Throw me your weapon," he coached. "Don't you see it's our only chance?"

Wolf read the indecision in Fennick's eyes, but still the fool failed to act. "Throw it," he commanded. "Before it's too late."

Fennick didn't react but Riana did. Hand reaching down to clasp the hilt of the sword, she began a low, rhythmic chanting. Fennick released his own grip as the blade began to glow. To his right, Vangarth mounted his horse, readying for the charge, but Wolf's attention was on his wife. Still chanting, she held the sword before her, not with her hands, but with an intent, focused gaze. It hovered there, glowing brighter, until it moved slowly upward, soaring through the air. Eyes wide, Fennick stumbled backward, falling over his feet to get away.

With awe, Wolf watched the sword come to his hands. All this time, he'd distrusted and belittled her power, yet here she was, using her magic for him, even as she'd done for her beloved Arthur. Properly humbled as he gripped the sword, he vowed he would fight to the death to save her.

Warm and still glowing, the weapon vibrated in his hand as Wolf turned to face the attack.

Charging at him, Vangarth saw the weapon and what Wolf meant to do with it but it was too late to slow his charge. He gave a bloodcurdling howl as he bore down on his victim, his own sword at the ready. Wolf stood his ground, knowing from experience that the force of blade hitting blade would knock his rival from the horse.

It was a monstrous collision, Wolf's rage meeting Vangarth's viciousness, felling and winding them both. Wolf recovered first, reaching immediately for his weapon, standing up to defend himself as Vangarth's men edged closer.

"Leave him to me!" Rising slowly to his knees, then feet, Vangarth snatched a sword from some lackey's hand. "Penawulf is mine."

Holding his blade up, Wolf watched Vangarth stalk him, his black eyes glittering with hatred and cunning. "Just so you know," he told Wolf, his lips curling in a sneer, "the bitch shall die as soon as I dispose of you. *After* I've taken my pleasure."

Wolf ignored him, knowing such taunts were meant to give his rival the advantage, but more importantly, knowing that Vangarth could do nothing to anyone if he himself were dead. With lethal concentration, Wolf focused instead on each movement of his opponent's body, waiting for the one move that would give *him* the edge.

With surprising swiftness, Vangarth lunged, but Wolf fended off the thrust neatly, as he did the next three attacks. With each failed attempt, Vangarth grew more and more irate, lunging at Wolf with increasing fury. "Fight, you coward," he cried, "or I'll have that bitch of yours dismembered before your eyes."

Worried for her safety, Wolf made the mistake of glancing back to Riana. As he should have anticipated, Vangarth took advantage of his momentary inattention. Pouncing at once, he sliced down with his blade, catching the unprepared Wolf across his left shoulder.

"Wolf!" Riana cried out in dismay, but this time, he did not look at her. Every nerve in his body was trained on defeating this monster. Blood trickled down his arm but he ignored it as he slowly circled his lifelong enemy. "I warned you, Vangarth, that I would see you dead before I'd allow you to touch my wife."

"You bore me with your boasts, it is time to make good on them."

For once, the man was right.

"To the death, then." Clutching the sword with both hands, feeling the power surge through him, Wolf went at his nemisis, cutting and slashing and intent upon mowing him down. It was Vangarth's turn to fend off blows, his efforts growing weaker and more desperate. Wolf nicked the man's arm, then thigh, and opened a shallow slice across his belly, until Vangarth tripped on his feet and went down on his back in the dirt. Standing over him, holding him in place with his foot, Wolf let the blade tip hover above the man's chest. "Pay your last respects to the gods before you die, Vangarth. Pray that they can forgive you, for I and mine cannot."

"Wolf," he heard Riana cry out, even as he was surrounded by Vangarth's men and the sword was ripped from his hand.

Cold and stiff with fear, Riana watched the brutes grasp her husband. Her first instinct was to rush them, kicking and biting, but she'd do no good by acting out of rage or panic. Now that the attention was no longer focused on her, she might better retreat to a position of greater advantage.

Creeping slowly up to the guard tower, she tried to remember all Ranulf and Wolf had told her about defending this village. Surprise, she knew, was her greatest weapon, but she was happy for the stout club she held in her hand. Entering the tower, seeing the guard preoccupied with the scuffle below, she summoned all her strength to bring the club crashing down on his skull. With a low moan, he slumped gratifyingly, then fell unconscious in the corner of the tower.

Reaching for his bow and arrows, she again prayed she would remember Ranulf's teachings. This was not the time to misfire. Wolf's very life could depend on her making the perfect shot.

She turned her attention to the square. Wolf still struggled against his captors while Vangarth rose to his feet, brushing himself off, as if he could thus regain the dignity he'd lost forever. He, like Wolf, bled from his wounds but neither so profusely he would die. Grimacing, she watched Vangarth stagger up to her husband.

"I've always known you to be a coward," Wolf spat out at him, "but never more so than today. You were bested in a fair fight, yet you refuse to die as a true man is meant to, with courage and honor."

"Might is what matters, you fool, not your noble nonsense."

To punctuate this, Vangarth snatched a club from a minion's hands, and brought it crashing against Wolf's knees. "Let's see how fast and far you run from us now," he said when Wolf's legs buckled.

Even in the tower, Riana heard the crack of the bone. Without his captors holding him, she feared, Wolf would drop like a rock.

"Strong, invincible Penawulf. How I have always despised you. So brave, so noble, but what good will those virtues do you now?" Laughing, Vangarth lifted the club again.

White hot rage exploded inside her as she raised the bow to aim and fire. She was too late to stop him from smashing the club in Wolf's gut, but not too late to deflect the blow to the head.

Vangarth yelped as the arrowhead buried itself in his shoulder, the club hitting Wolf's temple instead of crashing down on the top of his head.

"Bitch," Vangarth snarled, glaring up at the tower.

From the corner of her eye, Riana noticed Wolf had gone down, his captors releasing him to fall in the dirt, but her gaze remained on her quarry. "How do you like being the hunted?" she called down to him as she readied another arrow. "Go on, *you* try to run and see what happens."

"Get her," Vangarth shouted to his men as he yanked the shaft out of his shoulder.

"You might reconsider," she said quickly, holding the bow taut and aimed. "No one can get to me before I put this arrow through your heart."

Vangarth gestured his men to wait. "Am I expected to believe that you, a puny female, can fell me when you failed once already?"

Though Riana had her own doubts, she was not about to let him see them. "My first attempt was merely to catch your attention. My second, I assure you, will be far more lethal."

Vangarth grinned, obviously unconvinced. "Ah, but soon your arm will tire and the bow will quiver. I think that if you truly meant to kill me, I'd be dead by now. What possible use can be served by keeping us all in suspense?"

He meant to taunt her, she knew, and goad her into some rash action. If she shot, and missed, they'd be on her before she could arm the bow again. Indeed, she noticed uneasily, Fennick was no longer visible. Could he, even now, be creeping up behind her, even as she'd done to the guard?

She resisted the urge to glance behind her, fought the quivering in the muscles of her arms. Wolf's life was at stake here, as was the future of his village. For once in her life, she would be smart, patient and strong.

Was it mere hope, or did she hear boats on the river? Not daring to look, she said a silent prayer that it was Tad with reinforcements. Delay, just a few minutes more, and their rescue would storm through the gate.

"Come now," she told Vangarth, matching his arrogant tone. "Surely you can understand the pleasure I can derive, watching you squirm with uncertainty. Though let me assure you, my aim is true. Ironically enough, I have you to thank for my archery lessons for it was after your visit that my husband saw a need for me to learn to defend myself. Ranulf, before you killed him, made certain my skill matched his own.

Vangarth eyed her carefully, clearly unnerved. He might doubt her abilities, but didn't dare take the chance. "A stalemate then," he conceded. "But think, Moriana. You cannot hold out against us forever, and in truth, there is so much more I can offer you than your husband. In ridding us of Arthur, I've opened the flood-gates of England and left her ripe for the taking. Even now, Saxons are raiding the glory that was once Camelot. The prepared chieftain will one day rule supreme."

"But it's not Cerdric you mean to place on the throne," she said contemptuously, hoping the king was near enough to hear him. "Your visions are for yourself alone."

"Not alone. I would have you be my queen."

"Even were I foolish enough to believe you, my love and loyalty is—and always will be—for my husband."

Yet even as she made her declaration, what Riana feared most came true. Coming up behind her, Fennick grabbed her wrists, causing the bow to go tumbling to the ground below.

"Pity," Vangarth said with not even a tinge of regret. "I could have enjoyed matching wits with you. Kill her," he started to shout, even as with a guttural howl, Wolf leapt up at him, going for Vangarth's throat.

It was all the distraction Riana needed, for at the same time, she spun and kicked Fennick viciously in the groin. As Ranulf had taught, the man instantly clutched himself, giving her time to skirt free. Racing down the tower steps, she knew she must get to Wolf, to help him fight Vangarth until the rescue entered the gates.

To her relief, she found Cerdric there already. An angry Tad rushed to help his chieftain, though Vangarth looked more in need of rescue.

Separating the combatants, Cerdric ordered his men to herd all the miscreants back to his camp, where the council would hear the crimes and accusations.

"But that's unfair," Riana blurted out, appalled at the rough manner in which Wolf, limping badly, was being dragged through the gate.

"Riana, no," Wolf said, every word seeming an effort. "This is my fight now."

"Silence!" Cerdric commanded. "Do not make this any worse than it already is."

Watching Wolf be manhandled to the longboats, Riana curbed the urge to rant and rage, sensing it would get her nowhere with Cerdric. Like Arthur, he was king, and expected—nay, demanded—certain considerations. As such, she curtsied low before him. "Forgive my outburst, sire, but my fear for my husband is great, and I cannot bear to see him suffer any further. If you will, I can show you something that will make it easier for you to judge both men in their guilt and innocence."

He eyed her skeptically, but followed her to Vangarth's hut, to the horrid little room where he kept Sela and the children hostage.

Cerdric narrowed his gaze as the little ones cowered away from him, his jaw tightening as they named Vangarth their jailer. Leaving the hut, he swore under his breath.

"Will you now let Penawulf go free?" Riana had to ask as she followed him into the square.

Cerdric shook his head. "The trial must still go on, but I do not doubt your husband will be found innocent. He shall be returned to you as soon as possible."

Returned? "But I would go with him," she protested.

Cerdric gestured around them. "Knowing Penawulf, I would think he would want his wife here, helping his people. There is much to be done, I fear."

Riana swallowed, knowing the king was right. River Ford would resist her help, but they needed her, as did her husband, to see to the long, painful process of rebuilding the village. Until Wolf said otherwise, she was still the chieftain's wife, and this time, she would act the part. Whatever the hardship or heartache, she would surmount it, proving to them all—and even to herself—that she was worthy.

In this way, she would make her atonement. To River Ford, and to her husband.

"Fear not," Cerdric assured as he marched off. "I shall soon send Penawulf back to you, safe and whole."

Riana clung to that thought as she turned back to the village.

Twenty-six

Several months later, Riana clung to the same hope as she toiled in the fields, pulling the last weeds before harvest. In her mind, she knew Wolf was needed desperately by Cerdric to repel the marauders from their unsettled borders, but in her heart, she feared her husband's prolonged absence meant he had no further wish to see her.

Brushing her hair from her eyes, she thought of what she'd accomplished in his absence. After freeing the children from that horrid room, she'd watched them recover quickly, loving words and nightly stories soon bringing the smiles back to their young faces. Sela had been harder to reach, but Riana had gone to the woman's hut day after day to clasp Sela's hand and express her love and gratitude until she at last opened her eyes.

Nowadays, the old woman was up and about, acting more feisty than ever, but Riana far preferred the constant harping to the death trance and would have it no other way.

Winning over the village had proven every bit as difficult as she'd feared, but when River Ford saw how hard their chieftain's wife worked, how determined she was to rebuild the grand hall and the homes they had lost, one by one Wolf's people came to accept and help her. The village still had a long way to go to complete recovery, but working as a group, they'd made a grand start. Together, with faith and love, they'd rebuilt their homes and dreams, and now they began looking to the future.

All that was missing, Riana knew, was her husband.

Yet while she missed Wolf keenly, she now knew a sense of peace, of acceptance. Gazing out over the fields, she thought of the silly girl who had first come to River Ford, cursed with her impatience and haunted by her illusions of grandeur. She'd meant well, wanting to help Arthur, but Riana realized now she could no more singlehandedly save Camelot, than she alone could have destroyed it. Life was rarely comprised of a single, sweeping stroke; it was more often many little lines intersecting, at its best when those lines meshed together.

And she knew now that her lines had been leading her here to River Ford. It was much as Tad said, that long ago night she'd run away. Here, with these people, this was her home.

And though she yearned each night alone in her empty bed for the sound of her husband's voice, the feel of his strong warm body next to hers, she no longer felt despair. *Amazing things can be accomplished with the proper faith,* Morgan had told her. For once in her life, Riana was prepared to wait and be patient.

Especially now, she thought, touching her softly rounding belly.

This little miracle, conceived that night in the forest when she'd given her heart, body, and soul to her husband, was the symbol of her faith and hope, and her reward for learning her lesson.

Wolf would come for her, and when he did, she would be waiting.

Unknown to Riana, Wolf had already arrived. To him, his absence seemed to have lasted a millennium, and the sight of his village with its lush, ripening fields was a sight beyond comparison. Home, he thought with a rush of pleasure.

It still made his blood boil to think what Vangarth had done to his good friend Ranulf, and what the madman's lust for power might have done to the village, but he could rest easy knowing the man would bother them no more. As ever, Cerdric's judgment had been harsh and final, with Vangarth going to his grave screaming, suffering every bit as much as any of his victims.

With neither Vangarth nor Mordred to fan the flames, war between Saxon and Briton had become more sporadic, each tiny kingdom preferring to see to its own concerns as they had before the Pendragons took the throne. Perhaps another strong king would one day rise to unite England, but until then, Wolf was content to return to his own tiny part of the world and live out his days in relative peace.

While out securing Cerdric's borders, Wolf had come upon Sir Kay, who swore that his days of battle were likewise coming to an end. Most of the Round Table had disbanded, he'd told Wolf, and Queen Guinivere would devote the rest of her life to the convent. Nothing else remained of Arthur's world, he'd added sadly. Only this old soldier, missing the greatest king who had walked the earth.

On his journey home, Wolf had thought long and hard about the man who had ruled Camelot. A chieftain could do worse than to choose such a king as a model, or such laws for his people to follow. He had learned much from the Britons, much that could make life better for his people. Greta had been right; he and Riana did have much they could learn from each other.

And on that thought, he saw his wife, the sight of her stopping the breath from leaving his chest. By all the gods, he'd forgotten how incredibly lovely she could be, how even now, without the spell, he would yearn to rush up and sweep her into his arms.

Instead, he stood behind her, watching her work, letting the blood stir in his veins. It had been torture, staying away all these months, wondering if Riana would still be here when he returned. The fact that she was, that she stood in the fields she'd planted and tended, seemed a blessing from the gods. Wolf looked at Riana and saw his dream unfolding—his village, his land, the woman he loved, all stretched out before him.

And while he might also wish for children, one did not argue with a gift the gods granted. For Wolf, it was enough to have

Riana here at River Ford, safe and whole, and waiting for him to come home.

Taking a deep breath, he strode over to her, no longer able to wait. He had to touch her, hold her, sweep her up into his arms and tell her how much he loved her.

Nothing that had happened in the past mattered. From this moment on, life would begin anew.

Riana felt Wolf's presence before she heard him. Spinning to face her husband, she thought she might die of the joy at seeing him, so tall and proud, his raven hair and bronzed skin gleaming in the sunshine. Giving way to her emotions, she ran to the arms he held out to her, thinking only, *Now, I am truly home.*

He kissed her, long and thoroughly, and she clung to the sweet miracle of holding him again in her arms.

Too soon, he pulled away, his silver eyes searching her face. "Oh Riana, there is so much to ask, to say. The past, your magic—"

"I swear, I will not tamper with magic, nor ever again curse you with such an enchantment. I've learned that it's no good for a man to offer his love if it doesn't come from his heart."

Smiling, he took her hands and placed them on his chest, bidding her to listen. "Then hear the heartbeat of a man who's searched all over England for his woman. Magic spells or not, I will love you to the grave."

"You've forgiven me?"

Gazing down, drinking in the sight of her, he clasped her hands tightly. "You once spoke of atonement. Watching you that night in the guard tower, seeing you fight for this village, for me, I saw how wrong I was to ever doubt you. Perhaps we both have much to forgive and atone for, but I now have faith that one day, you and I will find understanding."

"Oh Wolf, I love you so much it hurts."

He nodded, clearly knowing that sensation. "I want to make our marriage a happy one, Riana. It doesn't matter about the children. We can build other hopes, other dreams."

Smiling, she brought his hand to cover her belly. "This is one dream I can make true," she said, feeling suddenly shy. "And this time, I shall guard this precious life with my own."

Wolf looked incredulous at first, but his joy was like a winter sun bursting free of the clouds. "A babe? Our babe? My beautiful Riana, you are the light in my life, the meaning, and I cannot live without you."

Sweeping her up into his arms, he swung her around, raining kisses all over her face as he carried her to the villa. Sharing his happiness, Riana said a silent prayer of thanksgiving. She'd been given a second chance and she would not waste it.

Someday she would explain to him about Arthur's dying request to keep his dream alive, how this baby, and the many others they would one day have would grow strong and proud, taking the best of both Saxon and Briton. How through them, she and Wolf would build a better England.

But right now, she had other, more urgent needs in mind.

"I've missed you so," Wolf said, as if sensing her thoughts and sharing them. "I cannot wait to touch you, join as one."

"Why should we wait?" she said coyly, nodding at the small copse on the path beside them. "After all, it would not be the first time we found passion in the woods."

Carrying her into the cover of the trees, he set her down on her feet. "Ah Riana, is it any wonder I love you?" Smiling tenderly, he gazed into her eyes. "I've begun to think that with or without magic, I shall always be under your spell. You are, and always shall be, my special enchantress."

Sinking to the ground with him, losing herself to the pleasure and joy he alone could inspire, Riana knew her mother had been right.

Love is indeed the greatest magic of all.

Author's Note

The true story of King Arthur is as shrouded in the mists as the mythical island of Avalon. Since the man who inspired the legend likely lived during the late fifth century, a time before history was recorded, the details of Arthur's reign lie in the imagination of whoever does the telling.

Like so many writers before me, I took the essence of the legend and walked that fine line between fact and fantasy, borrowing freely from both the Dark and Middle Ages, using the bits of each legend I enjoyed the most, to weave my own tale of myth and magic.

If you enjoyed *Enchantress,* please write me at:

Barbara Benedict
P.O. Box 4024
Tustin, CA 92681-4024

WATCH FOR THESE ZEBRA REGENCIES

LADY STEPHANIE   (0-8217-5341-X, $4.50)
by Jeanne Savery

Lady Stephanie Morris has only one true love: the family estate she has managed ever since her mother died. But then Lord Anthony Rider arrives on her estate, claiming he has plans for both the land and the woman. Stephanie soon realizes she's fallen in love with a man whose sensual caresses will plunge her into a world of peril and intrigue . . . a man as dangerous as he is irresistible.

BRIGHTON BEAUTY   (0-8217-5340-1, $4.50)
by Marilyn Clay

Chelsea Grant, pretty and poor, naively takes school friend Alayna Marchmont's place and spends a month in the country. The devastating man had sailed from Honduras to claim his promised bride, Miss Marchmont. An affair of the heart may lead to disaster . . . unless a resourceful Brighton beauty finds a way to stop a masquerade and keep a lord's love.

LORD DIABLO'S DEMISE   (0-8217-5338-X, $4.50)
by Meg-Lynn Roberts

The sinfully handsome Lord Harry Glendower was a gambler and the black sheep of his family. About to be forced into a marriage of convenience, the devilish fellow engineered his own demise, never having dreamed that faking his death would lead him to the heavenly refuge of spirited heiress Gwyn Morgan, the daughter of a physician.

A PERILOUS ATTRACTION   (0-8217-5339-8, $4.50)
by Dawn Aldridge Poore

Alissa Morgan is stunned when a frantic passenger thrusts her baby into Alissa's arms and flees, having heard rumors that a notorious highwayman posed a threat to their coach. Handsome stranger Hugh Sebastian secretly possesses the treasured necklace the highwayman seeks and volunteers to pose as Alissa's husband to save her reputation. With lost baby and missing necklace in their care, the couple embarks on journey into peril—and passion.

Available wherever paperbacks are sold, or order direct from the Publisher. Send cover price plus 50¢ per copy for mailing and handling to Penguin USA, P.O. Box 999, c/o Dept. 17109, Bergenfield, NJ 07621. Residents of New York and Tennessee must include sales tax. DO NOT SEND CASH.